Praise

"Every once in a while, a love story comes along that seduces all your senses, making you laugh, cry, and re-examine your own beliefs. Ray Bartlett's debut novel is all that and more. Told against the backdrop of stunning Yucatán, Mexico, the story examines the complexity of human love and nature, enthralling you from the very first page to the last."

– *Sena Desai Gopal, food/travel writer for the* Boston Globe

"While the setting is exotic, the human condition at the heart of the novel isn't. Bartlett focuses his compelling narrative about the nature of desire in the landscapes of Mexico. ... Bartlett has composed a deeply human narrative in prose as radiant as the sunset. This novel teaches us about the mind as it finds out where it would like to linger and where, perforce, it must continually turn. A beautiful and fundamental tale."

–*Meg Tyler, Boston University, author of* Poor Earth

"A sensual, sensory delight; a beautifully moving tale of love, loss, gain, and search for self."

– *Devon Ellington, author of* Tracking Medusa

"I was so drawn into the world Bartlett created that I read *Sunsets of Tulum* all in one day, shirking responsibilities and canceling plans. The added delight to this compelling book is the vein of intelligent eroticism that runs throughout, making it a one-of-a-kind, smart and sexy read."

– *Missy Brownson, author of* Hush Candy

"Reading *Sunsets of Tulum* is like stepping onto a glass-bottom boat floating downriver into the jungle. Everywhere you turn, the author fills the senses with his masterful prose, and the slow slip through the water soon becomes your life."

– *Todd Fahnestock, bestselling author of* Fairmist

Sunsets *of* Tulum

To Alison,
Enjoy!

Other books by this author include:

In the Sunlight of Sakurajima:
My Two Years Teaching English in Southern Japan

Look for these other titles
from Barrel Fire Press:

Summer to Fall, by Albert R. Waitt

Sunsets of Tulum

a novel

RAYMOND AVERY BARTLETT

Barrel Fire Press
Kennebunkport, ME
©2015

First Edition

ISBN-13: 978-0-9889390-3-5

Library of Congress Control Number: 2015944095

Cover design by J.Benitez,
99designs.com/profiles/1463359

Printed in the United States of America

One life, one encounter,
all we have is today

— *Japanese Proverb*

The stars do not align for lovers.

— *Anonymous*

Day Zero

In the Chopper

As Reed Haflinger shivered near the door in the Beverley airport lobby, he promised himself he would never let Dan talk him into this again. The early morning shift. No damn way. Global warming can't happen soon enough, he thought, trying to warm his fingers by wrapping them around the tiny cup of bitter, tepid coffee he'd gotten from the machine in the lobby. Where the hell was Booker?

When the pilot arrived—a full twenty minutes late—it was not Booker, the ex-Afghanistan Marine, but some kid Reed had never seen before. Dan had given him what looked like a teenager: some idiot kid wearing a hoodie and skinny jeans, probably just out of flight school. Someone who wouldn't inspire confidence even if he was behind the wheel of a Schwinn ten speed, let alone a news helicopter.

"I'm Rabbit," the boy said, extending his right hand. Reed hoped the bike messenger bag over his shoulder had flight plans in it.

"You're twenty minutes late. We've got a story to cover." For a moment he debated just letting the poor kid sit there, but then relented. "I'm Reed," he said, shaking hands. "You're going to freeze your ass off in that copter. Every bit of wind is going to go right through you."

"It's okay," said Rabbit. *Was that his real name? What kind of parent names their child after an animal that most of the world wants to eat for lunch?* "I've got a silk thermal layer on underneath. I'll be fine."

Silk thermal layer?

Haflinger wanted to laugh.

An hour and a half later, as the sun finally began its laborious climb out of the Atlantic, the chopper hung high over Boston as if it were an insect-collection dragonfly pinned to the perfect blue sky. In all the years he'd been in the news copter, he'd never gotten tired of that feeling of being weightless, above everything, as close as possible to being birds as man would ever be. That was about all he loved though. Mostly he was the camera for traffic snarls and fender benders, not the stuff he'd dreamed about in journalism class, where idealism eclipsed practicality. Back then he'd imagined being a war reporter or investigative journalist. Then life had happened, and suddenly fifteen years slipped by. For such a piss cold day, not much had been going on traffic-wise. A rollover on I-95 had closed two lanes out of three, traffic barely inching by. A mattress had flown off a truck north of the city. But that was it so far. He wondered what Laurel was up to, trying to remember the last time they'd had dinner together or gone out somewhere.

Then Channel 7 News requested something from over the Fenway Park stadium. Haflinger flicked the intercom.

"Rabbit, bring us over the ballpark. Need a shot with the sunrise for 7 News."

"Sure thing," the kid replied, banking the bird. Reed worked the camera controller panel in front of him, getting a last all-channel traffic angle before switching his attention to the upcoming task.

"Bring her in from the southeast. I'll need a couple good feeds there, then swing her around so I can get a view from the north."

"Sure."

The helicopter's nose dipped and the machine picked up speed, heading towards the iconic Citgo triangle, just barely visible out of the thatch of brownstones and university buildings that crowded the edge of the Charles River. Soon the stadium was visible, and Haflinger readied his position on the controls. The biggest challenge of being the helicopter cameraman was timing: arrive even a second too late and there'd be black fuzz on the TV screen when the anchor cut to a view from the chopper. It was one of the last arenas where television was still live.

Reed hit the intercom. "That's good. Hold it right here. Let's wait for the cue."

"Roger."

Haflinger turned on the camera and focused in on Fenway Park. Without zooming in, the baseball field looked like a little green bathmat. Yet with the push of a button Reed could see the numbers on individual seats in the stand. He'd been doing this for almost a decade and still felt lucky every time he got to fly. Even if the rest of the day sucked, he'd done something incredible for part of it.

A light on the controller panel turned from amber to red: the signal was live. Any poor slob who was up at 6 a.m. with their television on was seeing a few seconds of Fenway Park splashed by morning sunshine. All courtesy of Reed Haflinger and the rest of the Saber Traffic Team.

The light went from red to amber. The shot was complete.

Reed pushed the intercom.

"Got it. Now let's try a shot from the north."

"Roger," said the kid.

But instead of the usual dip into a new direction, the chopper's nose dropped like an elevator with the cable cut, descending so quickly that the heavy control panel in Reed's lap flew up and smashed him in the forehead. His cup of coffee splashed on the roof, and anything not bolted down was suddenly floating: pens, candy wrappers, the flashlight, papers. All of it suspended in the cabin, the chaos of an uncontrolled descent.

At the same time, instead of holding tight to the northeast compass point where it should have been, the nose of the copter turned a full three hundred and sixty degrees, stopped, reversed and did another full three-sixty. Instead of seeing Fenway Park below him through the bottom-mounted camera, Reed Haflinger was staring at it directly through the cockpit window.

Is this how it happens? was what came into his mind. *Is this how it happens?* Instinctively, he hit the intercom.

"We okay?!"

Nothing but the hiss of a live microphone feed.

"Rabbit?"

This is how it happens.

Reed could see the kid through the Plexiglas fighting with the controls. He saw Boston. What a beautiful city. He wondered if he and Laurel could have made it work out somehow. He thought about whether she'd put him in his folks' plot or somewhere else. He saw the sunlight scintillating over the mouth of the Charles and wished he'd found a way to let Laurel teach him how to swim. The kid they'd almost had; the kids they'd never had since. The rut they'd been in. Everything he'd let slip by thinking there'd always be time. Things popped into his head faster than he could process them. Not sadness but just an overpowering sense that everything had happened too fast.

Then: "I got this!" Rabbit's tone, a note or two below sheer panic, made it clear that even Rabbit remained unconvinced. "I got this! I got this!"

The helicopter's rotors howled as they struggled to gain purchase against gravity, and slowly, slowly, the trajectory of the chopper shifted away from vertical. The heavy control panel slammed down again onto Reed's thighs. He saw the readout. Only a few seconds had passed.

"We're good," Rabbit yelled again, as they began to rise, so close to the rooftops that Reed saw laundry strung on clotheslines and newspaper pages curled into rain gutters and a collared calico cat that hadn't thought to look up quite yet. He rubbed the sweat off his brow with the back of his hand and saw it was covered in blood.

Another news request came in and the nose of the helicopter dipped, they veered, and headed off to get the next live shot for Saber Traffic network.

* * *

When they landed back in Beverly, Reed stood on the tarmac long after the rotors had wound down and stopped, pressing a piece of oily rag onto the gash on his forehead and watching Rabbit walk all the way back towards the terminal, cinching up his hoodie against the cold. Just a kid, he thought. Just a poor fucking kid.

The sun hadn't burnt off any of the cold, but Haflinger allowed himself to shiver, relishing the sting of the cold air. Winter on its way. These sensations. Being alive.

Finally, inside, still shaking, Reed took out his cellphone.

"Reed," Dan said, answering before it even rang. "What can I do you for?"

"I'm taking some time off."

"What do you mean? When?"

"Now. Next two weeks. Hell, maybe three."

"You can't do that. Saber Traffic needs you."

"We had a goddamn tail rotor malfunction. Almost died. We were so close to the rooftops the pigeons were getting out of the way."

"Don't be melodramatic. You're still here."

"I mean it, Dan. And I'm not flying if I'm not with someone who's dealt with a couple crash landings under enemy fire in some Asian desert somewhere."

"Rabbit's green, but he's got potential. He was top of his class."

"At Acme Flight School? I want to see his log."

"Give him a chance."

"Rabbit almost turned us into stew."

Then a spontaneous call to Laurel. Voice mail. Which could mean anything: she was still sleeping, she was on the T, she was avoiding him, anything. Which wouldn't matter any other day, but something depressed him about leaving a message. He kept it short.

"Laur, call me back." He waited, willing words to come. "Something happened today and it gave me a crazy idea. Let's get away for a couple weeks. I know you're busy and there's a zillion things that you need to do but don't think it to death this time. Just say 'yes.' Pretend it's old times."

He hung up, staring out the plate glass at the brown leaves scampering across the asphalt. Even the Cessnas, wrapped in tarps and chocks on their wheels, looked cold.

Moments later, he redialed.

"I'm thinking Mexico."

Day One

Arrival

The 737's wings dipped on final approach into Cancún International, waking Reed from shallow, in-flight half-sleep. He rubbed his eyes, shifted position in the soft leather seat, and looked over at Laurel. For a moment, in that drowsy distance between dreams and waking, he saw his wife's legs as a complete stranger might: how impossibly toned they were, taut and sensual, too long even for the added room of business class. That the modeling career she'd seemed born for never quite materialized still seemed unjust to him, to both of them; it was criminal to keep those legs hidden away beneath the Channel 3 anchor's desk all day. She had draped herself across the window area with the entitlement reserved only for the dangerously beautiful, and—just for an instant—he saw those legs and felt a flicker of hope. That she'd agreed to come at all on such a last minute trip seemed like winning a small lottery. That she'd juggled her schedule and gotten the time off had to mean he wasn't the only one wanting to find a way to reconnect. The deep discounts thanks to it still being hurricane season were what clinched it for her. Even Laurel, thrifty to a fault, agreed they were too cheap to refuse.

These marriage issues were pushed back by something less important but more immediate: Laurel had closed the shade and fallen asleep soon after take-off, and now that the seat belt sign was turned on there was no chance to get up and look out from another part of the plane. Despite his fear of the water, or perhaps because of it, Reed had been imagining what the Caribbean would look like from above. With Laurel's pillow tucked against the opening, any attempt to lift it would involve waking her up, and waking her up would not end well.

Risking a reprimand from the flight attendants, Reed unbuckled his seat belt and lifted himself into an awkward crouch. Balancing so as not to bump his wife and disturb her, he reached toward the window shade until he could just barely hook two outstretched fingers onto the handle. If they'd been in coach it would have been simple, but the seats here were huge, and reaching over without placing a hand on Laurel or her chair took care and concentration.

With the slowness of someone defusing a bomb, he began to slide the plastic panel upward, behind his sleeping beauty's pillow. A horizontal beam of searing bright light cut the cabin air like a blade, little dust particles dancing in and out of it. He pushed upward again and the shaft broadened.

Laurel's face flickered, and she shifted position slightly. Reed froze. The awkward half-crouch he'd maintained was making his thighs hurt, but he stayed perfectly still until he saw her face drain of expression and relax back into whatever dream was drifting there beneath the eyelids.

This time Reed got the panel halfway open in one smooth push, enough that he could actually see something outside. As his pupils adjusted, the view below faded into focus like a photograph taken on Polaroid film. Reed leaned in over Laurel, and let out his breath so quickly that it was almost a gasp.

The plane hung only a few hundred feet above a spectacular swath of green-blue water with coastline so close he could count individual palm trees. The sand was smooth as a sugar cookie, its caramel edges crumbling into water too turquoise to be real. Vertigo swept over him. He inhaled sharply, as stunned by the brilliant azure below as by the chilling sensation that he was falling down into it, that he was somehow already underwater, sinking, down and down and down.

Craning his neck, Reed could see a long line of high-rise hotels lining the peninsula, the size of shoe boxes. Moments later he picked out the gold-and-black lion symbol that was the Grand Medallion's trademark. A sudden gust rolled the plane to starboard, sending a crew member apologizing into a surprised passenger's lap. Reed lost his balance and bumped Laurel's empty cocktail cup. It fell off the armrest, scattering the half-melted cubes. The blue plastic swizzle stuck to the carpet like a broken compass needle.

Laurel sat up. "I was sleeping."

"Look," Reed whispered, pointing outside. "Our approach is

going right over our hotel!"

She glanced out, disoriented. "That one? The pool looks tiny."

"No, the other one, the one with the three big circles." He laughed. "It looks like a big turquoise bio-hazard sign. Large enough to warn aliens away from space."

"Fitting description from someone who will avoid it anyway."

"I'm going to take swimming seriously this time. Learn to enjoy it."

"You'll treat it like it's a puddle of Ebola."

"You'll be proud of me." Reed let his hand drop to his wife's thigh. He began walking two fingers gently toward her lap. "And who says we have to spend all the time at the pool, anyway?"

Laurel let the hand linger long enough to get his hopes up, only to dash them by flicking it away. She nestled back into the chair, closed her eyes, and readjusted herself against the leather. "Wake me up when we land."

Reed closed his eyes and let the ocean's electric blue linger in his retinas. Laurel wasn't wrong to laugh about him learning to swim. How many times had he made that promise? Every trip to see her parents in Florida. Every visit they'd made to the Cape. Every time he signed up for the community adult education classes at the Y. Each time was going to be the time he learned to swim. But she didn't know what he knew: this time would be different.

The plane seemed to rise up for a half-second, and then the tires screamed against the tarmac. The blue faded as the plane revved itself to a stop.

Mexico.

They were actually there.

As the plane taxied to its place on the tarmac and Laurel stabbed at her eyes with a mascara wand, Reed checked his cellphone, pleasantly surprised to see bars. He expected something from Dan already, the urgent scoop that only he could cover, but for once there was nothing. Maybe even his boss understood that he was serious about being here. Reed put the phone away and waited until the cockpit bell signaled it was okay to stand up.

As passengers filed out of the cabin, Reed pulled their Coach Boston bag from the overhead and put it on the seat between them. He wrestled it through the narrow aisle to the doorway and stepped onto the gangway into heat so intense that a restaurant kitchen at the peak of summer would have seemed refreshing. The air was a near tangible wall that smelled of citrus and cinnamon and flowers and salt and sunshine, so hot that it seemed to suck the air right out of his lungs.

"Oh. My. God," Laurel gasped.

Holding the rail in one hand and the carry-on in the other, Reed descended and stepped onto asphalt that had the give of gummy bears. Passengers walked toward the customs entry in single-file groups of twos and threes like a line of Hawaiian-shirt-clad ants. Before they'd even reached the building, Reed broke into a sweat. He was glad when they opened the door and stepped into the polar chill of the air conditioning.

In the customs line, Laurel pulled out her phone and started reading *Cosmo.* Then she surprised him: She slipped her hand into his and gave it a squeeze.

Reed smiled and looked at her, trying to assess whether the warm hand in his palm meant they'd be making love at some point this week or if it was just familiar habit. They were in Cancún, after all. The most romantic place in the world. How could they be here for a week and *not* find a way to get a little crazy? The longer the hand stayed in his, the more he wondered if this was where they'd turn the corner and get beyond it all, get somewhere new and different and — he searched for the word — close. That was it. He hadn't felt close to her in years.

As Laurel buried herself in the phone, Reed picked up a pamphlet about adopting from a table with piles of info on tourist visas, time-shares, and customs forms. Reed wondered what it would be like to just swoop in and save one of these disadvantaged children. They had thought about that once, years ago, before Laurel's career took off and she'd decided on that over being a mom. Interested parties could call Sonrisa Children to set up an appointment. No commitment was necessary.

"Honey," Reed said. "Look at this. They have an adoption agency right here in Cancún."

She raised one eyebrow and stared at him.

"We could think about it," he said.

"Let's at least just make it to the pool, okay? Before we do any thinking."

"I'm not saying we have to do anything."

"Then fine," she said. "Take the brochure, but don't get any grand ideas."

Reed folded it in half and tucked it into his shirt pocket.

When they'd gotten their tourist cards signed and passports back and collected their luggage and weaved their way through the horde of taxi touts offering "free" rides or timeshare opportunities, a young man in a crisp starched uniform was waiting for them outside the gate. He held a placard with their names on it, and in moments he'd ushered them through the crowd into the hotel limo-van.

He sat next to her for a few minutes, then slid to the other window where he could look outside at the town of Cancún as the van bumped and bounced toward the hotel zone. Busty women in bright colors led skipping daughters along the crowded sidewalks. Teens laughed or lounged on corners. Old hunched men in cowboy hats with toothless faces made their way in the hot sun. Dogs panted in the shade. A scantily dressed lady with too much makeup stood in the threshold of a door. A grandmother laughed as she held the hand of a toddler. As the van pulled up to a stoplight, a young boy balanced a soccer ball on his knees, looked up and caught Reed's eyes, and waved, never letting the ball hit the ground. Reed waved back.

"Don't," Laurel said, "If you make eye contact, people will ask you for money."

"Friendliness is part of the culture."

"So is asking tourists for money."

The van pulled forward and turned onto a wider, cleaner road. High-rise hotels towered in the distance. A manicured median strip separated the going and oncoming traffic with fifty feet of lush Kentucky bluegrass. Signs in English. Tourists with wide-brimmed sun hats and khaki shorts bumbled along the sidewalks, none of them looking happy or comfortable. As the vehicle pulled into the hotel's parking circle Reed felt as if the trip to Mexico had already ended, and they'd arrived in Florida instead. He wondered if the adoption clinic was buried somewhere deep in the heart of Cancún proper and not in one of the hotels. Visiting would be a good excuse to see the real city again, if only from the window of a taxicab.

"Welcome to the Grand Medallion Cancún," said the driver. "Let me get your bags."

"Finally," Laurel said, as they got out and entered the lobby. "I will be so glad to get into the pool."

As the young man at the desk handed them two freshly minted keycards and a lovely young lady brought them each a welcome margarita in an ocean-blue, salt-rimmed glass, Reed felt a sudden ache for something undefinable, as if he were a caterpillar feeling for the first time that inexorable yearning for wings.

Day Three

The Third Girl

R eed found Laurel on the far side of the pool, a straw sun hat partially covering her face, one leg up on the chaise longue in a supermodel pose, her skin already a deep bronze in just three days. A tall glass of something pink and fruity was on the table next to her, and a dog-eared novel hung in her left hand. Nearby was a bowl of salted peanuts and an ashtray made out of a shell. A twenty-something waiter with chiseled biceps melted away from her as if a sixth sense told him that a husband was near.

Reed sat in the chair next to hers and for a while neither spoke, even though it was clear from the lack of turning pages that she was not reading anything anymore. An optimistic seagull was hanging in the sky above them, riding a micro thermal, as immobile as if it were a toy tied to a string. Only its head moved, the sharp eyes scouring the cement below for crumbs.

"I was looking all over for you," Reed said.

"I've been right here."

"You could have said you were going to the pool."

"You were already in the shower."

"If I didn't know better I'd almost say you're avoiding me."

Laurel looked at him. "I know what you want this to be," she said. "I'm sorry. We're not there. Or I'm not there."

"What's that mean? What do I 'want this to be'?"

She sounded more philosophical than sad. "*This*. This vacation. And it was a nice thing you tried last night. Getting the waiter in on it. I was touched."

"Not touched enough to actually dance."

"Because it was embarrassing."

"Not as much as being the guy who couldn't coax his wife up onto the dance floor. After all that. In front of all those people."

"You should have told me. Given me some kind of warning."

"So you could say 'no' right from the start."

"Probably true," she laughed. "It was sweet, Reed. That song will forever take me back to—" She stopped.

Reed smiled. "It's like our little time machine."

"Except, Reed, we're not who we were back in college anymore. Sometimes I don't even like hearing that song. It makes me sad."

"What's sad about it?"

"You're hoping I can be who I was back then."

"No, I want you to be yourself." He wanted to be in the helicopter, soaring up like the seagulls that were forever above the pool, high enough above the world to see the big picture and not worry about the little details. "I just want that person to also be wanting the same things in life that I do." He reached out and took her hand. "That's not impossible, right?"

"I don't think having kids is possible. Adopting, I mean."

"People juggle kids and a career all the time."

Laurel put her book down and looked out at the pool. "You know how it is. The moment an anchorwoman gets pregnant they're out. It changes everything. God, I still get butterflies thinking about how that felt when I got that promotion. It was a dream come true. I don't want that to crumble."

"I still get butterflies thinking about you," Reed said quietly. "But it's pretty easy to tell it's not mutual. Hasn't been for a while."

His wife stared out at something far away for a long time, then nodded slowly. "It's hard to think about...about disappointing you. Hurting you. But I'm not in that place right now. I'm not sure I ever was, but I'm not there now. I know you want me to be there. I'm just...my heart's not in having kids anymore. If it ever was." Laurel kept staring out, past the pool, past the seawall, somewhere far out where the blueness of the Caribbean met the mapping of her own mind. She started to say something and then stopped, tried again, then slowly stood up.

"Weren't you going to learn to swim this time?" she asked. "No, wait, you were going to learn to 'enjoy it.'?" She sounded tired.

"You're changing the subject," Reed said, trying to make it sound like he was laughing, but his chest felt as if someone were sitting on it. "Like you're onto the next news story. And I've always wanted to swim. I didn't say it like that."

"Enjoy it. Those were your exact words."

"Honey, there's a lot more that we could be doing here than just sitting by the pool."

"Sure. We could swim in it." She walked to the edge of the water and bent her knees.

"That's not what I meant."

Reed couldn't help admiring her dive: Barely a ripple, as if she'd sliced the surface with a blade and slipped inside. He watched the white patch of her swimsuit as it shimmered in the blue until she came up for air nearly three-fourths of the way across the pool, and he wondered what it would be like to enjoy staying underwater that impossibly long. She continued in a leisurely backstroke to the opposite side, then pulled herself out in one fluid motion and walked to the bar.

It took Reed a few moments to realize that the conversation, maybe the biggest one they'd had since getting married, was over. His hands were shaking.

"A drink, Señor?" asked a young waiter with "Carlos" on his name tag.

"Sure," Reed replied, sinking down onto the still-wet nylon webbing of the chaise longue. "Anything, just make it strong, tall, and cold."

No doubt Carlos was trained to watch for such situations and defuse them quickly with attentiveness and alcohol. Reed imagined that the boy had seen a thousand discussions just like this one, a hundred thousand hopefuls pinning their marriages on a week in this or that brochure's paradise pages. In a day or a week or a month, the actors would rotate, new actors flying in, the same little dramas would play out and end in divorce or sex or bitterness or reconciliation or something in between. But it wasn't like a week anywhere could wipe a slate clean, turn back time, or conceive miracles any differently than had the two stayed home.

Reed stared back up at the seagull, envying it the effortless non-mechanical loft. No rotors to worry about, no gravity that it couldn't handle, no pilot to send it plunging earthward. As the waiter left behind a stand of coconut palms, two young women appeared at the stairway railing, looking around at the pool. Hesitancy was the only thing that gave them away as non-guests.

The first was tall, five feet nine or so, with straight, honey-blond hair that reached the middle of her back, and an affable, friendly smile. A blue bikini top with strings tied in little bows on the sides barely covered the tan, curvy torso. The other girl was a peroxide blonde, a head shorter, pudgy, with a chiseled nose that looked too cookie-cutter perfect to not be surgically crafted. A black vinyl camera bag hung from her wrist, studded with what could very well have been real diamonds.

Reed was about to turn his attention back to the abalone shell and its mysteries when a third girl appeared. Her dark, shoulder-length hair was tied in a low pony tail, quick and careless, as if the only purpose was to keep it from tickling a neck as long as a sea lion's. Unusually bright lips glistened below a small, perfect nose. A loose, faded blue T-shirt hung over translucent white shorts that muted a greenish-aqua bikini bottom to a light mint green. Well-worn leather sandals protected her slender feet, and shimmery green polish made each toe look topped by a tiny seashell.

Reed stared at her as she slowly took in the hotel and pool grounds, seeming to commit the setting to memory as if she were going to reconstruct the scene later in her mind. When her gaze fell on Reed he tried to force his eyes away but couldn't, holding his breath as if he'd been suddenly pushed underwater.

Reed reached for his drink and realized it was gone. When he looked up again, the girl's attention was elsewhere, drawn to something on the beach or in the stairwell. She reached into her bag, unwrapped something and tossed it down out of sight to whatever hungry animal was below. Reed assumed it was a dog, maybe the same one he'd seen before. Dipping from the sky as if it had been shot, a seagull disappeared behind the wall, reappearing moments later with a tortilla in its beak. The piece flopped like a yellow sardine as the bird flew away.

She tossed a second piece down the stairs.

"If you keep doing that the stray will just follow you all day," the rich-looking girl said.

"I know, Cecily," the third girl replied. "But I'm going to feed it anyway."

"You could walk up and down the beach for a million years and not help every dog."

"I'm not trying to help every dog. I'm helping *that* one."

"Just wait until it gives you rabies."

Only when the girl was near enough for Reed to smell the piña colada of her sunscreen did he notice that her left arm hung strangely against her side. Just below the line of the T-shirt, Reed could see a band of skin pinched in around the bicep a little too tightly, making the contours of the wasted muscles beneath clearly visible. It was as if someone had placed a cable-tie around her arm and then pulled it tight. Some kind of childhood injury, Reed thought, or maybe a birth defect. The way she carried herself was so natural that he might never have noticed the injury had he not been staring.

"Is it okay if we visit the loo?" the tall girl asked the waiter, wincing as if to apologize for the intrusion. So that was why they had come, Reed thought. To scam a bathroom visit in the ritzy hotel.

The boy seemed confused. "You are here to see Mr. Loo?"

"The bathroom," Reed interjected. "They need to use the bathroom."

The waiter placed the drink on the table, then shook his head.

"I'm sorry. Bathrooms are for guests only."

"What, should we just pee in the fucking pool?" the rich one said.

The man seemed unmoved.

The tall girl winced again. "Please? We've got to get the bus back to Tulum, and it doesn't have a bathroom either."

"They'll only be a second, Carlos," Reed said, reading the name tag.

"The access is locked to prevent theft."

Reed fished in his pocket and pulled out a plastic card. "Then they can use my key. Hell, they can use my bathroom if they like. Room 1114."

"But if they go to a room, security might—"

Reed laughed. "If they take anything, I'll pay for it." He turned to the girls. "Just go."

"Thank you so much," the tall girl said, reaching out for the piece of plastic. She winked at Carlos. "Shhh!"

The third girl approached and stood directly in front of him, her hips in line with Reed's head. "Can you watch our stuff? While I steal the hotel diamonds?"

"Only if you split it, fifty-fifty," Reed said, feeling his face flush, conjuring something witty to his tongue.

She smiled and then followed the other two, the thumb of her left arm hooked casually into the pocket of her shorts. Reed shifted in his seat and stared, praying she would turn around just once more, hit him just one last time with another flirty glance. She did. *God.* He felt his chest constrict, and he reached again for the cold cocktail glass just to have something to do with his hands.

He took another long sip of the new drink. Leaning forward, he rested his elbows on the table and let his eyes drop to the girls' stuff before him.

Neither bag had any obvious clues as to what the girls' secrets were—no condoms or tampons or birth control pills. No medications. No visible money. A book blocked most of the view inside, but he could still see the tops of two bottles of sunscreen, Coppertone 30 and a Mexican discount brand of unknown SPF. A small towel, blue terry cloth and a flower pattern. The strap of a cellphone with a small Hello Kitty on it. They had to be college age at least to be traveling alone. It simultaneously thrilled and depressed him to think that if they were college freshmen he would be more than twice their age. A well-thumbed issue of *Cosmo*, the same one his wife was reading. Reed hoped that it didn't belong to the brunette. He thought of how the dark-haired one had smiled at him just long enough for him to think that she meant it.

"Thanks," the tall girl said, surprising him, already back. He hoped he hadn't looked as if he were snooping. She handed him back the key card. "You're a lifesaver."

She bent down and began to lift the bag, but lost her grip on one handle and it dropped. The stuff balanced on top fell off sideways, sending the camera and the third girl's bag to the floor, spilling the contents, scattering things under the table. There was a soft splash. Several coins rolled out across the cement, stopping eventually in ever-tightening concentric circles, a few dropping into the water and sounding like rain. The digital camera bounced off the hard terra cotta and came to rest near Reed's left foot. Without the book to act as a stopper, the tiny purse emptied: a Pandora's box of random tiny things onto the ground. Movie ticket stubs, coupons, two hair bands, a small comb, a foil and plastic package of small pills that actually did look like birth control, a wad of money that was not U.S. dollars and was not Mexican pesos. *Euros?*

"Shit," the tall girl said.

"Wow," Reed said, standing up, steadying himself on the table before moving to help. "Looks like you set off a grenade." They looked at each other. She giggled.

"Right?" He said, miming pulling a pin and tossing an imaginary incendiary over the pile. "Boom! Stuff all over the place?"

The other two girls pushed open the bathroom door, saw the mess, and came running over.

"What happened?" the peroxide blonde said.

"It was all my fault," Reed said, interrupting her. "I tried to hand it to her and somehow I just knocked the bag over. I'm sorry."

"He's just being nice," the tall girl said. "Saintly. First the bathroom, now taking the blame...." She touched his shoulder briefly.

Reed realized she was flirting with him and wished it were the enigmatic brunette instead. But the brunette was just standing back, watching casually, not seeming to care that her stuff, along with the others', was strewn over the cement.

"Damn it, Sharon," the short blond said. "You dropped my camera? If it's busted you're going to pay for it."

"Hah," Sharon snorted. "If it's broken just ask Daddy Warbucks to send you another."

"If you broke it, you fix it."

"If I'm buying you a new camera you'll be getting a one-time disposable. Something that fits my budget. Or...what, you think I should turn tricks on the corner to pay for it?"

"Did you even turn it on yet?" the third girl asked. "Stop bickering. It's probably fine."

They waited as the other girl hit the power switch. Reed heard the telltale electric whine of the autofocus.

"Does it work?"

The rich girl took a photo and peered at the viewfinder. "It looks okay. But if it turns out to be broken...."

The third girl looked at Reed, then silently mouthed "Drama," lengthening the "a"s.

Reed felt his cheeks begin to get hot, a heat that started in his neck and then spread upward and outward, all the way to his ears. The three coeds collected the dropped items, thanked him again for the use of the key card, and started to leave.

"Wait," said the third girl. "Where's my book? It was right here." She looked at Reed, as if he'd somehow hidden it.

"We're going to miss the bus," Sharon said. "You'll find it later."

"But it's not here." Again, a look at Reed. *You took it?*

After they'd gone, Reed settled back into his chair. He closed his eyes and saw that young woman's face swimming there in the darkness of his eyelids. He remembered the look she'd given him, how they'd shared that secret laugh at the other girls' expense. That feeling in his chest, as if some magician had reached his white gloves into the top hat of his torso and released a wild dove there. The idea that the last thing she'd ever think about him was that he'd swiped her book bothered him. The unanswered, "Why?"

Laurel returned right as Carlos was serving him another cocktail.

"What was that all about?" she asked. "Those girls."

"They needed to use the bathroom. I lent them my key."

She sat down. They looked at each other.

"Reed," she said, softly. "I'm going to go back tomorrow."

"Tomorrow? What do you mean? We just got here." He sat up and stared at her.

"I've got so much going on back home. You know. Important stuff."

"Oh, like this isn't important?"

"That's not what I meant."

"I think it's important. Us."

"I shouldn't have said it like that. It's just —"

Reed stood up. "I'm sorry but I think that's bullshit."

"People are staring," Laurel said, looking around.

"Let them look. I care about us. Having a future."

"Stop it, Reed. Now."

"We don't share anything anymore."

"I mean it."

"But don't you think we could —"

Laurel cut him off by plunging back into the pool. This time she popped up only a few yards away, and before she could say anything Reed cut her off. "So now you're just going to walk away? That's it?"

"I'm not walking away," his wife said. "I'm swimming away." And then she went under.

"What?" Reed yelled. Ripples seemed to mock him. He felt dizzy, but there was nothing to steady himself with. He curled his toes around the smooth lip of the edge. His chest felt tight. But she was still underwater, past the midway point to the other side. He wasn't going to chase her anymore.

He was turning to leave, planning to storm back to his room, when something in the water caught his eye: a novel — sodden and bloated — was clogging the mouth of the cleaning intake just a few feet away from the chaise where he'd been sitting all day.

He remembered the soft splash. It all made sense now.

"There's your book," he thought, as if explaining it to her. "It was there the whole time!"

He bent down and retrieved it gingerly, and the fight he'd just lost seemed very far away.

The Murakami Book

Reed stood there for a moment looking at the book the way a drunk might pick a winning lottery ticket out of a trash barrel. The colorful cover had blurred and the pages had thickened to nearly twice their normal size, the color and texture of papier-mâché.

"Waiter!" he called. "Can I get some help?"

Carlos came running over.

"I dropped my book," he explained.

Carlos looked at the sodden mess Reed was carrying.

"I can call bookstores. We find you another copy?"

"No," Reed said, shaking his head. "This one, um, it has sentimental value. But is there a way to maybe dry it out somehow?"

"I give it to Housekeeping? They, how you say, heat the pages with a hair dryer?"

"Wonderful."

When Carlos had left, Reed stretched out again in the chair, replaying the scene with the three girls, seeing that third girl's face, the way she'd mouthed the word "drama" to him.

He'd never see her again. The thought of having her book, of reading the same pages she'd been absorbed in, gave him a strange feeling like he was doing something improperly intimate with her.

Reed ordered another cocktail and another one after that, and as the sun turned the hotel structure into a sundial he watched the shadow as it lengthened and stretched across the triple clock face of the giant pool.

He picked up the abalone ashtray and again wondered how it was possible that a lowly mollusk could create something so beautiful. As the shadows reached the seawall a mange-ridden mongrel appeared at the stairs and began scouring beneath the empty tables for crumbs. Reed remembered the girl tossing tortillas and wondered if this were the same dog. It looked a little like his dog from childhood. Part beagle, part shepherd. He hadn't thought about that dog in a long time. *Poor thing*, he thought. He could see its ribs.

Reed tried to toss peanuts for it but it was too far away, and then a waiter noticed and shooed the hungry mutt with angry claps of his hands. The dog skittered away, rounding the corner of the stairs so quickly that it slid on the tile before dashing down the stairs to the beach below. Just hungry, he thought. The girl's scraps might have been its only meal the whole day.

The last thing Reed remembered about that evening was a glimpse of the moon suspended above the terrifying vastness of the ocean, a white thumb-smudge careening in wide circles around the inky paper of the night sky.

Day Four

Laurel Departs

Reed woke up to the sound of a doorbell. For a moment he thought he was in their brownstone in Boston, but the starch of the sheets and hard pillow gave it away. Laurel groaned and shifted the covers over her head. The doorbell rang again, followed by a soft knock.

"Housekeeping," someone called.

"Coming," he said. "Just a minute." He sat up, rubbing his temples. His head throbbed; he couldn't remember a hangover this painful since college.   As soon as he stood he remembered his leg was injured. Not putting ice on it was dumb: though the bleeding had stopped, it was red and quite swollen. Hot to the touch. He wrapped a white terrycloth robe around him and limped to the door, stopping once to steady himself on the back of the room's chair. A boy in the hotel uniform was standing there with a tray, and in the center was the book that the girl had lost.

"Your book, Señor. Luz María dried it for you."

He picked up the heavy hardcover and opened it. Tucked inside was a small card on hotel stationery that read: "We are sorry for the damage to your book. We could dry it, but some damage could not be repaired."

For a book that had spent an hour, maybe more, in the water it was remarkably repaired. Dry as if it had been baked in an oven. The binding was back in place; Reed could see a few spots where fresh glue, still tacky, had beaded at the top and bottom before hardening. The cover was warped and blistered from the long soak, and parts of the bird design had peeled off, revealing the cardboard underneath. But it was still a book, perfectly readable.

Reed imagined a matron in housekeeping bending over the soggy mess for most of the night until her back ached, her calloused fingers peeling each page carefully off and holding each one up for the hair dryer until it was crisp paper again. How many hours had it taken her to repair a book for someone she didn't even know? The book wasn't even his.

He put a ten dollar bill into the boy's hand. The youth's eyes grew wide.

"That's for you," Reed said. Then he handed over another ten dollars. "This one, I want you to give to Luz María. Tell her thank you. She must have worked hard."

" *¡Sí, Señor!*"

He watched the boy disappear down the long corridor and then stood at the threshold, bracing himself to favor his knee with one hand, while flipping through the warped pages. His eye fell on the inside jacket cover, where there was an old-style nameplate and a series of signatures below:

Property of the Welcome Wanderer
Read By:
Harold Ryan
Josephine Santos
Robert R. Redone
Louis Lafferty
Sara Borden
Kenji Matsuyama
Sarah Cortoni

It took him a moment to realize that this book hadn't actually belonged to the girl. It was property of the hotel she was staying at, part of a library for guests at the Welcome Wanderer, whatever that was. He stared at the seven names for a long time. He couldn't remember anything of what he'd said to Carlos, or what had happened that entire afternoon, yet he could picture everything about that third girl, every detail. The way she'd knelt right in front of him as they'd picked up the purse contents. The smell of her hair. Her delicate arm deformity. The way she'd walked up the staircase feeding that poor dog. Her saunter as she went toward the bathroom, as if her hips owned everything in the world. The word "drama" as it hung suspended and silent on the tip of her perfect tongue.

How was it that despite ten minutes of meeting her he hadn't caught her name?

Hobbling back into Room 1114, he closed the door, guiding it back and holding down the handle to make sure the sharp click didn't wake his sleeping spouse. He wrapped the novel in a clean face towel and tucked it into the middle of the pile of clean, laundered ones that rested on a stainless steel rack in the bathroom.

He slipped back into bed and lay there, staring at the ceiling for what seemed like hours.

* * *

Reed and Laurel ate breakfast in silence punctuated by knives hitting plates and utilitarian requests to pass this or that. Any conversation seemed to fall apart before it even got started. Laurel pointed out a hummingbird that buzzed and hovered at the flower bushes just outside the glass. Reed couldn't find anything to say in reply.

"What will you be doing when you get back?"

She shrugged. "Stuff for the station. It's a busy time of year," was all she could say.

"It's that important?" Reed stared at his glass of black coffee and took a few sips of orange juice. A croissant sat on his plate, untouched. The thought of eating anything solid made him feel nauseated. "The stuff?"

She stared at her plate.

"Stay," he finally said. "Please. Just stay."

Laurel looked at him. She reached over and put her hand on his.

"I'm not saying things are over, honey. I'm just not sure it's doing anything for either of us for me to be here."

"If you're not sure, then think about it some more. There's still ten days left."

"No," she said. "That's not what I meant. I've thought about it a lot. And I'm sure. It was a mistake to come."

"It wasn't a mistake. It was wonderful spending time together again."

"It was deceptive."

Reed shrugged. "You can't deceive me for another week?"

"You'd want that? Really, Reed? Even if I'm somewhere else mentally?" Laurel paused. "And physically?" She paused, carefully buttering a piece of bread before taking a bite. "It's not like I can't see what you want from me. I just can't give you that. Emotionally. I don't want kids anymore. I'm not sure I ever did even *before* we lost her."

"If that's all it is, we forget kids. Fine."

"I want to focus on my career...." She trailed off. "Explore options."

"After twelve years? Just toss in the towel?"

Now Laurel shrugged, a slight lift of her eyebrows and shoulders. "I didn't say that."

"What else is there?"

"We could try counseling."

"You want us to go to counseling again?" Reed laughed. "Because it worked so well the first time?"

"No," she said. "Not really."

"If your heart isn't here anymore, counseling isn't going to rebuild it."

"I was thinking about you, Reed."

"Me? You think I'm the one who needs counseling?" He suddenly felt dizzy. Pushing back the chair, he stood up. "I'll be up in the room. When you're done eating, let me know. I'll take you to the airport."

* * *

When the taxi cab pulled up to the airport Departures lobby, Reed let the driver heft Laurel's suitcase out of the trunk, still trying to favor his leg. The two held hands walking up to the counter. When they'd checked in and gotten the gate assignment, his wife gave him a quick hug and a peck on the cheek. "See you soon, honey. Enjoy yourself. I mean it. Take those swimming lessons they're offering at the pool."

And that was how they'd left it. Laurel turned once and waved at him through the glass after she'd crossed security, then walked directly to the gate, head high, pulling the little carry on bag primly behind her. Reed waited, his hand raised, but she went down the long corridor and turned right without looking back again. It took three Bloody Marys and forty minutes at the airport bar to calm him down enough to hail a cab.

On the way back to the hotel, Reed stared out at the dirty streets and the shabby buildings and wondered why he hadn't simply followed her home. In a sense, staying here just prolonged the inevitable. The discussions they'd be having. The figuring out of where they would live. Reshaping their lives. Or maybe he was already over-thinking it: maybe this wasn't as final as it sounded. Maybe Laurel would get back to Boston and miss him. He wished it wasn't so uncertain.

He tipped the driver and went into the lobby and pushed the "up" button on the elevator. As the doors opened, Reed stepped away and walked over to the long faux-wood check-in counter, where a receptionist in a neat beige uniform was typing something into a cellphone. Seeing a guest, the boy snapped to attention.

"How may I help you, Señor?"

Reed put his arms on the table.

"Have you ever heard of something called the Welcome Wanderer?" he asked. "I think it's a hotel in Tulum."

The other man scoffed. "Hotel? Sir, it's not a hotel, it's a youth hostel. Filthy. Not even a swimming pool."

"I'll be happy if I never see another swimming pool in my life."

"Sir, if you have to get there today, it's not impossible. A taxi will be happy to take you. It's only a two hour ride. Or, if you want to save money, the bus is very cheap, but we don't recommend it. It's not..." He paused. "Not hygienic enough for Grand Medallion guests. And then I can arrange for the hotel van to bring you from the ruin back to the hotel. I'll tell the driver to be on the lookout for you. But you have to be at the ruin parking lot at two p.m. sharp or he will leave without you."

"No," Reed said. "It's not important."

As he pushed the hotel keycard into the slot on 1114, he decided a little day trip was in order. In less than ten minutes he was back at the lobby, the Murakami book under his arm.

"How do I get to the bus station?" he asked.

An Orange from Paradise

The Cancún transit terminal was incongruously modern compared with the surrounding houses and one-story collections of little Internet cafés, pawnshops, and tortilla stands. The air smelled of chili and exhaust and flowers and roasting corn. Two nondescript dogs were trotting around in the traffic, noses to each other's rears, oblivious to the honks of the battered automobiles that were barely avoiding them. Reed winced as one taxi took a turn too quickly and clipped one of the dogs with its bumper. The animal yelped, rolled, then limped off around the corner, wiser but unharmed.

"You looking for a hostel, man?" a scrawny blond hawker asked in an Australian accent. "I got a great place, perfect for you — just ten bucks. You'll love it."

"Sorry, not looking."

"Come on, just let me show you. You need a place to stay, right?"

Reed pushed past him and into the terminal. A bus had just pulled up and people were disembarking, a stream of families with two, three, or even five children, all with dark skin and bright, sparkling eyes, wearing bright colors. A group of backpackers, their hair in dreadlocks and wearing Guatemalan print clothes, pressed by in a cloud of patchouli and body odor. Two women in their mid-thirties had matching bright-red roller suitcases, each with a big Canadian flag sewn onto the outside. They seemed at a loss as to where to go next. As they walked outside Reed heard the Australian start in at them with his need-a-place-to-stay harangue.

"Yes?" the girl at the counter said, from behind a Plexiglass shield. Small openings were cut at head level and at the desk where the money was exchanged. She was wearing a dark blue pinstriped uniform and had her ebony hair in a tight bun.

"Tulum."

"*Ciento veinte pesos, por favor.*"

"Are dollars okay?"

"Sixteen dollars."

He counted out a ten, a five, and a one and placed them at the semicircle cut into the thick Plexiglass. A draft sucked them through the opening, as if on cue. She counted them primly and smiled, then handed him his ticket.

"Gate number twelve, Sir. Next bus leaves in five minutes. You can board anytime."

Reed chose a window seat on the passenger's side, about two-thirds of the way back. He eased himself into the plush velour, surprised at how nice the vehicle was. The hotel clerk's description had made him expect something with chickens in the overhead bins, guys carrying goats, mothers with unwashed children. Instead, there was a bathroom in the back, three televisions spaced throughout playing a thriller with Alan Rickman, who was, of course, a deliciously nasty bad guy. No one did it better, Reed thought. Rickman's scorn was just as pleasing in the heavy Mexican dubbing, but it sounded so close to the actor's real voice that it seemed as if Rickman was speaking Spanish from the start. Reed reclined his seat, settled back in the soft foam, and smiled.

Laurel should be here, he thought. If she could see me now. Then he abruptly changed his mind. She would hate it. She'd be worried about getting some infectious disease from the seat cushions. And that's if she'd even allow herself to come on the bus at all. Which she wouldn't. If Laurel were here they'd still be there at the pool, fighting and frustrated.

Almost as soon as he'd thought that, he missed her. What if the bus crashed, what if something happened? Maybe she'd never know why he was on the bus or what he was heading off to do. It would be a weird final punctuation mark in their pages together. He should call her.

And then he remembered: his cellphone was still at the hotel, charging.

"Damn it," he hissed, standing up suddenly. "Excuse me. *Pardon...*"

As he pushed his way down the aisle, the driver climbed in, shut the doors, and there was a hiss of air from the brakes.

"Wait!" he said.

Everyone was staring at him. An old lady motioned with her hand for him to move to the front, that it was okay to get off. But he stayed in the aisle, stood there, his heart pounding. It was only a couple of hours. He could live without the cellphone. Just return the book and that would be that.

As the bus kicked up dust and backed out of the parking space, Reed found his seat and again sat down. It was out of his control now. Laurel or Dan or anyone could call, and if they did, they'd have to leave a message, that was all.

The reception here's just terrible. I'm only on one bar even now, yeah, just now, talking to you.

He could smooth it out, unruffle the feathers.

Just relax and enjoy the ride.

Seated around him was a mix of construction workers, women carrying produce in plastic grocery bags, and a few grubby tourists, mostly younger twenty-somethings with cameras and dusty carry-ons. Reed had grown up thinking you had to watch your stuff in these places, but no one seemed particularly concerned about theft. In fact, shortly after the bus engine rumbled to life, a girl's wallet slipped out of her loose linen pants and was immediately returned by the Mexican sitting behind her after he politely tapped her on the shoulder. Reed wondered how much of the "dangerous Mexico" he'd imagined up to now was all a creation of the American media, of stupid stereotypes ingrained into him from xenophobic sensationalists. Instead of feeling stressed, he realized that even in the busy bus station he'd felt more at peace than he had in a long, long time. It was already better than the hotel or the pool.

And fuck the cellphone: didn't every study show that people should unplug once in a while?

Reed pushed the seat back, wriggled into the cushion, and stared out the window as the bus rolled through the Cancún he would never have gotten to see. A flock of bright-green birds exploded out of a cluster of bushes like fluff-covered emeralds. The palms trees rustled, their fronds bending like a hula dancer's skirt in the breeze. Construction workers manhandled jackhammers, kicking up clouds of dust, which caught the morning rays as if the sun had trained a spotlight on them. A feral black cat, long and graceful, darted across the road. There could be big cats out there too, he remembered overhearing: jaguars, panthers, ocelots. Somewhere off to the west a lagoon held real crocodiles. He'd seen television programs about places like Yucatán, on public television, flipping through the channels at two in the morning after his wife was gone. All of it seemed like a haze. Was this the place where those giant lizards were? Komodo dragons, he thought they were called. Or was that Indonesia?

The vehicle slowed for a speed bump and was instantly surrounded by Maya ladies in their white embroidered dresses holding peeled oranges up for sale through the open windows. Two seats in front of him a woman bought a bag from a stunning girl, beautiful but barely five feet tall, whose long black hair reached down to the small of her back like rich molasses spilling from her shoulders. She saw him through the window and smiled.

" *¡Señor! ¡Diez pesos! ¡Diez pesos, por favor!* "

He shook his head, keeping the dusty window up. The girl put her hands together quickly in a "please."

"Okay," he said, and reached to open the window, but the bus had already started to move. It pulled away and the girl stared at him, smiling and shaking her head.

Too late, he thought. *Damn.*

The matron in the seat two rows in front of him sucked an orange. She turned back and offered him one over a young pair of construction workers wearing dusty jeans and flannel shirts.

"*Es bueno*," she said. " *¡Muchas vitaminas!* "

"Gracias," he said, nodding his head and taking the ice-cold fruit. It had been precut into six segments; juice was already running down his wrist. "Muchas gracias."

The construction workers were chuckling, making some comment to themselves that he didn't understand. Would the fruit make him sick? Should he worry?

He slipped one of the six pieces into his mouth. The orange was crisp, cold, sweet, and yet still tangy, nothing like any orange he'd ever tasted before. He offered a coin to the old woman who'd given it to him, but she shook her head. "*No es necesario. Es un regalo para Usted.* "

How many years since his two years of college Spanish? And why the hell hadn't he studied it a little more? He would take Spanish lessons when he went back. Going back made him think about

Laurel, and he stared out the window, suddenly regretting, again, that she wasn't part of this adventure somehow.

As the bus bumped southward, Reed again pulled out her picture in his wallet. Looking at it brought him back to that period in his life. He could look at it and remember all kinds of things that had happened. The cruise in Alaska they'd taken on their honeymoon. How they'd danced around their rented studio apartment like kids on Christmas morning when she quietly announced she was pregnant. He'd lifted her up in his arms and smothered her with kisses. They'd been so happy together at times. They really had. It was unfair, cruel almost, how happy they'd been then only to end up like this.

The bus slowed for another speed bump and Reed snapped back into the present. He craned forward, hoping to see another group of orange vendors. He was going to buy an orange and give it to the old woman this time, but this speed bump had nothing but a curled up, brown and tawny mutt, which only raised its head as the bus rumbled by. No orange sellers. In hesitating too long he had missed his chance forever. The bus picked up speed as it headed south, and on the left side of the bus Reed could see they were passing the other side of the giant lagoon. It was a mesmerizing blue—the same blue-green that swimming pools try to imitate, only this was real water and the bottom was real sand. Easy to see why this part of Mexico had become such a mega-resort overnight. But he wondered what it must have been like to come through the jungle for days and find it occupied by only a few fishermen. An unknown paradise.

The bus passed the airport, leaving the lagoon and the hotels behind. The jungle rose up around them, the trees and vines lush and heavy. Mangrove swamps became hardwood forests, thick and impenetrable. The kind of jungle that swallows people, makes them disappear.

Reed breathed in deeply, as if the air he were breathing inside the bus were piped right from the pores of the jungle vines. At least this was something different from yesterday. It felt as if his vacation was starting. He kept staring out the window until the bus pulled into the dusty Tulum station. As it swung around into the parking space he checked his pockets quickly, surreptitiously, making sure his money and hotel key were still there, and was relieved to feel their familiar weight pushing through the fabric of his pants.

The bus station had only enough room for four buses to park and a few rows of plastic chairs, the kind that were meant to be stackable, but they'd been pushed into wet cement and then left there. Now they were permanently uneven, some tilted slightly back, others forward or side to side, a miniature Stonehenge made of plastic and chrome. Above them sheets of green corrugated fiberglass provided scant protection from the elements except in the calmest of downpours.

Reed waited his turn as people filed off the bus, and smiled for the last time at the señora who'd given him the orange. The juice lingered on his lips like the taste of a kiss.

Gripping the book gently so it wouldn't fall apart, he stepped off the air-conditioned bus and into the heat of the midmorning sun, so intense that it felt as if he'd opened an oven and inhaled the hot air. He looked at his watch. It was only eleven and already the tar was sticky. Even the dogs didn't walk on it.

There was only one exit, two open gateposts with only hinges, no door. Beyond it was Avenida Tulum, a wide street made up of a central corridor and median, where the through traffic rushed on its way south, toward Felipe Carillo Puerto and Chetumal, or north back toward Cancún. On either side were smaller parallel streets, cobbled, that had parking spaces and sidewalks. A bunch of T-shirt-and-jeans-clad teens were clustered around a boy at an Internet café playing a video game, blasting away digital bad guys to his companions' cheers.

Reed walked back into the bus station and asked a mustached man with bright gold dental work if he knew the way to the Welcome Wanderer.

"Turn right," he said. "Just one block down. Can't meese it."

"Muchas gracias," Reed said, grateful that the man had answered in English.

The hostel was right where the man said it would be. A humble, almost shabby peach-colored facade with a big black sign over the doorway done up to look as if it were a school blackboard, the writing in fake chalk: The Welcome Wanderer! The door was propped open with a five-gallon water jug filled up halfway, but the place looked deserted from the outside.

Reed stayed on the corner for almost fifteen minutes, finally moving from the sunlight into the shade. Nobody came in or out. He shifted his weight from left foot to right, the book feeling heavy in his hands. Finally he turned around and walked back toward the bus station. When he got there he plopped the book into the rusty fifty-five-gallon drum at the entry way. It settled down among empty soda bottles and crumpled, oily papers.

"When's the next bus to Cancún?" Reed asked.

"You just missed one," the attendant answered. He was young, no older than twenty, with perfectly coiffed hair and a loud purple shirt. "Next one leaves in an hour."

"And the one after that?"

"Three thirty."

Reed nodded and sat down in the nearest plastic chair. After five minutes, he stood up and pulled the Murakami book out of the trash. Then he sat down again, flipping absently through it from back to front until he was again looking at that page with the names. He stared at them, unblinking, long enough for them to hover in green on his eyelids when he finally closed his eyes. Leaning back, he looked up at the green fiberglass, stretched, and stood up and went back out onto the street.

For a second time, Reed could not bring himself to enter the hostel. Instead, he ducked into a small coffee shop run by a girl who looked no older than fifteen. She had her hair up in a loose bun, with long eyelashes accented by turquoise eye shadow that reminded Reed of the lagoon they'd passed on the drive down here. The coffee was embarrassingly bland for a country that exported some of the richest, most flavorful beans in the world. He added milk and three packages of sugar, and sat at a table, sipping it until most of it was gone. Then he ordered another one. This time he finished it entirely, and he waited for a long time before crushing the paper cup, then put it carefully into the trash. After pressing a few coins into the girl's warm palm, Reed slowly crossed the street and went inside, his knees aching from the adrenaline and caffeine.

The Welcome Wanderer

"Hello?"

Reed peered into a surprisingly spacious inner courtyard. Large, smooth-barked coconut palms rose up like dinosaur legs from thickets of well-groomed hibiscus and prickly pear. Other thick-leaved, succulent jungle plants that Reed couldn't identify gave the enclosure an oasis-like vibe. The paths were paved with pea stone, which crunched softly underfoot.

The entire right side of the garden had been converted into a kitchen, covered with the same flimsy green plastic used at the bus station to keep out the rain. A small bar held an assortment of bottles, and next to that was a small desktop computer setup with a few chairs. An old 1940s-era refrigerator hummed loudly, condensation pooling on the rough cement, a permanent stain.

In the center were a few weatherworn picnic tables, and on a wall to the left were doorways marked "Bathroom," "Women's Dorm," "Men's Dorm," and "No Entry." At the back, colorful hammocks were strung up between trees. Unused, they looked like a gathering of big tie-dyed bananas. Even farther back was a small palm-roofed bungalow.

At first Reed thought the place was deserted. But just as he was getting ready to accept that this was simply not meant to happen, he realized that faint dialogue was coming from behind the door of the men's dorm.

Reed crossed and knocked gently before turning the handle. A wave of heat and locker room stench hit him. For a moment he stood there, his eyes adjusting to the light. The people kept talking. Either they hadn't noticed him yet, or they didn't care.

Two men were sitting on a wooden picnic table that served as the room's only desk. Behind them were two rows of shoddy looking bunk beds, some backpacks, and a few carelessly hung clothes.

"So I'm trekking through India with this nutso religious chick from Ireland, met her at a hostel in Calcutta, and we're trying to find out where the hell you rent elephants when suddenly she's holding my hand. I'm doing nothing, didn't hit on her, nothing. And she's holding my hand. I was like, what the fuck?"

"She knew you were married, right?"

"Sure, sure she did. I mean, there are two kinds of guys, those who take off the ring and guys who don't, and I'm the latter. If a girl wants to mess around, that's fine with me but I'm not going to pretend I'm available. She knew who I was. But get this: She'd been going on and on about God and her church for three fucking days. How 'He sees' everything and how she feels good that 'He's up there watching.' I was sick of it, but we were the only two foreigners there and I was kind of worried something'd happen to her if she went off on her own. I mean, she was sweet. Batshit crazy, but sweet. I'd have felt responsible if she woke up in a bathtub with her kidneys harvested or something. Not to mention she had a pair of tits so perfect they could pull homosexuals back to the home team. All my life I've never seen a pair that beautiful. And believe me, I've seen a lot of tits."

Reed's eyes adjusted to the light. The men were sitting near a small window that let in a lone shaft of sunshine as solid and tangible as a pillar of alabaster. Between them was a bottle of tequila balanced on the surface of a the table; inches away, a bowl was filled with limes. One of the two men was thin and dark, his skin an odd greenish color, with a finely trimmed pencil-thin mustache that seemed out of place until Reed decided he must be European.

The one talking was built like a Marine, with wide shoulders that seemed ready to split open the fabric of his shirt and a scalp that was shaved to a shine. He had piercing gray-blue eyes and a scar in his upper lip that pulled it into a slight sneer. Reed guessed the man was in his mid- to late twenties. Thirty at the oldest.

"Anyway, I ask her about it and she says she just likes holding my hand. So we hold hands the whole day. Then that night she knocks on my room door and wants to watch television. I'm still thinking that she's there to steal my camera, so I'm watching her like a hawk, but as soon as she's inside my room she strips off her shirt and instead of *CSI:Miami* I'm watching her sweet set of Irish casabas. She wants a massage. So I give her a massage—" The man paused, then raised a hand at Reed. "You trying to check in? Marisol's out back. There's a bell somewhere there on the counter."

Reed blinked. "I'm actually looking for...something else. Someone. I think she's a guest here."

"Well," the bald guy said. "I don't know who she is or where she is but I know where she *isn't* and that's here in the men's dorm. Not that I'd mind if she was!"

"Sorry to intrude."

"No, I didn't mean it like that. You can wait for her. Here, want a drink?"

"Thanks, but tequila and I have never really gotten along."

"You ever tried really good tequila? This is smooth shit, man. Like sipping cognac. We're not talking the rotgut crap they export for gringos. I got this just outside Guadalajara. Small batches, privately bottled. Can't get this anywhere but here."

Reed walked across the room and sat down on a nearby bed, the mattress bowing under his weight.

"I'm Lance," said the heavyset one. "Lance Canyon. I know, I know, sounds like a porn star name. But I never got that lucky."

"From the story you're telling it sounds like you're getting close."

Lance laughed. "I haven't even gotten to the juicy part, man. Stick around. It gets better."

"I'm Ambrose," said the other guy, interrupting. "From Amsterdam."

"I call him Styles," Lance said. "He's got a vitamin deficiency. Makes his skin glow in the dark."

"He's joking."

"You glow like a Pemex sign."

"Reed Haflinger."

Lance put his shot glass on the table and filled it, then held it out to Reed. "Lime?"

Reed shook his head, no, then tipped the shot into his mouth and let the warm liquid slide down. Hints of caramel on the tongue, and a finish of faint, perfect pineapple and, what was it? Clove? Lance was right. It was closer to cognac than he ever imagined.

"Wow."

"Good stuff, right?"

Reed nodded. His stomach felt warm, a heat that moved gradually upward, flushing his face, his cheeks, his ears.

Lance held out the bottle. "Another?"

Reed shook his head. "Sorry, I've got a bus ride back north this afternoon."

Lance shrugged. "Suit yourself. All the more for us."

"So what happened with the Irish girl?" Ambrose asked, pouring a new shot.

Lance leaned back. "No way I'm gonna keep my fingers off her perfect pair o' papayas. First chance we get we start heading around the bases, and she's just loving every minute of it. Moaning and arching her back and all that crap, so I think what the hell, let's go for the whole hog. Home base. And I'm getting her underwear off and suddenly she draws a line with her hand across her waist. Pulls the underwear up. I couldn't fucking believe it. Like she was in grade school or something. Off limits. A line," Lance's palm swept across his stomach.

"And?"

"I'm as blue-balled as a guy can be, but I'm not going where a girl don't want me to go. I whacked off in the men's room and we slept together. Slept as in 'in the same bed' together. Sleep. Biggest disappointment of my life."

Ambrose nodded. "Story of my life."

"It gets better." Lance held up the bottle. Reed shook his head. Ambrose snapped his shot glass onto the table like a poker player asking for a hit.

"The neeeeext night," Lance continued, "she basically does the same damn thing. Except this time, she tells me it's okay if I do her in the ass."

"Get out."

"Would I shit you? Why the hell would I shit you?"

"So you...?"

"So I slap on a rubber and dive into her mud. I'm digging through her like I'm a fucking coal miner, and she's moaning and shrieking and grabbing the sheets, and the whole time I'm hearing her voice in my head talking about how God is watching everything, and I'm thinking how that all fits — is it like God watches *everything*? Because jeez, if I was God, I'd have been trying to find anything to watch instead of watching *that*."

Reed's eyes fell on the large obsidian dial of Lance's diver's watch.

It was already twelve.

"Or does the Man Upstairs kind of watch certain things and change the channel for others? Or is that whole bit part of what got her so turned on? Maybe she just liked knowing God's her big voyeur watching me being in her back door? I never figured it out. I mean, she went on and on and on about how God was watching her, and then it's like she's giving him one hell of a peep show. That girl would do anything in bed. I've never seen anyone so horny."

The next time Reed noticed the time it was one-fifteen. Still no sign of the girl.

Lance refilled Reed's shot glass. Reed watched as a thimbleful of spill ran off the faded tabletop and soaked quickly into the floor. Lance topped off his own and Ambrose's glasses and all three lifted them to the air.

"To friends you meet on the road!" Lance said loudly, and they all drank.

Midway through pouring another round he stopped and held up a hand.

"Haflinger, I think I hear Marisol."

Returns of the Evening

Marisol was a short, curvaceous woman with lustrous, shoulder-length hair. Her neckline cut deeply downward to a silver sun medallion that floated atop her ample bosom like a piece of Styrofoam on the open sea. Reed guessed she was about his age, mid-thirties or so. She wore no makeup or lipstick, but her face was naturally striking, with long eyelashes that made her eyes appear dark and flirtatious. As he approached, she looked up at him and smiled.

"Here for a room?"

"Actually, no." He held up the volume in his hands. "I just came to return a book. I think a girl staying here left it at my hotel. Dark brown hair, slender, about this tall?"

She nodded and looked at the book quickly. "Nobody can read that book anymore. It's ruined." She pointed to a five-gallon bucket filled with paper and soda cans. "Drop it in the *basura* there. The trash."

"I'd rather...give it to her in person."

"Sorry. I don't allow guests inside the courtyard. If you don't want to leave the book, you'll just have to spend a night here. But we don't bite." She changed her tone. "Unless you want us to."

"This place is the fucking best!" called out Lance, poking his head out the dorm doorway. "The best! Marisol, you're awesome. The best."

"If nothing else, it appears to come well-recommended," Reed said.

Marisol winked. "Only the finest stay here."

"And how much does it cost to become 'one of the finest'?"

"Sixteen dollars."

He wished he knew when the last bus left in the evening. He

wondered what Laurel was doing. Did she miss him yet? At all? Images of scorpions and spiders went through his mind. Didn't all places like this have bedbugs? But at the same time he didn't want to argue with the price. Fourteen dollars was a sandwich and a cup of coffee back in Boston. Here it was a whole night's roof over one's head.

Marisol tapped her fingers on the desk. "Or one hundred sixty pesos. Money is money. All that matters is that you give and I receive."

"Here," Reed said, placing the cash into Marisol's hands.

"She's a pretty girl," Marisol said, catching sight of the wallet, where a photo of Laurel was encased in plastic along with several credit cards. "Your girlfriend?"

"My wife."

"She's not here with you? *¡Qué lástima!*"

He shrugged. "Long story."

Marisol smiled. "Oooh, I am invading your privacy, I can tell. You will have to tell me all about it later. For now, we have a decision to make: dorm or a single?"

"What's the difference?"

"If you choose a dorm," Marisol pointed to the room where Lance and Ambrose were, "they'd be your roommates. It's good if you're looking for camaraderie, bad if you're looking for..." she paused. "Privacy."

"I'm a light sleeper." He didn't care, really, since he wouldn't be staying. But he liked the idea of having a door with a lock on it. Some place that, if only for a few hours, he could call his own.

"A single, then. But be sure you get good and drunk first, because even the casitas have pretty thin walls. A light sleeper might have problems," she said, making quotation marks around "light sleeper" with her fingers. Then Marisol scribbled down some notes and tore off a receipt, which she handed to him along with a key.

"Let me show you your room."

She led him to the bungalow near the back of the garden, close to the row of hammocks. It was smaller than it looked from a distance, with round walls and a palm-thatched roof that was open around the edges. At one point someone had pressed mosquito netting into the gaps but it was torn in places, and on one whole side it had fallen away, hanging vertically like black gauze on a ruined veil, offering any biting insects free entry inside. Reed was glad he would be back in the Grand Medallion by nightfall.

Still, there was something touching about the care with which someone had tried to spiff it up. A tiny deck had been made with hardwood branches, stained a dark color that went nicely with the pastel peach walls. A hammock hung across the doorway, and Marisol slipped under it with the practiced ease of someone who'd done it a thousand times. Reed followed, feeling guilty for getting such an involved tour when he was only going to be there a few hours.

"Here," Marisol said, spreading her arms. "Your private piece of paradise."

The bed, a mattress-size area of raised cement with a thin futon and two almond-colored sheets, took up most of the walking area. A shelf ran along the edge of the wall above the headboard, and a small writing desk and chair were on the other side. From the center of the room a large white piece of gauze hung suspended like a giant spider web. A mosquito net. Looking up at the roof, he realized it was completely open—the palm fronds would protect from downpours, but the flimsy netting he'd seen outside would not prevent bugs from flying up and in.

"There's a lock on the door, but we can keep valuables at the desk if you have any. Nobody ever really steals anything here. But we take no responsibility."

"I didn't bring anything with me. I didn't expect to stay here. It's all at the other hotel. In Cancún."

"Oh, Cancún? Which hotel?"

"The Grand Medallion."

She giggled. "Oh, well then, I should have upped the rate just for you. If you like I can call and have them forward your things here."

"I can deal without them for a few hours."

"Suit yourself."

Nodding, the woman deftly undid one end of the hammock and tied it up so that it was no longer blocking the doorway. "Need anything, just ring the bell if I'm not there. The name is Marisol. It means 'sea and sun' in English."

"How could I forget? It's beautiful."

She laughed.

"Why is your English so good?" Reed asked, knowing it was rude but too curious to stay silent.

"Oh, I grew up in San Diego. Then my family got deported, and we came back here."

"Oh," Reed said. "I'm sorry."

"Why? It's not your fault." She turned to go.

"Sorry, one other thing," Reed said. "Do you have any wrapping paper?"

"What? You're already thinking about Christmas?" She paused. "Maybe I have some. I'll go look."

Laughing at him, the proprietress made her way back across the courtyard, looking for wrapping paper. A few minutes later she'd brought him a large sheet of blue shimmery paper that featured cartoon monkeys shouting "Feliz Navidad."

"It will have to do," she said, handing him the wrapping and a roll of tape.

When she had gone, Reed closed the door and then sat down on the bed. It was surprisingly comfortable, the cement underneath providing firm, cool support, the worn mattress had just enough cushioning and give. He placed the warped Murakami book into the paper and folded it as best he could, sealing it with tape. He set it next to the pillow and stretched out, letting his legs hang off the edge. His eyes lost focus, and in seconds he was asleep.

* * *

Reed awoke to the sound of Marisol's voice and a light tap on the door.

"Mister Haflinger?"

"Hold on!"

"Just letting you know your friends are back."

"Thanks, I'll be right out. Do you know what time it is?"

"Almost five o'clock."

How could he possibly have slept for almost four hours? It didn't make sense. He never did that. Not since college.

Finally he stood up.

"Turns out I'm staying after all."

Marisol poked her head in and smiled. "All the best do."

With Laurel gone he sure didn't have to be staring at the clock anymore. He'd stay here overnight. Wouldn't kill him. But already he saw the vacation he'd imagined a few days ago was over. Even returning home would be tense, uncharted. It would be strange trying to explain why he'd spent the night at a youth hostel. Even stranger would be feeling like he had to keep it secret.

He went to the rickety enamel sink in the cramped bathroom and stared at himself in the mirror. The bags under his eyes seemed darker, more purple than he'd ever seen before. Any darker and he'd look like he'd been punched in the face. Maybe it was the damn bed in that hotel room. Maybe he'd needed the sleep, just not realized it.

He undid his shirt and tossed it on the bed. Naked from the waist up, Reed turned the faucet and waited as the lukewarm water popped and hissed and finally turned into a stream he could wash his face with. The small bar of soap was the same brand they had at the Cancún hotel: Venus Rosa. It was bright pink, with a cloying fragrance that lingered on the skin for hours. He lathered his hands, still unsure if he'd turned on the hot or the cold water, and splashed his face, then finally let the water trickle down his neck and shoulders, before wiping himself dry with the clean but threadbare hostel towel.

Lifting an arm, he could still smell the pungent cumin of his body odor. It would have been wise to bring some toiletries, but how the hell could he have known he'd be staying longer?

He picked up his shirt, shook it, and put it on, buttoning it quickly, trying to calm himself but also think about the time. Grabbing the Murakami book, he walked to the edge of the doorway and peeked out through a crack into the courtyard. It was already dusk, the sun down, long shadows stretching out across the garden, which was flooded with people, a stark contrast with the emptiness he'd seen when he arrived. The bar and kitchen area was packed with couples and threesomes — some chopping onions or avocados, others frying things on the big black grill, others working in minute self-staked-out prep areas on the narrow counters. The two picnic tables were full, and there were even a few groups that had temporarily claimed the hammocks in the back for lack of space elsewhere. A Mexican pop tune was playing from an MP3 player that someone had hooked up to some speakers, and a girl with a fluorescent pink wig was dancing to it on the loose stones.

All he could catch of the song lyrics was, "*Mi amor, mi amor.*"

For a few minutes he just stood on the edge of the bungalow's shaded terrace, looking around at the people, hoping to see the brunette and her friends, but nobody looked familiar. Everyone there seemed to be with someone else, seemed to already have a group of friends they were traveling with. Reed realized that he might be the only person in the entire courtyard who didn't actually have anything he needed to do. No food to fix, no friends to talk to, no beer to drink with buddies.

He wiped his forehead, already so hot he felt dizzy. The sun had baked the stones all afternoon and now they radiated heat — they would remain warm until long after the stars were visible. Reed stepped off the patio and walked across, past the girl in the pink wig, who mistook him for someone approaching her for a dance. For a few moments he tried to get past her, first one way, then the other, while she courted him with an exaggerated belly dance. Neither of them spoke, and she finally let him pass by.

He went to Marisol and ordered a beer.

"I can't believe there are so many people here," he said, as she popped the top off and handed him a bottle.

"Everyone goes to the beach in the morning. By evening, people are hungry. Then at night, at night is when the party starts."

"So it's a party at the beach during the day?"

"No, mostly people just turn into iguanas. They stretch out, pull up some sand, and sleep. Most relaxing vacation in the world."

"I was doing that in Cancún and after three days wanted to shoot myself in the head."

"Why?"

"Nothing could be more boring than sitting by a pool."

Marisol laughed. "That's because it's just a pool. The beach? You're on the edge of something wonderful, this great life force, it's different every day. Dangerous, even. Different currents, different ships out there. You can plunge in and see fish and beautiful creatures. Ever go diving?"

Reed shook his head. "Everything you just said is why the ocean scares the hell out of me. Doesn't sound fun at all."

"Your friend's a diver. You should get her to take you diving."

"My friend?"

"Your lady friend. The bookworm."

"No, I'm not here to *see* her. Returning the book was just a good excuse to do something, get out into the real Mexico. I was dying there at the pool."

"What? A handsome guy like you came all this way...to get *away* from the pool?" Marisol looked at him.

Reed held up his left hand. "I'm married. Just returning a book."

Marisol laughed, batting her eyelashes. She leaned forward and put her arms together, highlighting her ample bosom. "If you're so uptight about rings and things then I'll give her the book and say it was dropped off by a very handsome but very anonymous and very married stranger. How's that?"

Reed felt his face flush in the silence.

"I didn't think so," she said. "Hold on a sec. I think she's in the dorm."

The beer was ice cold, a Pacifico, a mild Pilsner that reminded him of Heineken but still had a flavor all its own. Marisol had rimmed the lip of the bottle with a slice of lime and pushed the rest through; it floated, suspended in the yellow neck like a green shell. The best beer he'd ever tasted.

A heavyset girl in a lemon-yellow halter top and jeans came over to Reed carrying a plate of corn tortillas, salsa, an avocado, and refried beans. She plopped herself down next to him and split open the avocado with a paring knife, stabbed the pit with the point and twisted, popping it out neatly. Flicking the seed off into the bushes, she sliced up one half and held out the other to Reed.

"Want some?"

She held a slice up to Reed's lips, and waited. He took the piece with his fingers instead of opening his mouth, and she watched him as he chewed it and swallowed. "Good, right?"

"Delicious."

"This half's yours if you want it." She placed it on the table. "Where are you from?"

"Boston."

"I'm from Pennsylvania. So we're both from the East Coast."

"Never really thought of Pennsylvania as 'coast.'"

The girl laughed. "That's because you're actually *on* the coast. You get to be a snob about it. What I meant was that we're closer than if, say, I was in India."

"I guess it's a small world."

"I'm Cindy."

"Reed." He paused. "You didn't travel in India with Lance, did you?"

"With Lance? No, I just met him, here at the hostel. Why?"

"Nothing. Thought maybe it was a small world."

Cindy shrugged. "Isn't the avocado good? Here, have another piece."

She handed it to him. The flesh of the fruit was the texture of butter, soft and perfect, the place where she'd cut it already discoloring in the air. Cindy held out a wedge of lime, he nodded, and she squeezed it for him. He slipped it into his mouth, savoring the combination of sweet flesh and tart juice, letting his tongue move around the flavors, tasting it as if for the first time.

Marisol approached. "Found them. They're in the girls' dorm. You can't go in there normally, but since I'm okay with it, it's fine if you poke your head in. Nobody's changing clothes or anything."

"Go get 'em, Romeo," Cindy said, sounding sad.

Reed took a final swig of beer to calm himself, then went to the dorm and knocked.

"Come in," someone said, and he turned the handle.

The room was small and dark, with a row of bunk beds along each wall and a set of lockers. Someone had hung up three sets of panties on a coat hanger to dry. The three girls were on a lower bunk, sitting close together. One of them, the rich type, was crying. The other two were comforting her. A bottle of red wine with a dark blue label was at their feet, unopened, along with some plastic cups.

"Excuse us?" the tall girl asked, frowning. "This is the *girls'* dorm."

"Marisol said it was okay to ask you if...." He trailed off. "This is a bad time?"

The brunette looked at him, her face as unreadable as a beach smoothed by a wave. She could have been bemused or furious by the intrusion and he wouldn't have been able to tell. He felt his cheeks flushing.

"Kind of," the tall girl said. "Is it important?"

Reed shook his head.

"No, sorry. This can wait." He shut the door quickly, the book still in his hand. He returned to Cindy and sat down beside her.

"Crash and burn, huh?" she said.

He held up his bottle and Cindy tapped hers to it. They drank. He could see her watch. Twenty full minutes before the bus left gave him time to finish his beer.

"Don't feel bad. It doesn't matter."

"What?"

Cindy looked at him. "You okay? You need a back rub? I was studying to be a masseuse for a semester in college."

"No thanks."

"But I'm really good," Cindy said, reaching for his shoulder. He pulled away. Cindy's weight shifted away from him, and they finished their beers in silence. When he'd had the last sip, Reed excused himself and went to the bar.

"Another?" Marisol asked.

Reed nodded. "Can I get it to go?"

"Don't drown yourself in sorrows," she said.

"Here. Just tell her it's from me." He handed it to her.

"That's a sweet gesture," Marisol said. Then she handed it back. "But there she is."

Reed turned around. The girl had just closed the door of the female dorm and was walking toward the back of the garden. She had a thin journal under her arm. Reed watched her choose a hammock, pull the top over her head, then fall back into it, as natural as if she'd been born a Maya.

"You can tell her yourself," Marisol said.

"Give me a bottle of wine," he said. "The one with the blue label."

Marisol handed it to him. "I'll put it on your tab."

Reed swallowed, picked up the warped book in one hand and the bottle in the other, and crossed the courtyard. He realized he would be staying overnight in Tulum. The monumental implications of this fact passed quietly through his head as he walked toward the girl on the hammock, someone who probably didn't care if he lived or died, someone he might never see again. Yet even if he regretted it for the rest of his life, he was going to force himself to talk to her.

Clione Roux

Reed's footsteps crunching across the gravel made the girl shift position and look up from her journal. She'd been writing, and as she turned her expression seemed to shift from curiosity to annoyance. For a moment Reed thought he should just head into the bungalow, pass right by without even bothering to say anything. He could melt past, forget about it. Anything would be easier than trying to fumble through a conversation.

But as he glanced at her he remembered how her eyes had opened just slightly when they'd met his as they'd picked up the purse items under the table at the pool. The way everything had spilled. The way she'd mouthed the word "drama." Something had been there. And why had he even come here if he was going to let the moment slip away?

The girl looked at him, gently swinging the hammock back and forth, her bare feet hardly touching the ground. Her hair was wet and tied back with a green ribbon. Even from far away he could smell her fresh shampoo, the same scent he'd remembered when they'd been picking stuff up together by the pool. Coconut. Sea foam. A linen blouse just transparent enough for him to see a lavender bra. Her Guatemalan print skirt gracefully hugged her hips, and on an ankle as perfect as porcelain hung a thin embroidered friendship bracelet.

Reed didn't say anything. Their eyes met and he clung to her gaze, forcing himself not to look away even though it was brighter than staring into the sun.

"You remember me?" he asked.

"Sure," she said. Her glance flickered towards the reception desk. Reed imagined her making a quick calculus of how much time could pass before she leapt out of the hammock and ran for the door. "In Cancún. At the pool."

"I have something for you. A gift."

She took the package as slowly as if it were a bomb about to blow. "Feliz Navidad? Um, it's not my birthday. "

"Open it."

She unwrapped the paper.

"My Murakami book?" She flipped a few pages. "Jesus, what the hell did you do to it?"

"This is kind of a long story," he said. "But to understand how funny it is you have to know that I hate swimming. I really hate it."

She looked at him, her eyes slightly narrowed, the look of someone worried they're going to be asked to buy trinkets or sunglasses.

"I *can* swim," Reed continued. "I just, I don't know...there's something about it, about the water closing in around me that makes me panic. Even though I can keep my head above water I'll do anything to stay out of the pool."

"And this relates to your stealing my book, um, how?"

"Because I didn't steal it!"

"I'm listening."

"So it turns out my wife and I kind of had a fight," he said, recounting the events of how he'd found the book. "It was floating there like a dead opossum."

"How dramatic."

"I just couldn't live with myself thinking you'd forever and ever remember me as a book thief."

"I forgot and forgave. Mainly forgot."

"I didn't. And it killed me that I never got to even know your name."

Reed felt his knees shaking and leaned against the smooth coconut palm to steady himself. He became aware of the sounds of conversation in the dorm rooms, of the whoosh of a car driving by outside. A light wind crackled the palm frond leaves. The k-k-k-k of a gecko kissing the dusk. His hearing widened, deepened, until he could hear, far away, the crash of waves colliding with the shore.

The girl held up the warped book, looking at it as if it had started to smell, shaking her head a little from side to side. But she was smiling, too. A page fluttered to the floor like an oak leaf in autumn.

"I'm Clione," the girl said. "It's a shame you're so scared of the water. Because I'm going diving tomorrow and if you weren't such a fraidy cat about it, I'd invite you to come along. There's nothing more beautiful, nothing more magical than floating weightless over a coral reef. You should experience that sometime. Add it to the bucket list."

Clee. Oh. Nay. Clee. Oh. Nay. A heartbeat, a rhythm in the darkness. He felt a wave of panic wash over him. Suffocating. He couldn't breathe.

Another wave, a silence, a wave.

"I'm Reed. I *can* swim. It's not like I can't swim. I just don't like...the open water. Maybe I was a minnow in a past life? Retained that little section of DNA that says 'Be afraid of the water. Be very afraid.'"

"So come, then. If you don't face your fears you'll never get over them."

"I thought I *was* facing them. You know how scary it is to bring a total stranger a book they dropped in a pool?"

She laughed. "Why? You're also afraid of women? Do we bite?"

"Pretty ones, yes. Sometimes."

There was a pause. He took a deep breath and dove in: "Can I take you to dinner tonight?"

She pulled her head back, crossing her arms.

"Wow, I was not expecting that."

"Sorry," Reed felt the blood rush to his cheeks. His ears stung. "I'm not sure why I asked that."

"You were facing your fears?"

He tried to laugh.

Clione cocked her head and pointed at his left hand. "It's okay with your wife?"

"I don't think she cares who I eat with," Reed said, then paused. For all the frustrations, he suddenly missed her. She might have even liked Tulum. It was all so stupid, the fighting, the differences. And here he was, talking to a beautiful stranger. "But I'm not sure of anything these days."

"I'm not looking for anything," Clione said. "Not with a married guy. Or anyone else for that matter."

"I'm not looking either. Just dinner."

She looked down at the book. Reed could feel her thinking, weighing the fathomless options that swirl around an invitation from a total stranger.

"Eight o'clock?" she said. "I know an Italian place."

* * *

In the darkness of the bungalow Reed lay on the bed, staring up at the ceiling and looking at nothing at all. Each detail of their conversation burned into his brain, each lilt in her voice, each flawless half-smile, that amazing conversation that contained her magical name.

Eight, he mused. A bead of sweat tickled his forehead, and he wiped it away with the back of his hand. Talk about facing his fears. Swimming was nothing compared to the terror of asking a beautiful girl for a date.

Clee.

Oh.

Nay.

The syllables felt like drops of cool water on his tongue.

Reed couldn't remember ever hearing so lovely a name.

Entering the Water

"So, okay," Sharon said, pouring herself a third glass of the Montepulciano. "We'd just reached the end of things, and when you're at the end, you know, you're at the end. Brandon's a great guy and all, but he wanted me to go to law school, and I just figure that's something that's still waiting for me. Sometime. Does it matter if I start right after college? Or take a couple years and see some of the world? And he just, I don't know. He was always too worried about me, like he was my father or something. Way too jealous about guys hitting on me. Like what, I'm going to just sleep with anyone? There's a point where if a guy can't trust you when you're out of his sight, then who needs him? Unless he's nice enough to buy you dinner." She reached across the table and squeezed Reed's forearm. "Thank you so much. It's a treat to be able to dine here."

"Don't mention it," Reed replied.

Sharon giggled. "Then again, maybe I would sleep with him. Depends on the guy."

"So he was kind of right, right?"

"But him being like that is what pushed me away. And I wasn't actually sleeping with anyone."

"It's jealousy, not envy, that's one of the cardinal sins," Clione said. "There's nothing more destructive in a relationship than jealousy. If he was jealous, it means he didn't trust you. And that means he isn't happy with himself."

"Which is why he's becoming a lawyer," Reed said.

All three laughed. Reed was on his fourth glass of wine and the absurdity of the evening's events were playing out like a little movie in his head. A day before he'd been stumble-drunk beside a sterile resort pool; now he was having a romantic candlelight dinner with two young twenty-somethings, one of whom was the most perfect girl he'd ever met in his life. His heart had fallen a bit when he realized he wasn't having dinner with just Clione, but he'd gotten over it. In fact, having Sharon as a third wheel took tension away, made him feel more at ease.

All the little coincidences of the past couple days seemed imbued with meaning. The Murakami book, the girls coming to the pool, the orange that the woman had given him—and Clione, her spectacular eyes, her lips...*her lips*. Wine had made him hungry to kiss them.

The restaurant Clione had picked sat directly on the beach, with wrought-iron tables anchored firmly in powdery, white sand. The Sunflower. A light breeze was coming off the waves, smelling of salt and the sea, but it was not strong enough to blow out the white candles that the chef-owner had lit for them and placed on the starched white linen. Votives lit the sloping walkway from the tiny two-car parking lot, darkness enveloped the tops of the palm trees, their silhouettes like giant feather dusters against the pinpoint patchwork of vivid, pale-blue stars.

"So," Sharon said. "Clione said your wife left suddenly?"

"We had a fight. Sort of. She's been busy. Maybe it was me, crazy to think she could pull herself away from her life on the spur of the moment."

"What happened?"

"Long story." He told them about the helicopter's plunge, about how that had triggered the vacation, and how his avoidance of the water had ended up with him finding the book. "Actually, it surprised me that she came. Gave me hope."

"Was it your fault or hers? That she left."

Reed shrugged. "Hard to tell. I mean, you should try living with someone for a decade. It's the hardest thing you'll ever do."

"She doesn't appreciate you?"

Reed didn't know. "We're trying to figure some things out, I guess."

Clione was watching him intently, her wine glass in front of her mouth as if she'd blown a giant bubble of transparent gum. "What things?"

"Big things. We'd talked about having kids for years and then talked about adopting and had some appointments set up, and she backed out. I guess she's not as interested in it as I am. Or she's scared. Or maybe we both need space. I don't know. Maybe I pushed too hard on it." He paused, poured himself another half a glass of wine. "I pushed too hard."

"Is she pretty?" Sharon said, leaning in.

"She's the girl that makes every guy's mouth open when she walks into a room. She might have been a model. Now she's a newscaster."

"Wow. The newscaster and the helicopter reporter. It should be so romantic."

"I know. Kind of stupid of me, right? Me. Letting her go — "

"Not if she makes you lonely."

He sat back, glanced at Sharon, and then looked at Clione. "I should be devastated. But I'm not. Ask me tomorrow, maybe I'll be sobbing into my pillow, but right now? Tonight? I'm still in disbelief that I'm having dinner with the two of you."

"You don't sound happy with her," Clione said.

"When you're with someone that long you don't just toss in the towel and give up. You want it to work. They're a part of you."

"But you're not happy."

"It's not about being happy," Reed said, suddenly feeling defensive. He reached for the bottle and topped off his glass. "Besides, I'm happy enough."

"Are you?" said Clione. She stared at him, unflinching. He tried to stare back but quickly dropped his gaze to the wine.

"I think it's really noble to want to adopt a child," Sharon said, looking as if she were going to cry. She put her hand out and rubbed Reed on the forearm. "It'll work out. Things always do."

"Bullshit they do," said Clione. "Nothing works out unless you claw your way up a cliff to make it happen. And that includes happiness, too. It doesn't just happen because you think it should."

She sounded so bitter that for a few moments nobody had anything to add. Into the silence came the owner of the restaurant, a young Italian in a white apron and chef's hat, who approached and hovered over them, putting a large hand on each girl's shoulder.

"Everything to your liking?" he asked. "You must eat now so if storm Wanda hits you'll not be hungry!"

Clione patted her stomach. Her left hand was tucked in at her side, the napkin resting on the bent fingers, discreetly hiding them. "It was wonderful, just perfect."

"She's not kidding," Sharon said. "Deeeeelish."

"Bene, bene." He winked at Reed. "I envy you. A man between two beautiful flowers. You must promise to give me your leftovers." He winked. "And I do not mean the food."

"Ew," Sharon said, after he'd left. "Are there girls out there who actually think, 'Hey, now that he said *that* I guess I'm kind of hot for him'?"

"It must work," Reed said. "Otherwise Italians would have died out long ago."

The conversation stopped again. They all sipped their wine. Reed caught Clione looking at him over the rim of her glass, and this time he held her glance until she smiled at him.

"So what are you writing?" Reed asked. "I always see you with that book."

"Don't ask her that," Sharon groaned. "It's like asking a religious nut about God. We'll get sucked into it forever."

Clione shook her head, no. "Tell him what you would write then. See what he thinks."

Sharon laughed, then lowered her voice and spoke very softly. "Not me, not what I would write. But Clione should write a story about a female superhero. She's just like all the other superheroes. Has mad skills, can leap over tall buildings in a single bound, all that. But here's the kicker: she gets wicked bad cramps every time she gets her period. PMS so bad she has to lie down for like two days. That's like her kryptonite. You know?" Sharon leaned in close and dropped her voice even lower, to a whisper. "And then one day, the villain figures it out, right? And he times his heists perfectly: every twenty-eight days, just when the superheroine is gobbling down half a Midol bottle and lying on the couch all day. She's powerless, completely powerless. All she wants to do is watch soaps and sitcom reruns. And the townspeople turn against her, see?"

Clione wrinkled her nose. "It'd only work if she had a regular period. If she was never even a day or two late. Half the women in the world would be like, 'I wish.'"

"How does the story end?" asked Reed.

Sharon smirked. "The villain offers her a choice, right? She can trade her superpowers for a normal period! Light flow! Minor discomfort and no bloating! But," Sharon's voice quavered, "she'll never be a superhero again." As she leaned back, some wine escaped the lip of the balloon crystal and spread into the white starch of the tablecloth.

"That's the dumbest story I've ever heard." Clione said.

The tall girl shrugged, picked a strand of hair that clung to the side of her wine glass. "This would be bigger than Batman!"

Clione focused her attention behind them, pointing into the night.

"Is that lightning? From Wanda?"

They turned and stared at the ink-black sky. For a few seconds there was nothing, then came a flash and a yellow-orange flicker that spread out across the night like a series of strobes. It was too far away to hear the thunder.

"The storm?" Sharon said, standing up. "That would be so romantic, waiting it out by candlelight."

Clione shook her head. "No, I heard it stalled somewhere in the Atlantic. Must just be heat lightning."

Sharon looked at Reed. "It's a perfect night to go skinny-dipping, don't you think?"

"Sure," Reed said, staring at the center of the table. He looked at Clione. "Sounds...great."

"Let's go! This is just the perfect night to be crazy!" Sharon kicked off her shoes and started walking toward the waterline. "Aren't you coming?" she called, looking back. "It's beautiful!"

Clione put her napkin down. "Sorry about Sharon. I said I was going for dinner and she tagged along. She kind of likes you."

"Sharon's funny. I like her too."

"I mean she *likes you* likes you."

Clione finished her glass of wine and shook her head when Reed offered to refill it.

"Don't you feel like swimming? Trying?" she said. Before he could reply, she had pushed back her chair and followed Sharon's footsteps into the darkness, leaving Reed at the table alone.

Reed looked at the sky. Sure enough, out in the distance there was a yellow-green flicker, followed a minute later by a low rumble, like a truck going by on a far-off highway. He poured himself a glass of wine and listened to the light sound of the wind, the girls' laughter from out on the beach somewhere. Sharon let out a high-pitched squeal. They were playing in the waves.

He forced himself to focus on the wine. It made his lips pleasantly numb. His whole body felt light. Out of tune. The night, the girls, the dusty town of Tulum, the chickens in the road and the looming jungle and the sea out there. Two girls swimming naked in the darkness. The restaurant with its soft candlelight and ocean breezes, as if he'd stepped onto a movie set. His stomach tightened when he thought about trying to swim. He felt angry, as if he'd been cheated out of something important and beautiful. Something made him miss Laurel and resent her at the same time. He resented the owner too: He had cheapened the dinner, turned it from a fun night out with new friends into something sordid. He wasn't just another cliché older guy trying to get a fling on.

He paid the bill and walked out past the few remaining diners into the dark night toward the beach where Clione and Sharon had gone. The girls were nowhere to be seen, but he followed their footsteps, just visible in the still-warm sand. To the north, lightning flashed more frequently, illuminating the shoreline and the palms. His bare feet stepped on something soft: a sandal. He peered again into the darkness and realized that Clione was standing quite close by, crouched, her expression a mix of curiosity and amusement. When she saw that he was watching her she laughed.

"Took you long enough," she said.

"I thought you were already swimming."

"Sharon is. I waited for you." Standing up, she pulled her top off. Her taut breasts shone like alabaster in the silvery midnight. Tonight might be the last time he'd ever see this girl. As if a wave had broken over him, he felt out of control, swallowed up, simultaneously disoriented and devoured.

"Come in!" she said, unabashed, removing her shorts, then panties, one leg at a time. She dropped them on the sand. His eyes had adjusted to the darkness now, and he could see her nipples and the smudge of charcoal between her thighs. Her skin seemed to sparkle, and when she brushed her right arm through her hair he felt claustrophobic with desire.

He forced himself to look away. Curled up and tiny, her clothes looked like pieces of seaweed left at the high-tide line.

"I'll just watch the stuff. Make sure no one steals it." He remembered the travel advisories for Mexico, how most theft happens when stuff is left unattended.

"Steal our panties? Even if someone found it, who would want them?" She came closer and reached out for his hand. It was warm.

"Come. Swim."

His fingers felt cold and clammy. He felt as if he were drowning. "Is it safe?"

"It's like bathwater."

"Sure, I'll come in. In just a sec." He tossed his wallet into the sand beside the clothes.

"Race you!" Clione said, running to the surf. Not looking back, she plunged in, her body illuminated for a moment in blue-green phosphor. He envied that self-confidence, that utter lack of fear. He swallowed, his Adam's apple grating against his trachea. With her gone, he could breathe again. He inhaled the salty Caribbean air. Walking along the footprints she'd just left, he approached the water like a cat afraid to get its paws wet. The sand here was hard from the waves' moisture, and it was easy to see where the girls had entered the sea. White swirls broke heavily over the reef about three-hundred yards away. Between that line of surf and the shore he was standing on there was only inky darkness, a humid, pulsating womb.

Another flash of lightning and the beach became visible. The low line of cabañas, the swaying palms. Sharon had piled her clothes up neatly, far enough from the shore that there was no chance of the tide sweeping them away.

"The water's amazing, Reed. Why are you waiting?"

Sharon was standing waist deep in the water, hands on her hips in a Botticelli pose, all-but-invisible silhouette against the darkness. Reaching both arms up in an embrace of the night sky, she fell backward with a splash in the pose of someone making a snow angel. Again a flash of violet and green around her in the waves. She surfaced, brushed her hair from her face, and called out to him. "Pure freedom."

"We can't force you," Clione said, from somewhere deeper. "But it's your loss."

"Not forcing him?" Sharon replied, lunging out of the water. Amazonian, she ran toward him, her breasts bouncing up and down with each stride. Rushing him like a linebacker, she grabbed his arm, pulled at his shirt, sending buttons flying.

"In!" she screamed. "You're going to have fun whether you like it or not!"

Reed pulled away, trying to avoid contact with Sharon's wet breasts and thighs. Her hair hit him in the face like strands of rope.

He stepped back and Sharon shifted her weight, pulling him off balance and down into the sand. For a moment she was on top of him, then they were side by side. Sharon laughed and released him. "You're going in," she said. Somehow, in just those few seconds, he'd begun to get hard.

Desperate to keep his thin pants from turning into a tent, he ran the final few steps and splashed in until he was waist-high. He felt nauseated. The water was so warm it was hot, the temperature of urine, and he breathed quickly, in and out, trying to focus on the girls beside him and not on what was out there, what might be waiting for him. Images of otherworldly creatures flashed through his mind, the things that seemed like *Alien* with giant teeth and vestigial eyes that he'd seen on late-night television programs. He stepped on Sharon's foot and stifled a scream, thinking he'd surprised a stingray or crab or something larger that was waiting for him, something lurking out there. He fought against panic by forcing himself to breathe, to stop shaking, telling himself that people swam here all the time without being harmed.

In front of him, Sharon dove, the white of her buttocks showing briefly in front of him before the splash. She was so natural and relaxed. He realized Sharon was flirting with him, showing off. Clione was more reserved but clearly didn't care about being seen. These girls were as free as the ocean's waves. It felt right, somehow, that they accepted their bodies, that they were fiercely unashamed. Laurel didn't even undress in front of him anymore. It had been years since he'd seen Laurel fully naked.

Clione was still next to him. As they'd gone out, she'd been behind him but now somehow they were hand in hand, his left in her right. He felt the heat of her palm against his own, and wondered if she could feel how fast his heart was beating. They'd stopped moving, and the naked girl beside him looked up at his face. Her hair wet, plastered back against her skull, the tips of it hanging down at her shoulders, she looked much younger than a girl just out of college. Her full lips, the soft curves of her body, seemed more like someone fresh out of puberty.

"You're very beautiful," he said quietly.

She stiffened slightly. "Are you going to swim?" she said. "If you're not, you're missing something."

In response, he let go of her hand, took a deep breath, and dove.

His heartbeat mixed with the sound of waves, a rush of water and noise that overwhelmed him, disoriented him. Everything was a deep blue-black; he couldn't tell where the surface was. He put his feet down, stood up, feeling wetness between his toes, the stickiness of the sandy bottom. He was only waist-deep, but it felt like death itself were creeping onto him, weighing him down. He realized that not being able to see anything helped. He could do it, he told himself. It would be okay. It was looking out into the blueness of the ocean that paralyzed him. Like blinders on a horse that allow it to tune out the distractions of a busy street, if it was dark, totally dark, he could swim. It made it easier to ignore what might be out there.

Clione and Sharon were much deeper, already treading water and splashing each other.

"Come on," Sharon yelled. "The water's fantastic."

He swam dog paddle, his head up, fighting the sucking pull of the current, until he was deeper but could still touch the sand. It would be okay if he could swim without getting his toes wet, he thought. But that sensation of wetness was as intolerable as fingernails scraping at a chalkboard.

Too far away, the girls were still fighting, splashing. He was glad they were ignoring him. His head could slip beneath the surface and by the time they found him he'd be gone. If they could find him in the darkness. Finally, feeling a rush of adrenaline and terror, he pulled his toes off the bottom and kept swimming, sucking air in quickly, shallow gulps like a fish left on a lawn, until he reached the girls. He kept paddling, back and forth, like a dog.

"You made it!" Clione said, smiling as Sharon doused her. "Time out, time out."

"I win!"

"No way. It's time out. I have a visitor."

"Get her, Reed. Now's your chance!" Sharon sent another volley of water, dousing the both of them.

"All right," Clione screamed. "Now you're really going to get it!" Cupping her right hand in a tight V, she began shooting water at the other girl. She was precise and mechanical, aiming directly for the mouth and eyes, her powerful leg strokes keeping her head above water despite lacking the use of her left arm, but she tired quickly. Sharon laughed, sending volley after volley of water into Clione's face and eyes. Clione's left arm, with only a limited range of motion, was not good either for keeping her afloat or for splashing. She would kick, shoot a volley at Sharon, and then turn her head as Sharon mercilessly returned fire, until finally Clione started to sputter.

"You win," she said.

They returned to the beach, Sharon leading the way with a powerful crawl, Clione following with an uneven, weak sidestroke, and Reed taking up the rear with a dog paddle, the only stroke he'd ever mastered and one that kept his head safely out of the waves. When they reached the shore, Reed realized it had started to drizzle, a light sprinkle of drops that hit the water soundlessly, and the lightning was much closer, too. The storm would overtake them before they got back to the shore. He was glad when he felt his feet touch the soft bottom. By the time he was out of the water the girls had dressed, and the three of them darted back to the restaurant awning just as the sky opened up and it began to pour.

"I've got a bottle of wine back at my room," Reed said, as the three slid into the taxi. Sharon went first, followed by Clione, and Reed was last. Just sitting this close to her felt exhilarating, full contact from the bottom of his thigh all the way to his shoulder. He was sorry that the ride ended only minutes later when the driver pulled up to the youth hostel door.

The rain had left the courtyard empty, and they dashed across to Reed's bungalow. He let them in and then ducked back out to the bar to grab glasses and a corkscrew. Sharon was sitting on the bed when he returned. Clione was standing, looking uncomfortable.

"This place is beautiful," Sharon said. "How much is this?"

"Sixteen."

"I wish I could afford that."

Reed popped the cork, then filled each glass halfway.

"How much do the dorms cost?" he said, handing each girl some wine.

"Six dollars."

"That's nothing."

Sharon shrugged. "When money's tight, even six dollars seems like a lot."

Reed looked at Clione. She looked away.

He put the bottle on the cement floor and then went to the bathroom, where he tossed each girl a towel.

"Sit here," Sharon said, patting the bed. "That can't be comfortable."

Clione put her glass down. "I'm going to go."

"So soon?" Reed said. He stood up. "It's pouring out, can't you wait for—"

"No, I think I want to be alone." She went to the door and opened it, looking out for a second as the rain poured down. "Dinner was fun." Before Reed could answer she had darted into the night. The door swung slowly open again after she was gone.

Reed looked at Sharon. She looked at him. Neither of them said anything. Sharon took a sip of the red.

"Is it okay if I stay?" Sharon asked. "Just until the rain lets up?"

Reed went to the threshold. Across the courtyard he saw the girl's dorm open and a splash of yellow light across the garden as Clione went inside. Then it was dark again.

"I guess," he answered, closing the door and returning to the bed.

"More wine?" Sharon asked, shifting her weight toward him.

Day Five

Sun Worshipers

When Reed opened his eyes the next morning streams of light were sifting through the palapa. As sleep faded, he heard the soft breathing of another person sleeping next to him and realized that the arm across his chest belonged not to Laurel, but someone else. Twisting slowly, trying not to wake up whomever he was next to, he saw blond curly hair and realized it was Sharon.

They were both naked.

What the hell, he thought. Had he been that drunk?

Sharon turned over; her arm fell away, freeing him. Reed got out of bed and reached for his clothes. They were still damp. He winced as the cold fabric clung to his skin. Pieces of the night came back to him. He was naked because his clothes were soaked. The rain hadn't let up for hours, and they'd talked about her trip and her running out of cash soon and how much she hated to think about going back home. Sharon had gotten sleepy. It had been rainy and it was late and he just let her stay. He didn't remember having sex with her and was pretty sure he hadn't.

But whether he had or not, it was light out, and people would be waking up soon and he didn't want people doing any math about the two of them being there all night together.

"Sharon," Reed whispered. "Sharon, wake up."

The girl turned again, revealing large, soft breasts and smallish nipples. She was lovely naked. A Reubens nude. Half the hostel was probably dying to sleep with her and here he was hoping nobody thought they had.

Sharon sat up, rubbing her eyes, the sheet barely covering her waist.

"You need to get out of here."

Sharon giggled. "Did we...?"

Reed shook his head. "We didn't."

"We still could. What time is it?"

"Sorry, you have to go."

"Do I?" Sharon slid her legs over the opposite side of the bed and bent. She pulled on her T-shirt and stood up. Reed saw a flash of a pink thong between her buttocks before she zipped up her jeans. She crossed to the room and kissed him on the cheek. "This was so nice."

"Sure. Lovely. But you need to go—"

"You're such a sweetheart, Reed. It's not every day you meet a guy nice enough to let you sleep with him without having to *sleep* with him."

"I hope things work out with your travels. Sounds rough."

She still lingered. "Do this again sometime?"

"I'd like that," he lied. "We can talk at breakfast. Now go!"

When she had finally left, Reed closed the door and threw himself on the bed. He stared up at the ceiling and let out a long sigh. A gecko was wedged into a crack in one of the beams. Only its tail and a hind leg were visible.

What time was it? Reed looked at his watch. Six twenty-four. He went to the bathroom and splashed water on his face, then lowered his head and let the stream douse his hair. Stiff and salty, it stood up at odd angles. High time for a shower. Only two of the buttons still clung to the fabric of the Hawaiian shirt, and one seam had pulled out until the threads were visible. He realized it made no sense to go anywhere, so he took off his clothes and hung them up, hoping they'd dry before breakfast. He lay back on the bed, wishing he could take the whole evening back or rewind it and spend it with Clione.

He closed his eyes but couldn't get comfortable. Shafts of sunlight traveled from the top of the walls toward the bottom. Reed listened to the rustles of the gecko as it did its thing. The room grew warmer and warmer. Twice he checked his clothes and then realized he would have to wear them until they dried fully. After what seemed like hours he heard voices in the courtyard. In twos and threes, people came out to have breakfast and greet the day. And as they began to talk, bang pots in the kitchen, crunch over the stone paths, and open and close the dorm doors, Reed finally sat up, realizing that with all that had happened there was no way he'd be getting back to sleep that morning.

He reached for his cellphone and then remembered it was gone. It felt strange to be out of contact with the world, so disconnected.

He lay back on the bed and stared up at the rafters for a long time.

* * *

Reed waited until it was eight o'clock before going out himself. When he opened the door the kitchen area was packed with people. The aroma of fresh brewed coffee hit him and he suddenly realized he was starving. Lance and Cindy were talking, each of them swinging in a hammock outside, the same place Clione had been writing when they'd first met. Lance noticed the door open and waved. Cindy turned around and smiled.

"Heard you had quite a night last night, Romeo."

"What did you hear?" Reed could feel his cheeks getting hot.

"Two girls, one guy, lonely stretch of deserted beach?" She rolled her eyes. She handed Reed a cup of black coffee. "Here."

So at least she didn't know about what happened afterwards. Yet.

"Nothing happened. We just went to dinner and went swimming."

Cindy put a hand up and pretended to confide to Lance. "That's not all that happened."

"No," Lance said, shaking his head. "There's more to tell."

"Vivid imaginations, guys. And far too much time on your hands." He had to focus to keep from spilling the coffee.

"A little bird told us that three people went into your bungalow last night," Cindy said. She made a shocked face. "And only one person came back out?"

Reed felt sick. There was only one person who could have known that. Clione.

"Oops!" Lance said. "Looks like you touched a nerve."

Reed tried to smile. "I don't know what you heard, but nothing happened. And I hate to change the subject, but either of you know how to make a telephone call? I don't have my cellphone."

"Cell service sucks down here anyway," Lance said. "Here, take my Tel-Mex card. There's a pay phone outside."

Glad to have an excuse to get away from the hostel, Reed took the piece of plastic and went looking for a phone. The sunlight was already so bright that he had to hold his hand over his forehead and squint. Yesterday's rain had washed the pastel colors of the buildings, making them glow. The streets were cleaner too, and little channels of sand and twigs marked where the water had flowed. Even the dogs looked happier, their coats more glossy. Across the street, a man was setting up a small roasted chicken grill: just a fifty-five gallon oil drum cut in half, some charcoal, and wire across the top. The white, plucked chickens were laid out on a board nearby. Farther down the street, a metal storefront grate opened, revealing a young girl in a pink shirt and jeans in front of a pile of colorful Mexican blankets. She smiled at Reed as he walked by. Getting closer, he realized she was about five months pregnant.

"Like a blanket, Mister?"

"Not right now."

He walked to the telephone, inserted Lance's card, and dialed. Three rings and then Laurel's voice on the answering machine. The beep.

"Hi, Honey. If you're there, pick up." He waited. "Just wanted to make sure you got home safely. Had some phone issues here. No bars. Finally managed to get to a pay phone." A pause. "Guess you're not home. I'll try your cell. Love you. Bye."

Her cell number dumped him directly into voicemail. He didn't leave a message.

Next he called work.

"Reed! Hey!" Dan's voice was upliftingly cheery. Suddenly everything that had happened here seemed unimportant. "What's going on?"

"You want the long story or the short one?"

"The short one, of course."

"Well, we're well on our way to adopting a child."

"What?"

"I know. It's crazy but gosh, Dan, you go to one of these places and just realize how much good you can do just by saying to some poor kid they've got a loving home."

"And the wife's fricking okay with this?"

"So far."

"Because I'm not, Reed. Are you out of your goddamn gourd? You know what kind of work that takes? How much fucking *sacrifice?*" Reed could hear ice cubes going into a glass and the sound of a liquid being poured.

"How's Rabbit and whoever you've got covering me in the chopper?"

A pause that might have been Dan taking whatever he'd poured down in one quick swallow.

"Roland's on your shift, Reed, but the guy can't find his own dick in the dark. We need you back here. Did you hear about the Obama visit? Presidential motorcade going all over the city. That's prime stuff."

"Well, I can't come back yet. Laurel'd kill me now if I pulled us back to Boston. She even told her agent that she'd be here for as long as it takes."

"Why the hell does it have to be Mexico, for chrissake. Just adopt a crack baby from Dorchester. Or Southie. Not like there isn't the need."

"Touching, Dan. Sometimes you outdo yourself."

"You said you'd be coming back on Monday."

"Things changed."

"Why'd you even call?"

"Just wanted to hear your lovely voice."

After hanging up, he tried Laurel's cellphone one more time. It still went directly to voicemail.

"Hey, Laur." Pause. "I guess you're either not there or not picking up. Call me. When you can."

He placed the phone back on the cradle, leaving his hand on the receiver for a long time before pulling away. He sighed, running his hands through his hair, staring up at the sun until it seared his eyes. Then he kicked the metal stand of the telephone. The hollow aluminum pole made a faint ringing sound, and he felt a twinge where his leg had struck the edge of the swimming pool when he'd fallen almost a week ago.

Reed pulled Lance's card out of the telephone and turned. The smell of grilled chicken wafted over on the breeze, and he saw that the man had put up a sign: *¡Pollo Asado!* He walked over and looked at the grill. The featherless bodies of the birds were lined up like nude Vegas dancers in a chorus kick line. The man smiled at Reed and daubed some sauce over them with a hardware store paintbrush.

"No ready," the vendor said. "*Hasta la una.*" He held up his index finger.

"One?"

"*Sí. Hasta la una. Muy rica, el pollo. Muy dulce.* You like. Come back. Lunchtime."

"Here," Reed said, pulling out his wallet. "How much, you reserve one for me?"

"*Sesenta pesos por uno.*"

"*Sesenta.* Sixty?"

"*Sí.*"

Reed placed four wrinkled twenty-peso bills in the man's furrowed palm.

"*Muchas gracias, señor.*"

"*De nada.* I'll be back at one."

"*A la una, estará listo. Será perfecto.*"

The thought of good roast chicken made him happier. The time in the sun had dried out his clothes. He wondered what Laurel would think, if she were here, if she could see him now. She'd faint dead away, he thought. Immaculately sterile, Purell-toting Laurel would never imagine ordering a street-roasted chicken. And a youth hostel? No, if they'd come here together, he'd still be there at the edge of the Grand Medallion's pool, pretending the boredom was bliss.

He returned to the little store where he'd seen the blankets. The girl recognized him and smiled.

"You came back!"

"I did." He bought a Yucatecan-style shirt and simple linen drawstring pants from the girl, then crossed the street to where a woman sold pharmaceuticals, pawned items, and unisex underwear that came individually wrapped in boxes the size of lipstick containers.

"Do you have anything larger?" he asked.

She opened a turquoise pair and stretched it out to show it had plenty of waist room. Then, after a moment's pause, the woman pulled the crotch out, demonstrating that it had ample space there as well.

"*Muy grande,*" the woman said, nodding.

Reed bought two pairs.

"Condoms?" the woman said, pointing to a box so sun-faded he could barely read the label.

He shook his head and went back outside.

When he got back to the youth hostel many of the guests had finished their breakfasts and were either gone already or back inside the dorms. Wafts of eggs, bacon, salsa and Chiapas coffee greeted him as he returned to his room. Sharon, in a bright yellow bikini top and pink jogging shorts, waved from the sink where she was finishing washing up. Reed spotted Clione writing in her journal at one of the picnic tables. She had on the same outfit she'd worn that day at the pool. She was so absorbed in the writing that she did not look up as he walked over to the kitchen.

"How'd you sleep last night?" Sharon said, smiling. She dried her hands and gave him a hug. Reed extricated himself gently. Clione looked up. He nodded at her but she looked back down at her book.

"Have you seen Lance?" he asked Sharon.

"He's around. Probably already drunk, but around. We were thinking of going to the beach. You want to come?"

"Who's going?"

"The bunch of us. Lance, Cindy. Me." She turned to Clione. "You going with us to the beach?"

Clione looked up. "Maybe."

Sharon turned back to him. "So you in?"

"I was thinking I'd catch a bus back this morning. The beach isn't really my scene."

"If you don't like the beach," Sharon said. "There's the Maya ruin. That's pretty cool. We'll be right next to it. Seems a shame to come to Tulum and not see what made it famous."

"I guess I could see the ruin and then go back in the afternoon."

Sharon looked pleased. Clione watched him for a second, unfathomable as ever, and went back to writing as if Reed, Sharon, the whole hostel were as inconsequential as flies.

"We'll let you know before the van leaves."

He went back to his room. It had been over a day, and except for the swimming he had not washed or bathed. The tiny bathroom was a study in making the most of available space. A bare nozzle descended down to head height and had been covered with a large conch shell that had been stained brown, the same glistening color as a roasted chicken. There was no curtain or separate bathing area—the water just splashed on the entire bathroom and drained through a large hole in the floor that had been loosely covered with a rusted iron grate. He tried not to think about what might be living down there.

He twisted the "*Caliente*" handle and waited as the water popped and sputtered. After more than a minute, a trickle appeared, one lone stream that was no wider than a pencil. Iron ore had stained it a brownish-yellow color, and when Reed ran a hand through, it was piss warm. Thinking that the cold water and hot water might have been reversed, he turned the *"Fría"* faucet a quarter turn. There was a hiss like a steam vent exploding, followed by a spray of ice water so cold that he cried out and leaped toward the opposite wall. He turned it off and waited until the shower had returned to the urine-like dribble.

He washed his face, poured the contents of the plastic bottle into his hair and quickly worked the goo into a lather. Then he stepped underneath the thin stream, wondering if maybe he should just sleep with Sharon and be done with it. It wasn't as if she weren't attractive. He even kind of liked her. Was she as sassy in bed as she was in the garden? He turned and rinsed until most of the soap was gone and finally gave up, wiping off the remaining suds with a scratchy, line-dried terrycloth. If that were what he was here for then why the hell not?

To Reed's surprise, the old woman from the drugstore had been right: the bikini briefs actually did fit him, though he couldn't say they were comfortable. The linen pants were just the right length, and when they'd been secured with the drawstring they looked quite dressy. The guayabera shirt was airy and loose; just the thing for hot, muggy Yucatecan afternoons. It was easy to understand why the shirts were so popular here. Looking in the mirror, he ran his hands through his hair, smoothing it into something presentable. Just then he heard a knock on the door.

"Haflinger, you decent in there?"

"Come in."

"Here," Lance said, tossing a pair of swim trunks at him. "These fit you? I heard you're coming to the beach."

Reed fished in his pocket for Lance's Tel-Mex card and returned it to him, then held up the shorts. Lance's breath already smelled of alcohol. "Should work."

"Cool, brother. Just make sure they're cinched up tight. Don't want little Mr. Fuerte to make a surprise appearance if you get hit by a wave."

"That's okay. I'm not going swimming."

"Just lookin' out for you, Bro. Swim, no swim. I don't give a rat's ass but I don't want your junk appearing unexpectedly. You're gonna look pretty funny wearing those shorts with the guayabera, but you're not on a fucking catwalk, right? So who cares? And that shirt looks good on you. Most gringos can't get away wearing one, but you look all right. Get a cowboy hat and a couple hundred peasants to exploit and everyone'd think you're a fucking henequen baron."

"What's a henequen baron?"

"Henequen's what put this peninsula on the map," Lance said. He shook his head. "Long story, but if you're interested I can show you some old haciendas tomorrow. I'm driving out to the *ejido*; you could tag along." He stopped. "You could even help."

"Help with what?"

"I'm helping them build some houses. Maybe if we get enough money together we'll build a school. Nothing fancy. But you don't need much to be happy here. Not like anyone's going to freeze to death. Put up four walls, cover it with a palapa, you've got yourself a mansion. And if a hurricane hits you just put up another roof and it's as good as new."

"That's really admirable of you."

"That's me," Lance laughed. "One admirable guy." Then he left, shutting the door so hard that the bungalow shuddered. Reed heard his footsteps crunching on the gravel as he walked away.

The swimsuit was a little loose around the waist, but otherwise it fit fine. He tied the drawstring in a snug bow. In the mirror he could see what Lance meant: the shirt looked regal, gave him the air of dignity, and the oversize, flower-pattern surfing shorts took all that dignity away.

As he picked up his wallet to put it into the pocket of the new pair of pants, it opened again to that same worn photo of Laurel. He would call her tomorrow, he promised himself, carefully returning the image to its rightful place. But now the places where her face had worn were shifted, making the photo look as they sometimes did on newspapers that weren't quite printed right: The golds and reds and yellows of the leaves behind her were slightly off register now, like a blurry halo around the soft smudge of her smile.

At the desk, he saw Marisol.

"Looks like I'll need you to call the Grand Medallion after all."

* * *

As they drove out in a shuttle van belonging to the hostel, Cindy read sections from a guidebook she had:

The beach in Tulum begins at the northern tip of Yucatán, one hundred kilometers away, near the island of Isla Mujeres, the Isle of Women. Following the second largest barrier reef in the world, it extends unbroken all the way down the Yucatecan coastline into the country of Belize. The sand is brilliant, soft white powder. It drifts like snow, here and there reaching heights of five or six meters, and is anchored only by lines of coconut palms and some salt-tolerant succulents that can survive the harsh conditions. In the midday sun the temperatures on the soil surface are well over one hundred degrees; at night it dips down to the mid-forties, but winter northerlies drop the temperature further due to wind chill.

The water remains an even eighty degrees year round, and due to the chalkiness of the limestone bedrock it has a peculiar opacity found nowhere else in the world. Hit by direct sunlight few sections of water could be as green-blue, as beautiful. Even in rough seas the reef holds back the brunt of the waves, turning the water between it and the shore into a giant swimming pool. Islands of coral make dark dots here and there, each with its own microcosm of brilliant tropical fish, algae, sponges, and benthic vegetation. Pangas primarily zip out for diving excursions or to local fishing spots; they rarely come close enough to interfere with swimmers near the shore. Swimmers should exercise caution, as extreme currents can be deceptive and it is not always easy to return to shore.

The Italian restaurant where the girls and he had gone swimming was to the south, and as they approached the T in the road where it paralleled the beach, Reed wondered what the restaurant looked like in the daytime, without the candlelight, without the friendly darkness. They turned north, away from it, bumping over deep potholes, passing palms and cabañas and stretches of empty sand until they reached a small dirt parking lot at the end of the road. There was room for only three cars. A small path headed over the barrier dune to the beach, and another road headed even farther north, but was guarded with a locked gate so that cars couldn't enter.

They opened the back of the Welcome Wanderer shuttle van and Lance lifted out the large cooler. His muscles flexed as he carried the ice- and alcohol-laden container across the sand. Clione carried a towel over her shoulder, and Sharon got a tote bag of snacks, sunscreen, and other items. Reed realized it was the same bag she'd spilled that day at the pool.

The beach stretched as far south as he could see. Only a few other people were out this early. Tall coconut palms on the right and the water at the shore bounded the long strip of talcum-white sand. Reed felt queasy even looking at it. Farther out, at the reef, white waves crashed against the submerged corals, pounding them relentlessly until they cracked, fragmented, and were pulverized. A man in a flat-bottomed panga motored out slowly with what looked like a shrimp net piled high in the center. He maneuvered through a shallow channel, and headed out into the deeper water beyond the reef, the current sucking the craft through the narrow opening with surprising speed.

At the side of the parking area a buck iguana was pushing itself up and down in the sun. From its head to the end of its striped tail it was at least a meter long. It looked prehistoric, some leftover relic of the Jurassic Age.

"I've always loved the way they do that," Clione laughed, her hand touching his shoulder to get his attention.

"About last night," Reed said quietly. "I'm not interested in Sharon."

"I didn't say you were."

"We slept."

"Why are you telling me this? I don't care what you do. Or with whom."

"What's bothering you then?"

"I'm fine."

"You don't seem fine."

"I'm *fine.*"

She stalked over to the threesome and sat down. Out came the journal. Soon she was entirely focused on bringing whatever was in her mind onto the pages. Reed spread out a towel, eased himself onto it, and dug his feet in the sand. The breeze smelled clean and kept it from being too hot. To their left he could see jungle and the very top of an ancient building peeking out from above the palms.

Lance leaned back and took a long swig of tequila straight from the bottle, staring up at the sky. "How does it get any better than this, huh?"

Sharon turned up the music on her phone and then dug through the cooler, finally offering Reed a beer.

He shook his head. "It's not even ten a.m."

"It's *already* ten a.m.!" Lance said. "And you're not drinking yet? My blood alcohol's dropping to dangerously low levels."

"It's Mexico," Sharon said, still holding out the bottle. "Be uptight when you're back home."

So he took the bottle. The girl fished a lime wedge from a plastic bag and passed it to him. He squeezed the citrus and pushed the rind in through the opening, then took a sip. Maybe Lance was right. It didn't get any better than cold beer on a sunshine-splashed beach. He'd be home soon enough. And this would all be a memory.

"Reed," Cindy asked, handing him a bottle of sunscreen and turning her back towards him. "Would you mind being a gentleman and doing the honors? Every time I've asked Lance to do it his hands end up wandering all around."

"Hard not to have hands wandering toward a rack like that," Lance said. "Mammolicious!"

Reed took the tube of Coppertone and squirted a half-dollar-size puddle into his palm. Cindy had unhooked her bikini and let the straps fall off her shoulders. Reed worked the lotion into her back, moving his hands in circles over the tanned skin. He covered the area quickly and efficiently, then gave her a brief massage while the lotion dried. Cindy sighed.

"You have really talented hands. You oughta be a masseur. You have the touch."

When Cindy's back was evenly covered with lotion, Reed held up his greasy hands as an offering. "Clione?"

"No, I'm fine."

"I'll take some if you're offering," Sharon said. She traded places with Cindy. After he finished, Sharon stayed there, propping up her back against Reed's knees.

A Taylor Swift tune followed Jack Johnson. Cindy stood up and pulled Lance to his feet. Lance danced an Irish-style jig as Cindy grooved to the caramel vocals. When the song ended they both lay back down in the sand.

"Hey," Lance said. "Anyone want to come help me build houses tomorrow?"

"I'm not strong enough," Cindy said. "That stuff is hard."

"Yeah," Sharon agreed. "And why would I want to work when I'm on vacation?"

"It doesn't take that much and you don't have to be strong. You just have to want to help out people in need."

"I'll still pass," Sharon said.

"What kind of work?" Reed asked.

"What I was telling you about. Some old buddies of mine started this group that builds houses in Mexico for people who can't build them themselves. Things look nice now but get a good-size hurricane through here and people lose everything. And a lot of places, a lot of the villages, all the young people are gone. Living in Cancún or Mexico City. Trying to make money. A wall comes down and there just aren't enough strong people to put it back up. You should come. It'd be good for you. Meet the real Mexico."

Clione was watching him. He looked at her, trying to read a "do it" or "don't" into her expression.

Lance shrugged. "Or don't. Whatever."

"Is this because you're in some religious charity?" Reed asked.

Everyone laughed, even Clione.

"That's a good one, Haflinger," Lance answered, slapping the sand with his open palm. "Anything I volunteer for won't be having anything to do with religion. I'm all about *this* life being what matters. Not the next one. If more people thought *this* life was Heaven, they'd start treating the Earth like Paradise and each other like people instead of floaters in a toilet bowl."

"You just didn't seem like the type to be doing charity stuff."

"You don't have to be religious to help out people in need, man. You should come. You'll feel good about yourself. Make you feel like you've done something with your day if you can know that some kids are going to have a roof over their head because of you."

"Let me think about it."

"There's nothing to think about. You're either in or you're not. It's a bit of a drive, but it's a really cool spot. They've got a few cenotes too, these awesome cave pools you can swim in."

"Well," Reed said. "I'll pass on that part of it. Clione can tell you I'm not much of a swimmer. But sure, I'll help with the houses part. Count me in."

He looked over at Clione. She had stopped writing and was listening to them.

"Aren't you going back to Cancún?" Clione asked.

"Clione," Lance asked. "What about you? You in?"

"I've got diving class."

"Class is made for skipping, am I right am I right am I right?"

"Not when I'm paying for them."

"Come on," Lance persisted. "It's one afternoon out of your life.

And I promise we'll go swimming in the cenote when we're through."

"I'd rather see fish. Cenotes are pretty but nothing lives in them. It's not like a coral reef at all."

"Jesus," Lance said. "You'd rather go diving than help a few people in need. What's wrong with you people?"

"There's already enough people in the world, Lance," Clione said. "People breed like rats."

"Doesn't mean they don't need a place to sleep at night. And aren't there plenty of fish in the sea? You can go diving anytime."

"It's my second-to-last Advanced Open Water. There's a test. I can't miss it."

"Sure you can."

She shook her head. "Sorry."

Lance shrugged. "What if we go today?"

Clione paused. "Today?"

"Today. We could be there before noon."

"What?" Sharon said. "You aren't going to see the Mayan ruin? I made sandwiches. It was going to be a beach day."

"I do want to see the ruin," Reed answered. "But Lance, sure. I'll come help out. I'll go check it out now. Can you wait thirty minutes or so?"

"Sure," Lance said. "I can wait."

Reed started to walk back towards the cars.

"Hey, no, Reed, don't go that way. That's the long route. From here, just go around that cliff there, near where the girls went in swimming. It's only like a hundred yards and there's a nice little beach with a walkway that goes right up to the Temple of the Sun. Otherwise you have to walk all the way back to the car and then another ten minutes and go in the main gate. And pay the entry fee."

"You mean that cliff? Where the waves are?"

"Right."

"So you mean I have to swim?"

"It's not deep. It's just like wading. Knee deep. Maybe waist."

"Oh," Reed said. Everyone was watching him. Clione met his gaze and held it, challenging him. Reed swallowed. "Thanks, Lance. I'll give it a try."

Leaving the group, Reed walked toward the spot where Lance had pointed, hoping that when he got there he'd see some kind of ledge or walkway. But as he got closer, he knew that Lance had intended for him to swim. Or if it was wading, it was much deeper than knee-high. His stomach was already starting to knot up with the thought of the water touching his skin.

The beach curved slightly around a small promontory, and soon he was out of sight of the others. If he could stay less than waist-deep, he'd be okay. He could do that. But right after he'd gotten out of sight the beach dropped away, leaving only the tossing waves against the volcanic cliff side. They came in unbroken and slapped against the black, rough rocks, sending white spray high up into the air. Only knee-deep, Reed licked his lips, looked back at his footsteps, which were already being swallowed by the incoming tide. Was that it? The tide was rising? Maybe in minutes the entire hollow would be underwater.

He took a few steps farther in, forcing himself to relax as the water closed in around him, sucking him under. The ocean was even warmer than it had been at night, but the bottom disappeared quickly here; it wasn't the gradual slope of the beach they'd swam at before. Here there was a ledge, a ridge of sand that he didn't see until after a few steps he plunged down to his thighs. His heart leaped, and he felt himself sweating. It wasn't deep, he told himself. It wasn't deep.

The milky blue water was the color of jade and the current gripped his calves as strongly as if the pull was from actual hands. He fought for footing, felt a surge of panic, and reached out quickly to steady himself against the rocks. Something was there, something pulled at his leg, something moving, and he leaped backward, almost losing his balance, scrabbling for purchase on the cliff with his hands. He began to cry out, but water got into his mouth and suddenly he was choking. *It would look just great, wouldn't it, to have the girls see him fighting like a baby against a little bit of tide.*

When he pulled his hands away, they were bleeding, torn by the sharp olivine crystals protruding from the igneous jags. Above him, another prehistoric-looking iguana slithered into a crack.

He stayed there for only a few more seconds before turning around and returning to the beach. Forcing his legs through the current and the undertow, he felt safe again only when his toes dug into the heat of the dry, powdery sand. As he stood catching his breath, he tried to think of something, some excuse, some way to not embarrass himself in front of Lance and Clione. If the tide weren't rising he could have just hidden there for a few hours and pretended he'd gone to the Palace of the Sun. But already waves were lapping at his ankles. He had to go back around to the car.

The group had stretched out on their towels, everyone sunbathing except Clione, who was sitting with her back to the cliff, writing in her journal, the intensity punctuated only by looks at the horizon and the sky. He turned the corner and slunk back up toward the little parking lot, hoping nobody noticed him. As soon as he was on the hot, sun warmed sand he felt his blood return to normal.

Reed ducked under the gate and followed the paved path toward the entry fee booth, several hundred yards away. He paid for a ticket, received half of it back from the turnstile guard, and entered the site along with a group of schoolchildren. They were laughing and giggling, the boys in white starched shirts and gray tweed pants, the girls in white blouses and pleated gray skirts. Some of them had hats, others had backpacks. They pointed at him and chattered in Spanish. A few of the girls waved and then burst out laughing when he waved back.

Following the others to a low archway in the wall, he passed through and into the main grounds of the ruin. A broad expanse of grass spread out in front of him, about the size of a modern football field, dotted with buildings made from large limestone brick, more ruins than he could count. At the top of a low hill stood one that was taller and more substantial than the rest. The Palace of the Sun. There the Maya had indeed sacrificed virgins, cut out hearts at the command of the solar system to the frenzied chants and screams of the priests and onlookers. The buildings retained a sense of majestic splendor, though they were smaller than Reed had expected, certainly not the grandeur of pyramids he'd seen pictures of in brochures. But they had a presence, a power, that attracted him all the same.

He went first to the Palace of the Sun and got as close as he could to it without crossing the roped-off areas. If he'd brought the camera he could have taken a picture and emailed it to Laurel. They should have come here together. She would have enjoyed this. He decided to make do with a postcard later. He'd seen them everywhere: the classic Tulum ruin shot of the palace atop a cliff, the turquoise waves pounding the shore below.

The water behind the structure thrashed its white froth at the cliff. Reed overheard a guide discussing how the salt and wind had stripped the plaster from these edifices, destroying forever all but a few of the intricate paintings and designs.

As he neared the Palace of the Sun, he saw Clione sitting on a rock wall. She was looking east, over the ocean. She didn't see him until he put a hand on her arm. She flinched.

"Hey," she said.

"I didn't know you would be here. I thought you were writing in your journal."

"I was. Then I saw you slinking back toward the car and wanted to apologize. I could have told Lance you don't swim, but it was fun seeing you suffer."

"I *can* swim. Lance's route was perfect."

"I saw you going back toward the car."

"It was somebody else."

"It looked a lot like you. Not too many guys wearing board shorts and a guayabera."

"Okay. So what if it was me?"

Clione looked at him. "I wanted to apologize."

"You just did."

"No, I mean...There's a lot going on in my life and you're married, and I'm not okay with that. It makes me really uncomfortable."

"What does?"

She looked at him. "Us being together."

Reed nodded.   "Well, I'm sad I make you uncomfortable. But I'm glad you're telling me instead of just making me guess. I thought you were upset about Sharon. I didn't know my being married had anything to do with it."

"Sharon?" Clione asked. "She's just sleeping with you so you'll be her Sugar Daddy. Anyone can see through that. And you don't strike me as someone who is into someone who will toss you away the moment a richer person comes along."

"I'm not rich. And we're not sleeping together. She passed out in my bed."

"Even if you did it with her all night, what does it matter? You don't have to think about me." She broke off and bit her lower lip. "Do whatever you want."

"I thought you came here to apologize. Now you're sounding like

I've made you mad again."

"She stayed overnight."

"Because it was pouring rain."

Clione looked at him. "You didn't have to sleep with her."

"I didn't sleep with her," he insisted. "I slept *near* her. And I sure as hell didn't come all this way to bring Sharon a book that she'd lost. I didn't have the jitters in my stomach all that time thinking about taking Sharon to dinner. And you didn't have to invite her, right?" He waited. Clione allowed him just the barest hint of a smile. "Nobody could have been more perplexed than I was the way that night ended. You basically ran out of my room. You left me with her."

"She was all over you," Clione said. "And I can be quite the bitch sometimes."

"Okay. So we both have problems: I'm married. And you're a bitch. Maybe in our mutual flawed imperfection we can still be friends? Or if that's too close to the sun for you, fine. I can hop on a bus and head back. Though frankly, I'd prefer to be here in this lovely town than in that stupid resort. It's beautiful here."

The girl smiled, then pursed her lips and then looked as if she were going to say something. But she didn't. Reed waited, and Clione smiled at him again, and finally they just started walking, side by side.

They walked from the Temple of the Sun along the cliff's edge, looking down at the water. Swimmers were laughing and splashing in the waves.

Clione pointed. "That's where you'd have ended up if you'd kept on going instead of turning around. If you could swim. It's really beautiful when you walk up from the water and suddenly see all the palaces. The Maya that lived here must have felt the same way when they came back from swimming."

"Let's look around more. Somewhere not near the water."

She nodded. "I'll show you my favorite spot. Most people never find it, but I think it's kind of cool."

"Sure."

Clione led him back to where the cleared area began, to the base of a tall, central structure that from a distance looked like it was one story, but when they got close Reed realized there was a rough set of stairs going down to a second level entirely underground.

"I doubt many people know to look here. They just stick to the paths."

"Can we really go down?" Reed asked. At their feet, ancient steps led to a small, brownish puddle. The air smelled of urine. People probably came here to relieve themselves.

"Sure, we can go down. Just don't slip," Clione said.

"Your favorite spot smells like a bathroom? Are you aware of that?"

"It's just moss. Be careful and you'll be fine."

"It's mossy because people are coming down here when they can't make it to the Portajohn out at the main gate."

She slapped him on the arm. "Stop being so mean. Are you coming or not?"

Bracing himself against the cool rock wall, Reed lowered himself down onto the stairs, one leg at a time. Clione waited until he was stationary and then leaped in, landing like a mountain goat, securely as if she were on flat ground. She grinned. "Once a tomboy, always a tomboy."

"The tom may still be there but the boy is long gone," Reed said. He looked around. "So do these stairs lead anywhere?"

"Not far. But isn't it funny, there's all those people up there wandering around, yet this is like our little spot. Like we've been swallowed up by the ruin. I was here a few days ago and nobody came for two hours."

"I like it. Except for the smell."

"I wrote six pages here the other day. It's so cool and quiet and there was this perfect spot where a shaft of light made it possible to write. Did you know there are little tiny fish down there in the water?"

"Fish? In that brown goo?"

"Amazing, isn't it?" She pointed. "Look! There's some!"

Sure enough, Reed could see the glint and glimmer as they turned.

Clione crouched down on her knees and stared at them, her neckline opening enough for him to see the silhouettes of her breasts. "Wouldn't it be cool to be able to shrink down to that size, check out where that goes? I have this feeling like it connects to the cenotes, goes all the way out to the sea."

"Maybe it doesn't go anywhere," Reed said. "The fish just try to stay there, try not to think that there's so much more out there."

"Touché," Clione agreed. "Sure. And if they're stuck in that puddle and that puddle is all they'll ever know or ever see, maybe it's better that they *don't* know about the reefs or the cenotes."

"What are cenotes? Lance mentioned them too."

"They're amazing underground caverns filled with water. Unique to Yucatán. Sometimes there's giant tree roots that come down from the ceiling like ladders — you can climb up them and then dive back down. Shafts of sunlight knife through the darkness like a UFO's spotlight, and where the light hits the water it's an utterly amazing color blue. Some of the cenotes, nobody knows how deep they are or where they go. Yucatán has the largest underwater cave system in the world. Miles and miles. If you could hold your breath long enough, you could go all the way out to the ocean." She thought for a moment. "Lance could take you. You wouldn't even have to go in. They're just stunning even to look at."

"So you decide yet whether you'll come with us this afternoon?"

"I should study."

"You'll do fine. You were probably a dolphin in another life."

"Hardly. I'm not a strong swimmer, but I'm in love with the water. Totally addicted."

Reed watched the milky skin of her neck, wanting to kiss it. He would have tried, only she'd set things out so clearly that to make a move now would cause any budding friendship to crumble. He imagined the slight saltiness, the whiff of musk.

Her voice changed. "I want you to come out diving with me sometime."

"You really are a dreamer," Reed laughed. "Even that little puddle gives me the creeps. Those fish don't know how lucky they are. To be able to swim without fear."

"You swam with us last night."

"That's a bit of a mystery even to me. But there was some wine involved. And I seem to recall there were these two irritating girls who wouldn't leave me alone."

Clione giggled. "Must have been just terrible. So terrible that you went and slept with one."

"*Near* one. And I don't think I'll ever recover from the trauma."

"You *swam*." She said it firmly. "If you swam yesterday, you can dive."

Clione turned, climbed the remaining stairs, and waited for him to follow. He picked his way up the slippery steps and the girl extended a hand to pull him up. Her palm was dry and warm, and he was sorry she broke the grip after he'd planted both feet on the firm ground outside the hole. Reed felt as if he'd missed a chance for something there, as if he might have kissed her, but the moment hadn't ever been right. Or maybe it had come and gone, and he hadn't paid quite enough attention.

They exited the ruin and walked back toward the parking lot. Neither spoke. As they neared the gate, Reed saw that Lance and Sharon were just putting their stuff into the back of the car. Cindy had a bunch of beach towels in her arms.

"Who's ready for building some hovels?" Lance called, when they were within earshot.

"Clione, come with us," Reed said quietly. "Study later."

She looked up at him, tipped her head to one side, and then pursed her lips.

"It'll be different if you come," he said.

Clione turned, walking backward, studying his face.

"I'll go on the condition Lance takes us to the cenote *and* if you agree to swim in it. Not just watch. You can't be on the sidelines. You have to dive right in."

Reed stopped walking. He held up his hands.

"I can't, Clione. No—"

"So, that's a 'no.' Fine." She nodded. "See you when you get back."

"No, that's a...yes," he said, forcing the words out. "I'll go in. If that's what it takes."

"Promise?" She reached out her hand. "Deal? No going back, right?"

He shook it.

"No going back," she repeated.

"You didn't say I had to swim for long. Just that I swim."

Clione danced across the white sand like an otter pup that's just discovered a bank of fresh, newly fallen snow. Watching her made Reed feel dizzy, simultaneously thrilled and terrified, as if he were standing on the edge of a dock looking down into deep water and seeing giant shadows gliding by below.

The Community

The trip back to the hostel was subdued and silent. Clione took the passenger seat up front and Cindy, Sharon, and Reed sat together on the seat behind. Reed felt as if everyone in the van were watching him, as if they could sense a shift in the dynamics between him and Clione, that they all knew something had happened up there in the Maya ruin. Cindy and Sharon spoke only when spoken to, feeling they were being abandoned, even though they themselves had decided not to join that afternoon. Even Lance, usually jovial, kept quiet, his jaw tight as he looked out at the road, as if he were a frustrated father chauffeuring a carload of siblings who had just ended a fight. Finally, Sharon, sitting next to him, sought out Reed's hand. Too surprised to do anything, he let her hold it for a few seconds before disentangling himself. Sharon, knowing it was more than a snub, bit her lip and spent the rest of the car ride blinking as if trying to hold back tears.

As soon as Lance pulled the van to the entrance, Reed got out and went straight to his room. He stripped off the swimming trunks. This was all make-believe, he thought. At any point he could wave a wand and be back in Cancún. Then back in Boston in the time it took a Boeing to beeline there at five hundred miles an hour.

So why then did he feel so sorry for Sharon, he wondered. She was a sweet girl. If he hadn't met Clione he could easily have enjoyed sleeping with her. Almost as soon as he thought that, he checked himself. It wasn't like that at all. If he hadn't met Clione, none of this would have ever happened. He'd be at the pool. If that. He'd probably be back in Boston right now, covering rollovers on I-93 at fifteen hundred feet.

Sometimes you just meet someone and your whole world turns upside down. Nothing is ever the same again.

He was brushing his teeth in his underwear when there was a rap on the door.

"Haflinger?" Not waiting, Lance opened the door.

"Christ, I'm dressing." Reed grabbed for his pants and tried to put them on.

"Not sure what deal you made with the devil, but I admire you for persuading Clione to come with us." He watched as Reed fumbled to get dressed. "You hiding a ten-incher in your shorts or something? Jesus, those things don't leave much to the imagination."

"I didn't do anything to get her to come," Reed answered, ignoring the comment. "I just promised Clione I'd swim in the cenote."

"You're that scared to swim, huh?"

Reed buttoned the pants and threw on his shirt. "Terrified. It's hard for me to even look at a swimming pool."

"Not enough to let it come between you and a beautiful girl, it seems. I've invited her like five times, and she's never come before."

"Maybe she just likes me. And I *can* swim. Just don't like it, that's all."

Reed finished dressing and they crossed the empty courtyard. The air was cooler than it had been this time the day before, almost chilly, refreshing and good. Tiny lizards had staked out their spots to wait for the sun. Lance bent and coaxed one onto his finger, keeping his hand low to the ground so that the animal wouldn't injure itself if it got scared and jumped.

"Hey, little buddy."

"Is that a gecko?"

"No, those come out at night and eat skeets. These babies take care of the daytime buggies." He stroked it gently with a finger. It flickered its tongue, tasting the air. "I think it's an anole."

"You're good with animals."

Lance continued to the car and Reed crossed the garden to the girls dorm. He knocked on the door, and someone he didn't know answered. She had a towel wrapped over her head, a pink bathrobe, and big pink bunny slippers.

"I'm looking for Clione," Reed said.

"Hold on."

He heard the girl call for Clione. Instead, Sharon came out. They sat together at the nearest picnic table.

"Clione's in the bathroom. Little touch of Montezuma's Revenge."

They heard the toilet flush.

"So," Sharon continued. "Cindy and I were thinking about taking a trip to Holbox. Up north? You want to come with us? Take a road trip. See a different part of Yucatán?"

"I'll have to think about it," Reed replied. "I kind of like it here."

The toilet flushed again.

"You like Clione, you mean," Sharon said. She sounded sad.

"I'm married," he said. "I don't 'like' anyone. That's not why I'm here. It's just...."

"It's written all over you."

"Sharon," Reed said. "You're a sweet girl, but I — "

She held up her hands and laughed. "You sound like you're breaking up with someone. I'm just saying you should think about coming with us. You're missing out. Holbox is beautiful. It's famous for whale sharks. You can snorkel with them. They don't bite." She walked back to the dorm door and then turned. "And neither do I."

Reed waited at the table until Clione came, then they went outside. Lance stood next to a black CJ7 Renegade with a dusty soft top that the sun had faded from black to a light gray. The vehicle was jacked up for added clearance on oversize tires with knobby tread that had filled with hardened, reddish mud. A thick matte-black pipe came out the front quarter panel and ran all the way up above the windshield. If you were going to drive through the Apocalypse, Reed thought, this would be the steed.

Lance motioned and they got inside. The passenger's seat had a big X cut through the nylon; a lone coil spring protruded through the spill of cushion foam. From the rear-view mirror hung a pine-tree-shaped air freshener so sun-bleached that all that remained of the pine green color was a minty blush the color of sea foam.

"That seat's called the Anal Reamer. Watch out when you sit down."

Clione wrinkled her nose. "I'll take the back."

"Guess that makes you the lucky one, Reed. Hop in, get cozy, keep that sphincter clenched or you'll end up feeling like a convict who's dropped the soap in the shower."

Reed eased himself onto the edge of the seat and found that he could sit without too much discomfort if he didn't lean back. It was a good excuse to sit turned enough to see into the rear, where Clione was brushing off the seat as if it had been used as a meth lab. She finished and sat down next to some large plastic beer coolers. She peeked into one, revealing a tangle of diving hoses, regulators, weights, and nylon webbing. Under the seat Reed could see the gray cylinders of the air tanks. Parallel and glistening, the tanks seemed sinister, as if the car were rigged to explode.

"Are these night-vision goggles?" Clione asked, pointing to something Reed couldn't see.

"Yep."

"You've got more gadgets in here than James Bond."

"Must be a story behind *that*," Reed said, pointing to a large spider web in the windshield. In the center was a hole large enough to put a finger through.

"I was being stupid and learned a valuable lesson instead of getting what I deserved."

Clione laughed. "You always get away with everything."

"I do," Lance said, no trace of humor in his voice. "But that time was close."

Lance turned the key and the vehicle backfired twice, coughed, then came to life with a throaty roar. Several of the people on the street turned to look, and Lance waved at them as he pulled out into the traffic. He knew everyone, it seemed. Or else he just waved at anyone and they waved back. But Reed liked that: a town so small that everyone knew you, even if they didn't know your name. After a few seconds going south Lance cut the wheels hard and made a sharp U-turn. He punched the gas and the car shot forward, tires chirping. When they turned left at the Pemex, Reed got a whiff of rubber.

"Runs pretty well," Reed said. "Is that because of that smokestack thing in front."

Lance laughed. "That's not the exhaust. It's a snorkel. Lets air into the engine so it'll run even underwater."

"Why would you need it?"

Lance shrugged. "Mainly I don't. Not these days. But I do a lot of driving on beaches. Sometimes it's the only way to get out to where good sections of the reef are. Means you don't have to worry about tides trapping you in some remote location."

"So you're a diver?"

"Dive instructor. And a good one. I taught Clione everything she knows."

"Which isn't a lot," Clione said. "I just got my Open Water, and now I'm doing Advanced. But diving is something everyone should do at least once in their life."

"How'd you end up here in Tulum?"

Lance looked at him. "You writing my memoirs?" He glanced in the rear-view mirror. "I thought Clione was the writer."

"I was just asking. And if you're a dive instructor, why aren't you doing the test for Clione?"

"Ask her."

Reed waited, finally turning. Clione just looked at him and shrugged.

"I wanted a different instructor," she said. "Lance is too *Lance.*"

They fell silent. The road stretched out in front of them, straight as an arrow for miles, punctuated by potholes the size of trash can lids. Reed unzipped the plastic window and tucked it into the armrest, letting the hot air whip through. Sparse, straggly acacias and mesquites had replaced the palm trees and the lush, jungle underbrush. Trees here rose up from ochre earth that was cracked and parched. Low scrub was rarely more than four yards tall. The right side of the road had been roughly cleared, the yellow bulldozers nosed into the bushes at random like megalithic child's toys. One lone electric line paralleled the road, its poles made of weathered wood. Reed noticed that some of the green glass insulators had been replaced with broken beer bottles duct-taped to the wire. After ten minutes heading inland Lance pulled the car over into the gravel and pointed to the right.

"See that?"

Protruding up from the surrounding jungle were twin smokestacks, the canary-yellow paint peeling to reveal the rust beneath. Vine tendrils wrapped like tentacles around what clearly once had been a ship of some kind.

"Is that the Cozumel Ferry? Here?" Clione asked. "It's so faded I didn't recognize the yellow."

Lance nodded. "Hurricane Dean. Left it sitting on the palms. If you need any more convincing that what we're doing today is a help, we can get out and get a closer look at that ferry. The waves bent it in half and the surge came this far inland. Imagine what water like that does to a village."

"I believe you," Reed said. "It's Cindy and Sharon who need

to be here too."

"They're just here to play," said Clione.

"Isn't that why everyone comes? To get away from it all?"

"Some come to help," said Lance.

"Or to learn," replied Clione. "Learn Spanish, learn to cook, learn to dive, learn a new culture...."

Lance put the car in gear and pulled back onto the road. Reed looked back and could see the bow of the vessel sticking up from the jungle, the faded blue and yellow "Cozumel" still visible above the tree line. The ship looked as if it were sinking after having just plunged through a particularly deadly wave. Reed watched it through the window until the road angled slowly toward the west and the strange apparition disappeared behind them.

After about half an hour, they pulled over into the *ejido*, a ranchland township that was just a collection of roadside lean-to shacks roofed with palm fronds or green corrugated fiberglass surrounded by dry desert-like savannah. Intricately woven hammocks, rugs, and baskets made out of palm bark big enough to carry a small child decorated the one lone road that led to the village center. The closest shack was full of papayas, bananas, melons, gourds, and a few odd fruits that Reed didn't recognize. Across the street was a pushcart containing various parts of a pig, the head hung on a large hook above a tray of organs and entrails. Waxy and bloodless, it sightlessly surveyed the road in front of it as if it were a mask. The feet, all four of them, were lying like stacked shotguns beneath it, the hocks resting on the entrails pan that had already begun to bake in the heat, collecting flies. Next to the head, the liver, stomach, heart, and intestines were skewered on an iron spike like a giant shish kabob. A few children playing hide and seek around the wheels of the pushcart stopped their game and watched as the strangers got out of the car. Chickens scratched in the dust, and one lone turkey furtively crossed the road, fanning its tail. Near where Lance had parked the car an emaciated hound mounted a bitch and began thrusting.

Lance pointed, laughed, and shook his head. "Easy to see why Koreans eat dogs for their penile stamina. That mutt looks ready to keel over, but it can still get it up when it counts." He nodded. "I hope I can still fuck like that when I'm at death's door."

"I'm going to feed it," Clione said, pulling out her purse and getting a few pesos ready. "Poor, poor thing."

"Feed it when it's smoking a cigarette afterward," Lance said. "Don't interrupt them now, for chrissake. Those pooches are busy with the all-important task of making more pooches."

"I can see its ribs."

"Wait till you don't see its wiener. Then it'll be hungry again."

"Lance," Clione said. "You're not even funny. You're just gross."

Leaving them, Lance walked over to a ceiba tree and unzipped. His urine stream sounded more like a horse's than a human's. Cars drove by, some beeping, but Lance didn't care. He just focused on relieving himself, his back to the road.

Clione approached the two dogs and was flipping tortilla halves at each one in succession. They stopped their awkward thrusting and inspected the food. The sunlight shone in Clione's hair, turning it a rich chocolate, and her loose dress was just transparent enough that he could see the shadows of her legs inside. She turned around as Reed approached, and smiled.

"You look beautiful," Reed said softly. "With the sun behind you like that."

She wrinkled her nose. "Ha." She held out the tortillas. "Want to feed them? It's nice, knowing you're helping something."

Reed took a piece of corn tortilla and held it between his fingers. The male dog stared at it intently, ears pricked forward. It was a beige mutt with a patch of black on its forehead and on its two front legs, as if it had been dipped in tar. Up close, it looked healthier than Reed had thought: thin, but there was some flesh on it. Its muscles were still visible beneath the skin. One ear was torn at the tip, but its teeth were white and shiny. The remains of a previous morsel stuck to its whiskers.

"Don't tease it," Clione said.

"Here, boy!" Reed said, and gave it the food. The dog leaped on it, snapping it up in two quick bites, then turned its eyes again on Clione. The female also stared intently at the girl. Clione smiled at them and held up her hands, fingers outstretched.

"All gone." She sighed.

"Hey, you did what you could."

"At least their bellies are a little less empty."

"Get back in the car, dog Samaritans," Lance said. "There's real work to do."

Lance drove the Jeep slowly through the small village and a few minutes later stopped at a clearing in the jungle scrub. The road ended at a collection of small lean-to shacks. Here and there were square frames made of wood, some of them with bright colors being woven within them. About a dozen adults were visible, the men dressed in denim jeans and sun-faded guayabera shirts, the women in white tunics with colorful embroidery around the neck and hems. Two dust-covered boys, all grins, raced over to look at the Renegade, and circled it, kicking the tires and looking at it with the critical seriousness of someone about to buy.

"Are those rugs?" Reed asked, pointing to the wooden frames.

"The frames for the hammocks," Lance answered. "This *ejido* gets all of its income from selling hammocks and blankets here on the roadside."

Two men approached, raising their hands in greeting to Lance, who returned the signal.

"*¿Estás bien?*" one of them asked, when they'd reached the car.

Lance pulled the man into a rough embrace. "*¡Por supuesto! ¿Y tú?*"

"*Bien, bien.*"

"Diego, I want you to meet my friends. They're going to help today. This is Reed. And the girl is Clione."

"*Muy guapa.*"

"Well, if she wants you you can have her," Lance continued. "But don't get your hopes up. She's a hard nut to crack."

The men laughed.

"So, come on. It's this way."

The men led them along a small path to the home site: a ten-by-twelve rectangle had been drawn on the hard clay, with a double layer of cinder blocks already cemented in place. A pallet of the gray bricks was still in plastic sheeting off to the side. In the center of the room-to-be a wheelbarrow bed sat on the ground, filled with gray powder. The water was in five-gallon containers, three of them, glistening like blue grenades nearby. A scattering of ancient hoes, spatulas, and trowels littered the area.

"Let's get to work," Lance said, whipping off his shirt. The years of lifting dive tanks, fighting with the sea, and hauling himself and clients out of the sea onto pangas had sculpted Lance like a Rodin model. Reed felt acutely aware of his own sagging gut, barely covered by his guayabera shirt.

"I've never done this before," Reed said. "And I'm not very strong."

"You don't have to be strong," Lance answered. "You just have to want to do it. All you do is grab one of those gray things, put some cement on the wall and plop the block on top. Then repeat for five hours or until your muscles freeze up and you feel like you've been hit by a bus."

At first, Reed found it awkward to lift the heavy cinder blocks up and place them down on the soft cement. The sun beat down on him and he soon realized that only one of the three big water jugs was for the cement mixing. The other two were for them to drink. But despite the heat and the sweat and the unfamiliarity of the new tasks, Reed enjoyed being there. He learned that if he did it right there was a rhythm to it, a kind of dance, almost. Scoop the mortar, tap it once to free the trowel of excess, plop it on the brick. Two quick smears would spread it evenly over the surface. Then in a quick, choreographed move he would set the tool on the wall, lift up a block and center it on the midpoint between the two below it, the excess cement squeezing out like toothpaste under the weight. Two quick scrapes of the trowel to even the edges, and the process was finished, ready to start all over again.

They worked silently, talking little, stopping only to sip from the water tank or apply sunscreen. Diego and his cousin did the hardest labor, appearing with pallets of masonry when the current supply was about to run out. Every so often a mother would send her child over with pieces of fruit, which Reed would accept gratefully. Each child smiled shyly before scampering away.

"They're adorable," Reed said, as he paused to strip orange flesh from its rind. A girl approached with some freshly squeezed lemon water and they all stopped as she made the rounds. When she finished, she curtsied and then dashed off in a peal of giggles that floated around them like soap bubbles, coloring the air with childish glee. Reed paused to watch her as she ran out of sight.

"If you want a few," Lance said, "I'm sure some *madres* would love to get rid of a few mouths to feed. There's adoption agencies, but you could probably just pick one."

"I don't see you taking any."

They were quiet again. The only sound was the trees scratching at the sky. Even Lance seemed to sense that silence was the only way to reply. He picked up the trowel.

As the sun began its plunge into the horizon, the house stood before them, a gleaming eight-by-ten testament to their accomplishments that day. A door and two windows, one on either side so a breeze could go through. Reed could feel the muscles in his back and shoulders starting to tense up and get sore, but he felt proud, almost triumphant. Because of their work, someone was going to have a safe place to sleep at night. Because of his work, some family might have less to worry about if there were a hurricane. He couldn't remember when he'd done something like this before. Something this selfless. Something that felt this good.

Several of the families waved goodbye to them as they returned to their car, and the girl who had given Reed the orange gave his leg a quick hug. He tousled her hair and looked down at the bright smile. A lower tooth was missing, right in the center. Did the tooth fairy come in Mexico? he wondered. Something caught in his throat, and he suddenly had to focus on the home they'd finished to keep back tears.

"Bye," he said, as she dashed away to her waving mother. "You take care of yourself...."

One of the men stepped forward. "You need *hamacas*?"

Lance shook his head. "I already got one in the back."

"We got a truck full of beautiful *hamacas*. Two, three, four people. Diego's sister's kids made them. Very pretty."

"Hammocks?" asked Reed. "I'll look. Do we have time?"

"Sure," Lance said. "No problem."

"Hey, Amigo, you wait right here. I get the truck." The cousin disappeared around a corner, and a few minutes later pulled up in a brown 1957 Chevy pickup. The hood was dented and there was no windshield. The word "*¡Lávame!*" was scribbled in the dust on the side. "Wash me."

"Here, take your pick."

The bed of the truck was filled with a rainbow of hammocks, each neatly folded and placed in a plastic bag. The cousin pulled out a bright green one and in a few seconds, using the other man to hold one end, had stretched it out to show its full capacity.

"Ees a beautiful *hamaca*," the cousin said, his fingers running over the tightly knit threads. "Sleep three, four people."

"Five or six if they're couples," the man named Diego added, inserting the index finger of his right hand into a circle made by his left index finger and thumb. "If you know what I mean."

"You no like *verde*," he continued, "then we got *azul*, we got *morado*, if you gay we got rainbow *colores* so you can show your pride." The cousin laughed heartily. "We like everyone in Mexico. The only person we no like is person who no buy *hamaca*."

Lance laughed. "Well, I can't help you this time. I've got a silk-nylon blend in the back of my truck."

"You need a cotton one? Nice and cool on hot summer nights?"

"Nope, I'm all set."

"Cotton's cooler?" Reed asked. "What's the difference?"

"Sure, Amigo. Here. Look." Diego's cousin pointed to the threads. "See, these here are like a Mexican woman—flashy and not so thin. They made of nylon. Nylon also like a Mexican woman: she strong, she no mind the hot sun. Then there's cotton. Cotton is cool in the summertime, maybe you no want hot Mexican woman next to you in summertime, is too hot. You just want sleep. So cotton, is best. Then there is silk-nylon blend, is called *seda*."

"Which means silk," Lance interrupted. "But don't get confused. It's not pure silk. They don't make pure silk hammocks anymore."

"Seda, she like a beautiful *japonesa*. A Japanese woman. She thin and slim and elegant, but very expensive. She only for people who can afford her."

"Are any of the hammocks like Mexican men?" Clione asked. "Not that I've anything against sleeping with women. Just that I'd never thought of my bed in gender-specific terms before."

"It's the Mexican way," Lance said.

"Well," Reed said. "I'd like that green one."

"This one, Amigo? You like the color? We have others."

"No, that's perfect."

"Is big for one person. You have family? You sleep in this, you need a *mujer* and maybe four, five *niños*."

"I'll manage. It's a beautiful hammock. How much?"

"For you, I double the price." Diego's cousin laughed. "No, take it. You work in my village. I pay you with nice hammock."

Lance said. "Shit, Diego, this guy's rich. You don't need to cut him any deals."

Reed handed him five-hundred pesos. "Why don't I get two. The green one, and then a cotton one. Same size. So then I'll have one in the summer to use."

The cousin put the two hammocks into a larger bag. Tying it off, he handed it to Reed. "Bueno. Take whichever one you like."

Hands out the windows in farewell, the three headed home, following a shortcut route that Diego had mentioned that promised speedier access to the highway. It was a narrow road that Lance took so fast everything in the car bounced. Clione was trying to scribble something into her notebook; Reed wondered how she could even keep the pen touching the paper.

"You could go slower," Reed said. "It's not like we've got to be anywhere."

Lance shook his head. "If we don't beat the dark we'll be playing chicken with cows in the road the whole way home."

Clione pointed at the horizon. "Is that a dog way up there? Slow down. I can give it the last of these tortillas."

The small black dot she had noticed was clearly an animal, but as they neared it they stopped talking. It was difficult to imagine it was a dog. Staggering in the heat, its legs so thin it could barely lift itself, the animal was making its way along the pavement, seeming to not even hear the rush of the car as it approached. Medium size, it was a bit larger than the normal stray, but barely recognizable as a canine. Whatever fur it had once had was entirely gone, and the exposed skin was sunburned and dry, with large red fissures where the skin had actually split open. Two larger wounds, one near its shoulder and another on its ribs, looked as if they'd been caused recently by a blow from a stick. The dog's ears had fallen off; only small ridges protruded around the cavity of the aural canal. The tail was also gone. Ribs, backbone, and pelvis jutted awkwardly out from under the creature's hide, all muscle eaten away as the animal slowly dehydrated, like jerky that was still alive.

"Stop," Clione said. Her hand flickered across her face as she wiped away tears. As Lance slowed the Jeep she tossed the animal the tortillas. "There, you poor thing!" she said, clicking her tongue. "Eat your food! *Food!*"

The animal stopped and very slowly, its eyes focused on the car in front of it and the people inside. Then, unmistakably, the tiny curled nub of a tail twitched, then wiggled.

"Oh, God," Clione choked, wiping her eyes with her sleeve. "It just wagged its tail. Did you see?"

Reed nodded.

"We've got to go back. Lance, we've got to help it."

"Clione, there's nothing we can do."

"I'm not asking, I'm telling. I'm going to give it water. If you don't want to wait just drop me here and I'll walk home when I'm finished."

"Clione, it's too late for that one," Lance said. "I'm sorry."

"How can you say that?" Clione shot back. "It could still wag its tail. It knew we were trying to help it. So I'm going to *help it.*"

"There's water in the canteen. We're not going to take it to the vet or anything."

"We'll do what we have to. Turn the car around."

Lance turned the wheel and made a U-turn, running the tires over the dry brush that pushed into the road. The side of the car squeaked as a branch dug into the paint. Reed glanced in the mirror at Clione, who was fixated on the dog, her head following it the way a compass needle tracks a magnetic pole. A large truck hurtled past them, the rush of air behind it like a tiny typhoon.

"Careful!" Clione yelled.

It flinched, barely escaping being hit. Clione let out a sharp breath. They pulled the vehicle over several yards away from it. She was out of the car even before it had come to a full stop.

"Watch it," Lance said.

"It could have rabies," Reed added.

"It *could,*" Clione said. "But a vet once told me that the worst disease in Mexico is hunger. I think the worst disease in Mexico is indifference. It's just a poor thing in pain and nobody cares enough to stop and help it."

Reed opened the door and followed. The heat felt like a physical force on his skin, as thick as if a current were pushing against him.

Clione stalked toward the animal, carrying the canteen and two of the many coffee cups from the floor of Lance's Jeep. Before approaching the dog, she picked up small rocks so that their weight would keep the light Styrofoam cup steady while the animal was drinking. She then filled each cup with water, placing them close to each other and as far away from the edge of the road as possible. But on the rough, bumpy ground the cup would have instantly tipped over the second the animal tried to drink from it, so she put them in the hard gravel on the shoulder, between the tar and the wisps of tinder-dry grass.

"Here, pup," she whispered. "Water! Good, cold water!"

Seeming to hear her, the sightless beast honed in on the first cup and began to drink. Clione returned to the car and stood there, next to Reed and Lance, as the dog lapped feebly at the water.

"When it's empty I'm going to fill it up again," she said. "Was that so bad?"

As she said that, a small pickup truck appeared in the distance. It had three people in the front and two men sitting on the sides of the bed, holding onto some kind of furniture. They approached, one of the men waving at the foreigners.

From the other direction, an oversize luxury bus came hurtling down the one-lane road, leaning heavily to one side as it whizzed around the corner. The horn beeped twice as it tore toward the pickup and the dog.

"Slow down!" Clione gasped, her hand flying up to her mouth.

The two vehicles tried to pass each other on the narrow road, the driver of each swerving away from the oncoming lane, neither braking even for a second. The bus bumped over the curb and onto the grass, hitting the dog full force with its fender. The impact spun the animal like a wet beach towel onto the opposite side of the road. It landed yards away, scraping to a stop on the tar. The force of the collision pushed its skull entirely out through the dog's mouth, leaving the skin of its face bunched down around its neck like a turtleneck sweater. Lidless eyeballs stared out from scarlet pulp and waxy greenish bone. Its haunches and pelvis seemed to have been liquefied within the skin, yet the dog somehow managed to pull itself up on its front legs and drag itself for a few seconds before collapsing again in the road.

Clione screamed as if the blow had hit her instead of the dog. She screamed until she ran out of air and then screamed again.

Reed tried to fight the nausea clawing up through his intestines and esophagus but couldn't. He retched, a puddle of sour bile near his feet covering the grass in a thin sheen.

"Do something!" Clione said, still screaming. "It's still alive!"

Reed watched as the dog lifted itself once again and stopped, its front legs trembling uncontrollably. It could go no further. Its skinless head swung from side to side. Only then did it begin to howl, an agonized, unearthly wail unlike anything Reed had ever heard before.

"Get in the fucking car," Lance commanded, his voice sharp and gravely, the tone of a platoon leader ordering troops under fire. "Now!"

When neither of them moved, Lance whirled around and grabbed Clione roughly by the shoulder. He threw open the door and shoved her inside, his hand over her head as if protecting a president from an assassination attempt.

"I said move, Reed, goddamn it! *Move!*"

Reed stumbled over to the Renegade and Lance pushed him into the back beside Clione. She was cowering against the door, her knees tucked tightly up under her chin, her hands covering her ears. "I can't listen," she kept repeating. Her legs were shaking as if she'd been in frigid water for a long time.

Lance leaped into the driver's seat and slammed the door. Looking over his shoulder at the dog behind them, he threw the transmission into reverse and stomped his foot on the gas. The tires squealed, the car jumped backward, throwing Reed and Clione against the front seats. Before Reed knew what was happening, there was a wet thud and the howling stopped.

Lance continued in reverse for a few more seconds, then shifted into first and hit the gas again. This time the sound was like the tire had hit a rotten watermelon. Clione flinched as if someone had struck her, then threw herself at Reed, sobbing, her hands pressed even more tightly against her ears.

Reed held her, rocked her in his arms, ran his fingers through her hair. "It's okay," he whispered, unable to erase the image of the dog's green-white skull hanging out of that loose skin, the animal's own face draped around its neck. "It's okay, it's okay, it's okay." He said it like a mantra, soft and singsong, like a lullaby to a child, as Lance shifted into third, then fourth.

The Jeep hurtled through the gathering darkness for the full hour and fifty-minute return to Tulum, the passengers silent as spirits. Behind them the sunset seared the sky a deep red, but no one looked backward to see it. No one spoke until the familiar green-and-white petrol station sign that marked the edge of town appeared in the distance out of the blue-blackness of night.

"I just had to put it out of its misery," Lance said.

Reed nodded, but didn't reply. And only when they'd come to the stoplight did Clione lift herself from his arms and stare silently out the window at the dusty town of Tulum. When they parked she pushed herself over Reed and ran across the street to the hostel's open door.

* * *

In the oppressive darkness of the bungalow, Reed tried to force himself to sleep, haunted by what had happened that day. Each time he closed his eyes the animal's death cry kept echoing in his head, so he kept his eyes open, focusing on cataloging the real sounds he was hearing in hopes that they would push the other one away. Off beyond the walls some mariachi music was playing loudly, drowned out every so often by men's and women's laughter. A farm animal snorted. A car tore through town, its tires rumbling over the three speed bumps in staccato reports. Off in the distance he could hear the sound of waves. A light breeze was blowing, rustling the palm thatch above his head, making it sound like rain. Then, gradually, he heard soft footsteps approaching his door.

There was a tap, and he sat up.

"It's me," came Clione's voice, so soft that had he not been already listening intently he would have not heard it at all.

He pushed off the sheet and in two quick strides had opened the door, still half thinking that nobody would be there, that it was all his imagination. But Clione was trembling, and in the white splash of moonlight on her cheeks he could see the shiny tracks of tears.

"I'm sorry. Were you sleeping?"

"No," he said, pulling her inside.

"I just couldn't be alone—"

"Shh," he whispered. "There, there."

As the door closed and latched, she fell against him, clinging to him for support, for comfort. Not once had Laurel ever cried like this with him, needed him this way. A feeling welled up inside his chest, an ache, a yearning to take even the smallest bit of the pain away. He wanted to protect this girl, wash away the awful thing they had seen that afternoon. He held her tightly, rubbing her shoulders softly with one hand, pushing back her hair with the other.

Clione sobbed, her body shaking in little spasms, two or three sharp contractions, then a break for her to breathe. Reed gently moved her to the side of the bed and then the two of them sat down, their thighs touching as they had in the Renegade that afternoon. For a long time they just sat there, neither of them moving, listening to the darkness. Above them, Reed heard the now familiar rustle of the gecko scrambling around on the dry palm leaves.

Clione put her head on his shoulder. "I'm never going to look at water the same way again. I saw people washing dishes tonight and leaving the faucet on and I want to scream. And the cenotes. All that fresh water...it's right there. All that poor dog needed was water. Just a little to—"

"There was nothing we could do. You know that."

Clione sniffed, wiping her nose with the back of her hand. "We never made it to the cenote. They're so beautiful. I want you to see it sometime."

"We'll go tomorrow."

She leaned into him. Very slowly, Reed reached over and placed his hand on her shoulder. It was moist and slightly sticky from the heat, like just kneaded dough. Clione did not pull away as Reed pressed gently into her flesh and turned her toward him. He brushed away the stray wisps of hair that had fallen into her face with his hand. Her expression didn't change; her eyes stayed focused on another temporal plane. He felt as if he were adjusting a department store mannequin. He could see her nipples pushing out through the thin fabric of her T-shirt, like the tips of thumbs.

"Clione," he whispered. A part of him seemed to detach and drift upward, as if watching himself from above. He could see the two people on the edge of the bed, the girl stock still, the guy leaning ever closer, closer, as if in absurd play-acting, going through motions, moving his own lips ever closer to the soft lips that still hadn't and still hadn't and still hadn't and still hadn't pulled away.

Then they were kissing. His fingers shook as he touched her, a thousand questions tore through his mind. Still a part of him was watching, a voyeur. His vision blurred, as if someone rippled the water and now it was hard to see what the two people were doing down below. She shifted, moving ever so slightly closer, and he inhaled, held his breath, and dove in toward her mouth, tracing his fingers around her delicate earlobe as he pushed his lips against hers. They tasted of mint and mango, and her mouth was exactly the same temperature as his own. He was dizzy. It was hard to tell where his lips ended and where hers began.

His hand moved instinctively from her earlobe to her neck, tracing a simple, delicate design upon the skin. Clione opened her mouth a fraction, and inhaled as if he had become her air. She moaned, releasing that one tiny hint of contentment, and it was as if a vast damn had burst, a wall of water that was tumbling them together, crushing them and drowning them, a mix of terror and euphoria. They were devouring each other, their tongues licking like flame in a feeding frenzy of desire. She panted as he kissed her upper lip, her lower lip, her nose, her eyelids fluttering as delicately as moth wings. With each kiss she let out another sigh, as if he were sucking the air out of her; they kissed with the urgency of people about to drown.

Pressing harder against her, he bit gently at the soft pillow of her lower lip. She sighed, pulled his face closer to hers, their bodies still side by side, legs draped over the side of the bed, torsos twisted awkwardly toward each other. Her hot breasts pressed against him. His hands were on her shoulders, and he traced them down the length of her spine, following the contours of the vertebrae to her lower back. Through the loose fabric of her shirt he could feel the nub of each bone, the lines of muscle and sinews that clung to them. It was as if he were dissecting her with the tips of his fingers. She was not wearing a bra, and when his fingers reached the very bottom of the shirt he lifted it up, over her head, and she held her arms straight up to help him, like a child getting undressed at bedtime.

In the darkness he could make out the form of her body, the breasts and unusually large areola, nearly twice the diameter of a fifty cent coin. Her skin seemed too bright in the darkness, as if her body was collecting the ambient light, concentrating it, releasing it back into the night through her skin. He moved slowly down the landscape of her neck, kissing her jawline, her clavicle, the hollow at the base of her neck, her shoulders, and finally the hardened nub of her left nipple. He noticed a small indentation in her cheek, a mole on her neck just at the edge of her hairline. He kissed it gently.

Clione lay back, pulling him on top of her until they were pelvis against pelvis, legs intertwined. He had forgotten how much awkwardness was inherent in sex, the shifting and moving and uncertainty of caresses, the slow discovering of another human's needs.

He circled the nipple with his tongue, moving in radiating spokes from the center to the outside of her breast, as if painting a spider web. Each time he reached the nipple she exhaled and gripped his hair a little tighter. Shifting from the left breast to the right, he tasted salt and musk. Then, very slowly, he put his hand on the mound of her vulva, his palm on the pubic bone, and let his fingers find the wet syrup of her labia drenching the thin cotton of her panties. Even when Laurel had been turned on it was nothing like the tidal flood that he was exploring now.

Clione let him take off the rest of her clothes and then opened her legs wide, allowing him to slip his middle and ring fingers deep inside her. She moaned quietly, biting his earlobe and whispering something that he couldn't understand. He began circling his fingers inside her, pressing them against the rubbery G-spot that was tucked up against her pubic bone like a piece of kneaded eraser.

"Yes," she moaned, guiding him, her fingernails digging into his back. "There. Yes, *there.*"

He pressed harder, building a rhythm, feeling her body starting to move as it sought that universal human release. The bed began to squeak softly, then louder and louder. Louder, and finally she stopped and they both laughed.

"Let's not wake up anyone," she said, kissing his neck. "But don't stop."

"Let them wake up," Reed said, thrusting his fingers deep inside her. Clione gasped.

"I didn't know you were bad," she gasped.

"Bad...like good?"

"Very bad. Like very good."

"How bad?" he murmured, his lips grazing her ear while rippling his fingers around inside her.

"Awfully bad. Terribly bad."

"I should stop?"

"Don't you dare," she whispered. "Don't you dare."

She shifted position and looped her thumbs around his pants, then pulled both pants and briefs down to his ankles in one quick motion. Holding his penis between her thumb and index finger, she guided him inside her.

For a moment he held his breath; she was so hot it was as if he'd been splashed and scalded. Moving himself deeper, he sought her cervix with the tip of his penis, pressed against it, circled it, pushed until he could enter her no farther. She clasped her legs around his buttocks so tightly that he could not have pulled out even if he'd wanted to. Clione contracted herself around his penis as if clenching a fist. As she alternated ripples of pressure, he thrust rhythmically until the headboard began to bang against the adobe wall, dull, distinctive, and regular, building louder and more insistent. Sighing, she dug her fingernails into his back, running her nails across his skin, turning his entire back into an erogenous zone. He moved faster, their bodies building a rhythm. As she approached orgasm he felt her body became rigid, and finally she stopped moaning and began holding her breath, inhaling only in short gasps.

"Yes," she kept whispering, in-between breaths. "Yes, there. Right there...."

He felt the muscles in her walls began to spasm, tensing and relaxing at the speed of a strobe. His own climax overtook him like a gathering wave, devouring him, her, everything in its path. For a few seconds he lost consciousness, feeling his head go dizzy; when he could think again, Clione was quivering, her thighs relaxed and tense at the same time. It was over. They were as spent as driftwood tossed up onto wave-washed sand.

They lay together for a long time, moving only enough for each other to know that neither was asleep. Clione traced the braille of his back for a while, so lightly at times that it seemed more like the wind than any finger on his skin. Then she kissed his neck, his pectorals, bit at his tiny nipples and laughed when his body shivered at her touch. They did not speak. The magnitude of what had just happened took Reed's breath away. He felt washed in panic, dizziness, euphoria.

When Clione finished touching him and had pulled away, resting, he began to kiss her left arm. He began at the very tips of the gently curled fingers, exploring the digits with his tongue, feeling the atrophied muscles quiver and jump as he caressed them with his tongue. He moved to her delicate wrist and pressed his lips against the cobbles where her radius and ulna met her hand. Licking in long, straight lines, he traced his tongue up from her wrist to her elbow and back again, holding her bent fingers gently with both hands. Finally he reached the place where her skin tightened around the bicep and she nudged him away.

"That still hurts sometimes," she whispered. "But it feels good, what you're doing right now. It feels wonderful."

He put his head on her abdomen, listening to the thunder in her ribcage that was her heartbeat. His thoughts shifted away from sensations and again to what had just happened. The exquisite awkwardness of wondering what was going through her head.

He turned her over on her back, then put his arm across her; for a long time they lay cupped on the bed like nested silverware. Then, quickly and without saying anything, he entered her again, feeling her lift up toward him as he did so, helping him to enter, wanting him deep inside her. The moment he was inside her all his doubts disappeared. He felt stronger and more virile than he ever had before and his body shuddered when he came.

He stayed hard, slowly tracing patterns inside her. Her back was silvery from sweat in the dim moonlight, as if he were making love to a shimmering pool of water. She was utterly silent this second time, accepting him, working her buttocks and thighs for better friction against the shaft of his penis, which he thrust downward sharply into her G spot and then slowly followed through along the upper wall of her vagina until it reached the cervix and had nowhere else to go. They could not be closer to each other. It was impossible to know where he ended and she began. Sensation built and built, each level washing over his body, radiating outward like a wave, the rhythm frantic, clumsy, as if they were trying to kill something instead of make love. The sheets bunched up in her palms as she dug into the bed, clinging to it so that he wouldn't push her onto the floor.

He came again, the contractions violent, almost painful. He couldn't tell if she was feeling anything or not, and when he was done he froze in place above her, still inside her. They were fused together like statues, he arched over her back and gripping her thighs, pulling her against him. He could taste her mouth, the saltiness of her skin as he had run his tongue up and down her backbone. When he finally released her she fell limp onto the bed. He turned her over and, holding a buttock in each of his palms, lifted her to his mouth and ran his tongue up and down the moist flesh, tasting the chalky salt of his own semen, the tangy smooth lips of her vagina. His tongue flickered over her clitoris and her thighs shivered, and then suddenly she twisted herself up and pushed his head away.

"I can't," she moaned, snuggling against him. "I'm languid. I don't want to even move."

Reed's panic had faded into a giddiness so strong he felt like he was drunk.

"You're the most beautiful creature I've ever seen," he whispered.

Clione kissed him gently. "I'm a creature?"

"Something from the black lagoon."

She pushed his shoulders lightly, and he eased himself back onto the bed. She fluffed a pillow and tucked it under his head, then did the same for her. Reed wrapped his arm around her and fell asleep to the slow rhythm of her breathing, gently rocking like the roll of a ship out over the deep sea.

He dreamed of nothing, felt nothing, slept as if he'd been drugged.

When he awoke the next morning, the light was filtering in through the palm thatch. A gecko's footsteps crackled in the roof above him. The bed was empty. Clione had slipped out while he was sleeping. Reed wondered what time it was. Everything that night still seemed so unreal, it was only by looking at the bunched-up sheets that he knew she'd been there.

Sleep caught up to him again, and he fell back in the pillow, feeling more content than he'd felt in a long time.

Day Six

The Return

Reed woke up slowly from deep, dreamless sleep to the lacy pattern the sunlight made through the brown palm fronds and rafters. He breathed quietly in and out. The morning heat on the roof made it smell clean, like cut grass. The gecko rustled somewhere above him. Dust hung suspended in shafts of light. As consciousness came he remembered the events of yesterday. He felt his heart quicken as he thought about everything that the two of them had shared.

Reed smiled. What a magical girl, he thought. And everything about this morning seemed magical as well.

He sat up, stretched, went to the bathroom. After he dressed, he opened the door and stood on the veranda looking out at the courtyard for a long time. He saw Cindy and Sharon at the picnic table. They were hunched over their coffee, both talking, but as if they didn't want anyone else to hear. Reed felt a strange, unfamiliar fondness for this scene, this humble courtyard and the sweet people here. The parrots in the trees and the far-off crowing of the roosters. The smells of grilling chicken and coffee and the diesel of the freight trucks rolling by.

It all seemed precious, somehow, in a way that he hadn't understood before.

He went to the table and sat down next to Cindy.

"How was yesterday?" he asked. "You guys stayed at the beach?"

Both girls shrugged. Sharon stood up. "Sorry, I got to go." She went back to the dorm and closed the door, leaving her half-finished coffee on the table.

"What's up with Sharon?" Reed asked.

"Wonder what it could be," Cindy said. "I heard things went well yesterday."

Reed tried to read innuendo into the statement, but it sounded sincere. "We got the walls finished."

"Good for you."

"Hey," Reed said, hoping it sounded casual. "Have you seen Clione?"

Cindy shook her head. "I got up early. I think she was still in bed."

Marisol, over behind the desk, overheard them.

"Clione checked out early this morning," she said, coming over to the table. "She left."

Reed felt as if his insides had been filled with ice. "Clione? She's gone?"

Marisol shrugged. "Gave me her key. And she took her passport."

Reed tried to tell himself it wasn't because of what happened that night. Cindy was looking at him strangely. Shut up, he wanted to say. *Get the fuck away.*

"Was she planning on checking out?"

"You look so stricken," Marisol replied. "Surely there are other reasons to stay here besides that one girl. You could stay and make other ladies very happy."

"Christ, I'm not here for...that. Did you know she was planning to leave?"

"You don't need to shout. I'm right here. She didn't even take her deposit. She has another week all paid in full."

"I'll be checking out today too," Reed said, his voice a dry, cracked whisper.

It was as if everything inside him had turned putrid all at the same time. He ran to his bathroom and slammed himself down on the john. Diarrhea poured out, nearly filling the bowl. He stayed, hunched over, holding his head in his hands, until his legs felt numb. Only after the third bout did he feel ready to stand up. Sweat stuck the seat to his thighs.

Reed washed his hands, feeling weak and dizzy, then collected his few things and left the room.

Marisol checked him out, silently, watching his face but knowing not to ask questions.

"Come back and see us again soon," she said, and handed him a receipt.

He realized she must see this kind of thing all the time. Two ships pass as the sun goes down and are miles away from each other when it rises the next morning.

"Sure," he said. "I'd like that."

"Take this for your things," she said, handing him an empty plastic bag. "Otherwise you'll drop stuff. Lose something important."

He mumbled some kind of thank you.

"The door's always open," she said. "If you change your mind."

Reed nodded and as he turned to go, Marisol came out from the desk and hugged him. It felt as if he knew Marisol better than anyone back in Boston. He thanked her again and left the Welcome Wanderer. She went to the doorway and waved as he walked away.

It took Reed almost an hour to arrive at the bus station. At each doorway, each store, each establishment, even at what he was sure were people's houses he kept stopping and peering inside, hoping to see Clione writing in her journal in the shadowy recesses of a garden or sipping a coffee and watching the world from some second-floor veranda. It had to have been some kind of weird mistake, something that they'd laugh about when he found her again.

At the bus station he felt as if she would be there waiting for him. She had to be. She would look up from her uneven plastic chair with a shy smile then say she was sorry, explain the misunderstanding. Tell him that she hadn't meant to leave.

But the bus station was nearly empty.

Reed sank into the nearest seat and put his head between his hands. He would get on the bus, he would be back in Cancún, he would return to Boston and everything would slowly become a memory. If he was lucky he would patch things up with Laurel, and if he wasn't, that too would dissolve.

The bus came.

He got on, his legs heavy and slow. As soon as he sank into the seat he pressed his face to the glass, peering out the window, hoping for a glimpse of Clione. As the bus pulled out of the station he realized it was settled.

It's over. No book to help him find her this time.

He should be happy, he kept thinking. It had been the chance of a lifetime, more than he'd ever hoped for. He should appreciate it for the blissful moment it had been.

The tears came only when the bus reached highway speed.

* * *

By the time he left the bus station in Cancún, Reed had used the tiny cubicle bathroom at the back of the bus twice, and was sure he'd need to go again the moment he arrived at the hotel. He stumbled out into the terminal chaos past the same Australian tout trying to get unsuspecting travelers to go to his hostel. He saw the face of the taxi driver who picked him up, but barely spoke to him the entire ride to the Grand Medallion. He was glad there was no one else in the hotel elevator, and he slumped against the polished brass panel as it sped him upward to the eleventh floor. Nothing mattered except returning to Boston and somehow moving on.

The room was neatly made up, the bathroom as spotless as if it were in a showroom. The shade was half drawn and he pulled it aside and stared out at the ocean, feeling sorry for himself and wishing he'd left a tip for the chambermaid who'd had to clean everything. A sterile, empty room. His cellphone was on the nightstand, the charging light blinking like a pet that was happy he'd returned. He missed Laurel, would have done anything just to see her face in front of his. See her smile. Anything. He wondered why so many little things that didn't matter at all had seemed so important, as if they were insurmountable obstacles. What made sense was that they'd shared so many years together and somehow they'd pulled through.

But he didn't call her. Instead, he picked up the hotel phone and dialed the front desk. Listening to the ring, he watched the beach outside and his thoughts returned to Clione. Her skin, her voice, the intensity of her caring. How they'd clung to each other like steel wrapped around a forge, a glow so bright only water could make it cool. Far off, a few people dotted the caramel and vanilla sand, the size and color of peanut shells. She'd vanished. Gone in the light of day.

"Yes," he said, when the front desk picked up. "I need a reservation at the airport tomorrow. Boston. One way."

When the call was finished Reed lay down on the bed. The pattern of dots and bumps in the ceiling bothered him, as if it were a symbol-based language that he couldn't quite read. Everything seemed foreign, as if he'd come into a hospital room, a place designed for dying instead of sleep.

"Clione," he said out loud, just to hear the sounds of her name.

Reed reached for the remote and turned on the mammoth television. Dead, the screen seemed to loom like a predator over the bed, a giant bat-like thing with outstretched wings, ready to swoop in the moment one slipped into slumber. Press a button and the screen lit up the room with the hotel's bland introduction video. Reed watched the hotel channel for almost an hour, just staring and staring until his eyes finally closed.

When he woke up it was dark. The beach somewhere beyond was just blackness. His stomach stabbed him and he realized that it had been breakfast when he'd eaten last. He still felt queasy, as if he'd had too much to drink, and he decided a drink was exactly what he wanted. Not bothering to shower, he left the room and went down the hall to the elevator.

There was just one other person at the bar in the first-floor lounge, a woman in her fifties. She was heavyset but not unattractive, with long eyelashes and healthy skin. Reed sat down at the long slab of polished mahogany and glanced over at her. She brushed back her hair and smiled.

"A Tulum Sunset," Reed said to the bartender, a rail-thin Mexican with thick lips and permed hair.

The woman next to him raised her glass. "Good, aren't they?"

"Best thing about this place," Reed replied.

"I'm Louise," the woman said. Her nose was peeling badly.

"Reed."

"You were here a few days ago, right? With that lady?"

Reed shrugged. "My wife."

"My husband and I were near you at the pool. I think you and your wife had just arrived? When you fell in with your clothes on."

"That was me." He didn't remember her. "Looks like you got quite the sunburn."

"Yes," she laughed. "Oh, that was such a stupid mistake. You just don't realize how strong the sun is until you fall asleep. Then you wake up and you're as red as a boiled lobster. I even thought I'd put enough sunscreen on, too. If you can believe it."

"Where's your husband?"

"I'm taking some time for myself. Down time. Just a chance to get away from the kids."

Reed nodded. "Funny, my wife's doing the same thing. Only we don't have kids."

"We could start a single-spouses club."

Reed realized there was room for innuendo and backed away.

"What do you do back home?"

"I'm in advertising."

"A slave to the cubicle?"

"Not really," she said. "I own my own company." She fished a business card out of her purse and handed it to him. "I do websites. If you need a really good one, let me know."

"Thanks, I'll think about it."

Louise turned and looked at the darkness. "Listen to the ocean. It's so nice, isn't it?"

He nodded.

"I haven't been barefoot all day. You up for a walk?"

"It's late," Reed said. "Just wanted a drink. Was sick until now."

"That's precisely why you need some fresh air."

"I need to get the hell out of Mexico is what I need."

She looked at him and brushed her hands through her hair. "I don't feel safe going out there in the dark by myself. And it's my last night here. I won't bite, I promise."

"I can tell you're in advertising," Reed said, standing up. "Fine. We'll walk and I'll protect you from the evil beach." It sounded bitter, unfriendly. This woman hadn't done anything to him. She was lonely, probably just looking for conversation. Even if she were looking for more, could he blame her? Wasn't everyone, in some way or other, looking for something more from the world?

But anything she said made him think of Clione, who wasn't afraid of anything, who would have been happy to journey out into the darkness all by herself. She'd been so free. He remembered how she and Sharon had coaxed him out to swim for the first time. How pretty she'd been in the moonlight, how much he'd wanted to kiss her right then, but hadn't. If not for the dog's death she never would have come to his room and he never would have kissed her. That was who he was. Someone who held back until it was too late. Someone too afraid to really live.

Louise bought them another round and they waited as the bartender put down the tumbler he was polishing, mixed them their drinks, then returned to the chore, holding it up to the light to see better where the smudges were.

"To the beach!" Louise said, holding up her glass as she got out of her chair. "Let's go!"

She took his arm as they walked down the stairs. Reed stiffened, and she laughed. "Just steadying myself a little." But it had a wistful tone, and Reed wondered what family drama had occurred to leave her here while hubby returned.

They walked, listening to the waves and the sound of their feet in the sand. He had more in common with this woman than he ever would with Clione. How absurd to think that...to feel...to let himself fall in love like that with someone so unreachable. Clione was confused and immature. He was old and jaded. If he wanted someone, it should be someone like Louise. He took another sip of the Sunset and then, a little while later, took Louise's arm. She nestled into him, and they walked, their bare feet swooshing in the soft, sun-warmed sand.

They walked along the high tide line, following the winding trail of the flotsam and jetsam that the highest waves had beached there. In the moonlight they could make out the shells of molted crabs, dried seaweed, sun-bleached coral that was white as bone. Louise squealed like a little girl and bent to pick up a sand dollar, holding it up for him to see. It gleamed in her fingers like a doubloon.

Then Louise leaped toward him, her fingers digging into his bicep so hard that they hurt. "What was that?" she whispered. "Did you hear it?"

"What?"

"Something's out there." She pointed in front of them. "I heard something."

Reed peered into the darkness, unable to make out anything. Then, slowly, a shape appeared: A dog was scavenging, approaching them following the same high tide line, hoping to find anything edible.

"Ugh," Louise said, her grip relaxing only a little. "Don't get too close. It's a cur."

It came closer, nose pressed deep into the wrack. Here and there it would stop for a more intense sniff before moving on. When it suddenly smelled them it stopped and turned, as if ready to run, as if someone were going to pelt it. Then, despite the darkness, Reed could see the tail attempt a tentative, questioning wag.

It was the same dog that had come up to the pool area that day. The same one Clione had been feeding the first day they met.

"Hey, puppy," Reed whispered. He clicked his tongue. "It's okay."

Louise tugged his arm. "Don't encourage it."

Reed twisted free.

"It's hungry," Reed said. "I'm going to feed it, I'm going to give it water. If I can, I'll take it with me back to Boston." Suddenly everything felt right. "I'm going to adopt that dog."

He had never felt more certain of anything in his life. He remembered what Clione had said to Sharon at the pool: He couldn't save every dog.

But he could save *that* one.

Louise blinked. Her mouth opened, then closed. Then she straightened up. "Aren't there better things to do on the beach?"

"Sorry," he said.

"God, am I being stood up for...a stray dog?" She turned and walked back to the hotel. In a few seconds her shadow eclipsed the beach as she mounted the stairs, her body blocking the light that spilled out from the break in the sea wall.

Reed walked backward, keeping one eye on the dog, trying to make as little noise as possible. When he was far enough away to not scare it, he turned and dashed back to the bar. The bartender was still stoically polishing the flatware.

"I need meat and some rope, quickly!"

The bartender put down the glass. "Meat?"

"Table scraps, something like that? And rope. There's a dog down there. I'm going to adopt it."

The man pulled a plate from behind the bar. Half-eaten chicken breast and rice pilaf.

"You can have this. I don't have any rope."

"What about tape? You got any duct tape? String? Anything I can use to make a leash."

"Hold on, Sir," the bartender replied. He left the room, returning moments later with some jute cord. "Will this work?"

The dog was still snuffling along in the high tide line, and had found something that it was crunching on when Reed approached. The animal shied away at first, but the instant Reed threw it a piece of meat it shot toward him and gulped it down, as fast as a seagull.

Reed tossed it a few more scraps, then tied a slipknot in the end of the twine.

"Here," he said, tossing a piece much closer. "Food!"

But the animal stayed where it was.

He stepped away. Immediately, the dog crept toward the meat. Reed tensed, opening the noose wide. As it made a grab for the chicken, Reed tossed the loop. It glanced off the dog's ear, causing the animal to dash away. The leash fell on the sand.

The dog kept its distance, but Reed could tell it still wanted the morsel. Making the loop as large as possible, he placed it around the meat. Then he ran the remaining cord as far away as he could to give the animal some sense of security. Only when he sat down did the dog start to move toward him. Reed could see its nose twitching as it honed in on the location of the meal.

"That's right," Reed murmured. "Come on, doggie."

As the dog came cautiously closer, Reed clenched his hand tightly on the rope. He counted softly, trying to gauge whether the dog's feet were inside the loop or not. Reed had expected it to stay there quietly as it had before, but this time — perhaps sensing something amiss — the dog lunged for the chicken and tried to escape back toward the sea wall. Reed jerked his hand and felt the pull as the loop closed around the dog's hind leg. But he hadn't expected the animal to be so quick, and before he could do anything, the rope had pulled out of his hands. The dog dashed away into the dark, the rope tightly wrapped on its leg.

"Damn it," Reed said, the sound of his voice altered slightly as it echoed off the cement. He could hear the dog whimpering somewhere in the darkness. He wanted to scream: so close, yet despite all the noble intent, he'd failed. He'd let it slip away, and now the dog was not only afraid of him, it had a piece of cord cutting into its leg.

"By tomorrow," he thought, knowing how hard he'd pulled the noose, "the dog will have gangrene."

He looked back at the hotel. It had to be two in the morning now. The bar's lights had dimmed. Nobody was in the lounge anymore, not even the bartender. All the glassware polished. Not a ripple on the pool.

Another whine of pain from the darkness.

Reed took a deep breath, pausing as he tried to assess what he had gotten himself into. What the hell was he doing anyway? He would never see Clione again. The dog was just a pathetic mongrel that would be dead in a few days anyway. At least he'd gotten it some food. It might chew the rope off before the circulation stopped. Who knows. It was probably better if he just walked away. He could be on a flight in the morning, put everything behind him.

For a long time Reed stood in the darkness, the waves seeming to get louder, the humid night closing around him. Then he crouched down, and cupping his hands around his ears to magnify his hearing, he walked to where he'd last heard the dog.

He slipped off his shoes, knowing that bare feet would be quieter, then eased himself into a taut crouch. He stayed hunched over like that for so long that his thighs began to shake uncontrollably, yet even then he knew that he could not stand up. Shifting out of the crouch would have announced his presence, would have made it easy for the dog to see the approaching stranger and disappear in the night.

As it was, Reed found it before either of them saw the other coming. In a flash the dog—which had been focused on biting through the rope—leaped up. Tail between its legs, haunches down, it scooted sideways, trying to evade capture. Reed's crouch made it easy to sidestep, like a crab, and as the dog fled Reed leaped at the rope that was disappearing like a snake through the sand. He felt his body thud as he hit the beach and the burn as the coarse fibers of the rope abraded his palm.

With every ounce of concentration, he clenched his fists. There was a sharp tug and a searing pain in his right hand. Out in the darkness the dog gave a yipe.

His grasp held.

He had caught the dog.

Reed felt like a fisherman who had just hand-lined a tuna. The dog was there but the battle wasn't over. He had no way to safely take it with him. Slowly, trying not to scare it, Reed approached, keeping one hand firmly on the cord, using the other to take in the slack so the dog couldn't just keep backing away. It was surprisingly easy to get close: The animal had no strength left. It was shaking, spent, and as Reed came within a few feet it simply sank down in the sand and rolled over, its tail tightly wrapped over its belly in a last attempt to protect itself.

Reed wished he still had the rest of the meal. It was somewhere out there. The gulls would have it the moment it was light out. By the time bathers arrived, nothing would be left, just a clean dinner plate in the empty beach.

"Hey, sweetie," Reed said. "I'm not going to hurt you." He knew as soon as he looked at it that this dog would never bite him. "I'm going to name you Sam," he said. "Is that okay?"

Fearing that the dog might try to escape the second the leash was off, Reed used the other end of the cord and made another slipknot, which he looped carefully over the animal's head. Then he felt the femur and found the first one, slowly and methodically pulling at the fiber until it gave. After removing it his hands were sticky and dark: The cord had cut deep into the flesh.

"I'm so sorry, Sam," he said. "It's okay though. You've got someone to look after you now. It's going to be all right."

He took a few steps back to give Sam time to get back up on his feet, keeping pressure on the neck so that Sam wouldn't bolt the moment he thought he was free. Coaxing him gently, he walked Sam back up toward the beach, through the darkened lounge area, and into the elevator. Sam was shivering, and as they shot upward the dog scratched at the polished steel doors. Reed shushed him.

They reached the eleventh floor. Reed clicked his tongue, calming the mutt, and they walked down the hall. He turned the corner and his eyes traveled the length of the hall to where the door of Room 1114 would be. A person was there against the wall.

Even from far down the hallway, he knew that it was Clione. Only when he was quite close did she stand up, her expression a combination of sheepishness and curiosity.

"I didn't realize it was you," she apologized. "I wasn't expecting a dog."

"This is Sam." He pulled out the key card and fumbled with it. "Sam needs someone who cares about him."

Suddenly he couldn't see. "I didn't think I'd ever see you again," he said, barely getting the words out before sobbing.

"I got so scared," Clione said. "I'm so sorry. I just couldn't handle it. Anything. Even you. Especially you. I didn't even pass my diving test. Couldn't concentrate on anything, anything at all."

They opened the door. Reed let the dog loose and then locked them inside. He was still fighting to keep from weeping.

"Clione, I don't have to sleep with you. I'll sleep on the floor, I'll sleep down at the pool if you want. Just don't leave. If what happened last night meant anything at all to you, promise me that if you stay here at all tonight, you'll still be here in the morning."

"You think I left because I didn't like being with you?"

As if answering her own question, Clione led him, stepping backward, to the king-size bed. She sat down, then pulled Reed over on top of her, and then they wriggled farther onto the mattress, kicking off their shoes. She was as hungry for him now as he was for her, racing as fast as if a bomb were about to explode. He pushed up the fabric of her dress, felt the moist slick on her panties, pushed them aside and then thrust his penis into her, straight and smooth and urgent, coming almost instantly inside her. She arched her back, digging her ankles into his buttocks, using her thighs to pull them together. He stayed deep within her, piercing her, then he began to rotate his hips in slow circles, tickling the cervix with the tip as he explored.

"Reed," she whispered, clutching at his head with her right arm, steadying herself with the other. She worked her pelvis against his body, tensing the muscles, relaxing them, building ripples of sensation around him that became stronger and stronger.

She pulled herself to him, let him crush her against the cushions. Somehow they were already pressed up against the headboard, and he stopped for a moment so they could shift downward. She smiled at him. She kept her eyes open, staring at him as they grew closer and closer to climax.

"I'm going to make you come," she commanded. "You're going to come inside me. You're going to come."

He felt it burst inside him and moaned, arching his back and pummeling himself into her, faster and faster and faster as he ejaculated. His penis ached from the force of the explosion. She was still staring at him, her eyes intense and wild. She kept clutching his shaft with her thighs, shifting them rapidly, back and forth, back and forth.

"Reed," she whispered, her grasp slipping. She fell limply away from him and stayed there, her head turned to the side, still fully clothed. "I'm going to fall asleep," she whispered, turning to look at him. "You just do that for me."

Suddenly she leaped up, and slapped him hard on the shoulder. "How could you dare think it was the sex part that drove me away?"

Days Seven, Eight

The Day After the Day After

Reed woke up the next morning tangled together with Clione, the pristine starched linens rumpled, two of the five pillows on the floor. Sex seemed suspended in the sunbeams that were streaming in, and when he got up to shut the shutters, the splashes of sun on her skin seemed straight from an oil painting. The soft morning light, the contrast of her smooth skin and the sheets and her lustrous dark hair. Reed stood for a moment, drinking in the image, knowing it was all on borrowed time. He remembered the airline ticket that would go unused and smiled. She was here. They were alone.

He heard a tail thumping on the carpet and remembered Sam, who was still cowering under the dresser exactly as when they'd gone to sleep. Realizing the dog must be thirsty, he took a glass from the bathroom and filled it with cool water, then put it under the table. Almost immediately Sam started lapping it up.

Reed sat on the edge of the bed and shook Clione's shoulder lightly. She twisted, then opened her eyes.

"It's morning already?"

"Yeah, Honey. You okay if I make a telephone call?"

"I'm a big girl." Clione pulled a pillow over her head. Seconds later she was snoring.

He dialed their home phone and then picked up the extension in the bathroom, closing the door while the connection was made. It started to ring.

"Hello?"

"It's me."

"Hi, honey. How's Mexico?"

"How's Boston?"

"Cold."

"You could be here."

She paused.

"I'm taking," Reed's turn to pause, "swimming lessons. Just like I said. I'm going to extend my ticket. Stay another week."

"Wait, you're taking swimming lessons?" She laughed. "Here I was thinking I was the bad guy. Who is she?" A brief pause. "I'm joking. Actually, I'm impressed."

"I realized a lot of things, Laur. Maybe you were right in some ways. We can talk about it face to face."

Another pause. "Reed, you're not drunk, are you?"

"Sober as a priest."

"Because you always talk about swimming when you're drunk."

"Well, I'm not."

"So when will you be back?"

"You were the one asking for space. Now I'm giving it to you—"

There was a click, and the phone went dead. Reed stared at the receiver until the angry dial tone reminded him to set it back on the cradle. It was not clear whether she'd hung up on him but either way, he saw no reason to call her back. Let her worry for a little. Or not. Maybe she didn't care.

He went back into the other room and slipped in beside Clione. If she'd heard anything, she didn't show it or didn't care. He put his arms around her and she mumbled something. Reed's eyes stayed open as the shafts of sunlight traced their way down the walls, marking the sun's ascent higher and higher in the sky. At some point, he fell asleep too.

* * *

When they finally woke up it was almost ten o'clock. Sam, not yet housebroken, had decorated the rug with a pile of hard droppings that were full of crab shells. "I'll clean it up," Clione said, slipping on one of the plush hotel robes. "Just let me get some tissue."

When she was finished, she smiled. "It appears Sam needs to be short for Samantha."

Reed laughed, and the dog looked up meekly as if it knew all along that it was female.

"Samantha."

Clione smiled. They dressed and made it down to the dining room for the buffet breakfast just before it was about to close, leaving Samantha in the room, hoping the "Do Not Disturb" sign would keep the maids from discovering the mutt they'd left there. A fifteen-foot-long table held a near impossible array of breakfast items, from fruits to breads to cereals to yogurt. Nearby, a chef stood behind a lone propane burner, omelet ingredients in hand. Another table was lined with chafing dishes filled with scrambled eggs, Mexican chilaquiles, bacon, sausages and potatoes. As they filled their plates, a busboy and girl were already clearing the leftovers, dumping them straight from the table into the trash.

"See," Clione said, pointing after they'd sat down. "That kind of thing just makes me livid. Look at all that food. They're just throwing it away when right outside the hotel there's dogs that are starving. People who are starving. It ought to be illegal. All they need to do is put a tax, some kind of price, on the leftover food and bingo—hotels wouldn't waste a scrap. If they built that into the cost of running these places. If they made it affect the bottom line—"

"But you never know," Reed said. "Sometimes those kinds of taxes have unforeseen consequences. It's not certain that that'd actually end up helping."

"Well, someone should figure it out." She looked at her food. "I can't eat this anymore."

"Just because people—or dogs—are hungry doesn't mean you can't eat." He put his arm on hers. "Eat. Just enjoy it. We've got to bring some for Samantha, too."

Clione jumped up and ran over to the buffet. In a few seconds she collected a large plate of bread, sausages and bacon. "I almost forgot," she laughed. "How dumb would that have been, huh? Complaining instead of remembering to bring our dog some food!"

"What are we going to do today?" Clione asked, wrapping the meats in paper napkins.

Reed looked at Clione. "These days I'm having trouble planning anything beyond the here and now. The future's pretty hazy."

"I'm not talking about the future. I just mean today...like a few hours from now."

"Hazy, hazy, hazy."

Clione squinted. "You just don't want to make any decisions."

"Maybe I'm just happy where I am?"

"You're just making excuses for the laziness. But lucky for you, I know exactly what we should do."

"What's that?"

"Let's go back to Tulum."

As soon as she said it Reed knew that was what he wanted too. He missed the Welcome Wanderer, he missed Marisol, Cindy, the gecko in the roof of his bungalow. Even Lance.

"Grab your stuff," he said. "We're getting the next bus out of here. Will they take dogs?"

"Marisol might be okay with it, but it's kind of hard on other guests. This time, we'll rent a cabaña on the beach. We'll watch the sunrise. We'll get a bottle of tequila and get drunk in a hammock at night. Okay? And Samantha will be our watchdog."

Reed pointed. "That mangy thing? In our love nest?"

"Why not? Have some faith in poor Sam."

"Okay then," Reed said. "Tulum."

Returning the Favor

Marisol was behind the reception desk reading a book when they walked in, hand in hand. She smiled, closed the novel and nodded approvingly with the air of someone who has seen just about everything at least once, if not several times. Reed felt grateful that she didn't seem to be judging anyone or saying what was right or wrong. He wondered what Lance would make of it.

"Your stuff came," she said, pointing to a suitcase near her feet. Reed realized it was from his hotel room in Cancún: they'd sent it after all. He found it funny that he hadn't even noticed that it wasn't in the hotel room.

"Can I get it in a bit?" he asked.

Marisol nodded. "Sure. Who's your friend?" She walked over to the dog and tried to scratch it behind the ears. The animal shied away.

"This is Samantha. We need to find her a vet."

"You can leave her here. I have a friend who takes very good care of animals. She'll be safe here, too. Stay in the garden. Get lots of TLC from the guests?" She said it like a question, but Reed knew it was the right thing to do. He handed Marisol the makeshift leash.

"We'll be back in a few days."

While Clione freshened up, Reed walked outside. It was early afternoon, the sunlight like golden hay spun into the steel-blue sky. Hens scattered as freight trucks tore over speed bumps, and the same chicken vendor was there at the grill, a Thermos cooler full of carcasses ready to roast and sell. He smiled; Reed nodded in greeting.

"You want your chicken?" the man asked. "You order from me a chicken."

Reed laughed and put a hand to his forehead. "I forgot! Sí, señor, but not right now. Later."

"I save for you beautiful *pollo*. No forget next time. It is too delicious to waste."

Clione came out and wrapped her arm around his waist. She had quickly brushed her hair and had touched her lips with gloss, making them glisten. He'd been *inside* this girl, felt the hot oil slick of her body surrounding his. Her fingernails trails still showed across his back where she'd clung to him. He probably still smelled like her. Reed pulled her tightly to him, hips against hips. He wanted to crush her, become part of her so she would never slip away.

As the two approached him, the chicken vendor laughed. "I see why you no need chicken. You already have beautiful bird!"

Reed smiled. Just thinking about her made him want to turn around, march her back to the cabaña and make their bodies into one being. It was as if they were candles and Tulum were an oven and they had melted together somehow. Almost as soon as he thought that, he thought about Laurel. How strange to be without her when they'd been together for so many years. She'd hung up on him when he'd called, but that didn't give him the right to...he didn't know, didn't want to even define what he had with Clione in case it would be meaningless. It probably was. Just a fling, like that Italian restaurant owner had thought. She could wake up tomorrow and be gone. Or the next day. Or the day after that.

"Are we ready?" Clione asked. Her expression changed. "What's wrong?"

His doubts vanished. Her face was open, honest, kind. She looked at him with the trusting inquisitiveness of someone he'd known for a long time. There was no way she would ever do anything to hurt him. He felt sorry that his life back home was intruding on their day together. It could be their last.

"I'm changing my flight," Reed said. "That's okay, right? Staying a little longer."

"Why wouldn't it be?"

"Just checking that you'll still be here if I stay."

"I scared you."

Clione waited by the youth hostel as he made the call from the same telephone across the street. She looked younger today than he'd ever seen before, not a wrinkle anywhere, not a frown line, not a single mark of time. He suddenly understood what people mean when they say "my girl." How could he be the one lucky enough to be whisking her away from the hostel to have all to himself at the beach?

"Just don't fly back home without making good on your promise," she said.

"My promise?"

"We *are* going diving. Or I will hunt you down."

"There's a cab," he said, stepping into the street and waving down a white sedan with a red stripe. The driver was young, in new jeans and a spotless, candy-apple-red polo shirt.

"*El Mirador,*" Clione said. "*Gracias, amigo.*"

Reed put his arm around her, pulled her close. She'd put on some perfume, something light and fresh that made him think of rain in a forest somewhere. "I like how you can speak so much Spanish," he said.

"You can too. It's not hard. You could take lessons. It's what I did. Just park yourself here for a month or two, kick back, go to classes. It's easy to pick up."

"Somehow, my generation just skipped that whole travel thing. It's like we got lost somewhere. We're stuck inside, glued to our chairs, trapped in our cubicles. Even when we go on vacation it's to some place like Cancún, where everything's just the same as back home except for a pool the size of Rhode Island. And then we think, 'Why did I spend so much money when I could be back home not having the same amount of fun?' It's pathetic."

"Well, you escaped at least."

"Only because of you."

Clione laughed. "You wouldn't have come here on your own?"

"The second I saw you walk up those stairs something happened to me. I'd spent three days doing nothing by myself all day, and then I saw you and I just, I don't know. It was like I suddenly knew what I wanted. I wanted you more than the drink I was drinking, more than my wife, more than anyone I've ever known. I would never, ever have come this far, done what I've done. If not for you."

"My little stalker."

"I just got lucky with the Murakami book, and it led me to you."

"Good thing it wasn't an e-book," Clione replied. "Have you started it yet?"

"No."

"You should. It's about life, what's important. What we can't hold on to and what we can't afford to lose."

"What is your writing about?"

Clione smiled. "I guess my stuff is pretty much about the same thing. Ephemeral loss. I wish I could finish things. I start things all the time, and then they taper off. I get distracted. My journal entries are the only things worth reading."

"You write about what we can't afford to lose?"

"I think that's what all novels are about. All good novels anyway."

"And what's the answer?"

"'One life, one encounter. All we have is today.' It's a Japanese proverb."

"What's that mean? Carpe Diem?"

She shrugged. "It could mean a lot of things, but to me it means to make every moment count. Don't think you can feed a dog tomorrow just because it's there today. Don't second-guess yourself. Do things, do them right now. Because each moment we have never happens again." She was talking as much to herself as to Reed, staring out the window as the scenery rushed past.

The taxicab passed a flock of bright azure jays with black heads and yellow beaks, and Clione pointed to them as they collected in a treetop like ornaments. A pair of agoutis crossed the road, stopping momentarily to look at the oncoming vehicle. The taxi driver didn't hit the brakes, and at the last moment the pair split—one leaping left, the other right—disappearing into the woods. Clione shuddered, and Reed pulled her to him, knowing neither of them wanted to see any animal hit again. He kissed her softly on the mouth, and she left her lips parted and stared up at him after he'd stopped.

"I feel like I've come out of a tunnel into something." He paused, trying to fix the image of her there in his mind so he'd remember it forever. "Something amazing. Some world I never knew existed before."

Clione laughed. "You sound like you're forgetting all about your wife. And I'm not. There's a lot that I don't like about...us."

"Sure. She's there and I love her and, I'm sure you know it, I'm thinking about her and worried about her. But after meeting you I feel like there are two halves of me."

"What happened between the two of you?"

"Well, I already told you part of it."

"And the other part?"

Reed looked out at the palms and the sand and the sea. He took a deep breath. "She had a miscarrage. Six years ago. She was five months into the pregnancy. It just...it poisoned her somehow. Like she came to a bridge and looked at it and just decided she wasn't meant to cross it. She was just never the same. And we talked about adoption a little, tossed it around. Not seriously, but suddenly when we got here that started to make sense. At least to me. But when it came right down to it, she didn't want to. And maybe I didn't either. I should probably be there with her in Boston, but instead, I'm here. And here feels more real somehow than everything that's been going on at home. The longer I'm here, the less I want to go back. It's only been a week. What if I stayed two or three?"

"Well, you can't just leave her. Not for *me*. Sweetheart, don't take this the wrong way, but you're *not* falling in love with me. I won't let you. And," she stiffened, pushing herself away from him, "I'm the last person you want to be involved with anyway. I'm as messed up as an unmade bed."

Reed sat up straight, pressing his back into the cold, cracked vinyl. "Why do you say that? You're the most with-it person I've ever met."

"Hah!" she laughed. Then she smiled, cocked her head to the left and shook it back and forth, slowly. "Maybe I'll keep up the appearances for now. Disappoint you later. Some other time." She snuggled against his shoulder for the rest of the ride. "But don't make me into something I'm not."

The driver spun the wheel and the car pulled off the cracked pavement onto a dirt road so bumpy that Reed's head hit the window as they turned. A buck iguana hefted itself over the hot limestone and disappeared in the jungle, its long claws leaving little puffs of dust behind it that wafted like smoke up into the air. From somewhere came the thin strains of mariachi music, and then the car pulled into a small cantina on a cliff top. Down below, right at the waterline, were a collection of simple shacks with palm roofs nestled underneath the coconut palms.

"We're here," said Clione. "Welcome to *my* version of a fancy hotel."

Realizing they'd left the hammocks Reed had bought back at the hostel, they decided to rent one. The señora who gave them the key was a grandly obese woman with three missing front teeth, which gave her a singsong whistle as she spoke. She was also the source of the mariachi music, which was blaring from a boombox almost the size of a compact car. Three empty beer bottles were on the table in front of her, and Reed wondered whether she'd simply sat there all night or if a three-beer breakfast was part of her morning routine.

Clione did the talking, and for eight dollars they got a cabaña for a night with a threadbare hammock made of faded rainbow nylon. A rickety wooden staircase in the embankment led down to the beach, where a stand of wind-whipped date and coconut palms stuck out of majestic, bone-white sand dunes. Nestled among them was an L-shaped row of small shacks with palm-topped roofs, the walls made merely of sticks that had been trimmed and pounded deep into the sand. Rope had been used to make the door hinges, and each cabaña was locked with a small chain and a rusty padlock. Their key was to Cabaña 3, which was at the end of the short side of the L, closest to the beach.

"Isn't this great?" Clione said, pushing the door open and stepping inside. "It's as basic as it gets. And who needs more?"

Reed ducked as he went inside. "I can't believe they call this a hotel room." A few candles had been melted onto a lone slab of rock that served as a table. Other than that the room was entirely bare: just loose sand on the floor. He was still paying for an empty room in Cancún that cost hundreds of dollars a night.

"You don't like it?"

"I love it."

"Go barefoot. Let your feet feel the sand."

He pulled off his shoes and socks, tucking the latter in little balls into the toes. The sand was cool and light, as fine as chalk dust. He dug his feet in and watched Clione hang the hammock. She tied one end to a hook and wrapped the other around a support, using her left arm to hold the cord, then tied it quickly, deftly looping one end of the rope around the hammock's eyelet and pulling it tight with her right arm.

"You've done this before."

"I could sleep in one of these every night and not ever miss a bed. Mayans knew how to sleep." Finished with the tying, she pulled the rainbow-colored threads over her head and leaned back, kicking her feet into the air. "Come here," she said, stretching out. "Ever made love in a hammock?"

Reed adjusted the door and began to feed the thin chain through the hole where the lock was. Clione chuckled. "Why bother? People can see inside anyway, right?"

"I want to be alone with you."

"Forget the world, Reed. Just come over here, pull off my clothes, and let's do what people are meant to do to each other." She grinned and reached out for him. "Let's *fuck.*"

Reed forced the door shut anyway, dug it into the sand and left it there, hoping the door's own weight would keep it from swinging open. He turned around, pulled off his shirt, and eased himself onto the hammock. The support ropes creaked under their combined weight, but they held just fine. Clione ran her hands through his hair and then pinched his earlobes so tightly they hurt.

"What was that for?" Reed asked.

She didn't answer. Instead, she shifted her weight, putting one of her legs on top of him, twisting so that they were lying side by side.

Reed kissed her. "Are you ready?"

"Very."

Reed delicately put a hand on her vulva, feeling the cotton of her panties beneath the fabric of her sundress. The curve of the hammock pushed them together. He felt the warm heat of her thigh kiss his skin. Clione shifted and straddled him, opened, and suddenly he was inside her, his penis sliding deeply to the base of the shaft. Her vagina was hot, the muscles rippling as he moved through her. She brought her vagina up, bending his penis inward toward the G spot. He pushed himself as deep inside her as he could go. He took her left arm in his, drew the curled fingers to his lips, traced each nail with his tongue, moving to the knuckles and to the valleys where the fingers met the palm. Her hand quivered like a frightened bird as he moved his tongue along the salty skin. She shook her hips, clenched her pelvic muscles tightly around him, drawing him toward the G spot and the pubic bone. He shivered, feeling the first spasms of sensation. He licked her wrist, traced his tongue on the white skin, felt the blood contained beneath it. His own wife's forearms still had traces of the scars that had once been red mouths below her palms. Clione's wrists were so smooth and beautiful and young.

She moved faster, rhythmically, and he moved his mouth to her right hand, letting her fingers go deep, caressing his tongue, touching his gums. She seemed to send pulses of sensation out of her fingertips, making his whole head tingle. He gasped, pulled her down on top of him, grabbed her hips with both hands and thrust himself up into the soft fire, his muscles contracting again and again, until the contractions balanced the line between euphoria and pain. Clione kept moving, their liquids mixing together, anointing their thighs. When she began to orgasm, she held her breath, her body getting progressively more rigid, arching her neck back. Her legs trembled, her fingers dug into the flesh of his own. She seemed to have frozen on top of him, motionless as a statue, then she melted, sinking onto his chest with a deep sigh.

"I feel like I'm stealing something from you."

She nibbled at his ear. "You're probably the only guy on the planet who's *apologizing* because he gave a girl an orgasm."

He fell asleep, his body entwined in the hammock with the beautiful girl beside him, indistinguishable from any other pair of lovers.

Hibiscus Tea

"Shall I read to you?" Clione asked, sitting above him, the Murakami book in her hand. But instead of starting a page, she ran her fingers up and down his chest, waiting as he slowly realized he was still on a hammock and that everything that had happened yesterday hadn't been his dream. It was midmorning already. Reed felt the satisfying, bone-deep exhaustion that comes from making love.

Clione squirmed her way out of the hammock and dressed, slipping her things on quickly and leaving him still struggling to get untangled. By the time he was on two feet, she was off down the beach somewhere. He put on his shirt and pants and followed, finding her halfway up the stairs along the cliffside. She looked back at him and waved.

"Such a gorgeous view," she called, as he got closer.

They held hands walking up the stairway to the cement lookout area with its plastic Coca-Cola tables and pale green awning that served as a combo office and restaurant. Choosing a table overlooking the water, right on the edge of the cliff, they sat down across from each other and looked out at the view. Palms had grown up to the level of the scarp face, their bushy fronds seeming like green clouds. Here and there an emerald-colored parrot or a jet-black mynah bird investigated the canopy, announcing its findings with brilliant song.

"*¿Hay agua de Jamaica?*" Clione asked the matron, who was listening to an iPod Mini. The woman hit a button and waited. There were now four empty beers on the table. Whether she'd added to the three or started over from zero that morning, Reed couldn't tell.

"*¿Hay agua de Jamaica?*" Clione said again.

"*Momentito, por favor. ¿Quiere dos?*"

"Do you want to try hibiscus tea? It's delicious."

"Sure," Reed said.

Clione turned back to the Señora. "*Sí, dos por favor.*"

The old lady eased herself out of the tiny plastic chair and steadied herself on the table.

"*Dos Jamaicas!*" she yelled, to someone in the kitchen they couldn't see.

Minutes later a girl in a bright-pink dress brought the glasses, one in each hand. She could not have been older than ten, and had her hair done up in a matching ribbon, dressy as a flower girl.

"*Gracias,*" said Clione, taking the drinks. "*Y esto es para ti!*" She put a few coins into the Mexican girl's hand.

"She's adorable," Reed said, staring after her. "Like a little doll."

"I guess."

"How come you're so sour on kids, Clione? You'd be a good mother."

"Hah. Maybe if that was all I wanted to be. But if I had a kid right now, that would be it for my writing. I'd just be a mom, that's all."

"What if you became successful? Had all the money you could imagine? Couldn't you have kids then? Being a mom's a huge accomplishment."

"It's not the money. It's the time they take."

"But children are life itself. Everything depends on children."

"So have some. Have ten." Clione laughed. "I'm not against them in general. Just against them when specific to me. Why are you pushing me to have kids?"

Reed couldn't tell if she was angry or about to cry. "I'm not," he said.

She just looked at him, arms crossed.

Finally: "So how's the tea?"

They sipped their drinks quietly, Reed wondering if they'd just had a fight, if this was already the beginning of the end. Clione started writing. Reed pushed his chair back and gave her space, finishing the drink while watching the ocean. A slight breeze was caressing the coconut palms.

When Clione finished writing, she closed her journal and stood up, moving behind him. Resting her left arm on his left shoulder she pressed her right fingers deep into his deltoid muscles. He felt as if electricity were coursing through her, arcing out from her left arm, deep into his thorax, that she was catching the energy with her right hand. Completing a circle. Sucking out any tension that was stored there.

"Don't move," she whispered.

"That feels really, really good right now."

She stayed behind him, doing a dance with her hands. The pressure was different between her right and left hands, yet it was her left that felt better, as if the arm had gained in sensitivity what it had lost in strength. Within seconds she'd isolated a knot beneath his shoulder blade. She began to knead the muscle, pressing and smoothing, and Reed felt some of the hardness ease away.

He told her briefly about the conversation he and Laurel had had just before she left. She just kept kneading, silently. He looked out at the palm trees and the clouds.

"I'm sorry for being like this," he ended. "I'm not trying to tell you anything about your life. I'm just trying to figure out mine. It's funny, when I was your age I always thought that I'd know more about things when I was my age. And it seems like you're the one with all the answers."

"I don't have answers," Clione laughed. "You don't know the half of how fucked up I am."

"Maybe not answers. But you have a plan."

"I guess. But you can't beat yourself up. You feel the way you do." Clione laughed. She stopped massaging and came around in front of him. "It's nobody's fault. Sometimes bad things happen. Why does there have to be blame? Do what you're going to do. And eventually you die."

"I wanted to have kids," Reed said. "We both did. We just assumed it would happen."

"Well, you still can, right?"

"It's hard to have kids if you're not having sex."

"So have sex. Rut like rabbits and stop whining about it. Problem solved."

"After the miscarriage, she just...it's not there."

"That's a shame," Clione said. "You not having sex."

"Why?"

"Because you're good at it," she said. "I like it that you care about me, about making me feel good. Most guys don't know anything about how to explore someone. They don't know making love isn't really as much about the finish line as how much fun it is to get there." She kissed the top of his head.

"But it's not just me, just the guy. Good sex is something that two people create, Clione. What we had was so...It was sex, but it wasn't anything that I've ever had before either. I haven't had sex with very many people, and it was always nice, sometimes really nice, but last night...." He trailed off. The wind was picking up. At the horizon line whitecaps were breaking over the reef, a strip of white on top of toothpaste-azure green. "I can't even put what I want to say into words. But it's not me. Not you. It's us being together, here, right now, this capsule of time. That's why it's good. I didn't realize that before, that sex is about two people," he finished. He reached over to run his hand along her firm, smooth thigh. "I've never had that with Laurel. Sex, even when we were close, was always awkward. She never seemed to know what she wanted, seemed to expect that I should provide her with it. And I never could, so it was always strange. Sex should have made us closer afterward. Instead it made us feel further apart."

Clione continued rubbing his back. "It's nice, knowing that I made you happy."

Love, Scuba, and Murakami

When they got hungry, they went into town to find a place to eat. As they rode in the back seat of the hot cab, Reed wondered what it was that would bring him and Laurel back together. Or should they pull the plug and separate? It was as if he were splitting into two people, twins leading different lives. One was a husband committed to a marriage that would somehow pull through. The other was a traveler just starting to discover a lover more important to him than anyone he'd ever known. Sometimes he was one, then the other, and he felt it was impossible to know which path to choose.

What were Laurel's days like now? Was she taking long walks, reading, finding time to be by herself? Scrabbling to anchor the news each night? Fucking the producer as a way of getting back at Reed somehow? He couldn't imagine it. But it seemed impossible that the two of them could find happiness again. He felt sorry for her, yet he had no sense of what would pull them out of it. And yet this girl beside him, wonderful and kind as she was, couldn't provide him anything more than a night or two of throwaway happiness. Then she'd be gone, and he'd be as lost and alone as he'd ever been. She didn't want kids either, and he knew all he could hope for was a few more hours before the sunset brought their time together to a close.

What he wanted, he decided, as the car came to a stop at the Pemex intersection and they waited for the light to turn green, was for this day to never end.

That was the key, he realized: it was everything beyond the sunset that scared him. What he really wanted was to stay with Clione, stay in that little bungalow, stay here in Mexico, stay in this taxi even. He wanted time to stop and for them to just have one forever-long day.

Clione began tracing patterns on his thigh with her left hand, delicate spider webs that sent tingling sensations zipping across his skin. She stared intently out the window, looking away from him. Only their touch differentiated them from two strangers who had decided to share the same cab.

You can only fall in love, you can never reclaim it. He was trying to find a way back through the failures and frustrations to a place with Laurel where they were still in love, and it was never going to happen. How come he was realizing that just now? Was that why he'd left and let her go back to Boston? If he loved Laurel, he should have stayed, or should have gone with her, or fought to keep her in Mexico. He should have been on the next plane home. But he had let it slide.

So maybe that was it: You fight for the things you love.

Maybe he didn't love Laurel after all.

But he *did*, he told himself, staring out the window as if the answer would jump out of the jungle and leap at the car. He *did* love her. They had shared so much. The miscarriage. Laurel's failed suicide later that year. The good things too. Her promotion at the station. His shift from traffic news to doing the helicopter. They'd been happy once and even if that wasn't where they were now, they might find that again. He wasn't going to toss away twelve years of being with her just to be with someone for a few more hours. He just hadn't known things, hadn't been able to see as clearly. It wasn't Laurel's fault.

But if he wasn't going to leave his wife then it meant that everything now with Clione was meaningless, just transitory, as ephemeral as an ice cube in the summer sun. Which couldn't be true either. It *did* matter. It had to. Even just thinking about her made him feel alive. That had to mean something.

Clione.

He held the syllables in his mouth again as if her name were a sip of wine. Where there should have been regret, guilt, and disappointment, there was only a chamber filled with light and magic and a sense of possibility. He couldn't remember feeling happier or more free.

A flock of jays, maybe the same flock they'd seen earlier, startled and rose up from the palms, brilliant blue and black, their piercing yellow eyes beady and alarmed. Clione pointed and he nodded in acknowledgment. He watched their blue bodies penetrate the green and disappear.

"What's that look?" Clione asked him.

"I just thought of that Jimmy Buffett song, the one where the guy leaves and goes off to paradise. 'The Weather Is Here, I Wish You Were Beautiful.' You know that one?"

Clione nodded. "My father used to love that song."

She hummed a few bars, snapping her fingers.

"I'm the guy in that song."

"You're writing your own song. We all do." Clione pressed his hand with hers. "Don't forget that you and Laurel are just borrowing time, too. Just like us. We're all just borrowing time together, and it'll end, and we'll move on through our lives, borrowing time with other people or just staying alone. That's the way life is. It's the way it's supposed to be. I know you're not going to tear up that plane ticket. You're going to get on the plane and go. I'm okay with that."

"I was just thinking about how much I wish I could just stop time, just be here. Like this. Forever."

"Even if I wanted you to, you can't. And I don't. This can't last. But that's okay."

"This?"

"Us."

He looked at her. "Do you think if anything was different that it could?"

"You mean us be together in the long run? Or the short?"

"I don't know. Both?"

Clione stared out the window for a while. "In the long run, we die. And sometime after that the earth gets swallowed up by the sun."

"I deserved that," Reed said. "What about the short run?"

"We eat something in town, go diving, look at fish, and fuck. That's what life's about."

"You're avoiding the question. What about the middle run?"

Clione didn't answer for a while. The car slowed at an intersection, navigated the rotary. Finally she shrugged.

"I guess we'll find out."

"Do you want there to be a middle?" Reed asked. "I guess that's what I'm really asking."

"That depends entirely on how well you learn to dive."

* * *

Tulum Sea and Sport was a standard operation with tours going out in the morning and afternoon. It smelled of salt and wetsuit rubber. Lance was at the back of the narrow shop, filling tanks with fresh air from a throbbing compressor. When he saw the pair he nodded, then returned to the task while the owner talked on the telephone.

"There's nothing more important than fresh air," Clione said. "You fill a tank wrong, you get the air contaminated, a leak – all kinds of things can happen. You can't even let air sit in the tank for too long or bad things happen."

"Like what?"

"You can get drunk," she explained. "You start feeling giddy. Happens to people all the time, especially at lower depths. And if it hasn't been filled correctly your lips turn blue and you start acting funny."

"Just from bad air?"

"Sure. All it takes is a little moisture inside the tank, humidity even, and oxidation can start. Rust. In as little as three months, so much carbon dioxide builds up that it's like breathing car exhaust. Which is why you should always dive in pairs. One person can watch out for the other. Being under the water affects people differently. Some people get lightheaded even when the air is perfectly fine. But bad air or even stale air can be fatal. People say it's like a euphoria and you just never come up."

"This is not making me less nervous."

"It'll be fine," she laughed. "We're talking rare cases, like if you haven't refilled the tank in months or years. And Lance knows exactly what he's doing. If he had any ambition he would own that shop by now, instead of just working there."

"Yuv jest mist the murning dive session," the owner, putting down the receiver and coming over to them. He was a tall, burly guy with a beard and a thick Sean Connery accent. He pushed a half toothpick around in his mouth, letting it rest on his lower lip every time he spoke. "But we can take you out in the afternoon."

"He's a beginner, has never dived before," Clione said.

"We're used to that. He kin do a Discover Scuba course and be all sit. Or if he wants to, he kin do some stuff in the pool now and be ready for the whole thing by afternoon."

"But that's a little fast, isn't it?" Reed said. "I mean, to learn and absorb everything?"

"First time I went out," said the owner, "it was in a loch in Scotland in late October. My buddies handed me a taink and a regulator an sid to follow them, an we all dove in and that was it. I didn't even know I could inflate the regulator to go up or anything — just kicked an kicked until my buddy saw I was sinking like a stone an pushed the leettle button."

"Maybe I should wait."

"Point is, I was faine. I didn't know deeke squat about anythin' an it was faine. No bends, no problems, an I was utterly hooked from the moment my head went under the water." He sucked in, let his breath out, sucked in again. "It's like bein' high. But better than anythin' a chemical kin do for you. An I promise you, do a Discover Scuba session with Sea and Sport an you'll know everythin' you need to know to feel comfortable in the water."

"I'll be right there next to you," Clione said. "And Lance is a great teacher. He's an asshole sometimes, but he's serious about those tanks. He won't let anything bad happen to you."

The man behind the desk pushed a clipboard with some poorly photocopied pages on it, followed by a battered Bic pen with a thick ink blob at the nib. "Let's get started. This is the release form. Nothing will go wrong, of course. Riddy to sign your life away?"

Reed paused, waiting for the pen to stop shaking in his hand.

"Nobody's forcing you," Clione said, coming back to the counter. A pale mint bikini was in her hands, with so little fabric that Reed wondered if she'd only gotten one half. She put it on the counter and fished in her purse for some cash.

"You don't want to go?" she asked. "Don't go. But don't just stand there. Make up your mind about it. Go, or don't."

Mister Toothpick winked. "Nice suit you got there. A lass with some sass."

"Just give me my change." She pushed some peso bills at the man and pulled the bikini off the hanger. Unstretched, it looked like a crumpled party napkin left after a meal. Clione went to the door.

"It's probably better anyway, Reed," she said. "If you're panicking now, what's it going to be like when we push you off the side of a boat for the first time?" She shook her head and pushed out into the heat. He saw her through the window, walking out to a telephone pole where she leaned against it, arms crossed, mad.

Reed took a deep breath, grabbed the clipboard, and signed. The sweat from his palm left a wet streak on the countertop.

"You're goin' to have the taime of your life," Toothpick Connery said. "Trust me. Come back in tirty minutes and Lance'll take you to the pool."

Reed looked at Clione. She was staring at the road as if expecting life to come by and offer her a ride. He walked out to her and they looked at each other.

"Maybe get a margarita?"

Still silence.

"You're mad at me."

She turned around and looked at him. "The water won't hurt you. You're so, so scared of everything all the time. Scared of me, scared of your wife, scared of tomorrow, scared of the water...ugh. How can you live like that?"

He tried not to raise his voice but it got louder anyway. A boy across the street turned to watch them. "It's not like I can just turn fear off like a faucet or something. I *am* afraid. It's not rational, but it's there just the same. Doesn't anything make you want to run screaming away? I look at the water and I'm stark, raving terrified. I've always been scared of the water, and I know it's stupid, but it's just something. If you've never been scared about something like that, well, count yourself lucky. But...." he stopped.

"But what?"

"Being a mom scares you."

"Oh, you're such an asshole." She turned and started walking up the street.

He followed her. "Take every fear you have about having kids and that's what I feel when I look under water. I can't say why, but I just feel like something's out there. Waiting for me."

She kept walking. "Nothing's waiting for you, Reed. Except a really cool experience that will change your life. But if you're not into it, don't deceive yourself. Don't go diving just because of me. I'm not that special, and I sure as hell don't need your stupid puppy love. Or your patronizing crap about motherhood. Go diving because you really want to or don't go diving at all."

"I'm going diving because I really want to."

"Hah."

"I'm not just saying it," he said. "But if we're going to fight, can't we at least be doing it out of the sun somewhere? While we're sipping a margarita?"

She turned. The flicker of a smile played across her face. "Sure. Tell me what a bitch I am over a margarita."

They chose a place with a rickety second-floor deck made of rough planking and untreated wicker furniture, topped, like everything in Tulum, with a palapa roof. As Reed wondered if every tourist joint in the town was Italian-run, a maître d' led them up a spiral staircase made of metal so thin that it bent under each footstep. It wound up from the street around a telephone pole that had been carved with pseudo-Maya designs and then painted in Day-Glo colors. From the pole, a savage pink-and-lime-green face stared out at Reed as he sipped an over-salted, watery margarita.

"This is easily the worst margarita I've ever had," he said, after the third sip. For some reason he remembered the drink he'd had at the all-inclusive. "We should order a Tulum Sunset," he said.

"What's that?"

"It's the drink I was plastered on that first day we met. I'd had about nine of them, which was about seven too many."

"Okay," Clione said. "Let's get one."

Reed called the waiter over, but the man shook his head.

"I'm sorry, it is not on our menu."

"Well, it should be. It's the perfect tropical drink."

"We're in the shade, at least," she said. "We can stay here."

They looked at each other. Clione seemed to change each day. Her hair looked glossier than he had ever seen it, and it fell down across her shoulders like a shimmery mane. Her lips were full and flushed, her cheeks pink from sunburn as if she'd put on too much blush.

"So, where do we start?" Reed asked. "What's wrong? It just seems like suddenly we're fighting and I don't want that to happen."

Clione looked down, watched an old lady haul herself across the road with a bamboo cane. Her grandson, still only waist-high, scampered in front of her like a little puppy. "I'm sorry. I get like this sometimes. Maybe PMS? Or is that more woman stuff than you need to know?"

"Tell me anything. And if there's one thing that being married will do, it is teach you to endure the myriad facets of female biology." He paused. "I don't want you to be mad at me. So what's up?"

"Reed, you're great. I like you a lot. Maybe too much, in some ways. The thing that's unattractive about you is that you're like a piece of driftwood. Does that make sense? You're just kind of floating around, without any direction other than whatever current you're already in."

"Okay. Sure. I've always been that way," Reed answered. He took a sip of the margarita, winced, put the sweating drink back on the table. "I was thinking about that earlier today. There's only one thing I can remember actively pushing for...decades. And do you know what that is, Clione?"

"What?"

"You. I wanted you from the moment I saw you walk up the stairs at that godawful hotel. The moment I heard your voice, the second you looked at me. I just—blam—one look and you devoured me. I was gone. Sometimes that terrifies me, that I followed you here, that I felt that much of a pull. Part of me wishes I could just forget everything and return to Boston, return to what I have there. It's a decent job and a wife and things could be worse. But I look at you, Clione, and maybe you can't tell how much I've fought just to be able to sit here next to you. I want to figure out a way for us to stay together, to keep this day, and last night, to make it always be here."

He laughed. "Isn't that ridiculous? I know that can't happen. I know it, you know it. It's like watching a sunset that turns absolutely gorgeous for a few moments just before everything goes black. I'm watching you, you're the most amazing thing I've ever seen, and it's tearing me apart that it's going to disappear, that no matter how hard I try, I can't hold on to you."

Clione was staring at him, her lips slightly parted. Reed thought she might say something, but she just nodded, as if to herself, and waited for him to continue.

"And you know what else?" he added. "You see through me like my heart and mind and guts and all are in a goddamn sandwich bag. I'm terrified to go diving. I can't lie about that. Not just scared. Terrified. I don't know if I can do it or not. I'm lying to you when I say I want to go and you know that, too. But I'm more scared that you won't like me if I can't handle it."

"You don't have to go diving, Reed," Clione said. "If it's not your thing, that's just the way it goes. We'll figure it out."

* * *

An hour and a half later, Reed was waist-deep in what had to have been the coldest swimming pool in all of Mexico, water "cold enough," as Lance had warned them, "that your testicles will retreat toward your body cavity for warmth." Despite a thin rental wetsuit, Reed was shivering uncontrollably, goose flesh covering his arms and legs, as were most of the other people in the small dive group.

Lance, muscles bulging beneath his taut, bronzed hide, hadn't even opted to wear a wetsuit and didn't seem the least cold. There were three other people in the group: a couple in their late forties who were here on a honeymoon, and a guy in his mid-twenties from Paris. True to the breed, the man had donned a bikini that rivaled Clione's in size, and Reed found it hard not to be distracted by what was clearly one of the largest penises he'd ever seen, filling the tiny swimsuit to the bursting point.

"Quite the banana hammock," Clione whispered.

"If that guy coughs," Reed answered, "the suit's going to explode."

Lance demonstrated what the exercise was supposed to do. "You're underwater, okay? You're swimming, and suddenly you lose your mask. Someone kicks it off with their fin and suddenly, you can't see anything. It happens a lot, actually. Happens all the time." He turned around. "What are you going to do?"

Nobody answered.

"Drown?" Reed offered.

Lance slapped a hand down into the water like a teacher hitting a desk. "No! That's why we're here freezing our nuts off in this pool. So we *don't* drown. So we know exactly what to do in an emergency." He raised his mask, held it off his head and demonstrated in the same theatrical, rehearsed fluidity of a flight attendant giving the safety instructions just prior to take-off. "We go like this, and like this, and then we tilt it like this...." He held the bottom lip of the mask slightly off his face. "And then we blow. Exhale. What are we exhaling? Air. What happens when the air gets trapped by the upper lip of the mask? Huh? The mask fills up, you put it back on, you keep on enjoying the dive. Now, we do it underwater. Like this."

He bobbed under, and the class watched him pull the mask away from his face, then replace it. He blew a cloud of bubbles that obscured the view completely, but when he stood up, the mask was tightly back on his face with the water gone.

"Easy, right? Now you try."

They took turns. Clione performed the maneuver almost as fluidly as Lance had, bobbing up seconds after she'd gone down. She knew exactly what she was doing, as comfortable underwater as a sea lion.

Reed lifted the mask to his face and ducked under. The icy water stung his scalp and burned his face, but he stayed under despite the cold. Hoping to impress Clione, he pulled the mask away, slapped it back to his mouth, pulled the strap over his head, his ribcage contracting as if preparing for a breath. Tilt, blow, and then he stood up, gasping. The mask was still a third full, with water sloshing around at the bottom, but Lance let it pass.

"Not good, but good enough."

"You did fine," Clione whispered, squeezing his hand.

"I'm so cold," Reed said. "How is it possible this water can be so cold?"

"It's fed from the cenotes, dude," Lance said. "It comes right up from one of the biggest underground cave systems in the world."

"Couldn't they let it warm up first? I've been in warmer pools in Maine."

"People like it. It's refreshing. Let's keep moving, though. Next, we learn how to put a regulator back in if it's been knocked out."

They stayed in the pool for another forty minutes doing exercises. As he got colder and colder, Reed wondered if maybe the owner of the dive shop had the right idea: no training, just jump in. It seemed as if everything related to a buddy kicking off a mask or a fin pulling out the regulator, a tragedy inherent in diving in large groups. When they finally left the water, Reed was utterly exhausted, and instead of feeling that he knew what to do in an emergency, he had learned a long list of all the myriad things that can actually make a dive become a tragedy.

He hauled himself out and stood on the rough cement, shivering. Clione put her arm around his shoulder. "I'm proud of you. You were underwater just fine."

"But I can see the edges of the pool," Reed had explained. "It's when I don't know what's out there that I start to panic."

"We never know," Clione said. "That's the whole point."

They rode back with the other three in the dive shop's flatbed pickup, the gear and tanks jouncing around haphazardly at each turn. But when Lance pulled the truck up to the door of the office the Scottish owner was standing in the doorway shaking his head. A fresh toothpick was dangling from his lower lip.

"Something with the boat. Engine trouble. No can do on the dive today."

"What?" Lance said. "Can't we use Pedro's?"

"He's off fishing. Woont be back till seven. And b'then it'll be dark."

"Shit on a shingle," Lance replied, shaking his head. He turned to the five people who were still standing inside the pickup. "I guess we have to offer a rain check. We'll be going out tomorrow, though. No question."

The Parisian shook his head. "*Mais moi, je ne suis plus la, demain.*" He paused. "I am not here tomorrow. Today is my *onlee shaunce.*"

"Then we can give you a refund," Lance said. "Can't go diving if we ain't got no dive boat. That's just the way it is."

The other man shook his head. "You wasted my...zeese entire afternoon."

Lance shrugged. "Sorry. We no can do what we no can do."

"We can come back tomorrow?" Clione asked.

"We'll give you first chance for the a.m. session."

Reed felt Clione's fingers on his waist, then she pinched him.

"You're happy about this."

"Not at all. I'm devastated."

"You're euphoric."

They wrote their names down on another clipboard, said goodbye to Lance, and walked out to Avenida Tulum. The sun was starting its downward jaunt into the jungle behind them, but the shadows were still short, and Reed was happy, for once, that it was so hot: it took away the chill of the swimming pool. A beautiful gray turkey with an iridescent blue head strutted back and forth in an alleyway for a few minutes, flaring its tail at passersby until a Mayan woman in a white embroidered sundress turned the corner and unceremoniously pounced on it, picking it up by its feet before marching back inside.

Clione took Reed's arm and they walked side by side, back toward the Welcome Wanderer.

"Let's get the Murakami book," Clione suggested. "I'll read to you tonight."

"Let's get grapes, too, and you can peel them and drop them into my mouth. And a bottle of something?"

"Whatever you want. You deserve a reward for trying so hard in the pool."

"Didn't the Maya call tequila the ambrosia of the gods?"

Clione laughed. "I don't think so."

"The Aztec? Somebody must have thought it was."

"The ambrosia for frat boys, maybe." She smiled, pausing to tuck a strand of hair behind her ear with her right hand. "I'm sorry I was such a bitch today. This morning. I was, I don't know. Just everything was bothering me. It wasn't you. I just felt weirdly emotional."

They paused outside a pastry shop window and looked inside.

"Well," Reed said. "You didn't say anything that wasn't true."

They bought a liter bottle of tequila at a narrow, unlit liquor store not far from the dive shop. A thirty-something man was watching a soap opera on a snowy black-and-white nine-inch television. Wrapped up in the drama, he didn't speak when Reed handed him a single note and told him to keep the change. Carrying the tequila in a paper bag, they stopped in at the Welcome Wanderer.

The inner door was propped open with a wedge of wood, and the place was quiet. Suddenly, Reed decided that it would be nice if they just snuck in quickly and got his stuff and left. He didn't want to see anyone, didn't want to make small talk with strangers he barely knew. While Clione checked the bookshelves, Reed found Marisol. She was behind the bar, absorbed in a thick paperback with a shirtless couple embracing on the cover.

"You're back? Wasn't sure if we'd be seeing you again."

He shook his head. "We can't stay."

Marisol smiled. "It's nice to see her with someone good for her."

"She was with someone bad?"

Marisol shook her head. "No, no. She's the only one who can decide that kind of thing. I only meant it as a compliment about who she was with *now*, not as anything that's happened in the past."

Reed changed the subject. "I just came here to pay for leaving my stuff here. And to get a toothbrush. Maybe a clean shirt or two."

"It's your stuff, not mine. No need to pay."

She closed the romance novel and disappeared behind a door, returning a moment later with the box under her arm. It was bulkier than he remembered. How could he have needed all that? What was in there? The contents of his entire apartment?

He returned to Clione. All she was carrying was the Murakami book under her arm, plus a tattered paperback by Milan Kundera that she'd plucked from the hostel bookshelf. The small duffel bag was on the floor next to her. Everything she owned.

"Have you read this one?"

"Unlikely. Kundera?"

"He's Czech. Brilliant. Every word he writes makes me gush. And I mean that in all the meanings of the word. Gush bigtime."

"Maybe I should become a writer."

"Nobody should be a writer except a writer. Everyone wants to be a writer, but the reason most people aren't is that they start and realize exactly how much writing — the actual work part — just plain sucks. Even writers hate being writers most of the time. Except when they're writing. And then it's like someone else is inhabiting their skin for a while."

"So writers hate writing too."

"Exactly." She pointed to the box. "Get what you need?"

"Yeah, except now I'm thinking all I need is my toothbrush. I mean, I don't look that silly in what I'm wearing, do I? Do I need a new shirt?"

"This is Mexico. Who cares what you look like?" Clione sniffed the air near him. "You're not ripe. Yet. Clean underwear wouldn't hurt though."

"New boxers it is."

He opened the box. Three pairs of slacks were neatly folded at the top. Beneath them were short sleeve shirts, which the hotel had pressed and left in plastic wrapping. Two pairs of shorts, different shades of beige, which made Reed cringe. The classic fresh-off-the-cruise-ship tourist's uniform. Socks, rolled up into neat balls, and folded boxers. Some of the toiletries seemed like relics of another era: the travel-size can of shaving cream and the vibrating razor, the after-shave, the gel for his thinning hair. He felt as if he were looking through a box in an attic from childhood, each item a familiar novelty. Trial and full sizes of his favorite deodorant. A nail clipper and filing pads. His portable hair dryer.

He hadn't once thought about shaving, but now he rubbed his chin and the growth surprised him. He probably looked like a caveman.

"I should shave," he said, staring blankly at the box.

"Should you?"

"I'm here. If I don't shave now I'll end up— "

"With a beard! Horrors!"

"I think I'd just feel better."

Clione shrugged. "Do whatever you want. It's not like we have to be anywhere." She mimicked the Men Without Hats song. "You can *shave* if you want to...you can leave poor me behind...oh you can shave and if you don't shave, well, you're no friend of mine."

She was still singing as he picked out the razor, cream, toothpaste and toothbrush and went to the men's shared bathroom. It was a tiny, L-shaped affair with a scratched, stainless-steel mirror at the corner. A bulbless socket hung from the ceiling on a lone frayed wire; the only light came from a ventilation window near the roof, sending a shaft of brilliance down through the dusty darkness like a watchtower searchlight. A pair of flies orbited above the seatless toilet bowl. Reed remembered the sense of fear he'd had about the bathroom in the Welcome Wanderer bungalow and laughed, realizing how spotless that one was compared to what was in front of him.

Leaning in close to the dented, stainless steel mirror, Reed barely recognized himself. It was a trick of the dim light, certainly, but if he'd met himself in an alley in Boston he'd surely have crossed to the other side. But instead of the bags under his eyes, he noticed his eyes themselves. They burned back at him in the semi-darkness, intense and fathomless, his steel-blue irises unafraid, unapologetic. His hair looked thicker too, and for all the dirt, he was healthier and stronger. His cheekbones had become more prominent, the flaccid pudginess of the past two decades had left him. The rough stubble that had grown over the week gave him the look of Harrison Ford, in those rough-and-tumble, ready-for-anything Indiana Jones days.

He turned on the faucet, twisting the handle all the way before accepting the thin, tepid stream as the maximum that he would get. He cupped his hands and collected some water, then splashed his face, letting the liquid soak into his skin. Rubbing his cheeks, he felt the sandpaper skin, the whisker forest. He'd read somewhere that hair continues to grow long after death, that exhumed corpses are often unrecognizable masses of hair and fingernails. He pressed his cheekbones, ran his fingertips around his eye sockets, feeling a notch in the upper edge of his right eye that he'd noticed as a twelve year-old. Someday, that notched skull would be all that was left to testify that he'd ever walked this earth. Standing in his parents' almond tile bathroom he'd been frightened to have that swirl of mortality visit him, scared to visualize what his own skull would look like long after he was gone. Yet finding that same notch now made him feel alive, as if he were cheating death even if it would catch up to him sometime. He would die someday, as everyone does. But he was here *now*.

He splashed more water on his face, inhaled deeply. He brushed his teeth, spat, rinsed the bowl carefully, and then deliberately tossed the razor and cream into the trash.

Clione had put her hair up, curled it into a bun and stabbed it with a pair of chopsticks.

"You didn't shave."

"I didn't need to."

Nodding, Clione smiled, her expression a mixture of approval and pride. "Let's go read a book."

The sunlight was gone as they got into a white-and-red taxicab and headed back to the Watchtower's cabañas. When they arrived the sky in the east was a silky midnight blue, already dotted with pinprick stars. The white crests of the waves breaking on the reef were still visible offshore, but the wind had died. A couple with towels and an oversize beach tote passed them in the parking lot. The girl smiled at Reed, and he nodded.

"Beautiful night," he said.

"I love it here," the girl replied. "I wish I could stay here forever."

"I think most people who come feel that way."

Their cabaña was untouched, exactly the way they'd left it, with the hammock strung across the space like an upside-down rainbow. Clione placed three of the candles into the sand and then lit them, dripping enough wax onto the stone slab that she could stick the other three onto its sturdy surface.

"There," she said. "Now, Señor, I'll have a frozen margarita, salt, extra lime."

"We can do the salt and lime, but the frozen part won't be happening unless you happen to have a blender and three thousand feet of extension cord."

They sat facing each other in the warm sand, legs crossed, sharing sips of the alcohol bottle that teetered like a toddler between them.

Clione licked her hand between the thumb and forefinger and sprinkled it with a dusting of salt. Reed fumbled with a lime, attempting to utilize his thumbnail as a cutting tool until Clione handed him her diving knife. He halved them, then cut each half into thick, juicy wedges of green flesh.

Soon most of the bottle was gone.

Reed took it and tipped it skyward, letting the hot fire cleanse his throat. He realized he hadn't drunk this much since leaving the hotel. "Let's go for a swim."

"A swim? Am I...Is this the real Reed speaking? What? A swim?"

"This is the real, and the drunk — the real drunk — Reed Haflinger speaking." He stood up, steadying himself on the wall. "And I'm only asking once. You want to go for a swim?"

"Of course," Clione said. She leaned back and slapped her thighs. "You're definitely drunk. I like it. You were drunk when we had dinner with Sharon, too. Now I know! That's the secret. Some guys grow balls when they drink. You grow fins!"

"There hasn't even been time for the alcohol to absorb through my liver," he answered, knowing full well it was true.

"Drunk, drunk, drunk. If you are asking me to go for a swim you are dee-are-you-en-kay! Drunk."

"You should be proud of me, facing my fears."

"You said yourself it's not as bad when you don't look out at how deep it is." She giggled. "Drunk!"

The moon was enormous, hanging low over the sea like a silver serving platter. A breeze was rustling the palm trees, and from somewhere off in the distance a radio was tuned to a salsa beat.

"Music is the heart of Mexico," Clione said. "It's as if the song is urging even the darkness to dance. Come on."

Nobody else was on the beach, and the lamps from the café above had long ago been turned off. Clione's hand was warm in his, and for a moment Reed felt as if he were going to cry. In a few days he would be on a plane, would arrive in Boston with a tan and a T-shirt and a story he'd never tell.

Clione suddenly twisted and slipped one hand around his waist, putting the other straight out in a salsa pose.

"I'll lead," she said.

"I salsa about as well as I swim."

Reed felt her shift her weight and her foot came forward, through his body space, and as she moved, he stepped backward.

"That's right," she whispered. "Just let the music guide you."

He felt her foot come toward him and he stepped back.

"Keep going."

She took three quick steps, perfectly timed to the beat, sharp and crisp, and if he hadn't moved at the same time she did he would have toppled over, pulling them both into the sand. She moved to the side, then backward, then did a quick underarm turn, and Reed realized that he was actually dancing.

The music stopped midsong, and Reed and Clione froze, as if they'd been playing musical chairs.

"Still going to make good on that swim?" she asked.

"I'm a man of my word."

"Race!" Clione said, and scampered toward the surf.

The moon had risen a bit but looked only slightly smaller, and its light reflecting off the regular incoming waves gave the illusion of shimmery steps on a water-washed staircase, leading all the way up to the orb. Reed wanted to point it out, but Clione was already splashing, and he didn't want to yell too loudly into the peaceful night. For a few seconds it looked as if Clione could simply keep running, using the moonlight staircase to dance out across the water and up and up and up. She could keep going, step after step, until she disappeared into the sky. A panic hit him, watching her ascending the white staircase, heading for the moon. The back of his neck prickled for a second and then the fear passed. Everything was normal again.

Reed took a final look at the illusion, then followed the girl. She had already plunged in and was bobbing, several yards out. Reed reached the shoreline, felt his heart quicken as his toe touched the foam, but he steeled himself, swallowed, and stepped in. Water enveloped him, inch by inch, in its cold clamminess, and he decided that maybe he was drunk after all.

* * *

Later, in the hammock, Clione lay on top of him like a warm, heavy blanket. He was still inside her, their bodies slippery with semen and sweat. Clione traced her finger in a pattern on his shoulder as if sketching out a design for a tattoo. He ran his fingers gently around his penis in a slow perimeter, exploring the place where his body and hers were still fused. They lay for a while listening to the sound of the waves, the light breeze cooling them through the spaces in the cabaña walls.

"Why did you decide to become a writer?" Reed asked.

Clione shifted on his chest, and kissed him softly. "You sure you want to know?"

"Sure."

"You know that scar on my cheek?"

"I thought it was a dimple," Reed said. "It's a scar?"

"Well, when it gets light you can look at it again. When I was in second grade I wasn't very popular. I kind of ugly and —"

"I can't believe you were ever ugly."

"Well, maybe someday I can show you pictures. I was ugly, and of course I had this," she lifted her left arm and let it drop to her side, "which didn't help. I had braces and even with only one good arm I could beat up just about anyone in the class, even the boys, and I was smart and there was this one boy, I don't know, he just hated me. His name was Dick."

"Perfect name for a bully."

"Isn't that funny? I didn't even think of making fun of him back then, calling him names. But his sole purpose seemed to be to get other kids to hate me too. Dick used to spit on me, called me 'runt' and 'three legs' and 'gimp' and stuff like that. Sometimes he'd grab my left arm and try to twist it behind my back, but I learned to see it coming. If he got it though, it hurt terribly."

"He probably thought you were cute. That's why boys tease girls."

"Maybe," Clione said quietly. "One day he and four other boys caught me at recess. Our school grounds had a chain-link fence around most of it, but it was to keep the balls from going into the woods, not to keep kids from going out. There was this one place where you could push the link away from the pole enough to slide through pretty easily, and the older kids, fifth-graders, sometimes used that to go smoke their parents' cigarettes.

"Dick and his four friends caught me, and they dragged me through that hole in the fence, and took me into the woods, and Dick had a little penknife, see, and he said he was going to mark me, brand me, if I didn't shut up. It was probably just a bluff. He wasn't that mean. He just wanted to show off the knife, and I was his toy.

"I tried to scream for help, but they stuffed a T-shirt into my mouth, and when I wouldn't stop kicking and screaming, he held the knife up to my cheek to let me know he was serious. Only I couldn't see anything, I was so scared. I didn't even know they had a knife. It was like my vision had shut down or something. They were just trying to get me to be quiet but I was so scared and frightened, and I turned my face right into the blade, and it went through my cheek and lodged in the cotton of the shirt. I was lucky; if it hadn't been there maybe they would have sliced off my tongue. It had stretched out the skin, so the knife just went through my cheek like it was a piece of cellophane."

She stopped speaking. She stared at the pattern of light and shadow the walls made on the sand. Reed ran his hand along her back, waiting for her to continue.

"I still remember the taste of that knife. Metal has a particular taste, and we're used to it being in the front of our mouths. It was so strange feeling it, tasting it there in the side of my mouth. And I remember that, and the saltiness of the blood, and more than that I remember thinking that there was nothing more horrible in the world than *people*, that I would never let anyone do that to me, ever again. I would kill them first. Kill them as soon as they looked at me. The funny thing was that it didn't hurt at all. Not then. I guess I was just too scared to feel any pain. Just that peculiar taste and the look in Dick's face as the knife went through."

"What happened to Dick and the boys?"

"One of them puked, right there on the ground, and the other three went running. Dick stayed with me for a few seconds, trying to use the T-shirt to stop the blood like he suddenly realized what he'd done, but he didn't touch the knife or anything. It was still in my mouth, and when I started to choke from all the blood, he ran off too. I had to pull the knife out myself and walk back to school. Except I was too ashamed to go back. I went out into the street and tried to walk home. A neighbor near the school said she saw me wandering around, but I don't remember any of it."

"I'm so sorry."

"I still have the penknife. None of the boys ever asked for it, and I sure as hell wasn't going to give it to them. It's in my backpack now, but I wore it around my neck for years. It was the knife I was going to use to kill the next person who touched me."

Reed sighed. "You seem so normal now. I can't believe that's not what you were like back then."

"That's why I never want to have kids. Childhood is hell. I never want to put them through what I went through. This arm, you know, it could easily be in my genes. Maybe my kids will look like this and have to grow up with it, deal with it. I don't want to do that to them."

"But nobody who knows you cares about your arm. That's a silly reason not to want children."

"But I couldn't do it," she said. She shivered. "Something growing inside you? Like a parasite or something, feeding off your blood and insides? No way." She shook her shoulders as if she were cold.

"Maybe you'll feel differently someday," Reed said. "I didn't really want kids when I was your age. But you get older, you see a few of your friends have them and realize it doesn't change your life that much."

"I had my chance to be a mother," Clione said softly. "And I'm not a mother."

Reed looked at her. "You had an...?"

She nodded.

"I'm sorry."

Clione shrugged. "I can't change what's already on the page. If there's one lesson in life, it's that you can't undo things. You can change them. You can shape them. But you can't go back and do things over again."

Reed nodded.

Clione shrugged. "You seem to have a way of sucking these sorts of stories right out of me. You shouldn't be such a good listener."

Reed held up the empty bottle. "The blame lies solely with Señor Cuervo."

They sat for a few moments in silence.

"Do you ever regret it?"

Clione shook her head, no, without hesitation. "I made my choice. No regrets."

"You don't mean that."

"You know some rats eat their own babies? Just chew them up right after giving birth? Maybe I'm just like a rat. Something wrong with the chromosomes. I don't know. But I don't want to have a kid. Not now, not ever. I let them cut my baby out of me once, and I'd do it again if I had to."

Reed didn't say anything. The wind had picked up and sand was blowing in through the cracks in the cabaña walls. The waves sounded angry, smashing against the reef offshore. He shivered, realizing how cold it was with the ocean-chilled breeze.

"It might be too rough to go diving tomorrow," Clione said.

"That'd be just fine."

The wind was sculpting shapes from the melted candle wax, and Reed reached down with a foot to kick the hammock and make it swing. Instead of sand, his foot touched a book. He grabbed the cover between his toes and lifted it into the hammock. There was just enough candlelight for Clione to pluck the words from the pages. She twisted, adjusted her body on top of his and started at the beginning of the book, her voice soft and soothing, yet dramatic, bringing out the rhythms of the words.

"You read well," Reed murmured, curled up in her arms, feeling hollow and old and very far away from anything he'd ever known.

Day Nine

Underwater

R eed dreamed of Laurel as she'd been years ago, when she was about Clione's age. They were climbing scaffolding, gripping the cold iron pipes and laughing. Some kind of child's jungle gym at a playground. She was ahead of him, going upward, and every so often he caught a tantalizing glimpse of her thighs and even her panties as the wind flipped her sundress around. She knew he could see her—she was laughing, teasing him, enjoying the attention. Sometimes she would stop and let him catch up, but when he got there, she'd be off again, going up, up, up until they were so high up that the entire structure was swaying and bending, and the wind was tearing at them, ripping their hands off the slippery pipes, and then suddenly Laurel was just gone. He didn't know if she'd fallen or leaped or been plucked from the structure by the hand of God and gone into the sky. She was just gone. He was alone and then the structure, these frail pipes, were breaking, slow pops as the wind-weakened iron developed fissures and started to wilt, then fall. He could hear the structure bending, poing, poing, poing, and the scaffolding began to topple and below him was a vast, dark bay, an enormous whirlpool twisting and roaring and its eye opened up like a great blue-white mouth as he fell.

He awoke drenched in sweat, shivering. Clione was wrapped around him; the Murakami book had dropped into the sand. A strong wind blew over the waves, yet the sunrise had painted everything a flamingo-fire pink, the warm color beautifully incongruous with the frigid morning. Reed shifted in the hammock and stared at the girl sleeping next to him as if she were a stranger, watching her chest move rhythmically up and down, at times to the same beat as the waves. The shafts of deep pink light seeping in through the cracks in the wall made it look as if the cabaña were being licked by flames.

Reed traced his index finger along Clione's moist lower lip, very gently, and suddenly her whole body convulsed. She shot up, awake, breathing heavily. For a few seconds her eyes were wild, empty, then they settled on Reed and the hammock and she let out a half-laugh.

"You scared me."

"I wanted you to see this," Reed said, pointing to the sun and the strange light. "It's like the cabin's on fire."

"It's beautiful," Clione said, rubbing her temples as she looked.

"What's that old saying? Red sky at night—"

"Sailor's delight. Red sky at morning—"

"Sailors take warning," Reed finished. "Does this mean we won't go diving?"

"We're going diving," Clione said. "Today I'm not going to take 'no' for an answer."

"It's still early. You want to sleep more?"

Clione shook her head. "No, I'm awake now. Because of *some*body." She punched him in the shoulder, hard enough to make the hammock sway. "I'm awake. But I'm going to find a quiet place to write. It might be a while. I haven't been writing much lately."

"Sure. Go get some writing done. I'll mind the hovel."

Clione slipped her sundress over her arms, arching her body as she brought the fabric down around her. Reed felt dizzy. She turned around, holding the waist straps out so Reed could tie them into a little bow. He watched her leave.

Clione was a speck on the beach now, a tiny moving dot against the wash of pink sky, pink that was lighter, less urgent than even a few minutes before.

Reed locked the door of the cabaña and climbed the stairs toward the restrooms. The lone men's bathroom stank so badly that Reed held his breath as he went inside. The door was off its hinges, and the puddles on the cement made him glad he'd taken the time to put on his shoes. A handful of fat flies circled above the seatless toilet in lazy reconnaissance, and near the flush lever some unhappy guest had inked instructions: "Push here to flood the floor."

Reed turned on the tap and let the water collect in his palms. He splashed his face and studied it in the scratched, stainless-steel mirror. He looked good, felt good. Confidence that had never been there showed in his tanned face, in the features that had hardened, become more defined. He didn't mind the bathroom. Dirt was dirt.

Shit was shit. He thought about the sterile-surface mentality and the way that people back home weakened their immune systems by keeping everything so clean.

He squatted over the toilet bowl, did his business, putting the paper into the trash can as was customary so as not to stress the plumbing. He debated whether to attempt to flush, and finally pulled down on the lever. An impressively strong rush of water gushed up, and up, and up, and Reed made a hasty retreat outside as the water began spilling over the porcelain brim.

The graffiti warning had been spot-on: he'd flooded the floor.

Back outside, already even the iguanas were seeking shade. The little girl who'd brought them the beers the day before gave him a shy smile from the edge of a doorway, and he went down the stairway, past the palms, and peeked into the cabaña to see if Clione was back yet. She wasn't, so he grabbed the Murakami book and walked to the stand of palm trees closest to the path. Sitting far enough away from it to avoid being hit by a falling coconut, he stretched out in the ragged shade. A few early sunbathers were already staking out their piece of paradise with towels and coolers and bottles of sunscreen. One girl slipped off her pink bikini top, stepped out of her bottoms as casually as if she were alone in a hotel bedroom, and lay down, face up, wearing only a pair of thick sunglasses. Reed decided she must be European. Americans were too scared of their nakedness, too paranoid that someone else would be watching, so fearful of everything that they forgot to look around and live.

He opened the book and began to read, pausing every so often to stare out at the sunbather. But the book drew him in: The narrator's wife was mysteriously missing. Dreams were built up with details into spectacular realities. Turning the pages, he found instant connection to the character. The plot seemed simultaneously odd and very natural. His own wife had "gone missing" in a way. It wasn't hard to feel for the bewildered Japanese salaryman who was lost and realizing the world was nothing like what he imagined.

He was several chapters in by the time he heard Clione's footsteps coming toward him in the sand. She was smiling.

"Good book, right?" she said.

"Not good. Great."

"Come on, let's get going. The wind is looking stronger. If the morning trip leaves there might not be one again in the afternoon."

* * *

When they got there a half an hour later, the door was shut. A sign in the window said "Excessive wind: all diving canceled today."

"Bullshit," Clione hissed. "Just bullshit. That wasn't much wind at all."

"Maybe it's trickier than it looks. See the whitecaps?"

"You've still got your Discover Scuba to finish." She bit her upper lip. "They can't do that! It's not like we're going to be able to do this forever."

"It's okay," Reed said. "I don't need to dive."

"This isn't the only dive shop. We can see if someone else is going out. Maybe it'll cost a little extra but that's better than sitting around for another whole day."

They walked down Avenida Tulum. By now, midmorning, the street was bustling. Backpackers were arriving at the bus station, tourists from the cruise ships had come in vanloads to see the ruins, the air smelled of wood smoke and grilling meat and hibiscus flowers. The *panadería* windows were full of amber loaves of freshly baked bread. A girl on the street corner was selling melon waters and rice-based *horchata*, the pinks, oranges, and reds of the liquids seeming even brighter in the rays of the sun.

A few streets over, they found another dive shop, open, but it too was not sending boats out. The owner was short and beefy, with a hooked nose and a thin T-shirt; his forearms were the size of dinner hams. Were it not for deep crow's feet at the corners of his eyes and a few streaks of gray in his jet-black hair, Reed would have guessed he was in his thirties.

"Sorry, the boat has to leave from shore," he said, sucking air in through his teeth sharply, as if he'd just seen a scary part in a movie. "Waves like this, no is possible."

"But what if we can just get out to the reef?" Clione asked. "Is the current bad? Is it dangerous to actually dive?"

"No, not so dangerous right now if you do a shore dive. Just dangerous for the *barcos. La lancha.*"

"So, if the boats can't go out, where's a good shore dive?"

"Hssssssss," the owner said, another hiss punctuating the thought. "In Tulum, we no have close *arrecifes*. Close *arrecifes*, you need to go toward Punta Allen. Is difficult road. Lots of, how you say, potholes."

"So, we go to Punta Allen!"

"You have a four-wheel-drive car?"

"We can rent one."

"If you have a car, if you have equipment, then I think you can go diving today."

"Can't you rent us some?"

The man laughed. "I no have rental gear. You rent from Sea and Sport. They have plenty rental gear."

"But they're closed."

The man shrugged. "Then maybe you just go diving tomorrow." As if to make a point, he flipped the sign on the window over to "*Cerrado*," then slapped his hands. "Come back tomorrow, okay? Mexico is playing against Argentina today. Maybe you should watch the game?"

"Fine," Clione said, storming out, almost slamming the door on Reed as she hurried into the street. She stood there, breathing heavily. "Damn!" she finally exclaimed.

"It's not his fault. He's just—"

"Hell," she said. They turned back toward Avenida Tulum. "He just didn't want to rent us anything. He wanted us to buy it."

"If it means that much, I'll buy it."

"I'm not going to give him my business. Not after that."

"But it really is windy. Even he said so."

"I've seen them go out on days that are windier. Everyone's just making up excuses because they want to watch the soccer game." Her lower lip trembled as if she was going to cry. Reed walked a few steps behind her, not knowing what to say. Then Clione turned around and looked at him. She had the look of a fox that's just noticed the latch on the chicken pen is broken.

"Yes!" she said, slapping her hands together.

"What?"

Clione smiled. "I think know where we can still get diving gear."

"Where?"

"The Welcome Wanderer."

"They rent diving gear too?"

"Not exactly."

* * *

When they got back to the hostel the first thing Clione did was look around for Lance. His car was there, parked across from the hostel, two wheels up on the sidewalk. Marisol shook her head.

"Maybe he is watching the game somewhere?"

Clione nodded, her lips pressed tightly together. "Probably."

"He knows where you can rent gear?" Reed asked.

"In a way."

"So, no diving today?"

Clione shook her head. "No, we just have to do a little problem-solving."

Reed followed her outside to where Lance's Jeep was. She looked in through the window. Reed remembered the steel tanks there underneath the rear seat, along with Lance's other diving gear.

"We're not going to take his stuff, Clione. It's not right."

She opened the door. "Of course not. He's going to lend it to us."

"He'll go nuts if he finds out. Lance is one of those guys large enough that I don't ever want to see him when he's really mad. Especially when he's going to be mad at me. No way."

"Reed, it's nothing to worry about. Lance and I...let's just say I have a teeny-tiny trump card that I plan to use. Believe me, Lance will be only too happy to let us use his stuff."

She pointed to the ignition. "See? Keys! He's going to lend us his whole car."

She went inside and asked Marisol to give Lance the message. Reed stood by the car, shifting his weight from foot to foot, watching the traffic pass by and imagining how angry Lance was going to be.

Fifteen minutes later, Reed and Clione pulled off Avenida Tulum, turned to the ocean, and began to parallel the shoreline, heading south toward Punta Allen. Reed was still shaking his head, wondering what would happen when they came back. Clione sensed how angry he was and kept silent, staring straight ahead, occasionally pointing at something—almost to herself—as they passed by.

Soon they were at the Italian restaurant where Reed and she had eaten with Sharon that first night, the night they'd gone skinny-dipping. A few minutes later they zipped by a few more cheap, tourist-get-drunk restaurants and a variety of cabañas, ranging from upscale ones as nice as posh hotels to others that were clearly competitors of the El Mirador. Then the road turned to dirt when it entered the Biosphere, and after a few kilometers a solitary ranger came out to greet them and collect the park entrance fee. Not two hundred yards past the guard post, the road narrowed, the jungle seeming to leap up around them, the thick green leaves getting darker, blocking out the sun. To the left was the ocean, a shimmering azure that filtered through every so often. To the right was mangrove thicket deeper and darker than any Reed had seen on the trip thus far, the tannin-laden water beneath it an inky rust. Someone had been murdered near here, Reed remembered. Decapitated. A drug killing. He suddenly imagined Lance stumbling onto a drug deal and wondered if that was how the bullet hole in the windshield had gotten there. Maybe someone would mistake them for Lance. But he kept driving anyway, knowing that they had already long passed the point of no return.

"We might see an ocelot, or even a jaguar," Clione whispered. Even she seemed nervous to be so entirely alone. From time to time, the brilliant blue jays with black heads and yellow beaks would burst from the foliage, screaming out avian profanities. Later on an agouti loped awkwardly across the road like an escapee from the island of Dr. Moreau. The road looked like it had been bombed: a series of deep, mud-filled ruts that sucked at the tires and forced Reed to shift into four-low more than once. Some were so deep that the transmission ground out, making them both wince. The foliage thickened and darkened, pushing into the two dirt tracks as if the jungle were a living organism trying to close a wound. If anything went wrong, if a snake bit them or they broke a leg, it would be impossible to get to a hospital in time. Reed looked over at Clione, surreptitiously, trying to watch her without her knowing it. She was leaning forward in her seat to avoid having to sit on the open springs. The posture made her seem girlish, her hands on her knees, her gaze alternating from left to right to front, as if expecting a jaguar sighting around every curve.

"If something happens to the car we'll be trapped here forever," Clione giggled. "You better know how to make a fire with sticks."

"Don't jinx us," Reed replied.

For another two hours they crawled along, trying to avoid rocks and the eroded areas big enough to devour a whole tire. Then the road slid out of the jungle and paralleled the beach, a rough, jagged shoulder made of chunks of bleached coral the same size and color of catacomb skulls. He eased the vehicle over reef pieces the size of watermelons and through soft tracks of sand. They passed the hulk of a rusty Honda Civic, early '80s vintage, its hood and windows—

long broken — covered with thick, waxy leaves of some kind of vine. Its tires, flattened and melted off the rims, were sunk two-thirds deep in the sand.

"A hummingbird," Clione said, pointing.

The biggest hummingbird Reed had ever seen was hovering in and around the old auto wreck like a mutant emerald bee. The beak alone was two inches long. It darted in and around the car, feeding off some thin, pale white flowers that Reed hadn't noticed before. In a flash it disappeared, as quickly as it had come.

"Awesome," Clione said. "Hummingbirds were revered by the Maya. Maybe it's our good luck sign." She pulled out her journal and scribbled a short note.

Reed shifted the car back into first and pulled forward, feeling the tires slip a bit as they inched out of the sand. "Maybe that means we won't get stranded here."

Then the road disappeared entirely, the soft sand so windblown that the only indication of the trail was simply the direction they were traveling in. The shoreline curved inward, a gentle scythe, two promontories at either end of a shallow bay. Stands of ragged palms looked like armies of inverted feather dusters, dotted here and there with an avocado or wild papaya tree. The angry froth that marked the reef seemed closer, only a few hundred yards away. A frigate bird, distinguishable by its V-shaped tail, soared above them in the pitch-blue sky. From the bird's vantage point, the spot would have looked like a letter D, with the reef forming the spine. Far ahead, Reed saw what looked like a rickety bridge they'd need to cross, but before they arrived Clione told him to stop.

"That's the reef, right there. I think we can just park here and go in from the shore. Looks perfect."

"Looks deep."

"Deep? Not for a diver."

"I'm not a diver."

"Reed, you can *do* this. It's not going to be bad. It's shallow here, a perfect place to learn. We won't even need to bother with decompression or anything. It'll be just like snorkeling, except you won't need to come up for air."

"I hate snorkeling, too. Can we go home now?"

"Funny. Let's get moving."

They unloaded the gear, tanks first, then the nylon buoyancy vests, then finally the regulators, carrying it all over the beach to the ocean's edge where the sea gently swooshed along the water-hardened sand. In places the bleached coral bones cut sharply into the tender soles of his feet. Clione changed, naked for a moment, like Botticelli's Venus without the scallop shell. She slipped on the mint-green suit she'd bought the other day and smiled.

A flock of tiny sandpipers landed behind her, blending immediately into the brown-and-tan shoreline. The remoteness of it all overwhelmed him. He had never been this far away from civilization before in his life, this absolutely alone. Laurel and her problems, his whole life back home, in fact, seemed impossibly far away, as unreal and strange as this perfect bay would feel the moment he stepped off the plane back in Boston. He felt disconnected from both realities. For Clione, at least, this was real. She could live here if she wanted. She, Lance, Marisol, even Sharon. They could stay for as long as they liked. For Reed, it was as if anything he did had a clock looming above it, ticking out the seconds until it was over and he would have to go home.

The immediacy of his first diving expedition and the terror that accompanied it brought him back to the present. The water seemed hungry, waiting. If it weren't for this crazy girl, he could be in a hammock reading a book, safely on dry land. Instead, he was letting her take him diving. Not just swimming. *Diving.*

"Okay," Clione said. "Remember what we talked about at the class. Check your air, check your regulator, check your octopus...." She went through the steps with the routine of an army instructor, someone who's done the same thing so many times it becomes second nature.

Reed tapped the mouthpiece and air rushed out.

"Air's a good thing," Clione said, nodding. "Now check the octopus and make sure you've got the right amount of weight in your weight belt. You want to add about fifteen or so pounds."

Reed pressed the second-stage regulator, a bright high-visibility yellow so someone could more easily rip it out in an emergency. Reed had forgotten all the math, the calculations about atmospheres and depth and time and nitrogen loading, but he remembered that he couldn't hold his breath, even for a second, or the pressurized tank air would rupture his lungs. Breathe in and out, in and out, in and out, he reminded himself, as his heart began to beat faster. No matter what. In and out.

Clione was grim as she double-checked the gear, slowly and methodically. Finally she nodded.

"Ready to see things you've never seen before?"

"Ready as I'll ever be."

Reed lifted Clione's tank-vest-regulator up and she looped her arms through the straps, tightening the Velcro webbing so it was snug but not restrictive. She helped him into his own gear and checked to make sure he'd put it on correctly. They walked to the water, waiting to put on their fins until they were waist-deep in the warm sea.

"Don't forget to spit in your mask," Clione reminded. "Otherwise it'll fog up as you dive."

It wasn't until he sat down, mask on, the second stage of the regulator firmly clamped between his teeth, that Reed felt the fear take full control of him, as if some creature had cupped his heart in talons and given them a squeeze. How had he done fine until then? He'd been pushing doubts out of his mind the way he'd been pushing away Laurel and Boston, and as the clammy water enveloped him he felt his heart jump and a throbbing pain shot into his right temple, making the vision in his right eye cloudy. He tried to focus, and the pain subsided. Bending down to put on a fin, he lost his balance and toppled over into the water, the tank pulling him down from behind. He forgot to breathe, inhaled too quickly, caught water, and came up splashing and sputtering. He tore the mask off his face and stood, one fin half on, his other foot digging into the jagged coral, fighting for balance. A thin trail of blood, blackish in the water, rose up from his heel like a wisp of smoke from the first licks of a forest fire.

"Don't panic," Clione said, coming over to him. "It's okay. One, we're waist-deep. Nothing's going to happen. Two, you're not under pressure yet. It's only when you get deeper that you really have to worry about decompression. We'll never get that deep."

"So I would have been fine? It wasn't my lungs exploding?"

"No, just you starting to panic. Relax."

"It's just hard to —"

"This is *easy*. Remember that. It's not hard. It's easy. Now just take a deep breath, okay?"

He did, letting the air expand in his chest until it began to hurt.

"Let it out."

He exhaled.

"Now do it with the regulator."

He put the rubber mouthpiece between his teeth and wrapped his lips around the stale-smelling rubber flange. He breathed in, listening to the Darth Vader-esque hiss as the lever opened and the diaphragm let the regulated air rush in. He exhaled, felt the lever shut, heard the air escape out the bottom of the mouthpiece. It was working.

"Now just stick your head underwater and try it again. The same thing. There's a rhythm to it."

He put on his mask, adjusted the tension so it was snug but not too tight against his face. Clione gave him the thumbs-up sign, and he bent his shaking knees and allowed the water to take him. After the initial moments of terror as he felt the water compress around his ears, seeping inside them, pushing out the air, he relaxed and inhaled. There was a whoosh, and when he exhaled, bubbles burst upward. Everything around him was green-blue, bent by the refracted light, seeming larger and more luminous. Clione's eyes, the only things recognizable beneath the alien mask and regulator mouthpiece, were wide and intent. She gave him the okay sign, the universal three fingers and thumb-forefinger O.

Are you okay?

Yes, he replied, repeating the gesture. He slipped one fin onto his foot, then the other. The trail of blood was like a blackish vine in the water, curled by the current into tendrils.

Follow me, Clione pointed, using the signals he'd learned in the class. She took his hand and began to swim, keeping her body motionless, using only her legs as propulsion. The bottom of the bay sloped gently downward, and he felt his bowels churn as he realized they were already so deep that he could not stand up if he needed to.

Below them, only six or seven feet down, a few small fish flitted around, as streamlined as if they were electric arrowheads above giant plates of scallop shell coral. Others drifted around in schools of three or four, with vertical patterns of white, black and yellow. As he looked longer, he realized that everything was alive, that there were fish everywhere: black ones, tiny schools crowding in close to the swaying purple sea fans, bright orange-and-white clownfish as cute as the Disney character. Shimmery fish that looked like blades tucked themselves into the surface waves and became all but invisible. Little spindly shrimp crept along, transparent except for their intestinal tracts and delicate pink claws. Passing above some huge brainlike coral, Reed felt as if he'd swooped in on a surgery in progress, that he was looking directly at organs of some giant creature that was breathing, palpable, and alive. Even the water itself was not water, but a thick soup of microscopic drifting things, primordial and unchanged since life on Earth began.

He felt his heartbeat quicken as a trio of larger fish appeared out of the blue, swam past them and then disappeared like silent torpedoes. Clione's hand clenched twice, and she pointed to where a giant spiny lobster had curled itself into a hole. She tapped her buoyancy button, releasing a burst of air, and began to descend. He followed her lead, holding the tube above his head as they'd been taught in class to allow the air to escape. Underwater, time was measured in breaths, not seconds: the constant rhythm of inhale, exhale, as regular as a stopwatch. At some point, if they could not get to the surface, that rhythm would slow, stop, and they would die.

For the first time, Reed felt oddly at peace underwater, that same sense of calm he had hanging above Boston in the helicopter. Clione was right: There was no describing the beauty of this astonishing landscape, the myriad of colors and shapes and sizes and contours. It had nothing of the regularity one sees on land, the order that comes from plants adapting to different quantities of light. Here there were no shadows, no canopies, nothing to prevent this coral from rooting and growing on top of that one, this anemone over that one. No gravity to force shapes to conform. When Reed sank closer it was as if he were closing in on a zoneless cityscape of neon chaos where anything that could possibly be built had been constructed, and where nothing was ever torn down. A sea peach, its bulbous polyp slowly shaking in the current, had sprouted off of some antler coral, and on it, a collection of barnacles, and on them, three black shrimp that were meandering about their benthic pasture like tiny Holstein cows.

Clione let go of his hand, and the two of them swam deeper. A cliff opened up beneath them, a dark purple void in the blue and green. Reed felt that he was weightless, as if he were soaring above a canyon, able to rise or sink to any level with the same freedom as a bird of prey. Clione let out more air and sank into the trough, her body swallowed up as the depth ate the sunlight. Reed watched the ineffable curves of the stretched mint bikini fabric that had worked into the cleft of her perfect behind. Again, he remembered how he had been inside that body that morning. He knew its inner contours, the feel of her cervix, her softnesses and the hardness of her pubic bone. He'd felt her muscles contract around him as they had reached orgasm. He had tasted her sweat, her skin, had drunk from her as if she were a chalice.

The warm sun on his back, the strange sensation of weightlessness, the astounding variety of things to see put Reed into a kind of trance. He wondered why the fish didn't flee as he loomed over them like a giant, lumbering UFO. He became aware of sounds, odd cracks and poppings, crunchings, the tinny whine of an outboard engine somewhere far away. Clione's inhaling and exhaling, as well as his own. He felt as if he'd slipped back in time, as if he were watching the Earth as it must have been hundreds of millions of years ago. These coral polyps spreading, covering surfaces, paving them with soft tissues that could be consumed by other organisms, which in turn would struggle to thrive and be consumed. This glowing, shimmering, spectacular display in essence was nothing more than a monument to reproduction, millions, maybe billions of years of life reproducing life, shifting and changing; the sole object was to create more of yourself before you yourself were consumed. It dawned on him that reproduction alone was the meaning of life itself; it was all that mattered, our closest thing to immortality.

A simple act, a few minutes of movement, an orgasm, the release of a quarter billion sperm. And from that, new life. Tender, helpless new life. Creating more of himself before he himself is consumed, before the container of his own body breaks, the electric spark of life sputters and dies, before the body returns to the earth and molds that tear apart the molecules and recycle them. To reproduce was to cheat death, to continue something beyond the confines of one lone life. To reproduce was to participate as a link in a long, ever-branching chain that would keep fanning out, wider and wider, like a river delta before it finally reaches the vastness of the sea.

He remembered that he should check his air gauge, and he tugged it free and held it out in front of him. Only ten minutes had passed. The tank was still almost full, the needle only a fraction shifted from its spot at twelve o'clock. When it pointed to six, Clione had said, they would start up. Give them plenty of time.

Clione eased herself up out of the crevasse, rolled over on her back like an otter and gave him the okay sign. He returned it. He was having fun, to his complete surprise.

Suddenly, Clione's body jerked around and she pointed with urgency to something in the distance. At first, Reed saw nothing, his spine singing as he scanned the fathomless blue. For what? Had she seen a shark? A barracuda?

But she was swimming toward it, her powerful legs propelling her body in sharp thrusts. He followed as best as he could, terrified that she would leave him behind, trying to let the fin's elasticity do the propulsion work for him. Breathe! *Breathe! Don't hold your breath.* Breathe!

He saw the bubbles before he saw the thing itself, a swirl of whitish green, as if a child had just jumped into the sea from the edge of a swimming pool. They were now deeper, the water fading into a blackish blue beneath it, the reef only barely visible below as a mosaic of shadows. Clione was ten yards or so in front of him, and as the creature turned he finally realized what they were looking at: a manatee.

Its face had a strangely human expression, with deep-set eyes and a bristly, walrus-like snout, the cleft lip running from the mouth to just beneath the nose. Its eyes were back farther in its head than Reed expected, more like a whale's than a dolphin's, giving it a myopic expression that seemed comic yet mournful. The look of a Shakespearean court jester, the wise fool. It rose up, broke the surface for a breath, and sank down a few feet, worked the tonguelike paddle of its tail twice, and continued swimming. As he got closer, Reed saw that its hide was covered in barnacles and algae, which grew up around the back and shoulders like a green mane. Two deep speedboat slashes had cut through the skin, the whitish scars standing out clearly against the rough topography of uninjured hide.

Clione slowed, then stopped, floating without kicking so as to not frighten it. They watched it swim slowly toward the shallows. Reed felt as if he were watching it in slow motion, every move seeming deliberately slowed, sluggish, heavy; it was incongruous with the weightlessness of being underwater and the freedom Reed was feeling for the first time.

Then, in a burst of bubbles and with a rapid flick of its tail, the manatee spooked, leaving a cloud of bubbles that disappeared slowly with the currents. In two or three seconds the strange animal disappeared into the maw of the blue.

Reed's spine tingled, his awe replaced by a sudden, growing realization.

Something had spooked it.

Clione seemed to be asking the same question, for she was slowly rotating her body around, looking up, down, right, left. She looked at Reed, shook her head, shrugged. *Okay?* She mimed.

Reed kept looking, straining his eyes to make out what was lurking there. The manatee must have noticed something. His mind took in details as if the situation had tapped into some deep, long-buried snippet of his DNA: Before, there were fish, the sergeants and some other nondescript silvery ones, thin and shaped like arrows. Now it was just them, two divers and a whole lot of empty, terrifying blue. Chills rippled up and down his spine.

Something *was* out there.

He just knew.

Then he saw it: bigger than he ever imagined, a telltale silhouette gliding through the blue, a huge, streamlined, triangular torpedo with a distinctive shovel-shaped head. A hammerhead shark. Reed felt the blood rush to his head and he remembered how he'd cut himself on the coral when they'd waded out. He looked down. Sure enough, the thin purple thread was still unwinding.

The shark wasn't coming for the manatee.

It had sensed fresh blood.

Suddenly, it was as if the entire ocean's weight were crushing him, pressing down on his head and chest like a car compactor. Reed inhaled, sucking far too deeply on the regulator than the slow, even breaths Clione had advised. Instead of the measured breath of air, suddenly he couldn't breathe at all. He felt his eyesight start to go dark, the way it did when he was really, really angry: blackness in the peripheral vision, encroaching, collapsing inward on his sight until all that remained were two pinpoint spots of bright light.

Oh, God, he thought. *I'm drowning.*

He clawed at the nylon webbing, trying to release the weight belt, but nothing was happening. He was going down, sinking. He couldn't hold his breath, but he couldn't breathe either. *Help!* he thought. *Help!* Clione hadn't even noticed. She was still swimming in the same direction as the manatee.

Reed felt something rip, the weight belt's hook and loop webbing, he hoped, and he thrashed around trying to get it free. In the distance, the shark, sensing distress, turned sharply and began swimming in a direct line toward him. It was coming in for the kill. From the side it had seemed enormous; now, with the shark coming head-on, its profile was all but invisible. Had Reed not already seen it before, the darker skin on top and the lighter skin below would have made it invisible against the backdrop of inky blue. A perfect predator.

The regulator slipped from his mouth and Reed wrenched free, realizing as he lurched toward the surface that he had released not only the weights, but the entire tank assembly. The mask slipped from his face, he inhaled water, and he clawed blindly toward the pure white light that was the surface. Things were white, then black, then white again. He swallowed water, coughed, swallowed more. The last thing Reed remembered was hearing the sound of the shark's razor sharp teeth grabbing the steel dive tank below him, a squeak like fingernails on a chalkboard, and feeling the blow as something—its fin or tail—sliced against his thigh, the texture of rough sandpaper, and everything melted into something impossibly blinding and bright, yet he couldn't look away.

Returning

L aurel seemed to have lost ten years. She was prettier than he'd ever seen her; they were deep in some kind of deciduous woods, walking hand in hand along an old road, two ruts leading deeper and deeper into the forest with huckleberry bushes and briers that had grown up in the middle, as if the road, through disuse, had become two parallel paths. A new kind of understanding had passed between them, something that he'd never felt before, a happiness, a sense of everything being complete and whole. It made everything in the forest seem dappled with sunlight, as if light clung like raindrops to the edges of each of the leaves. Laurel whispered something to him and touched her belly: She was going to have a baby girl.

"A baby girl?" he said, and his voice was far off, hollow, echoing strangely in the forest. "How was that possible?"

She was too old to have a child, yet there was her stomach, smooth and already starting to stretch taut like a beautiful drum. It seemed to be growing larger as he watched, but he couldn't say anything. He felt unbelievably at peace. The woods were never greener, so bright and full, and there were birds flitting here and there, chirping. One came right down and pulled an inchworm from a branch, close enough to touch. He could see every single feather.

A red squirrel scampered out across a thin limb with a green pine cone in its mouth, saw them, dropped the cone, and chirred. The woods ended and a field began, and they were walking. Laurel turned and her eyes were full of tears. She turned and kissed him. Her mouth was softer, the lips more full than he'd expected.

"Are you okay?" she whispered.

"Of course, I'm so happy."

"Reed!"

Now there was an urgency in her voice, a desperation that seemed out of place, unreal. As they walked, the sky got brighter and brighter and then gradually everything disappeared.

"Reed, are you okay?"

Clione's features formed out of the face that had seconds before belonged to Laurel. She was biting her lip, and her cheeks were stained with tears.

He was on the beach, sharp coral points digging into his shoulders and hips. He coughed, his chest heaving, and water came out. Everything tasted salty. His foot stung as if he'd been burned.

"What happened?"

"Thank you," Clione said, wiping at her eyes with the back of her hand. "Thank you thank you thank you. Reed...I'm so sorry. You scared me...."

Then he remembered: the shark, the desperate climb upward into the air.

"I got attacked."

She shook her head. "You panicked."

"It came in at me. My toe was cut. It was going for the blood."

She was stroking his hair, pushing it back out of his eyes. He just lay there, looking at her. "No, Honey. I saw everything. You just saw the shark and started bolting upward."

"No, it came at me. It did. It was the blood in the water."

"Sharks don't attack people, normally, even when there's blood in the water. It came in to look, swam right by, and left. The next thing I see is you in a cloud of bubbles, dumping your gear and then practically drowning."

"Really?"

She nodded. "It's okay. It's my fault. I shouldn't have taken you out."

"I'm glad you did," Reed said. He sat up slowly. "My chest feels like you've been pounding it with a sledgehammer."

She put a hand up to her face and held it there. "Then I shouldn't have taken you out over your head so soon. We actually weren't deep. Just six feet or so under the surface."

"I felt like we were miles down," Reed said. He stretched, rolled his neck from side to side, until the muscle tension eased away.

"Are you mad at me?" she asked.

"No. It was unbelievable. It was beautiful down there. Like a different world. I almost wet myself. But it was beautiful."

"You really thought so? You liked it?"

"I did. Still makes me want to wet myself, but I did."

Clione punched him softly in the thigh. "I was so worried." She kissed him. Then she stood up and looked out at the water. Reed stared at the sand, suddenly looking at it for the first time. Here it was more granular than anything he'd seen before, full of tiny shells and wave-sanded stones. Pink and orange and white and red, as if someone had shattered a sunset they'd been watching and scattered its shards across the beach. The sun was already low on the horizon.

"We should get back," Clione said. "It's already late."

"What happened to Lance's tank?"

"I got the mask and snorkel. But the rest," she shrugged. "I think it's gone. Lance is going to kill me."

"Could we try to find it?"

Clione looked at him. "I just spent a half-hour getting a friend out of the water and I'm a bit tired. It's out there. Somewhere. Be my guest."

"So we buy Lance another set of diving stuff. Rather, I'll buy."

"It's my fault too. I'll pay my half."

"You work on making sure he doesn't put us in jail for stealing his Jeep. And I'll handle whatever the vest and gear cost. Deal?"

Reed pulled himself onto all fours and stood up. His chest still hurt, but he could breathe more easily now. He stretched again, still testing the soreness for signs of injury.

"I guess we go back?" he asked. "Maybe to a place with a real bed tonight? Is that okay?"

Clione picked up a palmful of sand and threw it onto his legs. "Sure. If a hammock's not good enough for the fancy-pants city boy."

Reed laughed. Clione put both palms on his cheeks and held his face in front of hers for a few seconds, as if seeing all the features again for the first time. She brushed her lips to his and pulled away, hefting her tank up to her shoulder, the sinews of her arms tense. She looked ready for anything, a heroine in a sci-fi movie, the tank a weapon for fighting aliens. Her pectorals were taut under the perfect breasts that strained to burst the bikini top. Her stomach seemed larger than before, full and round, womanly. He felt another rush of desire.

With her free hand Clione brushed back the strand of hair that had fallen into her eyes. She motioned toward the car. "It'll be dark soon."

Working together, silently, they repacked the Renegade. Clione scanned the beach for forgotten items, then hopped in. Reed did a wide U-turn, the tires leaving deep ruts in otherwise pristine sand. He eased out on the clutch, keeping it in low gear.

"So you really think the shark didn't attack me?"

Clione shook her head. "More like you were attacking it. But you did okay today. It could have been better but it could have been way worse."

"We saw the manatee."

"I wanted to talk to it," Clione whispered. "Apologize for those scars on its back."

"You didn't make them."

"But we did. Humans have messed up everything."

"Not intentionally."

"It's still messed up. That's just an excuse. Intention has nothing to do with it."

He glanced over at her. She'd rolled down the window and had one slim arm draped out over the side, two fingers hooked on the mirror to keep her skin from touching the hot paint. A sun-drunk iguana wobbled out of the way, plopping into the brown mangrove water with a splash.

"Clione," Reed asked. "Are you like this with everyone?"

"What kind of a question is that?"

Reed shrugged. "Just a question. Forget it."

"Why would you care? Isn't it more important how I am with you?"

"I like you a lot more than I ever expected to. I just don't know what it's going to be like when I leave."

"Does who I've been with or how I've been with them change who I am with you?"

"That's not how I meant it."

"How did you mean it?"

"Just forget it. I'm sorry."

"I think you need to go back to Boston, Reed. You'll put one foot forward, then the other, you'll enter the plane, recline the seat, watch a few stupid movies, and you'll be home. You'll pick up your lovely wife, you'll live happily ever after. You'll forget me the moment your feet are off the plane."

"You really think that?"

Clione shrugged. She was silent for a long time. The car was already deep in the jungle again before she spoke. "No. But what I do with my body is my business. Not yours."

"I know. I said let's forget it. It doesn't matter."

"Then why ask the question to start with? Who the hell cares? I'm not asking you if I'm the first young thing you've sampled, am I?"

Reed looked at her quickly, surprised to see the bottom of her lip trembling. Her eyes were wet. She bit her lip and stared out the window. Reed hit a pothole straight on and the car ground through it, the iron squeaking and protesting as it scraped over the sunbaked mud.

"Why don't you watch the road," Clione said. "We've had fun, and you'll go back to Boston. End of story. So just drive."

"If that's what's going to happen then at least give me your address."

Clione's eyes flashed. "Of course. The obligatory Christmas card. To the slut. I forgot."

"Stop," Reed said, slowing the car. He put it in neutral, and pulled the parking brake. "I'm not saying that. Not at all." He turned and looked at her. "I still don't know what you ever saw in me. I don't know why you chose me, why any of this happened. But I know that when I think about it ending, I want to run this Jeep into a tree. My life back home is nothing and I feel like I *have* to go back. There's nothing obligatory about hoping we stay in touch. It's all I have to cling to."

"Don't stop. Can't you talk and drive at the same time?"

Reed shook his head. "Not about this. Not about you."

"Fine. I'll give you my address."

"When?"

"Sometime. Can we go home now?"

Reed slammed the CJ7 back in gear, and started driving again, spraying gravel behind them. Clione kept the window down, but her hand creeping up to her cheek every few moments told Reed she was crying. He let her cry. It reminded him how young she was. An immature, stupid, selfish girl. He'd followed her blindly, let her persuade him even to steal the car. Suddenly he wanted to see Laurel, his implacable Narcissus. The rock in the storm. Forcing the Jeep haphazardly over the bumps and skidding through the turns, he thought what he needed to do was to dump this girl off at the youth hostel, toss some money at Lance for the lost equipment, and then take the next bus back to his hotel in Cancún.

The End of Something

The two of them let silence fall between them along with the gathering dusk. Reed couldn't think of anything to say that wouldn't come out sounding stale and stupid, a thinly disguised conversation starter. It occurred to him that they had probably already made love for the last time, that everything was unraveling between them as quickly as it had begun. Even if they were making love it would be different now. A tide had turned; it was ebbing.

He kept his eyes on the road, yet in his peripheral vision he could see Clione's body shaking, the moist puddle at her lap spreading out on the thin patterned cotton, dark as a bloodstain. He wanted to know what made her cry when she knew as well as he did that they could never create something longer, larger together.

"I need to tell you something," Clione said, as they passed the gate that marked their departure from the Biosphere preserve.

"Can't it wait?" He glanced at her sideways. Her lips were trembling. She shook her head, dabbed at her eyes with a finger, then scrambled through the glove compartment looking for tissues and finding none. Finally, she picked at the hem of her dress and ducked to wipe her eyes. Reed caught a glimpse of the bikini, an inverted mint triangle tucked between her thighs.

She glared at him. "Don't make this harder than it is."

"So talk, Clione. Talk."

"Reed, it bothers me that you're always treating me like I don't love you. Or that I don't care about you. This was a very special time for me. You mean more to me than maybe you'll ever know."

"I could say that same thing about you." He said it angrily. Meanly. Where did this come from, he wondered? This anger.

"Don't make this about you."

"We can pull over and talk if you feel like talking now." The

Jeep slid into a turn, the back tires spraying the shadowed leaves with gravel.

"No, Reed, listen to me." She brushed her hair out of her face. "There's something, something I've been trying to tell you. It's hard to talk about, but I don't want you to hear it first from someone other than me."

"Just say it," Reed said. "Whatever it is, you can tell me. Okay?"

"I'm late," she said flatly.

"Late?"

She repeated the word. "Late. My period hasn't come."

As the meaning of the words sank into Reed's consciousness, the road seemed to slip out from underneath the car, as if the vehicle were floating above the dirt, wheels spinning but without traction on the ground. It bucked hard, tugged at Reed's hands like a dog on a leash as the passenger-side tires pushed off the shoulder and bumped over the rocks on the side. Reed swung the wheel, fighting the car back before oversteering, and the Jeep fishtailed to the right and to the left before finally straightening out and stopping, ninety degrees to the shoulder.

"Jesus," he hissed, his foot hard on the brake. He turned the tires and pulled the vehicle over to the side. A cloud of dust spread out and lifted up around them.

He looked at her.

"I kept thinking," she added, her eyes wide, fixed on the road as if it had just tried to kill them, "that I wouldn't have to tell you. You were only going to be here for a week. Then things changed. You stayed."

"How can you be late? We've only been together — "

"I don't know if it's you, Reed. It might be someone else. But it might not be."

Reed could barely hear her as she continued.

"My period is usually like a Japanese train. Arrives and departs within thirty seconds of the scheduled time. This month was different. 'All aboard' should have been about two weeks ago. When we met I was already a little late. Enough that I didn't worry about us using protection. I thought I was past the danger zone and my period was going to come like that day. Or the next. But it didn't come and it didn't come and it didn't come." Another sob escaped her. "And it didn't come."

Reed swallowed, his throat dry, constricting in on itself, making it hard to breathe. "You can't be thinking about—"

Clione's voice was hard and flat. "I'm not going to be a mother. And it might not be yours anyway so don't try to tell me what to do or not to do. I know you think I'm all fucked up and I know you're leaving. But I felt like you should know, before...." She trailed off. "Telling you was a mistake."

Reed felt paralyzed, as if something were wrapping itself around his throat and choking him. He tried to open his mouth to say something and no words came. He struggled to turn his head and look at her and couldn't. His vision narrowed into white light and then shifted to a coral, a blood red. *I'm dying*, he thought. *I'm having a stroke and dying.* But he was still there, still in the Renegade, his brain still picking out the screams of the jays and the far-off wash of waves. All he could think was that he had to get out, had to get away from it all. He lifted his heavy limbs and twisted the key, hearing the spark long after the ignition had caught and begun to grind against the starter. He threw the Jeep in gear, pushed the gas pedal, and the vehicle shot forward so suddenly that Clione's head snapped back and hit the whiplash cushion.

"So you don't need to worry about keeping in touch," Clione sobbed. "You think I'm just a slut, I know, but I just didn't expect to—"

"To what?"

"To love you, Reed. I know you don't believe me. You don't believe me because you don't believe in yourself. But I fell in love with you. And I can't believe you're leaving any day now."

Reed didn't answer. In his mind, neurons were firing in patterns that called up high school biology textbooks, cycles of the moon and sun, the wash of tides and the odd fallopian fingers that cupped the orb of ovary. They were pulling him through a journey where egg bursts through flesh and slips into inexorable current like an autumn leaf dropping from a maple branch onto a stream, into deepening, powerful flow. It might be his own sperm that had twisted past this bend or that, homing in on a signal that grew louder and louder the closer it approached. All of history depended on this simple journey of a few inches. Only this journey lets us cheat death. Only this voyage saves the human race from extinction.

Reed felt something like a scream rear up from inside him, a dragon asleep that suddenly shifts and breathes out fire. He opened his mouth and nothing came, only silence. He turned left onto the long beach access road, left again at the rotary, and pulled up in front of the Welcome Wanderer. Clione's hand scrabbled at the door and she slipped out, still sobbing, not saying a word.

Reed stayed in the Renegade, hands on the wheel at ten and two, staring into the night that seemed to build itself, darker and stronger, with every passing second. The stars pierced through the darkness, cold and distant and timeless, then the low moon, with its sad face lifting up over the pueblo's cement walls and corrugated plastic rooftops and its rebar and dust. Mariachi music came from somewhere to the left. Tourists arrived off the bus and humped their backpacks to the Welcome Wanderer.

Still Reed sat in the stale heat of the car, his hands at ten and two.

Flamingos and Sunset

When Reed finally entered the Welcome Wanderer it was as if the entire cast had been replaced with near duplicates — save for Marisol and Lance. And Samantha, who leaped up on him, wildly wagging her tail. Cindy and Sharon and Ambrose and the Danish girl, everyone had slipped away, and in all likelihood Reed would never see them again. But there was a new shabby balding guy sharing a bottle with Lance and a different heavyset-but-cheerful gal in the kitchen, and the Sharon look-alike seemed plucked from the same carbon-copy backpacker sorority. Marisol's bright smile made everything that had passed over the last few days seem that much worse. He patted Samantha as he thought about how he was fucking up his life, throwing everything away. He didn't deserve a smile.

Lance, parked at the picnic table with a two-thirds-empty bottle of tequila, lifted his head when he saw Reed standing at the entryway.

"Take my Jeep for a joyride, huh?" Lance called. "If your little Sea Angel hadn't smoothed things over I'd kick your fucking ass."

"Mister Reed," Marisol said, from behind the bar-reception desk. "Are you here to stay?"

"Is it okay if I talk to Clione for a while?"

"Not unless you're paying for a bed."

"Can I purchase an hour or two?"

"You know the rules. You can purchase a bed, or the cabaña, Mister Reed Haflinger from Boston," Marisol replied, her hand sweeping the courtyard to point out each. She shook her head, coyly, as if she were flirting instead of giving him a refusal. "But not an hour or two. We are not a brothel, and we surely would be if we rented by the hour."

"Fine, I'll take the cabaña then."

"*Perfecto.* Your passport, please."

He pointed to the computer. "Okay to use it for a bit?"

Marisol waved her hand. "It's yours. Ten pesos per hour."

"It'll just be a minute." He pulled out ten pesos and handed them to her. She shook her head.

"If you're quick, it's free."

The faded swivel chair wobbled as he sat down, threatening to topple him to the floor. He double-clicked and waited for the web browser to load. The computer's plastic had yellowed to a deep ivory and the keyboard was missing its Q and W. He hadn't seen a system like this for at least a decade. When the browser finally loaded, to the page of a popular search engine, Reed brought up his email provider and logged in. There were only three messages in his inbox, all of them from Dan.

He opened them in order, oldest first:

Three days ago: "WTF, Reed. This isn't like you. You and Laurel get abducted by the Sinaloa cartel?"

Two days ago: "Still hoping to hear from you. We need you back here before the presidential visit." Presidential visit?

And last night: "Reed, give me a call as soon as possible. Had some funny pain in my arm this morning. Turns out it was a heart attack. Minor one, nothing serious. But I'm laid up at Mass General for a whole damn week while they run a bunch of tests. I know you're all adopting a kid, but I need you back here. ASAP. Call me anytime."

He shut off the computer and took out his phone. Still no service. Taking the box of things the hotel had sent, he thanked Marisol.

"Do you sell Tel-Mex cards here?" he asked.

She nodded. "Sure."

"I need one with enough juice to call the U.S. for at least thirty minutes."

"100-peso card is the highest I've got."

"Give me two of them."

Marisol handed him two cards.

"Everything okay?"

Reed shook his head.

"Anything I can do?" Marisol asked.

"No," he answered. "But how could anyone get too worried about the world in a place like this?"

"Especially when it's run by such a sweet and classy lady!" she answered. "If Clione doesn't treat you right, Marisol will."

"You're already treating me like I'm a king," he replied.

"Oh, but you haven't gotten to the good parts yet."

Reed laughed. "Do you flirt like this with all the guests?"

"Only the males."

* * *

The telephone was still warm from the sun's heat even though sunset had been hours ago. It had to be ten o'clock already back home, but Dan had said to call no matter what. Pulling up the right number from his cellphone contacts, he heard the click as the connection went through. The ring tone of "It Had to Be You" on the line told him he'd gotten connected to the right number.

"Reed!" Dan said as soon as he answered. "Finally. I was almost starting to think we'd be sending out a bunch of sniffer dogs and CIA men to find your decapitated body."

"I'm fine, just busy and my phone doesn't have bars. I got your emails. Are you okay?"

"Fine. Felt like I'd had a bunch of bad seafood. Wouldn't have even known it was a heart attack."

"They say why? You're not overweight."

"Cholesterol. LDL in the wrong place. Something like that. Anyway, you gotta get your ass back here like yesterday, Reed. You're the only person who can get that video footage."

For a split second Reed wondered what it would be like to just tell Dan to fuck off. That his boss had earned his heart attack, that working in that news company was worse than living in a rat hole. He thought of Clione and what it would be like to have months or years to spend exploring Mexico with her, instead of hours.

"When's the visit?"

"Next week."

"I'll be there. I can fly back on Friday so there's the whole weekend to prepare. And I'll come see you Saturday morning so we can go over the flight plan. If you need anything from the office let me know and I'll bring it to you."

"There's a bottle of scotch in my desk drawer. Bring that. If I had that I might be able to choke down more of this hospital food." Then Dan's voice softened. "Hey, how's the adoption going?"

Since when did Dan ever care about anything that was going on behind the scenes? "We can talk about it when I get there. But good.

Yeah. It's exciting."

"I was always rooting for you two. How you managed to nail a looker like that always threw me, though. You must have a dick the size of a fire hose."

"Classy."

"See you Saturday."

He put the receiver back in the cradle and left his hand hanging there as he bent over, suddenly so tired he could barely stand. He hung on the phone for several minutes before straightening up. Still dizzy, he returned to the hostel and went inside.

* * *

His room was just as he'd left it, and he wondered if that was just from good housekeeping or if there'd actually not been any guests here since he'd left before. He placed the box on the bed and then, opening the top, flipped it upside down and watched the contents spill out. The random jumble seemed inappropriate for the clean cabaña, and as soon as things had settled Reed wished he'd just put the box on the floor.

He heard footsteps, then three soft knocks.

"Yes?"

"It's me," said Clione.

"It's open."

Clione poked her head in, letting her eyes adjust to the light. She saw the jumbled mess on the bed and raised her eyebrows, then walked over to the bed and picked up a shirt. She folded it, put it back on the bed. She picked up another.

"You don't have to do that."

"I know," she said. "You going back to Boston?"

"My boss had a heart attack."

"I'm sorry. Unless he was the kind of boss you hope that stuff happens to. In which case, I'm not sorry at all."

"He's fine. He said he didn't even know it had happened. Stress probably caught up to him. But I have to cut things short. The President is going to be in Boston all next week and I have to be in the chopper."

"So you're going back."

"Have to be there by next Monday."

Clione looked at the bed. "Less than a week from now."

"It's not like I want to go."

Reed waited, hoping the silence would flush out more from her, but she just stared at the bed.

"Clione, we don't have time to play games. Tell me what's on your mind."

"Goodbye just began," she said. "And that makes me sad."

"Goodbye doesn't happen for five days. And I've got a lot to see before I go."

"Road trip?"

"Anything that doesn't involve water. Or sharks."

"We could go to see the flamingos in Lagartos lagoon. They're a special color, rose or something, not the pale pink like in Florida. I've never seen them. Always wanted to go."

"Flamingos," Reed said. "Sure."

"Or the ruins? There's one called Ek' Balam that sounds incredible." She leaned over and gave him a soft peck on the cheek. "But this time we rent a car instead of stealing one."

She caressed his neck and they kissed, letting their lips linger. Then Clione was quiet for a while, and when Reed went to kiss her again he realized she was asleep. He folded the thin cover over her and kissed her hair softly. She murmured something but did not wake up.

When he was certain she was asleep he quietly opened the bungalow door. Latching it behind him, he crossed the courtyard and returned to the telephone out in the street. Stars had come out but only a few were bright enough to peek through the town's illumination. The Mexican chicken seller waved amicably and motioned at a few birds still smoldering on the ashes.

No, Reed shook his head.

"*Muy rico,*" the vendor replied. "Good for the heart and for the —" he made a motion with his fingers that was clearly obscene. "You know?"

"Actually, I'm just fine in that department," Reed said. He went to the telephone, inserted the card, and dialed the number. The sweat on his palms made the receiver slippery and he tucked it between his ear and shoulder, pinching it into place with his neck. Using the card had become routine. He dialed home and, when there was no answer, Laurel's cellphone.

"Hey, Laur. It's me. I would have called sooner but the service here is spotty. I found out Dan from work had a heart attack, not sure if the news got to you yet. He's okay. Nothing serious. Just sobering because he's young, my age. But I'm coming home. I'll call when I know which flight I'm going on. Probably from Houston, since by then I should be able to use my own damn cellphone."

A click, and everything had been decided.

Friday, everything would end. Clione was right: It was the beginning of goodbye. Reed stood with his hand still on the telephone, watching the chicken vendor pile the last few birds into the back of a pickup truck and start breaking down the grill. The man seemed happy and carefree. Reed thought about that simple, quiet life and the joy that a few dollars must bring after a long day. No deadlines, no stress, no getting up at four in the morning and waiting in the freezing cold. The man had pride in that simple profession that Reed would never have in his. He liked flying because it made him forget. It was like drinking. In the air nothing mattered until he touched back down. But it was just an escape. He hated Boston and everything with Laurel and him was shot. And in twenty more years, Reed would have his own heart attack.

The vendor scattered the hot coals in the street and then doused them with melted ice from the plastic cooler that held the beverages. Steaming and hissing, the coals sent plumes of vapor up into the night, and as cars passed it seemed as if they were pulling pieces off, wicking the moisture behind them as they passed. Reed watched the steam spiral upward, upward, into the night. A curiously shaped cloud turned the almost full moon into a jagged blade, like a rusted hand-scythe hanging over the town.

Reed smiled and pointed at the sky to the chicken vendor. The man looked up and bent backward, pausing for two entire minutes to just stare, noticing it too.

"¡La luna está magnífica!" the man exclaimed, shaking his head. "¡Magnifica!"

"¡Sí!" said Reed. "¡Sí!" He walked closer, stepping over the smoldering coals. He pointed to the cooler with the iceless beers and sodas. They were still cold, sweating in the humidity of the night.

The vendor suddenly stared at Reed, then bent quickly and took one of the remaining chickens, wrapped it in wax paper, and handed it to Reed.

"Es for you, *señor*."

"For me?"

"Is your chicken. You pay me for chicken, I wait for you. But you no come."

Reed laughed. "I'm sorry. I forgot. I was doing something else."

"Es good chicken. You eat," the vendor slapped his stomach. "You get strong like me!"

The two men laughed.

Reed pointed at the drinks. *"Bebida.* How much?"

"Ten pesos."

"That one, *por favor,"* he said, pointing to a clear bottle with yellow liquid inside. Jarritos brand. *Piña.* The Mexican popped the top off and handed him the beverage, nodding and smiling. Reed put the mouth of the bottle to his lips and tipped it back, relishing the coolness of the golden liquid. It was less sweet than any American soda he'd had, made with real sugar instead of corn syrup, with a nice hint of fresh pineapple.

"Very good!" he said to the vendor. "Gracias!"

"De nada," the man replied.

Reed finished the bottle in four long gulps, letting the tickle of carbonation soothe his throat, calm him. Remembering how every bottle gets recycled here, he handed the empty back to the man instead of tossing it in the trash. Then, instead of leaving, Reed bent and motioned that he would help. Together the two of them hefted the heavy cooler onto the truck's dusty, dented bed. Then they broke down the grill, the handles still hot to the touch, and put that in too. Reed jumped up in the truck for better leverage, then leaped out over the side as the man slid the grill in. The two men laughed for a moment, and Reed nodded.

"Gracias," he said.

"No," the Mexican replied, *"gracias a Usted."* He pointed to the moon. Already it was whiter, more clearly visible.

Reed shook his head, then took the Mexican's outstretched palm and clasped it firmly. "Thank you."

"You're a good man," Reed said quietly, as if to himself, and returned to the youth hostel, the chicken wrapped in paper tucked under his arm.

Clione and Lance were standing near the picnic table, their posture suggesting two teens pushed together because their parents were close friends, not because they wanted to be next to each other.

The bottle of tequila between them on the table stood at attention, half empty. As Reed approached, whatever conversation they'd been having stopped. It felt like midnight already, but the clock said it was just before ten.

"Hungry?" Reed said, looking from Clione to Lance. He held up the wax paper package. "I've got a chicken, be happy to share."

"No, buddy, not at all."

"Maybe later," Clione said.

"Can I have some of that?" Reed said, pointing to the bottle. Lance nodded, and Reed took three quick gulps.

"Was thinking of going dancing tonight," Clione said. "At Abacus."

"What's Abacus?"

"A nightclub. There's a pretty good crowd even on Tuesdays."

Lance nodded. "If you want it, I can get you both some decent 420."

Reed shook his head, no. So did Clione. Lance shook his head with a "What am I going to do with you?" expression.

"A little reefer to take the edge off?" Lance persisted. "What's wrong with that?"

"You know I hate the stuff," she replied.

"I'm asking Haflinger here. He looks like he needs to smoke a spliff the size of a cucumber."

"I'll take more of that tequila," Reed said. "But no pot. Thanks." He took a swig and then another before handing it back to Lance.

The other man waved his hand in front of his face as if swatting at a mosquito. "Fine. But this stuff came from Marrakesh. You two go have your little dance. Do your little thing. Be square as sponges for all I care. Me? I'm going to enjoy life while I've still got it to live. Sit on a sand dune and get so high I think I'm on the moon."

"Lance," Clione said. "Smoke all the shit you want but I won't be joining you and don't even pretend like I'm missing anything. Reed, see you or not at Abacus. I'll be on the dance floor."

Reed and Lance watched her walk to the girl's dorm.

"That is one amazing specimen of the female species," Lance said, lifting the bottle to his lips and draining it, tapping it to get the final drops. He set it back down on the picnic table with a thud. Reed nodded. Lance slapped Reed on the back, then the two of them bent over, laughing and laughing as if they had already smoked the Marrakesh.

The absurdity of everything made Reed's eyes sting, and he watched Lance hitting the picnic table with his meatloaf-size hands, thumping the weathered boards until it seemed as if the whole table were going to fall apart. Reed steadied himself, then another spasm of laughter almost pulled him to the ground. He buckled, calmed down, buckled again, and finally sat on the picnic table bench and braced himself until he could finally breathe.

"We should start a website," Lance finally said, still chuckling. "Clionefans dot com."

"She's incredible."

"Ain't that the truth, the whole truth, and nothing but the truth," he said. "I changed my mind. Gimme some of that chicken. Few birds are better than a good *pollo asado*. You're in for some sweet meat."

* * *

Abacus Bar was closer than Reed thought, as close as the hostel was to the bus station, just in the opposite direction. It was a tiny enclosure with rough-cement walls and a postage-stamp sized dance floor, all flashing strobes, the music a mix of techno, hip-hop, and ska. Outside it was non-descript, a shabby exterior in need of some paint. Inside, it was far more stylish. Small pedestal tables lined the walls, illuminated by neon tubes that hung from the ceiling and ran in long, erratic floral designs, like giant day-glo palms. At the back was a giant glass fish tank, the water an eerie velvet-blue, glowing behind polished bottles of liquor that shone like a futuristic apothecary in the black light. In the tank, tetras and angelfish hung motionless as if suspended by string.

The bartender was tall, easily over six feet, and thin as a barracuda. Waiting for a margarita, Reed wondered whether the fish could sense the beat, understand the tension, know what archetypal scenes were played out here every night. Or did they just swim, oblivious to anything outside the tank walls, their days and nights measured out by the sprinklings of food flakes onto the shimmery surface?

Clione was in the center of the dance floor, surrounded by a trio of American twenty-somethings wearing muscle shirts and baggy, loose jeans. One had a faded tattoo on his bicep. Their shirts had been turned into purple blurs by the black light and strobes. Reed envied them their youth, their over-testosteroned confidence. Even in his twenties he could never have danced with a girl like that, a complete stranger. He steadied himself on the bar, feeling the solid, cool wood, running his fingers on the unsanded grain.

If Clione was aware of the guys gyrating around her, she was ignoring them. Her eyes were closed, and she was dancing in a slow circle, her right arm up in the air, her left tucked into her pocket. The posture accentuated the perk of her breasts, the dot of each nipple clearly visible through her tight baby-doll tee. She had changed into a pair of cutoff denim shorts, and her dance consisted mainly of slow twists of those magical hips, rocking them side to side, the beat exactly twice as fast as her motions. Her movements were a kind of alchemy: She was constructing a cathedral around herself out of beat, movement, and sound. It was hypnotizing, and as other girls sidled up to the trio of worshippers it was clear that no one could hold a candle to her smoldering flame.

One guy reached out behind her, placing a hand on each of her hips, trying to match the movements of that perfect pelvis with his own. She shuddered as if hit with ice water, her eyes wild and angry. She stared him down until he raised his hands in a "don't-shoot-me" pose and backed away. His buddies were laughing. Clione noticed Reed at the bar and instantly pushed her way through the crowd and sat down next to him.

"You came after all."

"Don't stop dancing. You look gorgeous. You were like Salome out there." Reed took a sip of his margarita. "Something to drink?"

"Want to go somewhere quieter? Just talk for a bit?"

The two of them squeezed through the crowd back out into the street, then walked side by side, and at some point Reed took her hand. She moved closer to him, and they just walked together for a while down the empty streets. Reed looked for the moon but couldn't see it, and he realized that clouds were rolling in, blurring lights in the distance, making everything seem enchanted and eerie at the same time.

"Will you come with me to see flamingos?" Clione asked. "It'll be a great trip."

"Sure," he said, letting her change the subject. "Why wouldn't I?"

"Can we leave tomorrow?"

"As soon as the rental agency opens."

"Stop teasing." She put her hand in his. "This has been fun, Reed.

It's been really, really nice."

"You make it sound like I'm already gone."

"You basically are."

"What if I weren't? What if we could just keep on going?" he asked her, suddenly imagining that he could keep traveling with her. Just kept on going, past the flamingos, following the sunset. Chiapas, Baja, La Paz, Hawaii. Japan. Just keep going and going. An endless sunset, never let the night come. "Just like this. Like we're always traveling. So there's always something new and unexpected. Something to see."

"Reed," Clione said. "I like seeing you get passionate about something but I wish it weren't me. Because we can't do that, and you know that, and you know you're going to wake up tomorrow with a splitting headache and you're going to look at me and you're going to think about her, and you're going to choose her. You're always going to choose her. And I know that because I'm not naive, even if you don't know that, or don't know it yet. The moment you get back home your real life will be waiting for you and this will all have just been a fun little dream."

They had reached the end of the divided street and the two lanes merged into one. A truck pulled up to the speed bump that marked the edge of town and pulled slowly over it, the rusted leaf springs creaking. The driver craned his neck to look at the couple, then waved as he hit the gas.

"I'm coming back," Reed said. He was with her because she was here, because she was beautiful, because he'd been lonely. He just hadn't imagined he would end up falling in love. "You'll see."

"I won't believe it till I see it," she said, and kissed his cheek.

Day Ten

The Salt Factory

By eight-thirty the next morning they were on the road, the wheels singing over the hot pavement as they picked up speed. Clione had a dog-eared Lonely Planet *Yucatán* open and was thumbing through it, page by page. They were heading west, and the morning light deepened the green of the jungle, sending long shadows out over the already-shimmering tar. They opted to not take the highway, willing to trade the speed and convenience of an interstate for the chance to see something interesting or stop in the little towns along the way. It was the same road, Reed realized, that they'd taken on that day when they'd seen the dog die. Silence bound them, comfortable and relaxing, as if they were an old married couple instead of lovers thrown together for a few days.

A flock of parrots, ten or fifteen of them, burst out of the bushes on the left and circled, screeching and cawing. Reed was used to them by now. They seemed as normal as crows. The road curved, dipped down into a low gully with water on either side, visible only for silvery glimpses through the thick verdure. A heron, startled by the car, took awkwardly to the air, flapping its heavy wings and uttering a disgruntled squawk. Reed watched it in the rearview mirror as it looped back behind them and settled again onto the bank.

"It occurs to me," Reed said, finally breaking the silence, "that just about all I know about flamingos is that they are sometimes plastic lawn ornaments. What exactly is a flamingo, anyway?"

Clione stretched her feet out on the dashboard, her toenails painted a fresh coat of silvery green. "A bird? What do you mean?"

"I know they're a bird. But what do they eat? Do they migrate? Are they tame?"

"They're ferocious as tigers," Clione said, her voice low. "They attack without the least provocation. Tourists have disappeared, ripped to pieces by a sudden swarm, you didn't know? Trampled by an angry herd."

"Birds don't herd. They flock."

"We may need to buy a gun."

"I'm serious."

Clione shrugged. "The guidebook says that the ones here are different, uniquely colored. I know they're shy. We should be careful not to scare them. Sometimes if they all fly in a burst their wings get tangled and they can get hurt. I'd hate for that to happen." She read some more, silently. "We should have brought binoculars."

"Next time."

"I think they eat," Clione continued, "like little critters in the water. Isn't that right? Brine shrimp or whatever the Mexican equivalent is."

"Mexican jumping shrimp. Also highly dangerous?"

They lapsed again into silence, Clione taking out her journal and scribbling, Reed watching the road. The land had gotten drier, more hilly, and every so often they passed the crumbling remains of the henequen plantations that Lance was so fascinated by. Clione hunched over her pages, scribbling quickly in a light scrawl, turning the pages silently, with purpose. When they slowed for the tiny villages, she'd look up, roll down the window, and toss out tortilla scraps for any roadside dog. Little children laughed and pointed, and Reed waved back. Clione seemed not to notice them.

Marisol had copied the map for them, single lines indicating the roads and dots where the important villages were. At Valladolid they were to turn north, and when they reached Tizimin they pulled into a parking spot at the central plaza. Several giant ceiba trees shaded a cracked rectangular courtyard about fifty by one hundred meters square. At one end was the old cathedral, a majestic, crumbling ruin dating back to the era of the Spanish conquerors. The thick stone walls were cracked and one part of the steeple had given way, leaving the building lopsided, unbalanced. It looked like an old elephant, injured yet still standing, watching over a troop of lesser beasts. A drunk was lying in the shade of the cathedral, empty bottle tipped over on the ground. Nearby him, two scruffy-looking mutts lethargically licked spots in their fur.

It was so hot that the air rippled off the hood of their car. They stretched, then crossed the street and had breakfast at the Buenos

Días Café, a combination breakfast joint and pizza parlor with an Internet café upstairs.

The waiter was shy and seemed nervous as he served them, giving Reed the impression that tourists rarely frequented this part of Yucatán.

"*Chilaquiles,*" she said. The waiter nodded quickly and licked his lips. He glanced at Reed and then stared back to the kitchen as if expecting them to produce a translator.

"*Motuleños,*" he said, hoping he'd pronounced it right.

The waiter nodded again. "*Y... ¿bebidas?*"

"*Café.*"

The coffee, when it came, was a packet of crystals to be stirred into hot water. The cream was powder too. Reed mixed them both slowly and then pushed one chipped mug across to Clione, who looked up just briefly to acknowledge him. Absorbed in note taking, she stared periodically through the dust-smeared glass to the plaza and the beautiful ceiba trees. He felt she was avoiding him. Her face was placid, unreadable, and then something would occur to her and she'd spring upon the pen and scribble, her nose almost touching the page. Reed wondered if she were nearsighted, or was she shielding what she wrote so that it would be harder for him to see?

It occurred to him that there was nothing more destructive than indecision. That was what had plagued him, would always plague him. In a way, it didn't matter if he fought to make Clione have the child or fought to make sure she didn't, or decided that his position was to let her make the choice entirely on her own. It was the not knowing that made his intestines churn. The stress came from the thought that perhaps ten years later he *would* know, he would have realized that whatever path he chose right now would have been the wrong one.

"Clione," he said, staring at the empty plates. "Do you think you'll regret this?"

"Eating breakfast? No."

"Being with me."

"Not for a moment," she said, without hesitation.

"Would it change anything if you knew the baby were mine?"

She shrugged. "Don't go there."

"Even if it wasn't, I could —"

"Reed, I love you. Don't crush that, okay? Isn't that enough...for now?"

"No," Reed said, shaking his head. "It's not." A lump rose in his throat. He pulled out twice as much money as the meal cost and put it on the table, then stood up.

"I'll be outside," he said. He pushed open the door and stumbled into the street. A sob tore out of his chest, so loud that it startled an old woman who was crossing the street. She looked at him as she passed, her eyes curious and wide.

He walked into the plaza and sat down on a bench, his fingertips at his temples as if they could massage the past events away and make everything okay. The shade was tranquil, calming, and he took deep breaths of the jasmine-scented air. He tried to void his mind of everything and focused on the boys dashing after the dusty soccer ball. He realized it was like the scene back in Tulum, the children, the dust, the endless chase after a soccer ball. Centuries ago in the days of Maya splendor the ball had meant sacrifice, death to the winning or losing team, hearts ripped still beating out of the chest cavities to be fed to the sun. Now the same blood coursed through children's veins, the ball was bigger, the court a bit different, but nothing signified finality or victory or defeat. Life just bounced along like a ball, kicked this way or that, until the game ended or the sun went down. New children appeared when others were grown up enough to have them.

What if he never went back, he thought. What if he just stayed here in this town forever, built a soccer field for the kids, found a sweet woman to marry and have kids with. Just start over, wipe the slate clean. A few sparrows landed in front of him, chirped, and began washing themselves in small holes in the dust that he hadn't noticed before. They rolled into the sand at the shoulder, on their backs, then wriggled up and shook themselves off in a tiny cloud. Reed imagined an unbroken line of sparrow ancestry, parents and children taking dust baths back to the time of Archeopteryx. The trees, the pollen, the children playing soccer, the insects busily hanging onto the open blossoms of the vines that draped over the bushes. Gourds filled with seeds that would ripen and rot, splat their fertile contents to the hard desert ground, the seeds pushing themselves into the cracked earth and shooting skyward at the next rain. The hammocks swaying as lovers clasp themselves together at the hips, the sighs and releases and tears and blood and pain. The miracle of new life.

Reed felt like an empty shell on a sun-scoured beach, something hollowed out, devoured and bleached, but still there. He thought of Clione. How could anyone not want to see herself mirrored in a tiny face, see her own fingers reborn in an infant's tiny grasp, feel her own heartbeat quicken when the child cries? He thought of a beautiful and solitary and friendless girl, shaped by forces within and without her, who had learned that she was the only person she could ever truly depend on. He wondered whether anything would change in a decade, if Clione never made it as a writer, if the dream slowly slipped away, worn down by the rut of a nine-to-five. Would she be the same? Would she abort the novels and short stories that lived inside her and choose, instead, the role of being a mom?

People are just breaths of air to her, he thought. Nice, necessary sometimes, but gone as soon as she exhaled. And there would be another breath after that one, just as important, just as temporary. If she inhaled without exhaling, she would die, but that was love — inhaling a person and never again being able to breathe. And she would never love anyone, never truly love him, until he'd extinguished the writer that burned within her. And when that was gone, she'd be gone too. He couldn't imagine her without that passion, without that curiosity to know and understand the world. But that was what kept her submerged, in a different world from his. She came up, breathed, dove down into the depths of a story or an idea, pushed it until her lungs burst, returned, gulped air, then went back down. All he was to her, all he would ever be to her, was a breath of air. Vital for a few split seconds, then gone.

He felt fingers on his back, firm pressure in the hollows of his shoulders and clavicle. Clione was standing behind him, and as she massaged his arms she leaned down and gently kissed his neck. The sparrows disappeared, as if blown away by a puff of wind. Reed looked up at her and she looked down. She wore just a hint of lipstick, and her eyes seemed darker and more accented, the halo more intense than ever before. She smiled at him, simultaneously siren and angel.

"I'm sorry," he said. "I shouldn't have walked out. I don't know where I'm going anymore."

"North," Clione said. "You're going north. That's where the flaaaamiiiiiinnnnnngos are."

"That's not what I meant."

Clione moved around beside him and sat down, their thighs pressed together on the narrow bench. "You don't have to have all the answers. Not now. Things will get better."

"You don't love me, right?"

Clione smiled. "Not the way you want me to."

They drove north, Reed pushing the pedal to the floor, so fast that their stomachs hung suspended in air as the rental Chevy popped over the peaks of hills. Each held on to their own individual fictions, pretending in their own silent ways that this day would be perfect and that tomorrow would never come. They sped past wizened woodcutters on battered yellow pedal-tricycles, their rusted machetes slung across their backs, straining against the pedals with their firewood loads. After an hour of driving the jungle abruptly thinned, the trees disappeared, and they entered vast pampas plains with tall sedge grasses that bent in the wind and muddy water-lily- and hyacinth-choked pools. Egrets clustered on bone-thin tree branches like ornaments hung from a long dead Christmas tree, motionless, the same shocking white of fresh snow. Small herds of goats watched them from the tall grass. Now and then a cluster of brilliant yellow butterflies would appear like a puff of magical levitating leaves, dancing this way or that before disappearing.

The air was hot, oppressive, and Reed wanted to be there already, to have reached the destination. The tar was a straight line from the dashboard to the horizontal border between the green of the land and the blue sky, making a perfect T as the road met the horizon. He swerved into the empty oncoming traffic lane briefly to avoid a large turtle, as black as a pothole. Clione nodded.

"Thank you for missing it," she said. "Some people wouldn't even swerve. Some wouldn't see it. Others wouldn't care. Others would justify hitting it by saying it's too dangerous, that they could have hit an oncoming car."

"Of course I'd try to miss it."

"You're a good person, Reed. You're not just good. You're very, very special. If I wanted to get married, you'd be a wonderful person to be married to."

"You up for a wedding?"

"You up for a divorce?"

Reed didn't answer. The road made a gradual bend to the right, went over a rough bridge made of metal grating that whirred against the tires, and ahead they saw a few small shacks with corrugated plastic roofs and thin, wind-battered walls. Mangrove swamps replaced the pampas grass, their dark leaves and thread-like root-tangles unmistakable, the water stained as red as bergamot.

"Looks like the map says we should turn here."

"Where?" Reed asked. "There's no place to turn yet."

"Did we miss it? Was there a side road?"

"Nothing that I saw."

Clione pressed the map out on the dashboard and scrutinized it. "I guess we should keep going. But if there's a right, we turn."

"Flamingos, thataway."

The shacks grew more frequent, and soon they entered into the town of Río Lagartos.

"Weren't we going to go to Ek' Balam first?" Clione said.

"Shit. Maybe we missed the turnoff?"

"We can catch it on the way back. Let's keep going now."

The road dead-ended at a small sea wall, beyond which spread a chalky green bay. Reed nosed the car between the faded lines of a parking spot. A lone pier extended quite a way into the water, the low-beamed panga-style fishing boats rocking and bumping in the wind. A pelican was perched on each of the pilings, wings outstretched, as if in some odd prayer to the sea. To the left, a group of swarthy men was playing cards and smoking cigarettes.

"I'll ask them where the flamingos are," Clione said. "Wait here."

She hopped out, holding her hands down on her thighs so the breeze wouldn't catch the hem of her sundress. Several of the men stood straighter when she came over, and one of them put out his cigarette and ran a hand through his hair. In a few moments their gruff expressions disappeared. They nodded, pointing and shaking their heads, until it was clear that Clione had gotten the directions right. She nodded, thanked them, and returned to the car, smiling.

"I got directions and an offer of marriage," she said. "Who would have expected it? Two in one day."

Reed laughed. "Hey, nothing like a good Plan B."

"I could do better," Clione said, as Reed turned the car around. "But I could do worse." She waved out the window at the men and one of them fell to one knee, his hands tightly clasped at his chest. The other men laughed.

Clione turned back to Reed.

"So where do we go?"

"We go back to the bridge, then turn left, and follow that around until it enters the preserve. And we should watch for crocodiles. They said be careful if we get out to take a picture and get too close to the lake."

"It's kind of amazing to think we're in a place that's so wild you could actually end up being eaten by a crocodile."

"Now that would be a death you could be proud of," she said. "Eaten by crocodile. It's authentic. Real."

"Actually, it sounds kind of unreal." He slowed down. "We're back at the bridge. The road's on the left?"

Clione sat forward, looking intently. "Should be, but I don't see it—no wait, I think that's it."

Two thin tire tracks, separated in the middle by overgrown grass, headed east, only faintly visible through the surrounding weeds. As they sat there, a burro pulling a four-wheeled wagon labored out from a side road, turned onto the dirt road, and eventually appeared at the intersection. A lone Maya woman in the traditional embroidered white dress was sitting in the back of the cart, one hand on the reins. She smiled at them. Behind her was a pile of cactus pears, freshly picked.

"She must be bringing them into town," Clione said, waving to her. "She's so beautiful."

When she had passed, Reed eased the vehicle over the shoulder and onto the two-track lane. The soil was drier than he expected, quickly lifting up above the swamp onto a raised mound. The mangroves they'd seen earlier were replaced by stunning yellow asters the size of silver dollars, bursting on bushes that were head-high, as if someone had set the shrub on fire. From a distance it looked as if the edges of the road were covered with yellow mist. Here and there the ground got wetter, the vegetation clustered in, grew taller, and dark pools of sedge-rimmed mud appeared. A few were covered with water, and ibis, storks, spoonbills, coots, rails, herons, and egrets hunted for food in the muddy shallows.

The difficulty of navigating the road gave Reed an excuse to focus on keeping the wheel straight instead of letting his mind wander back to what had happened over the past few days. Even a four wheel vehicle would have foundered if the undercarriage was flush against the mud. Clione helped by pointing out rocks that hid in the tall grasses. She kept her right arm tightly on the hand strap above the passenger door, as if expecting the vehicle to suddenly roll, intently peering into the grass in front of them. Twice they surprised jack rabbits, which leaped off to the side in long, deerlike bounds. Another time they stopped to let a coiled viper slither out of the sunny track it had been sleeping in. The pattern on its skin was a mix of black and green stripes. He felt relieved that he'd been able to slow down in time to let it get into the weeds.

"Going home will be good for you," Clione said. "You'll figure things out."

"Good for me?"

"For the two of you."

The conversation died. The trees grew thinner and thinner, the grasses spreading out in ever-widening patches. Soon the road pulled right and began to parallel the beach, visible only for seconds behind a high barrier dune. Giant agave leaf spikes dotted the sand, and here and there a seed stalk rose twenty or so feet, branched at right angles like a wireless telephone pole. Orioles flashed their bright orange plumage, sitting for seconds and then flying in low loops off into the bushes. A light wind had picked up, enough to make white wisps of sand dance across the silvery dune.

"Do you think we passed it?" Clione asked. "We've been driving a long time."

"If we see some, we see some. If we don't, we don't."

Clione smiled and nodded, and the conversation died again. Neither of them wanted to feel like the day had been a failure, that their sightseeing adventure had all been just a waste of precious time. Reed wondered what they'd be doing if they'd just stayed at the hostel.

They drove for another hour, stopping the car at times and getting out to look at the road. It had been paved in sections, yet high water from a hurricane must have washed it out, leaving a jagged patchwork of tar, loose sand, drifted dunes, and, in places, only gullies. From the tire tracks, Reed could tell that some large machinery had been along here: The giant wheels' teeth had chewed into the sand and mud, making it all the more impassable for an average car. Here and there stretched odd paved patches of crumbled hot tar that shimmered in the heat for twenty or thirty yards before disappearing into the dirt again. How could anyone have thought this road could warrant paving? Yet there it was, proof, a testament that hope had once been there for a future that never came to pass.

Coming over a small rise they caught their first glimpse of the lagoon: a wide, nickel-silver halo to their right, as if someone had airbrushed out the grasslands and turned it into a mirror of mercury-blue. From their viewpoint at the narrow entryway, which went under the road and connected with the ocean outside, it appeared to be a rough oval, slightly flatter at the opposite side. At either side were two thin tributaries, S-curled and graceful, which connected to even smaller pools that they could just see shimmering in the far distance. The edges of the estuary were an odd pinkish color, and the small opening where they had paused the car was rimmed with a forest of dead stumps and stunted brush. Here and there trunks poked out of the shallow water in pained postures, as grotesque as burn victims frozen after a bomb had dropped. Aside from a few sandpipers, there was no life at all that they could see. No fish, no birds, and no flamingos.

And it was easy to see why. Behind the desolate foreground was an enormous factory and what appeared to be a giant, displaced iceberg — a whitish mountain rising hundreds of feet into the air, lopsided and lumbering, like a Maya pyramid that had been recently constructed with the white plaster still intact, brilliantly reflecting the sun. Its jagged sides seemed gnawed at, the top unblemished, smooth and creamy, with wisps of brown like an enormous meringue. It dwarfed the small, rusting factory at its base, with the lone elevator rising up at a forty-five-degree angle like a crane arm. Squinting, Reed could see several trucks at the base of the giant pile, as small as Tonka toys.

"What have they done here?" Clione asked, her voice a whisper.

Reed shook his head. "I don't know. It looks dead."

They got back in the car and followed the road, which dropped down into the lagoon, becoming moisture-hardened sand, much easier to drive. In twenty minutes they had crossed the vast perimeter. Except for a few solitary frigate birds soaring on the ocean side, they didn't see a single creature. Just the factory, looming closer and closer.

The road turned sharply toward the ocean again, rose up, and now Reed could see that there was a network of long feeder tubes running out for miles into the lagoon. In places the water level was already so low that they were visible, like long, dark varicose veins against the pinkish sand. They were sucking out the water, carrying it to the factory.

And then Reed realized what the function of the tubes was.

"Salt!" he said. "They're draining the lagoon to make salt."

Clione nodded. "They must pump in salt water, let it evaporate, then suck it up—"

"They don't care at all about the lagoon or anything living inside it."

"Just suck out whatever they want, leaving it barren." Clione's voice was quiet.

The road turned again, passing through a small cluster of plastic roofed shacks, abandoned completely, the doors and windows gone. Drifts of salt and sand had piled up in the entrances. At the far end, a fishing panga lay facing the sea, the sand around its bow like stationary waves.

"Pull over," Clione said. "Look at that."

Leaving the engine in neutral, Reed pulled the parking brake and they hopped out. Clione pointed to the surfaces of the nearest shack. The prevailing, salt-laden winds had coated it in a milky glaze, as hard as sugar frosting. It had built up over time, layer upon layer upon layer, the wind twisting the edges into soft ripples and bumps, like wax drippings from a candle. Reed saw twisted faces in the patterns, grimacing gargoyles that had been frozen midscream. He felt as if they'd stumbled onto a sacred cemetery, a place that shouldn't be violated.

Clione tapped at an edge of the strange salt and shook a piece off into her hand. It looked like a knife blade, the edges serrated and dangerous, the surface shimmering like snow from the reflections of the crystals.

"It's salt. You're right," she said, touching the shard to her tongue.

"I'll take your word for it."

"This creeps me out," Clione said. She let it slip from her hands and it shattered into three shards. "Where are all the birds? This is supposed to be a wildlife preserve. Where's all the wildlife?"

They were close enough to the factory to see there was motion: Trucks were backing up to the mountain, front-end loaders were carving into its sides. A thin white puff was blowing from the very top of the elevator where the dry salt crystals were being deposited onto the pile. Its bed full, a massive yellow dump truck pulled away, belching diesel smoke as it picked up speed, and headed toward them. They watched it approach, and it slowed down to inch past their car in the narrow roadway. Reed could have stood inside the wheel wells of the tires.

"*¡Perdón!*" Clione yelled, over the roar of the engine.

The truck's air brakes hissed and the vehicle stopped.

"*Amigos,*" the driver said. He wore a frayed Boston Red Sox cap, a dark-blue flannel shirt, and his entire upper lip was buried beneath a mustache so thick and bushy the man might have pasted an entire rabbit onto his upper lip. His forearm, which hung out of the open window, was as large as an Easter ham.

"*¿Qué pasó? No se puede pasar por aquí. Es propiedad privada.*"

"Flamingos?" Clione said. She looked at Reed. "I don't know the word."

"Flamingos?"

"*Es un ave muy grande y rosada.*"

"*¿El flamenco?*"

"*¿Es un ave?*"

"*Sí, había muchas en el pasado.*" The man shook his head. "*Pero ahora no. No hay. Hace dos o tres años que no los veo.*"

Clione nodded. "*Gracias a Usted.*"

"*De nada, señorita. Adios.*"

The man put the truck in gear and eased it forward past their car. A cloud of oily smoke descended around them, twisting and contorting in the wind currents until it was devoured.

Clione looked at Reed, her eyes blank and frightened.

"How could they do that? He said there used to be lots of flamingos here. He hasn't seen any for years."

"Let's head back," Reed replied. "Being sad isn't going to change anything."

"But we came all this way. For nothing. Can we make it to Ek' Balam, maybe?" Clione said, walking around the hood to her side of the vehicle. "By sunset? It'd be nice if we could see the sunset from the top of a pyramid."

"I don't know," Reed said, and looked at the sky. "If we hurry and if it's not too far?"

"It'd make the trip worth something."

Reed made a three-point turn.

"I miss Lance," Clione said. "Lance knows this area like he was born here." She stared out the window, deep in thought, as if the salt factory had shifted her viewpoint on something, opened her eyes to something she'd never quite realized before. "He'd know where the flamingos are. If any are left, that is."

Silently, they backtracked out along the same route they'd come, the landscape reversing: beach into mangrove, mangrove into marshland into field. Clione, absorbed in her own thoughts, did not help watch for rocks this time, but Reed had a general sense of where they were from driving in and they reached the pavement without incident an hour and a half later.

"Ek' Balam, right?" Reed asked. "Are you okay?"

Clione nodded. "Fine. Did the plan change?"

"You sound upset, like we should be talking about something."

"I'm not upset."

Reed shrugged and hit the gas. It was a relief to see the speedometer creep steadily upward. Fifty, sixty, seventy kilometers an hour. The tires hummed on the late-afternoon, sun-softened tar. They passed another woman on an ox-pulled wagon. Or the same one they had seen before? Things were blurring together now, shifting, one memory into another into another. Reed focused his eyes into the gathering dusk, pushing the car faster and faster, hoping to outrun the sun.

The Majesty of the Ruin

They reached Ek' Balam, pulling into the parking lot just as the sun's rays were deepening. Light sat on surfaces as if it were brushed on by Monet. The shadows gathered, crouched, turned from black to blue to lavender. The daytime birds flitted nervously in the lush canopies preparing for the jaguar nightfall.

They pulled up next to a small white Eco-Tour van that was waiting for its seven tourists to get into the air-conditioned vehicle. Overweight and sunburned, each was toting binoculars and blue fanny packs with the tour logo emblazoned on them.

"And now," said the tour guide, a thin, attractive Maya girl with short, bobbed hair and a black mole on her cheek the size of a raisin. "We've just got time to visit the fifth ruin in our tour, the spectacular Chichén Itzá, where we'll enjoy dinner and a laser show, and—" The door slammed shut.

When the van left, they were alone, save for a pair of puppies near the ticket booth and the park ranger. Not wanting to lose his cellphone clambering around the ruins, Reed took it out and noticed the signal indicator light was on.

"Hey, what do you know?" he said, putting it into the coffee cup holder. "Ek' Balam's even got bars!"

"Power of the pyramid," Clione said. "Don the tinfoil hats."

The guard nodded when they paid the admission fee, not bothering to count the bills they'd presented him, then warned them that the park was closing in an hour.

"I thought it was open until seven," Clione said, in Spanish.

The guard shrugged. "Tonight, close at six."

"We were hoping to watch the sunset."

He looked at them. "I no here when you come back. I home with family. Stay is okay, but no touch, no steal."

236

Ek' Balam was only the second ruin Reed had seen the entire trip, yet it seemed far more familiar to him than when he'd wandered around in the sea of tourists at Tulum's excavation a week ago. The map on the sign at the entrance showed that this site was also roughly a rectangle, with the buildings set around a central plaza, with temples of varying height, splendor, and reconstruction on all four sides. Unlike at Tulum, where all ruins had been cordoned off and were inaccessible, at Ek' Balam they were free to climb and clamber wherever they wished, providing that they stayed off walls and did not remove or disturb the stones. Several areas, the places where the frescoes were the best preserved, had been covered with palapas and roped off to prevent vandalism.

"I want to see the Gates of Hell," Clione said, marching toward the largest of the structures. "It's got a jaguar mouth pattern around the outside, and it's an entrance to a deep pit. And at the bottom of the pit?" She looked at Reed, waiting for him to fill in the blank. "Do you know what's there?"

"Giant killer crocodiles from outer space? What?"

"Sharpened stakes. The sacrificed were pushed in, impaled and left to die."

"Ugh."

Clione nodded. "Just another way of seeing the world. We kill people too, with gas chambers or bullets or ambivalence about poverty...." she paused. "Or we just kill time. We just don't think of it as bad. They were probably the same way. It was justified. Even the ones who were sacrificed, they were okay with it."

"Is anyone ever really okay with death?"

She shrugged. "Never know until it happens, I guess. And then it's too late to write down."

They reached the base of a steep stairway that led upward. The steps were rough, pocked limestone, dotted with pinkish algae and darker gray lichens. Here and there wisps of grass grew up from the cracks, the tassels of seed like tiny flags.

Reed followed her lead, walking up the steep, uneven steps at an angle so as to reduce the chance of falling. What would happen if one of them fell? Reed wondered. The pyramid at Chichén Itzá had recently been closed for climbing because a tourist had died. What if there were a viper sunning itself beneath an overhang? Or a scorpion? Or a poisonous spider?

They were the only two people at the ruin. If anything happened it would be hours before help would arrive.

He watched as Clione picked purposeful steps up toward the Mouth of Hell. Gate of Hell? He had already forgotten. But he felt as if he were ascending toward something genuinely evil, a terrible and impenetrable blackness. A tingle of fear went through him as he realized that all it would take would be a misstep or a push, and one of them could fall onto the spikes themselves.

"You okay?" He heard Clione ask. "You look strange."

Reed exhaled, inhaled, held his breath, exhaled again, his blood like drumbeats throbbing in his ears.

"Winded," He paused. "I'm just going to sit down here for a bit."

Reed fell to his knees on the ancient steps, wondering at what horrors must have happened here. Sacrifices, bloodlust, chanting sun-worshippers that time had simply erased. Now the courtyard held no power; it was just an empty field, long forgotten, rimmed by decaying monuments, unused for centuries. A jay left one tree and flew in short arcs across the space to the far side. Reed felt intense fondness for this sweet, kind girl who had allowed him to share so much of her over the past few days. They had done so much together. And tomorrow, he would leave forever and everything they'd shared would become like this empty ruin: a monument to a memory, something no longer alive.

Clione scampered up the remaining steps and disappeared for a few moments as she peeked into the hole.

"Be careful," Reed called.

"Kind of disappointing," Clione said, reappearing. "I couldn't see anything. Just pitch black. Heard a few bats squeaking but couldn't see even one."

She walked down the steps and sat to the left of him, so that she could leave her left arm in her lap. With her right arm she traced a line up to Reed's shoulder and left it there, warm and intimate. It was when she touched him, he realized, that he felt everything they had wasn't just going to disappear. When he couldn't feel her skin against his, everything became fuzzy again.

"I love it when you touch me," he said.

Clione smiled. "Let's climb to the top. It's going to be an amazing sunset."

Reed nodded, then rose to his feet.

The very top of the temple was flat, with three coffin-size stones that had been inscribed with hieroglyphs, partially worn away and unreadable, one to the east, north, and south. They sat facing west, watching the sun abandon the day. The thick jungle canopy below and around them was as irregular as cumulus; Reed felt as if he were in an airplane, looking down at green clouds. The sun became a giant glowing coin in the yellow tablecloth of sky. Parrots shrieked, settling into the canopy for the night, jockeying for best position on the branches. A series of shrill jays rang out with similar calls. Clione pointed as the birds erupted out of one tree and circled in a wide loop, screaming as they went, finally disappearing to the east, into the darkness. Other smaller birds that he couldn't recognize darted about. A lone vulture circled lazily above the trees, lower and lower, until the purple-green forest canopy swallowed it up as if it were the sea.

"Look over there," Clione said, pointing back into the jungle.

The branches were moving. It was dim light but Reed could just make out a few forms, small bodies and arms and fingers, traversing the branches as if it were a kind of highway.

"Spider monkeys," Clione whispered, even though there was no reason to lower her voice. "Oh, look at them. How cool is that! They don't even know we're here."

The sun seemed to tip for a moment like a sinking ship when it reached the horizon, staying afloat, afloat, afloat for far longer than seemed possible before the last ray finally winked out in adieu. The night seemed to gather up its forces, stretching and awakening with a low growl.

Reed looked at Clione, brought his lips to hers, and kissed her. Her mouth tasted like guava and pineapple, and he let his mouth linger on hers for a long moment before slowly pulling away.

Clione's eyes were still closed.

"I have to say something," Reed said softly. His heartbeat was loud, the blood rushing in his ears, louder than waves. "I'm probably not going to say it very well, either. But here goes."

She pulled away slightly and slowly opened her eyes.

"Maybe it sounds crazy given that I'm leaving Friday. But I love you more than anything I've ever known before. You are...." he paused, shrugged, shook his head, and just looked at her. He shook his head again, took a deep breath, and put a hand quickly to his eyes.

"I just love you. I love you so intensely that it makes everything else I've ever done in my life seem pale. I can't go back to how things were before and just be with Laurel. I'm never going to be happy with her. It's like asking someone to be happy with the moon when they've been dancing with the sun. I'm never going to be with Laurel and not think about what your lips felt like against mine those nights, how you moved your body when we made love. How your skin tasted, how incredibly warm you are. Like your skin was burning up because it was touching me. It's like I've walked out of a building through a one-way door and I can't just turn around and go back in. I never knew what love was until meeting you.

"And for you," he continued, "it seems like you're swimming around and came up and I happened to be the breath of air you got that time and now I'm there inside you, feeding you, we're somehow connected. But you'll come up again soon, take another breath of air, find someone else to be with for a while, and keep on going. I believe you. I believe every word you say. But I can't believe in you, in us, even though I want to."

She swallowed, as if remembering a kiss before opening her eyes and shattering the memory. "I might love you too, Reed," she said. "But I don't know. And whether I do, or whether I don't, either way makes me scared. There's a part of you that terrifies me because I don't want to end up normal, just another family mom living just another family life. I want to be different, and being with me might make it impossible for you to be happy."

Reed took both of her hands with his, held them in his lap. He moved his fingers, massaging hers as he spoke.

"I can love you even if you're the most wacko person in the world," he said. "As long as I knew that you were there waiting for me to kiss you, hold you, make love to you. I don't mean fidelity. I don't believe that's at all what's right for us right now. But if you think you love me, let's figure things out now. How we can be together. Or be together more. Clione, I love everything about you. I love that you're so passionate about everything. I love that you want to be a writer so much. I love your mouth and the way it opens up when you kiss me. I love making love to you and I love being with you afterward, wrapped together so tightly that it feels like we're two towels that have been twisted up in a washing machine. You challenge me to do new things I never thought I could do. I want to go diving with you again. Really, it's because of you that I did all of this, and now it's like I'm waking up and realizing what everything really could be. What life is. It's because of you that I've changed so much."

"It's not because of me," Clione whispered.

"It *is*. And Clione, I don't know how to say this, but I love the fact that it might be my baby you're carrying inside you. It's your baby, but it's *our* baby. Even if it's not genetically mine. It's my baby too because I'm the person with you and I'd be its father if...well, if you changed your mind. I'm ready to embark on that part of life, but I can't force you to. I can only hope that you realize how good a mother you'll be someday. How much a child will look up to you, believe in you. You're smart, you're fun, you're so...." Reed's throat went dry and he stopped, almost choking. "I just love you so, so, so much. I know that you don't feel that way about me. That's what tears me apart every time we're together. That you'll never love me like that."

Clione pulled away and shook her head. "Why wouldn't I?"

"Because I'm nothing special. I'm not particularly attractive or funny, I haven't done anything special with my life, I'm not strong like Lance, I'm old and — "

She continued to shake her head slowly, from side to side, staring out at the setting sun. "You are so insecure about yourself, you know that? You're so, so stupid sometimes. Maybe that's what I like about you. That you're stupid sometimes. Stupid, stupid you." She giggled. "Because you're wrong, Reed."

"Wrong? About what?"

"I knew from the moment we were picking Sharon's stuff up under that table at your hotel that there was something I liked about you. And I mean *liked*. It wasn't just that I thought you liked me. *I liked you.* Remember that. If I didn't want you, if I didn't like you, if I didn't love you, you'd have never gotten near me. That stupid thing with the book. If it hadn't been you, if it had been that waiter or someone else from the hotel or one of those guys dancing at the bar, I wouldn't have given them the time of day. I'd have been creeped out and felt they'd hunted me down. Because it was *you*, Reed, I was flattered. I liked you from the instant I saw you. That doesn't mean I wanted to instantly sleep with you. I wasn't sure I wanted complications and I'm still not sure. But that night when we did make love? When I came to your room? It wasn't like I was making love out of charity or something. I wanted you. I needed you. Not just *someone*. I needed *you*."

She lifted up her journal. "I never show anyone my journal. It's for me, my special place to have the world all to myself. But I'll read you something. Okay?"

Reed nodded. "If you want to read it to me. You don't have to."

"I want to," she said, flipping for the right page. "Here." She took a breath and marked the spot with her finger. "*I saw a man today and something about him reminded me of Chris. He doesn't look anything like him of course, and he's older, but he had such beautiful eyes. Really wonderful eyes, I almost drowned in them. I want to put his eyes into a book someday, they were so striking. I wish I could draw them, paint them, fall into them. I wish his eyes were paints so I could splash them onto canvas, show them in a gallery. Is it possible to fall in love with someone just for their eyes? Is that where love at first sight comes from? Is that how we know love is really love? He kept looking at me and looking at me, and I think for the first time since Chris I might be really ready to swoon for someone. Swoon, it's such a strange word, archaic and yet so beautiful for something as strange and powerful and overwhelming as love. Swoon. Like swim and moon combined.*"

She paused. "Should I keep reading?"

"It's beautiful," Reed whispered. "Please."

"*Somewhere I read that the human heart has room for only three great loves. First love and true love and the love one has for one's child. I know my first love taught me what I never want to do again. Could I be ready for the next? I wonder if he's ever looked that closely at his eyes? There was a little halo of gold around the outside, like the corona when the sun's being eclipsed by the moon. How nice to feel a ripple of something in my heart again, after such a long time of wondering if my insides could ever be the same.*"

Reed shifted and his eyes dropped to the pages she was reading from. In place of any writing, he could clearly see she was reading from a blank page. There was no text, just a sketch of a dog.

"You were just making that up," he said, pointing at the journal.

Clione closed the book suddenly. "I read it from memory."

"You think you have to shield me or something?"

"That's what I wrote."

"The page you were reading didn't have any text."

She looked at him. "Everything I said was true. I've read that part over and over these past few days."

Reed stood. "I don't know what to believe, Clione. Let me see it."

He moved toward the journal and she picked it up, and held it far away, her eyes blazing.

"Reed, the only time you'll ever have permission to look through this journal is after I'm dead, okay? You do not touch this. You do not look at it. If it is accidentally left open, you close your eyes and you close the book or I will never love you and we will never, ever be together. Understand?"

Reed snorted. "Sure, Princess. Play whatever games you want to play."

"Reed, I've loved your eyes from the second I met you, saw that when we picked up stuff together in that hotel. It's how I feel about you. You're wonderful for me. I've never felt so comfortable being around someone. And you're genuinely nice to me, you want to make me happy, not like every other guy I've known. I like how naturally you make love to me, and no, I don't just mean the sex. I mean, it's like we're becoming the same creature when we're making love. It's deeper than just the sensation. It's like, like a meditation. No, it's not meditation. It's love. That's what love is. Fine. It is. Something spiritual and important and ineffably beautiful and I've never felt that before with someone. Can't you tell how scary this is for me too? I love the way you make me feel when we're making love, and whatever you say, maybe there are other men out there who can do that, Reed, but I haven't found them. Not yet. And I don't really want to. You're everything I could possibly want in a lover. You just attract me, deep and physical and intensely spiritual. That's it. Maybe you think that's shallow and meaningless bullshit from someone too young to know the difference. But it means something to me. Nobody else in the world has held me the way you do. And I like feeling like you value me, like you care about what I have to say. You're a good lover, Reed, and you're a good listener. I loved you, right from the beginning. Don't you see? *I loved you too.* Seeing you there in the hostel with that book in your hand, thinking that you'd come all that way to find me...it was the most romantic thing that anyone will ever do for me. My whole life I'll remember that no matter what happens to us, to you, to me. No matter what direction we go. I'd love to think we'll have that story to tell together, but I'm not stupid. And I'm not afraid to love you anyway and know that tomorrow comes and we have to go our separate ways."

She stared at him, waiting. "Do you need to hear more? Really? Isn't that enough already?"

Reed looked at her for a long time, staring into her eyes as the light slipped away and the purple-blue shadows in her cheekbones deepened.

"Yes," he finally answered. "That's more than I could ever hope to hear."

"Do you believe me now?"

He nodded. "I do." It sounded like a marriage vow.

"Your leaving doesn't mean it has to be the end. If it's meant to happen, if we both want it to happen, it will happen. It has to happen. Us, I mean."

"How could it ever be the same?"

Clione shrugged. "It won't be. But it'll either work or it won't. I want it to work. You'll know if you want it to work after you figure out things in Boston." She reached into her pocket and pulled out a small piece of paper. It was folded up in an origami pattern. A crane. She put it in his palm.

"My address. Are you upset?"

"No," Reed said. "The opposite. I feel like everything is opening up and I'm just starting to see what's been in front of my eyes all this time. But it's hard to know what will happen in a couple of weeks or months...or a year. Maybe that's why so many people want marriage? So they can forget that the future is always unknowable, something we can only hope for, but can't control?"

Clione slipped her hand into Reed's and squeezed. "Let's make a pact. Let's say that in a year, exactly a year, we'll come back here no matter where we are or who we're with, and we'll watch another sunset together, and at least you'll let me hold your hand. Even if you're still married. Even if *I'm* married. We'll come here by ourselves and hold hands. Just like this. We'll have *this* again."

"Just a sunset?"

"An amazing sunset."

"No sex? No fireworks?"

Clione leaned back, palms on her thighs, the points of her nipples showing through the thin cotton of her dress. "Okay, sure, we'll claw at each other like tigers on the top of the pyramid here until one of us screams louder than a howler monkey and the guards drag us away."

"Deal," Reed said. "One year. Here. Sex so loud the monkeys get jealous."

"And if one of us doesn't show," Clione looked thoughtful. "Then the jilted needs to toss himself or herself into Hell's Mouth, get impaled on spikes."

"Love or nothing," Reed said. "You better show because I'm not big on wooden stakes and all."

Clione extended her hand again. Reed shook it firmly, then kept it cupped in his own. He stroked the delicate veins, traced them as if following the contours of a river through a jungle map.

"It's so beautiful," Clione said. "The sunset. If you're lucky you get to see one spectacular show each day before the night comes."

They stood up, still holding hands. Some yellow still clung to the sky, a condensed stripe along the horizon, bright enough that the dark jungle below seemed a paper silhouette. Blueish night hung like a giant hand above it, pushing down, inexorable, sweeping the light away. They were silent as they descended the phantom steps, silent as they walked in single file back through the deserted pyramids to the parking lot. The guard had already left for the night; not even the dogs were there anymore. Just the lone car sitting in the deserted gravel lot, the blackness of the trees, and the blue canopy of night above them. A strong wind was blowing, dark tendrils of cloud wisps already blotting out the pinprick stars.

They got back in the car. Reed was about to ask where they should go next when he noticed the cellphone, its green missed-call indicator flashing like a firefly. He flipped open the phone and pushed the button for voice mail. For a few moments he couldn't recognize that the person at the other end was Dan, the voice was so angry.

"Reed, what the fuck is going on? Laurel's had a car accident, she's in the hospital. Mass General Hospital. Two floors below me. Which leaves me wondering how the hell she got *here* when you gave me all that crap about adopting a fucking kid. Probably she'll pull through but yesterday was touch-and-go. What the hell is going on? They called me because some EMT found one of your business cards in her purse and called the office looking for you. You get your ass on a goddamn plane and get back here. Your mancation is *over*. And whatever excuse you've got it better be so goddamn good it wins the Nobel fucking Prize."

Lance's Highway

Reed threw the car into gear and stomped on the pedal so hard that Clione had to grab for the handle to keep from being thrown against the door. A cloud of dust and gravel sprayed out behind them, then the car jumped forward as if hit from behind, turning so fast that Clione's head thumped the passenger's-side window. Neither of them said anything as Reed retraced the way along the unpainted road back to the main highway. When they reached the double lanes Reed pushed the pedal until it stopped against the floor. He flipped on the high beams and tightened his grip on the wheel as the tachometer needle moved into the six thousand range, from yellow to red. The tiny four-cylinder engine struggled to a top speed of one hundred and ten, and Reed kept it there, tense and ready, praying there wouldn't be anything in front of them as the vehicle devoured the night.

"Be careful, Hon," Clione whispered, still holding the door handle. "There could be anything out there. Potholes, animals."

Dogs.

* * *

The trip out had taken almost four hours; when Reed screeched to a stop at Tulum's only stoplight, sweat was beading on his forehead and his hands were shaking, but they'd made it back in just under an hour and forty-five. Clione slowly took her hand down. With her left arm she touched his thigh.

"Nice driving," she said, even though they both knew it had just been luck.

They waited for the light to turn green and realized that people were flooding the street, unusual for this time of night.

"Look," Clione said, pointing across the street, where at least forty cars were waiting all the way into the street. "Why's there such a long line for gas?"

The light changed. A few minutes later they passed the supermarket. There, too, the parking lot was full, the lights on inside. People hurried in and out of the supermarket carrying bags of groceries and plastic bottles of water, filling the beds of beat up pickup trucks with timber, plywood, and supplies.

"It's after ten," Clione said. "Something must be wrong."

Reed nodded. Taking the speed bump fast enough to catch air, he gunned it down the Avenida and pulled the car over beneath the youth hostel sign, bumping the passenger-side tires over the curb.

Marisol was waiting at the door. Her hair was loose, her usual serene expression replaced by a look of genuine fear.

"What's going on?" Clione asked, hugging Marisol. "You look terrible."

When Reed approached Marisol hugged him as well.

"You heard the news? The hurricane is heading directly for us," she said, her eyes wide. "It's already killed many people in Jamaica." Behind her he spotted Lance, naked to the waist standing on a step stool, sweat on his muscled arms gleaming in the lamplight. He was covering the courtyard windows with thick pieces of plywood, working at a frenzied pace, driving each nail in with two quick strokes, a short one to set the point in the wood, a second one to pound it home. The sound was like a heartbeat, thu-thump, thu-thump, in the background. He saw them and nodded briefly, then returned to the work at hand. "It's a Category 5," Marisol said. Her mouth trembled.

Reed remembered the images of Louisiana after Katrina. That was only a Category 4. He thought of the Watchtower, all its beachside cabañas. The entire town was only a few feet above sea level; the marshes and estuaries that once protected the land had been carved up for timeshares and hotels. A direct hit would wipe the town off the map.

"Marisol, I need to get home. Are there any more flights today?"

"You're leaving now? The buses, no, I think it's impossible. The buses are totally stopped. Everyone's preparing for the hurricane."

"I have to get to the airport. Tonight. Does Tulum have an airport?"

She shook her head. "No, the closest is in Cancún, but I think you're stuck. Planes are being canceled already."

Reed shook his head. "I *have* to get out. My wife's been in an accident. She's in the hospital."

Marisol pointed north. "Maybe just stay at the airport and see if you can get out if there's a lull?"

Lance, his torso glistening with sweat, came down from the ladder and crossed to where they were huddled in the entryway.

"You guys back already?"

"Reed has to leave."

"You should have stayed on the other side of the peninsula. This is one hell of a storm."

"I've never seen a Category Five storm," Clione said. "It's probably incredible."

A large convoy of military trucks rumbled past, beeping at the smaller vehicles to get out of the way. The wind picked up a newspaper, sending it fluttering upward, the pages separating one by one, up and up into the night until they were gone. Somewhere a donkey was braying, nasal and high-pitched and afraid. Reed felt a chill run down his spine. Marisol stepped into the road and stared after the vehicles.

"They're closing the roads, for sure."

"Somebody going somewhere?" Lance asked.

"My wife's had an accident. I have to get home. Tonight."

Lance looked out into the darkness where the trucks had gone.

"You're not going to get past the roadblocks now," he said. "So you're out of luck. Unless...." He paused.

"Unless what?"

"I haven't driven it in a couple of years," he said, using a T-shirt to wipe off the sweat. "But there's another route that leads to Cancún."

"Can you show me?" Reed said. "I've got everything here in the car."

Lance looked at the tiny rental and laughed. "You don't understand. I'm talking about a road that's not on the maps. For good reasons."

"This have anything to do with that bullet in the windshield?"

Lance shrugged. "Let's just say I'm confident the cops won't have roadblocks on it. But it ain't exactly a highway."

* * *

When they had said their goodbyes to Marisol, Lance led them to the battered CJ7 and held open the door for Clione. She pulled herself up, using her left arm for balance, doing most of the work with the right. Reed got into the passenger's seat in front of her, pushing his box of possessions up on top of the giant dive bag.

Lance hopped into the driver's seat, pulling the door shut and turning the key in one quick motion. After a check in the mirrors he pulled forward over the sidewalk and out onto the street.

A loose chicken scooted out of the way of a vehicle, got caught by a gust, and was twenty or thirty feet above them in the air, unable to make it back to the ground. The awkwardness of the bird, its unnatural height, the few feathers that came loose as it struggled to land itself, seemed unworldly, unreal. It had the same upward drift as a loose helium balloon.

"This storm's going to be a whopper," Lance muttered, tightening his grip on the wheel as the wind buffeted the vehicle. "We're already seeing just the very edges of it."

A palm leaf did cartwheels across the road in front of them, end over end, flattening itself against the metal grate of a closed storefront. Reed eased himself back into the worn nylon seat, holding the cardboard box so that it wouldn't knock around. In a few minutes they had left the lighted, four-lane stretch of Avenida Tulum and reached the Pemex. Twin lines of twenty or thirty cars waited for gas. Children played in the parking lot while their sisters supervised. Mothers clung to babies while burly, mustached fathers in cowboy hats and flannel shirts or guayaberas tapped impatiently against the rolled-down windows, smoking cigarettes that disappeared too fast, fiddling with seventies-era battery-powered transistor radios while nervously watching the sky. Children stood on the curbs trading mp3s on their cellphones, unconcerned about or even excited for the storm.

Beyond the gas station there were no streetlights. Reed knew the road made a straight line from Tulum through Playa del Carmen, Puerto Morelos, and finally to Cancún. He wished that the storm could track more northward, demolishing those ugly resorts. Let the damn insurance companies pay for it all. That's what they were there for, right? Why did the storm have to hit here, this beautiful, dusty town, with its simple, sweet people? Cancún was just a soulless tourist resort. Let the wind toss the Jet Skis through the plate-glass hotel windows. Would anyone except the insurance companies weep if all of that were to disappear? Couldn't the storm wipe Cancún clean, return it to coconut palms and jungle as it once had been?

Maybe then, Reed thought, he'd try going back there.

Nobody spoke as they traveled northward.

"See that?" Lance asked. His finger drummed against the windshield. In the far distance, Reed could just make out a reddish glow and the faraway flicker of strobes.

"That's the roadblock," Lance said, as he killed the lights. "But we're turning here."

Making a sharp right, Lance veered the Jeep off the highway and down a ravine so steep that Reed thought they were going to flip over. His head hit the roll bar, and he could hear Clione bouncing around in the back. The diving tanks thudded against the undersides of the seats.

"Jesus," Reed hissed.

"We'll turn the lights on again in a bit. We just have to get far enough away from the road."

They hit the bottom, splashing through a wall of water that drenched them completely. The engine sputtered, coughed, sputtered again. Lance worked the gearshift and popped the clutch and the ignition caught. There was a roar as the throttle opened, and the Renegade kept on going. In seconds, Reed's feet were wet. Water was seeping in from under the doors.

Only then did Lance turn the lights on, and then only the running lights. The dim yellow illuminated a sight like nothing Reed had ever imagined. All around him were the tangled gnarls of mangrove branches, some of the trees as thick as human thighs. Yet from where they'd entered and for as far as Reed could see into the darkness ahead of them was a single car-width channel cut so precisely that even the corners were square. It was exactly big enough for a Jeep.

A Jeep full of drugs, Reed realized.

Lance put the vehicle in neutral and pulled the emergency brake up. He reached down in front of the gearshift and pulled out a heavy plastic bag. He handed it to Reed.

"Ever shot a pistol before?"

Reed shook his head. "I'm not going to shoot anyone."

Lance laughed. "You won't have to. I don't think anyone uses this tunnel anymore and even if they do, tonight they'll be tending 'crops' in preparation for the hurricane. The gun's for gators. I've got to lock the hubs."

He checked the magazine, undid the safety, and shot a round off into the darkness. Reed and Clione jumped at the sound. A curl of powder residue lifted into the air. Reed smelled sulfur.

"It's easy. Point, pull, bang. Just get the gator before it gets me, because if it has a chance it'll do a death roll and I'll come up without a leg if I come up at all. "

Reed shook his head. "I don't think I can do it."

"Hopefully you won't have to."

Before Reed could say anything else Lance was waist-deep in the water, ducking under for fifteen seconds at the front driver's-side tire. Reed peered through the darkness trying to see anything. Lance came up, took a breath, walked to the other side of the car, and did the same thing for the passenger's-side hub. Even underwater, there was a faint click as the axle engaged with the wheel.

Lance got back in the Jeep, took the gun from Reed, flipped the safety back on, and tucked the pistol back in the hidden spot in the dash.

"Just FYI, nothing you've seen tonight goes out of this car," he said. "You guys never saw this highway. Never saw the gun. Memories go into vault. Close vault door. Toss key."

"You were a drug runner?" Clione asked. "How else would you know about this place?"

"It wasn't that I wanted to run drugs, Clee. Just that I was in love with staying in Mexico long before I fell in love with staying alive. It's not hard to change a windshield. Takes all of two seconds. But that bullet hole is like a tattoo. Reminds me to stay alive."

Lance put the Renegade into gear and it began to slosh and bump through the semi-darkness of the secret mangrove channel, climbing over sodden logs or submerged stumps with mule-like stability. Ghostly white egrets, surprised during their nighttime roost, lifted up on sleep-drugged wings and took off into the night like enormous albino bats. Twice Lance pointed out crocodiles. One was a tiny thing, smaller than an iguana, that plopped off a branch into the tea-colored water and disappeared. The other was so big that Reed couldn't tell where it began and ended; by the time they got close enough the water seemed to explode as the animal spooked.

After forty minutes the ground gradually dried out and became a two track stretch through tall, wispy scrub. They were doing at least fifty when Lance locked the brakes, fishtailing to a stop in a cloud of dust and leaf litter. Reed jounced and scraped on the seat spring, ripping a hole in his pants. A black cow completely blocked their path. It was inches from the hood, surveying the passengers with monastic serenity. Lance beeped the horn twice and the animal snorted, shook its hide, and finally sidled over to the edge of the road. Reed noticed two other cows peering out from the shadows.

"Way too close," Lance said. "Anyone shit their skivvies?"

"I didn't even see it. Nice braking. Glad I wasn't driving or we'd have hit it full on."

"Ugh," said Clione.

"That's why I say never drive at night here. You gotta expect an animal around every corner. Because one of those corners you're going to be right."

After another twenty or thirty minutes, their friend slowed down and took a sharp left. Chain-link fencing ran along their right side, topped with barbed wire. Only then did he put on the actual headlights, and after a minute or two they were back on the main highway. Reed let out a long sigh, glad to be back on asphalt again.

Clione took out her journal and began to write, scribbling more quickly when a car's headlights passed, illuminating the page, pausing when it was too dark to see. Twice Reed caught her looking at him and smiled. He wondered if his face showed a fraction of what he felt for her. He wanted to lean back, slip his hand through the space between the door and the seat, and hold her hand, caress her thigh, something, anything, to show her what he felt. But she was writing.

Looking at her, at the intensity, he could see it happening. Clione was right. She *was* going to be a writer. Because she already was one. He could help her, provide for her, protect her. She'd get novels written and published. They'd travel. Together they could work things out, maybe raise a family sometime. But not now, he thought. Not yet. He wanted her to be ready, ready enough to be able to love the child. It was okay, he realized. Everything was going to be okay.

Lance steered the car around debris and passing cars as if he were playing a video game, always with a smooth savoir-faire that Reed admired with a mix of bewilderment and awe. This man he hardly knew was doing so much to help him, help them, when exactly a week ago Lance had been jealous of him for stealing Clione away. Lance seemed to have everything he needed, in part by focusing all his energies on what really mattered. Tequila notwithstanding, there was no excess in Lance's daily routine. It was simple and rewarding, and gave him exactly what he needed. Lance had found stasis, peace. Reed wondered if he ever would.

As the car neared Playa del Carmen the traffic increased, slowed, and finally stopped. In the distance strobe lights were flashing, and eventually they inched past an accident in the median: a pickup truck full of people had rolled over into the oncoming lane. A woman lay uncovered at the curb, her torso split open, her face staring upward and unblinking into the night sky. In the flashing blue and red strobe Reed saw bloodstained family members holding onto each other, their faces contorted in grief. Nearby, someone was sobbing on hands and knees near the body of a small child.

"Don't look," Lance said quietly to Clione.

But Clione had already fixed her eyes on the scene, her face pale and her eyes wide. She craned her head as they passed by. Taking in details, Reed realized. Always *writing*. To Clione, this hurricane was just another experience to live through, just another event to pull details from, to remember so as to faithfully record.

The three were silent for the rest of the ride, each absorbing the details of the ride in his or her own way. When they reached Cancún Reed told Lance what hotel to head for, and they pulled onto Boulevard Kukulkán. The trip had taken only an hour and a half, but already the wind was blowing in more frequent gusts, whipping wraiths of sand up into the air, tossing plastic beach chairs into the palm trees or scattering wicker furniture into the immaculate hotel pools. The surface of the mangrove-rimmed lagoon had turned from the heavenly azure Reed remembered to a frothy slate-gray. Whitecaps ripped across the water, their tops torn off and flattened by the sharpness of the wind, and a beach umbrella, turning end over end, galloped across the road, leaped the small mangrove barrier like a gazelle, then sank quickly into the water on the other side. Reed remembered how unreal the ferry had seemed surrounded by jungle. Despite the wind he was seeing now, it still seemed unimaginable.

As they turned the sharp corner at the southern end of Kukulkán, Reed realized that there was a different attitude here. Tourists were laughing, plastic traveler cups full of beer in their hands, heading from beach to bar in their shorts and polo shirts as if nothing was happening. A baseball cap blew off its owner's head and went sailing across the street in great leaps, animated, like a wounded rabbit attempting escape. It was just entertainment for them.

They pulled up into the wide, manicured driveway of the hotel and stopped. Lance kept the engine running, waving "no" to the timid valet who had approached, looking askance, apprehensive about being required to park such a dirty vehicle amid a garage full of spotless Beemers and SUVs.

"He's just checking out," Lance said.

As Reed opened the door a gust of wind caught it like a bat's wing, and with a loud snap pulled it out of his hands, wrapping it around the front of the car. With effort, Reed managed to secure it back in place, though the force had bent the window frame, leaving an inch open at the top where the rain would get in.

"Don't worry about it," Lance said. "Just get your stuff, pay, and let's get to the airport."

* * *

The room was as sterile as it had been when they had left it, but it smelled stale, unused. The maids had left his stuff neatly on the luggage table, the open suitcase like an giant oyster on the half shell, clothes neatly folded inside. Looking at it, he felt a sense of revulsion, dread. The polo shirts and pressed pants seemed to mock him: This was the world he was returning to. If only briefly. It was what he had been, whom he had been.

He emptied the cardboard box into the suitcase, shaking the contents out quickly and then closing the latch, not bothering to arrange them further. He'd be home soon enough, he thought, and picked up the suitcase. He left the card key on the table with a twenty dollar bill under it and, after a quick look around, walked into the corridor. It smelled of carpet and cigarette smoke and men's aftershave. Reed returned to the elevator, luggage in hand. This time it was already packed, and he had to squeeze in and hold the bag up over his toes to fit. The elevator doors barely missed him as they closed.

Checkout was automatic: a swipe of the credit card at a computerized kiosk, a verification of the charges, a click on the screen, and it was done.

The CJ7 was where he'd left it. Lance was outside, trying to repair the damaged door with duct tape.

"Sorry about the door."

Lance shrugged.

Clione was now sitting inside in the front passenger's seat. She looked up briefly at Reed and smiled, then kept writing.

"Got everything?" Lance asked.

Reed nodded.

He lifted the heavy suitcase and slid it onto the seat, then climbed in afterward. Lance hit the gas as soon as the door was closed.

"When's your flight?"

"Tomorrow, seven a.m."

"No way will that flight run. You gotta get out tonight if you're gonna get out at all, man. If you wait, you'll end up stuck in the airport until the storm passes. And who knows, you might be stuck here until they've fixed the airport."

"I have a good feeling about it," Clione said. "He's going to make it."

"Nice to have a clairvoyant along, but when chickens are being ripped apart by the gusts most planes don't fly."

Clione shrugged. "I just think everything's going to be okay, that's all." She craned her neck back around and looked at Reed. Her lips pursed quickly in a kiss. Reed smiled. He wanted to lean forward, crush his mouth against hers, but it was impossible with Lance there. Love was a private thing, something meant for two people and only two. Not for spectators.

"Let's hope you're right," he said, holding her gaze, hoping she could see how much he wanted to kiss her.

Clione nodded. Lance pulled out into the oncoming lane to pass a pickup truck that was going too slowly, then veered sharply back again as soon as possible.

The airport was even busier than Reed had thought it would be, with a long line of cars waiting to find parking spaces, and dazed, frustrated tourists lugging hastily packed suitcases toward the terminal like a hive that had been disturbed. Lance pulled the Renegade up onto a grassy curb, bumping the two right wheels over the cement barrier. "I'll stay here," he said. "Make sure they aren't going to tow me."

Reed realized that Lance was really just making up an excuse for Clione and Reed to have a few moments alone inside.

"Thanks."

Lance shrugged. He extended his hand. Reed took it, shook it, and the two men smiled.

The wind whipped around them for a moment, so strong that it made the lampposts hum. Reed pulled the suitcase off the seat and let it drop with a thud, the plastic roller wheels sinking into the grass. Clione opened the door and slid out, the sudden wind lifting her sundress all the way to the middle of her thighs. The smooth skin seemed like alabaster in the cold light of the argon lamps. She kept her journal and pen in her hand as they walked inside. The air smelled wet and heavy and sweet, like crushed flowers.

Then a period of calm, as sudden as the wind had been, eerie, unnerving.

"You should change your ticket first," Clione said, slipping her fingers into his. It was her bad arm, the fingers limp and soft, like a baby bird. He held her hand gently, reassured by the warmth, by the fact that she felt comfortable enough to offer him her weak hand to hold. He slowly lifted the arm up to his mouth and kissed it. Clione blushed.

"You're silly," she whispered.

"I love you."

Clione nodded. "I know. I love you too."

The line for the ticket counter was a long snake that looped several times before entering the marked-off area. In front of him was a family of four, and every single one of them could have lost half their body weight and still needed to diet. The father was so wide that he barely fit between the tape-marked aisle. The mother, behind him, was only slightly thinner. She wore a tropical-print muumuu that hung like a tent off the precipice of her breasts, hiding everything but her toes. The son and daughter, both plugged into iPods, seemed so tuned out to anything else around them they might have been on drugs. Or maybe they were. In front of them was a thirty-something couple, also fat. Reed quickly scanned the aisle and realized that he and Clione were the only thin people there. Was that America? A country so full of excess that it couldn't see how obese it had become?

Everything seemed so perverse. A country full of liposuctions, of stomach-stapling, a country that had come unhinged like a giant ship with a broken anchor line. Everyone searching for happiness in drugs and therapies and promises of gluttony without consequences, when there *were* consequences. There always were. A country where politics had become a baseball game, a faith-based choice of this side or that one, forget the issues, forget the concept of information. Even the news media lost in a struggle to win ratings, to make money, to sell, sell, sell.

"I don't want to go back," Reed said.

Clione smiled. "You don't have to apologize."

"I don't want to leave you."

They waited, the line moving slowly toward the ticket counter. Uniformed girls with plastic ID tags and white gloves directed human traffic to this line or that. Loudspeakers blared information and flight cancellations that were unintelligible, lost in the din of the nervous, clamoring crowd. Neither spoke.

Finally they reached the counter, where a thin Mexican man with dark blue circles under his eyes took care of them.

"We have only a few flights tonight, Sir," he said. "All are delayed, of course. We can change your ticket but you will have to pay extra, almost the full fare."

Reed reached for his wallet. "I just need to get out of here as quickly as possible, so I can come back as quickly as possible." Clione gave his hand a little squeeze.

The man looked confused. "You need a round trip ticket?"

"No," Reed said. "I'm going back. I just plan to come back as soon as I can." As soon as he said it, it felt wrong. He should stay. He should *stay*.

The man frowned. He pecked at the computer, waited, pecked again. Eventually he nodded. "I can get you standby on the next flight," he said. "If there are no seats on that, then there is one other flight scheduled for tonight. But," he said, shaking his head. "I do not think it will make it. The storm too close. Is already very dangerous, you know. Right now."

"When is it boarding?"

"Right now, Sir. You should hurry."

"Right now?"

"Yes, Sir. If you don't want the seat I will give it to the person waiting behind you."

Reed paused, feeling robbed. He wanted time to sit with Clione, wanted to tell her something more. He'd imagined some time in the airport to just say a few last things, a lingering kiss.

He should stay.

"He'll take it," Clione said quickly, making the decision for him.

The man nodded, tapped in something on the keyboard, and printed out a boarding pass.

Only when they arrived at the security gate did Clione pull away.

"Take care of Sam, okay?" Reed said.

"She'll be waiting for you at the hostel."

"I guess this is goodbye." He swallowed.

"No," Clione said. "It's goodbye *for now*." She tucked her journal against her body with her left arm, then ran her fingers through his hair. "Whatever happens, we had a wonderful time together. Right? Nothing can take that away. And we'll get together soon. You'll figure things out. I will too. And in a year we watch the sunset at Ek' Balam."

Reed nodded, swallowing hard, trying to sound normal.

"Or toss ourselves onto the stakes."

Clione nodded. "Of course. So see you for a sunset. Top of the pyramid. Love or nothing."

"Right," Reed tried to laugh. "Love or nothing."

"Sir, please," a uniformed guard said. "You're holding up the line."

Reed bent and tasted her lips one last time. Her eyes were still closed when he pulled away, as if she were trying to remember the moment, fix it in her mind.

"Bye," he said. "Clione, you're the most magical person I've ever met."

"Catch your plane, Reed."

He turned, placed the contents of his pockets in the plastic tray, removed his shoes. When he turned back, she was still standing there, watching. She raised her arm, waved, kissed the air. She looked very young, suddenly, like a fifteen-year-old saying goodbye to an older brother going off to college for the first time.

"Bye," he said, knowing she couldn't hear him.

I love you, she mouthed. *Bye.*

He walked through security, returned his things to their appropriate pockets. He waved one last time, lifting himself up on his toes to better see her through the crowd. She still had her arm raised.

I love you too.

Day Eleven

Boston

When Reed stepped off the plane into the stale chill of the terminal ramp, he felt a hollow ache inside him from exhaustion far deeper than the lack of sleep he'd had because of the turbulence of the plane ride. Lance had been right: The Mexican pilot had gotten the plane out of Cancún, but just barely. After waiting for two hours on the runway, the wind howling so hard it made the plane's wings hum, twice they had been told they would return to the gate. Then, the plane bucking and shuddering like a mechanical bar bull, the pilot had gunned the engine and the machine had taken off, clawing its way up into the dark, wind-tormented night. For a full hour the gusts hammered at the fuselage like fists. Two of the overhead luggage racks cracked open, sending the contents showering down on passengers. Flight staff stayed strapped into their chairs, lips pressed together, eyes wide. But eventually they'd outrun the storm. Halfway through the flight they'd announced that it was safe to move about the cabin and people collected their scattered carry-on items as the attendants tried to serve drinks. One person nursed a lip split from a falling bag. Reed had eased back the seat, tried to stretch his legs in the cramped coach-class seat, and prayed for sleep. Clione had been right. He'd made it.

Only when he saw the familiar skyline of the Hancock and Prudential towers from the plane window, the Charles River, the Zakim Bridge, did he feel a sense of calm; something settled within him again that had been gone the whole time he'd been away. Looking down at Boston from above. This was his home. He wanted to be in the copter. He didn't deserve to be anywhere else but Boston. He deserved to be cold and dreary and depressed.

Even though he knew Laurel wouldn't be waiting for him at the

261

gate, he still somehow expected to see her there, a remnant of happier times when she'd always wait for him in baggage claim, whether or not he had checked luggage. They'd have Thai food at a cellar-level greasy spoon across from Boston University before going home. The memory came back sharply. They would eat Indonesian fried rice and laugh about how spicy it was. Laurel would chatter like a songbird about what had happened while he was gone – how the cars were acting, which light bulbs she'd had to replace, what he should call the landlord about. Mere minutiae, but somehow it always made him feel he was home. He realized that he'd been happy with her, really happy. Once upon a time. There was more to being with someone than keeping the downstairs neighbors awake with your noisy headboard.

Now Reed waited in the packed baggage claim area, cold, tired, and alone. A hundred other bedraggled tourists milled about in the stale airport air, perking up at the buzzer like a pack of Pavlov's dogs. When his suitcase arrived he noticed the wheels were still clogged with dirt from being dropped onto the grass at Cancún International. One was permanently maimed by the dirt and went clack-clack-clack in a semicircle instead of rolling.

Reed lifted his arm and flagged a taxicab.

"Mass General Hospital," he said to the driver, as the man eased into traffic.

"You return from vacation?"

"You could call it that."

Reed leaned back in the seat and stared out the window at the green copper roofs and brownstones, at the cherry trees with their cold, leafless fingers scraping at the sky. He stared unseeing as people walking their dogs picked up poop in sterile baggies to invert and put into the trash. Someone behind them beeped as soon as the light turned green, and Reed had a sudden urge to leap out of the taxi and shout at the guy. The horn should be used out of fear, he thought. Not frustration. Don't people have meaningful things to care about? He opened the window a crack, letting the icy air calm him. It seemed as cold as it had been that morning in Beverley. The near-crash seemed impossibly far away now, as if decades — not weeks — had slipped by.

As they neared the hospital, Reed's palms and mouth went dry. The car pulled up, parked. Reed paid the driver two twenties and told him to keep the change. He stood at the emergency entrance, watching as the taxi made a U-turn and sped off to catch the yellow light before it changed to red. On the curb there was ice already, slick gunmetal gray buildup that would need rock-salt or it would be there til May. Had it snowed already? Stepping carefully to avoid slipping, he picked up his suitcase and walked into the fluorescent glow.

A receptionist looked up. "May I help you?"

Laurel's Accident

Laurel was lying on her side with her back to the door when the nurse practitioner had shown him to the room. A translucent nasal cannula was strapped in place with satiny tape. Beside her, an intravenous bag hung from a wire rack. Reed braced himself on the threshold for a moment, his knees threatening to buckle under him. Somewhere under there was Laurel.

"Honey?" he whispered. "It's me."

For a few seconds he thought she was asleep. Then she shifted slightly.

"Reed?"

He went to the side of the bed near the window so she didn't have to turn over to see him. He crouched down and smiled at her. She looked so gaunt and thin and pale.

"What happened?"

She blinked a few times and moved her mouth as if to say something, but Reed couldn't catch any words.

"Just take it easy. Everything's going to be okay."

"Reed," she whispered. "Hi, honey. It's good to see you."

"Shhhh," Reed said. "Just rest. We've got all kinds of things to talk about. But it can wait."

"I was with...a friend."

"What?"

"I was with someone. Is he okay?" Laurel raised herself slowly up on one elbow. "He was driving and I think if he was okay they would have told me."

It was the insistence in her voice that told him everything. He would learn the details later: how his wife and lover had slid on black ice inside the Big Dig tunnel, how the car had been so mangled it was a miracle both of them survived. But he felt nothing, really, and he breathed in and out, in and out, in and out, as she spoke. Instead of anger, he felt as if his entire insides had become blackboard chalk and husk, mixed with mild relief, mixed with the longing to have never gotten on that plane. He'd left the girl he loved to...to go through some official rite of leaving, some obligation that assumed Laurel to be blameless, pure, and needing him.

He stepped back from the bed and leaned against the cold plate glass, looking at the person in front of him. "You could have told me," he whispered.

"I'm sorry," she said.

"Let me find out for you," he said. "Let me find a doctor. You just rest, Laur."

Reed pushed open the door with his shoulder and stumbled out into the sick ward to find the answers Laurel was looking for. He walked down the corridor for what seemed like days until he found a desk and receptionist.

"I need to find answers about my wife's accident," he said. "Can I get them from you?"

She was looking at him as if she were a bank teller and he'd just slipped a note that said to put all the cash in a bag. He imagined a secret button beneath the counter she could press, where seconds later security would arrive.

"My wife. Laurel Haflinger. Room 314."

"Hold on, Sir. I'll get someone who can help you." She picked up the phone and dialed. "Someone will be here right away."

He waited, wondering what kind of distraction led to the accident. Was it wrong to think they were lovers? How had he missed the signs? And for how long? It didn't matter, really, nothing mattered, he just wished he'd known, known way back before, so there'd have been time to...to what? To fix things? To cut it cleanly? Everything was muddled and gray.

A man in a white coat turned a corner and approached from a different corridor. He was tall, young, and had bright orange sneakers that matched his I'm-too-busy-for-this-now attitude. He introduced himself as another nurse's assistant.

"Her friend? We can't release his name."

"But he's alive."

The man squinted. "He's in intensive care. An induced coma. He may make it or he may not."

"Where is he?"

"Sorry, I can't offer more without violating HIPAA laws. I know you're concerned."

"Will my wife be all right?"

"She was lucky. Got knocked around a bit but the airbags probably saved her life. She'll pull through."

"How soon until she's out of the hospital?"

"Weeks, not days. But whether it's two or seven depends on how fast she heals." An alert came over the intercom and he looked down the hall. "I've got to get back to my rounds. She'll be fine."

By the time Reed went back, Laurel was asleep. He sat in the room's only chair and watched the machines suck and pump and keep her alive until at some point he fell asleep, too.

Day Twelve

The Wait

B ecause it was closer to the hospital than their apartment, because
it was right on the T and they no longer had a car, because he
didn't want to field calls from Dan, and because he couldn't bear
to return to the apartment they'd shared, Reed checked himself into
the Kenmore King Hotel, a fancy new place with faux European
molding that overlooked the B Line tracks and the neon Citgo sign.
He and Laurel had found it appalling and ostentatious and made fun
of it each time they'd passed by; he'd sworn never to stay there, but
four hundred thirty-seven dollars later, he was overlooking Kenmore
Square with gin-and-tonics downed and a third sloshing around in
his glass. Below him the square was empty, the Sox fans hibernating
until spring training began.

The next morning he woke up to a headache and a driving rain
slamming against the window panes and eleven more missed calls
from Dan. Reed watched as cars splashed pedestrians down in the
street below and the giant triangle illuminated the square with red,
white and blue neon. He opened the bar cabinet above the sink and
scanned the skyline of green and brown bottles in front of him. Each
bottle was like a skyscraper in miniature. He imagined a city made to
look like a liquor cabinet. Why not? People could talk about the
Tanqueray building, the Bombay Sapphire, the delicious café at the
top of the Myers Dark. He pulled out the heavy green bottle of gin,
uncapped it, and filled a tumbler half full and topped it with tonic.
He carried the drink into the living room, sat down on the couch, and
turned on the television.

Guys in spandex briefs were hurling each other around a boxing ring.
Click.
An evangelist bemoaned loss of family values.
Click.

A diamond ring could be *his* if he called now.

Click.

Then the news. A giant storm was over Yucatán peninsula, the satellite image a swirl of fury, the winds highlighted in spokes of pink and blue. He finished his drink in three long swallows, watching images of palm trees snapped like toothpicks, of Volkswagen Bugs tossed through walls, of fishing boats lifted up and carried miles inward by the twenty-foot-high storm surge. He felt sick to his stomach. He reached for the remote control and lost his grip, and he watched as it skittered across the rink of the coffee table before landing softly underneath the couch.

He left it there. Reed stood up, got the bottle of gin, returned to the couch, and stayed on the couch, staring at the ceiling, balancing the bottle on his stomach as if it were a baby. From time to time he lifted the bottle to his lips, took a slash, returned it to the coffee table. The alcohol began to make his fingers and toes tingle, normally a pleasant sensation, but before the feeling moved up through his body the bottle was empty and he felt nauseated. He kept balancing the green glass cylinder on his stomach for a while, nudging it this way or that with a finger when it was about to topple. And it eventually did, slipping off to the right, contacting the hard oak edge of the coffee table and exploding, the scattered shards jungle-green, like parrots.

Reed lay on the couch, getting up only twice to crunch, crunch, crunch across the floor to the bathroom. Once to pee. Once to vomit.

At some point he drifted off.

Boston. Home, sweet home.

Day Thirteen~Day Eighteen

Damage

Laurel improved slowly. He would go to the hospital, say hi, try to keep the topic away from anything important, anything he really wanted to say. On the third day she confirmed that his guesses were accurate.

"I'm sorry," she said, sounding infinitely tired. "I don't want to throw everything away. I didn't mean to hurt you. We were both yearning for something, right? I wasn't making you happy, I needed some freedom — "

"You weren't letting me be a part of your life anymore," Reed said, partially rising up from his chair. "You pushed me away and pushed me away and pushed me away. Don't make it out like anything's *my* fault. I was trying everything I could to keep us together. And the moment I stopped trying, that's when it fell apart." Reed wondered why he was even arguing. He didn't care if he won or lost, was wrong or right. All he wanted was to end things and leave. "Anyway, all of that doesn't matter anymore. Because I met someone too. She took me diving."

Laurel focused somewhere through Reed, several rooms behind him. She gently pulled off the translucent green mask that covered her mouth. "You went swimming?"

"Not just swimming. *Diving.*"

"Diving?! You? In a mask and tanks and — " she stopped and laughed. "I wish I'd seen it, honey."

"I wish you had, too."

"If she got you into the water, you love her more than you ever loved me." Laurel sat forward and then slowly slid back against the pillow. She put the mouthpiece back in and closed her eyes, breathing heavily. "I can't call the kettle black."

"I'm in love with her," Reed said. He felt acutely aware of the sounds of the machinery: drips and ticks and humming. "I'm taking the next plane I can get and I'm leaving Boston. We'll figure everything out, okay? But I'm leaving. I'm moving to Mexico."

* * *

Reed called Dan on the subway back to the hotel, the phone again dropping the call twice as it had when he'd first arrived in Mexico. He let Dan yell at him and simply held the phone away from his ear until there was a pause long enough for him to speak.

"I'm sorry, Dan. Really."

"You better be. Because dammit, you know what this damn hospital has done to me? All that time to think? I've been thinking that maybe it's time for me to move up in the world. And by that I mean retire."

"Retire?"

"Yes. I've got things I want to do, Reed. Maybe I seem like my whole life revolves around this station but there was a time way back when, when I wanted to travel. See the world. I'm thinking it's time I started checking off some of those items on the bucket list before I run out of time."

"What's all this got to do with me?"

Dan paused. "Until you went fucking AWOL on me I was pretty sure that you'd be the right person to replace me. I don't want to make it sound like it's tomorrow. But in six months, a year. Maybe we can get you out of that chopper and — "

"Dan — "

"Hear me out. I know, I know, you don't know what to say and don't know how to thank me, it's fine."

"I'm not staying, Dan. I quit."

There was a long pause.

"What?"

"I'm leaving Boston. I'm moving to Mexico."

"You've got a cruel sense of humor to play tricks on a guy with a bum ticker. Don't fuck with me."

"I'm done. That's why I called."

Dan's voice changed. "Reed, ah, I know what you're doing. You're upset about that message I left. You know how I get."

"I haven't listened to it, don't need to, don't care. I'm not even listening to you now, Dan. Being in the chopper is the only thing I ever loved about this job. And I've worked my ass off for a decade and what's it gotten me?"

"It's gotten you *ahead*, Reed. You're the best cameraman the station's got."

"It's gotten in the way."

"In the way of what? Being poor?"

"In the way of being happy."

"Reed, we need you. You've got an obligation to the station. To me."

"I wish I could help, Dan. But in a way, we're kind of in the same boat. Only I'm going to start checking off my bucket list twenty years sooner. So there's time to live before I die."

"This is about pussy, isn't it? You're in lust. Okay, take another couple weeks, get the fucking out of your system, and we can talk about it when you get back."

"Goodbye, Dan. Been nice working with you."

* * *

Returning to the hotel in the rain, Reed put the "Do Not Disturb" sign on the door and lay on the sofa, watching the news as the Category 5 hurricane exited Yucatán. In what little coverage there was of Mexico, reporters all said the same thing: "Luckily, the tourist resort of Cancún has been spared." Reed wondered if Clione and Lance had made it back to Tulum. He flipped the channels so frequently that after the third day his thumb was sore. By then most forecasters had, in their meteorological narcissism, returned to local forecasts. Once he saw a report showing footage of the ferry that Lance had shown him: The newscaster, safely out of the dangerous eye of the storm, was passing off shots of that ancient vessel in the jungle as if it were current news, put there by this current storm. Only a Mexican channel in Spanish kept broadcasting footage of the actual devastation. Reed watched the images of bodies and buildings crushed as if they were eggshells, of dogs left bloody and terrified on rooftops, of fire burning on oil and gasoline slicks.

He wept until the tears stopped coming; he prayed.

Periodically he would dial the international operator and ask the computer-simulated voice to place a call to Tulum. The call would go through to a busy signal, and he would listen to the beep-beep-beep until the line clicked off and went silent. He was not hungry: When there were no more peanuts in the minibar, he stopped eating altogether. When the gin was gone, he drank whiskey; when the whiskey was gone he drank the vodka; when that was gone he drank crème de cassis and Drambuie and finally the bottle of Rose's grenadine. When he needed to vomit, he staggered into the bathroom and sat on the edge of the tub, propping himself up with his elbows above the splattered porcelain bowl. Sometimes he woke up with the damp, musty bathmat pulled beneath his head like a crumpled pillow.

He didn't shower; he didn't shave; he didn't shit.

The maid came to the door, dropped a fresh newspaper through the door slot, knocked and asked if the room needed making up and Reed always answered that he was fine.

On the sixth day of getting that busy signal, Reed threw the telephone into the wall, leaving a baseball-size hole in the plaster and spewing the receiver's silicon insides around, shattering the emerald-green plastic populated by transistors and resistors and capacitors, neatly arranged, like ants collected into military formation.

It was dark out when he woke up. He didn't know the time or what day it was. Stabbing pain tore through his right temple, worse every time he moved. He stared up at the drop ceiling so long without blinking that everything went white, then orange, then white. When he held his eyes closed he saw the ceiling in perfect detail, the overhead light, the framed Doug West silkscreen print in neon blacks and blues, like staring at a film negative.

He lifted himself into a sitting position and stayed there, cradling his head in his hands. The yeasty scent of the empty liquor bottles made his abdomen contract. He retched, a stream of thin, colorless bile trickling onto the rug. He wiped his mouth with the skin of his forearm.

He crossed the room and sat down at the large mahogany writing desk that was the centerpiece of the room. It had curled legs that ended in carved animal feet and drawers that slid open and closed silently, effortlessly. The center lifted up on a ratcheting slide to offer the writer more or less of an angle, and a thick piece of maroon blotting leather offered just the right amount of yield for a pen to smoothly glide.

It was a reproduction of a desk very similar to one that had been given to him by his grandfather, one that had been passed down for generations. His grandfather's, his grandfather's father's, his great-grandfather's father's. He ran his fingers over the wood, missing the age-feathered chamois of the leather blotting pad on his one back home. He lifted up the center and felt it lock into position, about a ten-degree angle. He wanted to give that desk to Clione. She would love it, she would love writing at it. He could picture her tilting her head as she thought about something before touching her pen to the paper. Its shelves filled with journals of a hundred thousand travels.

In the drawer to his left he found a pad of pale green stationery with the Kenmore King logo across the top, and a collection of matching ballpoint pens. He selected one, shook it to get the ink flowing, and scribbled to make sure it would write. Then he began a letter. Halfway through he tore the sheet off the pad and started over again. Soon the floor was littered with crumpled pieces of paper.

> *I love you, Clione.*
>
> *I love you, and I never knew what those three words meant until I met you and shared what we've shared.*
>
> *From the moment that our eyes met that day in Cancún at the pool, to the last moment when we parted in the airport, to the moment right now that I sit here, hung over and heartsick, I have loved you. I feel embarrassed, ashamed almost, at how deeply I fell into love with you. I'm not a religious person, but perhaps I was a martyr in some past life, I must have been, to be lucky enough to have met you. To share everything we've shared.*
>
> *Whatever Laurel and I had, we had it years ago. The biggest reason she and I stayed together is because we somehow just felt we were expected to. I told her as much as she needed to know, and I was happy to be gone. The irony? She was with someone too.*
>
> *I don't know what you'll think when you get this letter, what part of your life you'll be in. Maybe you've already moved on. But I don't care whose child you're carrying, I don't care if you feel you can't bear a child right now. I want to help you become the writer you know you can be. I can support you, help you financially, be whatever you need. It's funny, somehow the one thing I wish I could*

> bring with me is this massive writing desk that's been in
> my family for years. I want to see you sitting at it, think
> perhaps it inspires your next great work of literature.
>
> And if you need me to leave you, or you realize that
> I'm no longer the person you love, I understand. If
> you love Lance, I'll understand. He's the other possible
> father, right? I like him. He's a good man.
>
> I'll accept anything, go on through the motions of
> my life, as long as I know you're out there somewhere,
> writing and living and flashing your magical smile.
>
> I feel ashamed putting any of this into words.
> You're the writer. No matter what happens, know that
> those few days we had together were the best thing
> that every happened to me. They always will be. Thank
> you for showing me the depth of the meaning of that
> special word: love. I never understood it, never
> understood anything, until meeting you.

He paused for a long time, his hand over the pages as if ready to crumple them. Then he finished, his hand shaking as he continued:

> Yours, but while I know you say we never own
> people, we only borrow them, share them for a while, I
> want to thank you for letting me borrow you. I also
> want to be yours. Yours in whatever way I can be,
> even if that's just to be your postcard friend. But I
> can't wait to hold you, kiss you, be with you. I hope
> that's what you want too.
>
> Yours, yours, yours. Forever and always...yours.
> Reed

When he finished writing he folded it twice and put it into an envelope, not daring to read it over again. He ran his tongue along the glue, moistening it, and pressed the flap firmly down onto the paper. The folded paper crane she'd given him was sitting on the surface of the desk, so polished that it almost looked like there were two.

But where should he send it? Had she made it home? Or was she still in Yucatán?

He shook his head, pressed his hands to his temples to try to stop the pressure in his brain.

Think.

Just think.

She would still be in Yucatán, but had she gone back to Tulum? Perhaps the Welcome Wanderer could forward the mail to her. He had to send it there. He dug in his pants pocket for a receipt from the Welcome Wanderer. He pulled the crumpled piece of paper out, smoothed it with his fingers. The address was smudged but readable:

> *Clione Roux*
> *c/o The Welcome Wanderer*
> *Avenida Tulum*
> *Tulum, Quintana Roo, CP 77780*
> *MEXICO*

He sat down again and, tearing open the envelope, he copied the entire letter again, word for word. Clione had written a smiley face next to her address in the origami crane she'd handed him on their trip to Ek' Balam. He copied the Oregon address exactly onto the other envelope.

With the two letters in his hand, Reed left the hotel for the first time in a week. The sun made him squint, and for most of the walk to the post office he had to hold his hand over his forehead to keep the stabbing pain away. He had no jacket, and the late-autumn air made him shiver. Branches were bare. Gusts of wind pushed brown leaves into cartwheels. Mothers pushed baby carriages with their infants wrapped up tightly. Young professionals walked dogs. Squirrels hopped here and there, digging in the ground to bury acorns for next spring.

Reed was hunched over and shaking by the time he reached the post office. There was no line. The blond postal worker took a step backward as Reed approached the counter, as if she were about to be mugged. She was pudgy, with long, well-manicured nails. A button advertising Star Wars Postage Stamps was pinned above her name tag.

Reed spread the two letters out on the counter top.

"What's the fastest this can get to Mexico, Evelyn?" Reed asked.

The woman looked at him a moment before punching a code into the computer. "Well, first class would get it there in — "

"I need it there tomorrow," Reed interrupted.

"You need Global Express Guaranteed."

"And that can get it there tomorrow?"

"It's our fastest service, Sir. You can track it online too."

"But can it get there tomorrow? There was a hurricane. I need to get it there as quickly as possible. Is that the fastest way?"

"I'm not familiar with other mail delivery options. Perhaps they're faster. But if you want to use *our* services, Sir, then this is the best way to go. The computer's telling me it will be there tomorrow, and you can track it online if you have a computer."

"How much?"

Her fingers clicked on the keypad. "Fifty-five dollars." She handed him a cardboard envelope with red and gray stripes. "I'll need you to fill out the address on here, Sir. And a customs form."

"It's just a letter. I have to fill all that out just for a piece of paper?"

"They treat it like a package, Sir, because it's going Global Express Guaranteed. Just fill out the form."

"How about this one?"

Evelyn checked the postal code. "To Oregon? It would be seventeen fifty-five."

She nodded.

"It's the same letter," he said, smiling faintly. "She's the girl I'm in love with. I just don't know which place she's in."

Evelyn paused before pressing the postage label onto the upper right corner of the envelope. "That's very interesting, Sir. Covering all the bases. Very thorough."

"Also Global Express Guaranteed?"

Reed nodded.

* * *

Ten minutes later, shivering again, Reed pushed open the glass door of the university travel agent. Several racks of brochures lined the walls, along with posters for exotic island destinations. There were two agents, their makeup done perfectly, their hair tied up in prim buns. One had hawkish features, a sharp nose and tight lips that gave off an aura of prim rigidity. The other had jet-black hair and was Asian, maybe, her hair so glossy he could practically see his reflection. She was compulsively twirling her pen in a way that Reed found annoying. The girls exchanged a quick glance as soon as Reed entered the door. The Asian girl motioned for Reed to have a seat in front of her.

"Can we help you, Sir?"

"I need to get to Mexico as quickly as possible. Cancún. Tulum, actually, if I can fly direct there."

The girl shook her head. "Everything's canceled right now."

Reed took three hundred-dollar bills out of his pocket and placed them on the counter. "This is a bounty. I don't care how you do it. I don't care if you route me through India first and then to Rio before I end up in Cancún. I don't care if you charter me a helicopter and it drops me into Tulum by parachute. Just find me the very first plane out of here."

The girl stared at him, then looked quickly at the other agent, who shook her head almost imperceptibly. The Asian girl slowly pushed the money back toward Reed.

"A bribe isn't going to get you there any faster, Sir. It's just that there aren't any flights."

"Will you take the money and keep checking until there is one?"

"I'll keep checking for you. You can keep the money."

She pulled a keyboard out on a sliding tray beneath the desk.

"Now, what's your name, Sir?"

"Reed, Reed Haflinger." He gave her his name and address, contact info, and she assured him they'd get him on the next flight possible. He nodded silently as she went over the details of the arrangement, and shook her hand when he was through. The handshake caught her off guard, and for a moment her fingers went limp as he shook, then instead of removing it, she left her hand there until he finally released his own fingers.

She smiled again, brushing back her hair.

"We'll do the very best we can for you, Mr. Haflinger."

He returned to the hotel room. Housekeeping had done its work: The bed was spotlessly made up and the bar completely refilled. He opened a new bottle of Tanqueray and sat down again at the desk.

> *Dear Laurel,*
>
> *I am deeply and profoundly sorry about what's happened to us. Love between two people can be defined only by two words: whatever works. What we had stopped working long ago, and we tried for a while to fix it or pretend that we could rewind our lives, then we tried to ignore it, but in the end, we were just two hollow husks moving through our lives. I can't blame you for what happened when the same thing was happening with me. I just wish we could have done things differently somehow. Kept what we had. But we didn't. Right? That's really all we can say. We*

> *didn't.*
>
> *I didn't choose to fall in love again, if that helps at all. Love chose* me.
>
> *I am going away, for good. I will write in a few weeks regarding the apartment. Basically, with a few minor exceptions, I think everything in it should be yours. I will stay in Mexico. Start a new life there with the girl I met. What's here in Boston means nothing to me.*
>
>   *Apologies and fondness.*
>   *Reed*

He took out his wallet and removed Laurel's photograph. He folded the paper in thirds and then slipped the photo into the middle. He licked the envelope and sealed it. After searching for his sister-in-law's name in the address book by the phone, he wrote Laurel's name and "c/o Audrey Lafferty" on the outside. He peeled a stamp from the roll and pressed it onto the upper-right-hand corner. He was done.

The telephone rang, the loudness of it making him jump up from his chair.

It was the woman from the travel agency.

"There's been a cancellation," she told him. "It will be expensive, but we can get you on tomorrow's flight."

"Book it," Reed said. "I'll be there."

Day Nineteen

Arrival, Again

Cancún airport looked almost the same as it had when Reed left, save that in the parking lot a few palm trees had uprooted, and as he walked through the crowd of touts he saw that a few panes of glass were cracked and others had been covered over with plywood. A large yellow bulldozer was nosing around behind a line of parked cars, but if Reed hadn't been looking for evidence of the hurricane, he wouldn't have known the airport was doing anything but routine construction.

It was an hour south, as the bus passed Playa del Carmen, that Reed felt the hair on his neck prickling from fear. Every single tree was damaged; those that remained rooted had large branches missing, and the canopies were marred by gaping yellow gashes in the trunks where limbs had been stripped away. Smaller trees had toppled or been broken. Leaves on the fallen branches were already turning brown. The storm had torn every leaf off the mangrove trees, leaving them as bare and naked as if they were winter oaks back home.

Construction crews were already repairing the road, sawing up the trunks of trees that had been pulled off to the side. Swarthy men, shirtless and sweaty, were winching abandoned cars out of ditches, pulling the vehicles onto 1950s-era flatbed Fords and Chevys so they could be inspected and repaired. Vehicles that could not be salvaged would be left where they were in the jungle. Creeper vines would cover whatever didn't sink into the *manglar* swamps. In a few months, new branches would bud from the base of the torn trunks, and thick emerald foliage would emerge to soak up the sun.

The bus lurched as it crossed over the median into the other lane. A long stretch of Highway 307 had simply disintegrated: The water and wind had simply ripped up the tar like a person pulling a runner of carpet off a flight of stairs. Large pieces of sun-softened asphalt hung in the trees, draped over the jungle canopy on the leeward side like pieces of whale blubber that had been cut up and left to dry.

The passengers were quiet, dirty, tired, scared. Many carried possessions tied up in sheets or pillowcases. One old woman sat in the front, sobbing softly, with two boys and a little girl crammed into the seat beside her.

The driver slowed at a speed bump and a young boy got on. Reed remembered it as the same place where the old woman had given him the orange, weeks ago. The youth was wearing a brilliant white button-down shirt and a gray cowboy hat with a wide brim that seemed too large for his head. He had a battered, nylon-string guitar, and after a short introduction and thank you, he began to play. Reed remembered what Clione had said at the Watchtower: Music is the heart of Mexico. As he listened, Reed felt odd, the combination of exhaustion from the flight, the stress of the trip, the anticipation of the return made him dizzy. He felt as if he were in church: The bus seats turned to pews, the song a hymn, the boy elevated from busker to the voice of God. The child's face, so young and pure, the richness of the song, and the simple melody made something well up inside Reed's chest, and he began to weep. He turned his head to the window, put his hand up to his eyes to shield the tears from view.

The boy sang three songs and then made a brisk pass through the aisle, his cowboy hat extended like a collection plate. Reed had not remembered to change money at the airport and put a twenty-dollar bill in among the ten-peso coins. The boy nodded a brief, professional approval and continued to the back, then got off the bus at the next stop. Reed watched him scoop the money into his pocket and cross the street, as cocky as a crow.

For a short time, Reed nodded off into dreamless darkness.

When he opened his eyes as the bus pulled into the station in Tulum, Reed felt as if he had awoken into the apocalypse.

After the Storm

The iconic green Pemex sign that had acted as the unofficial welcome beacon to the town of Tulum was lying like a downed soldier among green shards of emerald plastic. The head of the sign was snapped off; the inside cables spilled out like a giant arm that had been deveined, sparks still dancing inside the bird's nest of wires. The gasoline pumps had been tipped over, some of them covered with grayish-white foam where the extinguishers had activated. Behind, in the jungle, a pump hose snaked through the tops of the trees, the handle poised perfectly like a python about to strike.

Someone had pulled off the heavy iron lid to the gasoline holding tank, and a small group of children was lowering a battered plastic pail down into the depths to withdraw the liquid inside. Only one car was there waiting; behind it was a line of men, women, and children lined up with tubs and buckets and old pineapple juice cans, all waiting for a fill.

As the bus pulled past the rotary, Reed could glimpse the damage to the town. Giant blocks of wave-scrubbed concrete were strewn across the sidewalks, hastily deposited by military backhoe and front-end loaders to allow passage on the road. Several army trucks were stopped to direct traffic safely around obstacles that hadn't yet been removed.

No building taller than one story was still standing; many had been flattened completely, just square patches strewn with garbage where houses had been. The storm had stove in balconies, torn off entire second stories, lifted bookcases and beds and shattered them against the neighboring walls. As the bus pulled nearer to the station, Reed saw one store he remembered, the place where he'd bought his guayabera shirt. It had been slashed by the storm as if the building were the stomach of a samurai: its contents, colorful blankets and clothing and piñatas and ceramics, littered the surrounding debris like entrails.

When the bus pulled up outside what had once been the bus station, Reed's hands were shaking. He stumbled down the steps and into the baking sun. The row of plastic chairs still waited for passengers, covered with a layer of mud that had dried and pulled away, like slabs of thick animal hide. Moments later, he was at the Welcome Wanderer. He hardly recognized it. The entire front facade of the hostel had been flattened, leaving the inside courtyard at the mercy of the wind and the waves. The picnic tables where he'd first met Lance and Ambrose were split and crumpled at the far back wall. The storm had torn off the palapa roof of the bungalow, then crushed the walls, leaving only round piles of debris that had once been such wonderful cabañas. Books, their backs broken, pages ripped and mudlogged, lay in piles where they'd settled as the floodwaters had receded. A lone pipe, complete with oversize shower head, stuck up from one pile of wreckage like a steel sunflower.

Carrying his small bag in one hand, he stood for a moment in the dust and diesel, trying to imagine how this could have been the same location he'd been only few weeks before. Reed sat down where the bar had been, sitting on a concrete block, a rainbow of broken glass at his feet. He put his head between his hands, overwhelmed with sorrow.

Where was Clione? Marisol? Lance?

What had happened while he was gone?

Dread tickled the base of his neck and his spine. He had to talk to people, find out what had happened. Leaving his bag against one of the inner courtyard's crumbled walls, he walked back out to the street.

Not a single building had remained unscathed. Most were unrecognizable, as ruined as the Welcome Wanderer. He felt a tap on his shoulder.

"Reed? Reed, is that you?"

Reed turned, and for a moment didn't recognize the slender Mexican woman in front of him. Her hair was tied back beneath a bandanna, and she had no makeup—her dusty face looked pale and faded, and a deep gash ran from her cheekbone almost to her ear. Dirt had dried in the wound.

It was Marisol. Seconds later Samantha leaped on him, covering his face with sloppy kisses before flopping to the floor for a belly rub.

"Oh, oh Reed," she said, collapsing into his arms. "It means everything to see you." She began to sob, her fingers digging into his back for support. He held the shaking woman in his arms, feeling again the sense of disembodiment that comes with disbelief. "We...it is all," her voice broke again, then, as if she were drowning, she gasped. "All gone."

"Where are the others?" Reed asked quietly, stroking Marisol's hair. She stayed buried in his arms. "Are they okay?"

The girl didn't look at him. Tears welled up in her eyes. "She's gone," she sobbed. "She and Lance...they're both gone."

Marisol closed her eyes and began gently rocking back and forth, foot to foot, as if she were floating on the water instead of standing on firm ground. Reed waited, holding her in his arms but feeling as if he were a balloon that had slipped from a child's fingers and was floating up, up, up into the stratosphere. He felt as if he could see the town below him and its people working like ants to rebuild, he could see tiny toy trucks and bulldozers pushing dirt around. He floated higher and higher until the whole Yucatan peninsula stretched like a map below him, a mitten sticking up into bright blue water, dividing the Caribbean from the Gulf of Mexico. He kept floating upwards until he was in the cold, empty blue-black of space, the world below him a curious glass bead, its people and its problems impossibly insignificant and small.

* * *

Later, back at the Welcome Wanderer, they sat on pieces of the broken inner wall, sharing a loaf of hard bread and a bottle of red wine that had miraculously survived. Samantha appeared, wriggling back and forth and rolling over and trying to lap Reed's face with her tongue. They tore chunks of the crusty loaf off for each other and washed it down with gulps of the thin, flavorless wine until the bottle was empty and the bread was gone.

Finally, Marisol began to tell her story.

Hell's Flood

"We were prepared for the wind," Marisol said, her lips trembling as she remembered it. "We are used to the wind. Tulum, the government, everyone knows what to do in a hurricane. We were prepared for the wind.

"But not for the water. That's never happened before. The tidal surge came so fast we thought we would drown, Reed. We moved to the chairs, then to the tables, then we were trapped, there was nowhere higher we could go. But Lance found a cinderblock and smashed a hole through the ceiling with it, then helped us up so we could escape to the roof. When we got up there the wind was howling so hard I thought it would rip me away. I never want to hear wind like that again, roaring like a freight train. The smell, too, it was like Hell had overflowed and risen up around us. That wind, it wanted to tear us off, wanted to carry us *up* into Hell. Lance built us a shelter." She stopped, bit her lips, and looked at Reed, her eyes dark and terrified.

"Lance fought against the wind and the water and the rain, like some god in a movie, some superhero. I tried to help him, Clione too, but the wind was too strong and her arm, her arm was too weak. She needed all her strength to keep from being blown away.

"Lance made us sit and he wrapped a rope around his waist and went around on the roof, pounding nails into pieces of wood until there was a structure strong enough to block that wind. He grabbed things floating by, anything—tables, plywood, pounding nails in with the same cinder block he used to make the hole for us to escape. Sometimes the wind tore things from his hands. One time the nails pulled out suddenly and the wood scratched him across his shoulder, like he'd been clawed by a jaguar, a jaguar of the storm. But just looking at him, we knew everything would be okay."

She paused. Reed held her hand. She smiled faintly.

"Thanks to Lance and his carpentry, we didn't drown in the rising water or get blown away. The three of us were shivering together, but our three bodies were warm, and we held each other so tightly, as if we were family. Samantha too. Lance made a raft for her out of plastic bottles and tied them around her neck like a string of giant beads. The poor *perrito*, she hated it, kept struggling and struggling, but it kept her safe. She just floated when she got too tired. Like a seal in the aquarium sticking its head through a ring.

"The wind howled and the rain stung us like bullets, but the wooden shelter, it was okay. We watched the water rise and cover the houses, and we couldn't see anything, we couldn't hear anything but the horrible wind in our ears. We couldn't speak, we could only wait, hold each other. Only when I pressed my ear against Lance's chest to hear the heartbeat could I know he was alive. And Clione, you know how she is, she was terrified and shaking from the cold but in her eyes I could see that to her it was all still just an adventure, something to look at, something that filled her with awe."

She took a breath. Reed asked about Clione, but she shook her head. She looked directly into Reed's face.

"I know why they call it the 'eye,' now," she said. "That's when the storm is only half over, there's still so much more damage to be done, but you get to look around and see the full horror of it for the first time. You're too blinded when the storm hits. But that calm, the eye, it was like we'd been surrounded with everything that Hell could form. I saw a tiny child floating past us like it was a doll, its eyes open, glazed over in death. I saw dogs shivering in sunken palm trees, clinging for dear life, some swimming in circles until they drowned. Some were mad, crazy like, their eyes all white and foam streaming from their lips like they were rabid. Samantha was so lucky. Without that necklace of bottles, she would have drowned, too.

"Houses were burning with people trapped inside. It seemed impossible, Reed, but the houses would be burning under the water. Lance told us it was oil or propane, something about it being heavier than air, sinking, filling up the rooms. My explanation was more simple: We were looking at Hell. How can a house burn underwater? No, it was everything evil come up from down there...." She broke off, leaned against Reed, and gently sobbed.

Marisol straightened herself and looked up at the sky. "How could God let something like this happen here? To us? To this simple town?"

For a long time she shook, her face in her palms, her body shivering as if she were very cold. Reed put his hands on her shoulders, rubbing his palms across her back, feeling the heat of her skin through the thin cotton shirt she wore. He felt a hot ache inside his chest, centered below the diaphragm. Each breath pained him.

"When the storm passed, Reed, you could not believe the destruction. Lance and Clione and me, we did nothing except bury the dead. Women, children, men, dogs, cats, chickens. The sun, it came out like nothing had ever happened.

The military arrived quickly; even before the storm they had troops ready to help, they trucked people in from all over Mexico to assist in the rebuilding. But even they were surprised this time by the force of the storm.

"For two entire days, we helped. Night and day, we buried the dead, looked for the missing, tried to reunite children and parents. We worked so hard. My back was so sore I couldn't sit down, so I walked and walked, and when I had to sleep I leaned myself against a wall and just slept standing up. Lance found a radio, and he and Clione heard that out at Punta Allen the bridge had collapsed. So the village at the tip of the peninsula, it had nothing. No food, no water to drink. It was completely cut off from the world. And Lance and Clione, they went to help rebuild the bridge. Because Lance's Jeep, it can go anywhere. It can drive underwater even."

Reed nodded. "I know."

"It was something to do," Marisol continued. "Something to give the village hope. I wanted to go, but I was tied to this hostel. I was trying to find things, trying to think about how to rebuild things here."

"They were gone three days helping that community. The third day, right at dusk when the sun was so bright, a van comes down the road, bumping and weaving. It was full of people, relatives of the villagers in Punta Allen. From all over. Mérida, Cancún, Chetumal, Mahahual. Everyone coming to check on the village, make sure their family is okay. Bringing food, beer, candy and clothes for the children. But the driver, he lost his wife and his baby in the storm and he'd been drinking. He didn't see the bridge was broken, with the sun in his eyes or maybe because he was drunk. He wasn't paying enough attention. And the van went into the river and the passengers, they started to drown.

"Lance and Clione were right behind them. They following the van and saw everything happen and they had to help. Lance, he dove in first, he tried, he swam out there but some of the passengers were too panicked. They clung to Lance, with terror that makes them superhuman strong, too strong, and Lance...they all went under."

Marisol stared, her mouth open, the lower lip moving oddly, as if the nerves were firing on their own. Reed put his arms around the shivering woman, pulled her close to him. Marisol bit his chest, dug her fingernails into his back, as she tried to summon the strength to continue her story.

Still in his arms, Marisol finished.

"Clione tried to help him too, they say. She rushed down the embankment and tried to wade in and save him, but the river, it eroded the clay and it crumbled when she stood on it. She fell in too. And the current swept her out into the darkness." Marisol's voice broke and she began to wail. "I still can't believe they're gone, Reed. I keep thinking maybe if I'd been there, if I'd gone too...maybe they'd be alive. I still wake up thinking Lance is right next to me. That I'll walk around a corner and see Clione smiling, writing in that journal of hers."

"It's not your fault," Reed said, feeling hollow, fighting for consciousness against a wave of agony that built inside him, a deep, roaring blackness that seemed to engulf him, tear him apart. His limbs felt numb, his breath was short and erratic, and were he not still holding Marisol he would have fallen to the ground. Very slowly, he sank, his knees giving way, and he collapsed, gouging his knees on the rough gravel as he went down. Marisol held him upright, kept him from toppling completely, and guided him to a sitting position against the crumbled wall.

"Reed," Marisol whispered. "Oh, Reed, Reed, Reed. We lost our brother and sister." She ran her fingers through his hair, brought her lips to his forehead and kissed it as if she were his mother. The jasmine musk of her perfume was all that came through the inky void.

Day Twenty

A Different Story

R eed and Marisol hired a driver to take them out to the place
where Clione and Lance had drowned. They were silent the
entire drive, both of them absorbed in their own worlds,
reliving their separate memories, linked and haunted by their
shared ghosts. Boston seemed as far off as a fairy tale, but even
the torn trees and dust-covered, salt-savaged foliage seemed two-
dimensional, like part of a meaningless dream. He wanted to
wake up, to discover himself in Clione's soft arms. He wanted to
kiss her, hold her, find a hammock for the two of them to fall into
and make the afternoon disappear.

Three times during the trip, Marisol began to cry, silent weeping
that he didn't notice until he saw moisture on her hands. Then he
would touch her, leaving his hand on her shoulder or back. There
was nothing to say. As the taxi maneuvered around the potholes,
scraping the gas tank and transmission over the sunbaked mud,
Marisol slipped her hand into his and kept it there, warm and soft
and trembling, and when the taxi driver eventually pulled up at the
site of the accident, neither of them pulled their hands away. Still
clinging tightly to each other, they got out of the car through the
passenger's-side door, hands clasped rigidly together as if they were
marm-scolded schoolchildren crossing a street.

The bridge was constructed of old railroad timbers that had been
held horizontal by gray, weathered poles, poles which now poked
out of the water like a broken stepladder tipped on its side. A few
men in cowboy hats were trying to pull the timbers out of the way
with ropes so that there'd be room for fishing pangas to pass into the
wide, mangrove-lined lagoon behind the road, its placid water the
same milky green color of Chinese jade. The water was peaceful now,
glassy except for a breath of breeze on the surface, but the ragged

edges of the water-carved earth and the toppled poles told of the current that had coursed through the narrow channel only a few days before. The millions of gallons of storm surge would have had only a few places to escape back to the sea. No one could have swum against it, not even Lance. Clione, with her weakened arm, could never have made it back to shore once the embankment gave way.

Reed kept Marisol's hand in his and together they walked closer to the ragged, crumbled edge. Lance's dusty Jeep was pulled into the bushes, and when they peered over into the water they could see the passenger van still half-submerged in the muddy swirls. Driftwood, trash, storm-torn mangrove shoots were caught in the broken windows of the vehicle, as random and colorful as the collection of crucifixes, flowers, and images of the Virgin that were placed on the shore. It was as if the river too were creating an offering for the lives it had taken away.

Marisol pulled away from Reed and went to the Renegade, opened the door, and stood there for a long time, not moving, her head down, one arm still on the handle. Reed shifted his gaze from the beautiful weeping Mexican woman to the crisp, meaningless, ice-blue of the sea. Only a few miles north, he and Clione had gone diving. Now this same stretch had become her grave. There, three hundred yards out, stretched the second-longest reef in the world. The beautiful, sensual, electric body that he'd made love to was now drifting there beneath the blue.

His throat caught, and he felt his knees sink into the damp soil. Clione.

He could still feel her, he could hear her voice, he expected to see her come out from the bushes, grinning, laughing at him, as if it were some cruel joke. But Marisol was not a joker; no face could fake that much pain.

Clione.

Several minutes passed, and he felt Marisol's hand on his shoulder. He turned up, saw her tear-stained face, and saw that she was carrying a leather-bound notebook. Reed knew instantly it was Clione's journal. Tucked inside the pages was the letter he had written. She had received it after all.

Marisol left without speaking, and Reed sat for a while on the bank, his hands trembling as he debated whether to open it. Finally, holding his breath as if he were about to dive underwater, he opened it to where the letter was tucked like a bookmark between the pages. He took it out, trying not to glance at what she might have written inside. It seemed a violation. But the letter was tucked into the book and he couldn't help glancing down at the page.

> *I saw a man today and something about him reminded me of Chris. He doesn't look anything like him of course, and he's older, but I find after Chris I crave maturity over anything else. He had such beautiful eyes, and I found myself staring at him as the two of us picked up Sharon's stuff under the table. I want to put his eyes into a book someday....*

Reed remembered exactly when he'd heard these words before, sitting on top of the pyramid at Ek' Balam. He turned the page, looking at the weeks of entries leading up to the dog sketch she'd drawn. And weeks of entries before, with no pages torn out or inserted. Clione hadn't been lying to him when she'd told him she wrote those things. She really had been reading it from memory.

He heard footsteps and softly closed the book.

Marisol sat down next to him, and he put his arm around her, and she put her head on his shoulder, and the immensity of their combined loss seemed to push inward on them, join them closer than if they had been making love. After a while, Reed took the crinkled, translucent airmail pages from the envelope and pulled them out, like petals from a sunflower, holding them up, letting the wind pluck them from his fingers. He watched the pages flutter upward, tumbling and circling. In seconds they too had fallen into the sea.

Marisol looked at him.

"It's her letter," Reed answered. "I'm just making sure she always has it."

One of the workmen came slowly toward them, approaching shyly, hesitant to interrupt a pair that so obviously needed time alone. He was dressed in a red-and-black checked shirt and dusty brown pants, with smears of mud as thick as face paint on his cheeks and hands. He took off his cowboy hat and ran a hand through his graying hair.

He stopped several feet away from Reed, as if waiting for an invitation to speak. Reed looked up, and the two made eye contact. Deep lines made it impossible for Reed to guess the man's age. He could have been thirty-five or sixty. Something about the man was familiar, yet Reed was certain he had never met the man before.

"My brother," the man said, in broken English. "he sell you a *pollo*, a cheeken."

Reed remembered: the roasted-chicken vendor near the Welcome Wanderer.

"¿*Sí?*"

"He say me you good man. He like you. He say you very lucky man to be with the beautiful girl."

Reed didn't reply. He didn't care, didn't want to talk to this man about anything, least of all chickens.

"My brother, he say you help him clean up at end of day."

"Are you wanting money? I'm really, really tired right now and—"

"He happy for your help that night. *Alegría en el trabajo*. Pleasure in work. That is all life has to offer."

"Give my regards to your brother," Reed replied. "But we'd like to be alone for a little while."

The man nodded but stayed where he was. "Someday, I will see him again and pass on your greeting. I pass your words to him but it will be a while because I do not want to die soon. He died in the storm."

Reed remembered the street vendor's twinkling eyes and how carefully he'd arranged the chickens each day. "I'm so sorry for your loss," he said finally. People were stumbling through their lives, reconstructing them from fragments. "I was rude."

The man continued as if he hadn't heard. "My brother, he love chickens. He love eating them, he love the taste of the oil on his fingers. He love feeding them in their pen, he thankful that these birds give him a house for his family, a job, something to do each day. It just a simple life, but it made him happy. He die doing what he loved."

"He was a good man."

The brother nodded. "The girl who die, she was your wife?"

Reed met the man's eyes again and briefly shook his head. "Just a friend." It sounded hollow, unfair. *Just* a friend? He turned his head. "She was my lover, my *novia*." he said roughly. "I came back to spend the rest of my life with her. Can't you please leave me alone?" He felt Marisol's warm hand on his shoulders, patting him slowly, as if she were patting a dog.

The two men said nothing for a few minutes, each of them contemplating the ghosts and memories, the Mexican still turning his hat clockwise in his work-worn hands as if waiting for something. Finally, the man put his hat back on and nodded as if taking the hint.

"You should know, your *novia*, she saved a young boy's life," he said. "So when you see her again in Heaven, please thank her for my boy."

Reed turned. "What?"

"Your *novia* saved my son's life," the Mexican said again. "She break window on the van, pulled him to safety. He was only five but he old enough to tell me everything."

"No," said Reed, standing up and shaking his head. He felt lightheaded, as if he were going to faint. "No, you're wrong. There was another person there. A man. *He* was the one who saved your son. His name was Lance. Your son made a —" Reed paused. "There must be some mistake."

"That's not the story my son told me." The Mexican shook his head. "Come, I show you the van. It still in the river. Easy to tell which story is true."

He led Reed back to the bank, where the rain and mud and footsteps were all mixed together. Pieces of rope were coiled like smashed serpents in the soil, and the windows of the half-submerged van were shattered. Dark maroon bloodstains still stuck to the sides like blistered paint. Beneath the bridge, Reed saw soft depressions in the ground where bodies had lain before the families could come to take them away.

"My son was there," the man said, pointing to the rear window. "He always love to watch from the back of the car. That day no different. He in the back, with his momma. He watching the Jeep behind, he wave at the driver and the pretty girl. When the van go into the water, he suddenly trapped. You can see. There no escape except for if someone smash the window."

"But she couldn't have done it. She didn't have the strength."

"My son, he said two people try to help. One man, he strong and powerful. He open the door and he let people in the front escape, many people saved before the river take him. *Pero mi* boy, he in the back, with the water coming up. Nobody save him. Nobody see him. My wife, she hit her head, she killed when the car go into the river, maybe. But my boy, he was alive. Look, amigo, look at the way the van is in the water. See?"

The man pointed to the rear of the van, which stuck up slightly higher in the water. Air would have been trapped in the back, just enough for a small boy to breathe. But he would have had to dive under the water to reach the front, which was the only escape.

Reed followed the man's finger and saw the dirt smudges on the roof, footprints far too large for a boy's and far too small to be Lance's. The crushed safety glass was still partially attached, lapping in the water like a dog's tongue. Reed could see the four distinct impact spider webs where the person, balancing on the outside of the vehicle as the water rose, had beat until the glass had given way. It had taken four tries.

Reed knew instantly what the man was showing him. If it had been Lance there the window would have been only one hole. His powerful arms, stronger for the adrenalin coursing through them, would have stove in the window as if it were made of cellophane. And surely, in the darkness and confusion, Lance would not have seen the tiny, terrified face of a boy cradling his dead mother, pressing his face upward into the glass as the water levels inexorably rose. Only Clione's keen writer's eyes, taking in everything from the bank in perfect detail, would have locked onto the terrified face of a little boy about to drown in the back of a van.

A sob raked across his ribs as if he were being clawed. He fell down, digging at the warm mud until his fingernails bled. Still struggling, he felt strong hands pull him by the shoulders and drag him as if he were a drunkard up the steep ravine toward his car. A door slammed, and then he could feel Marisol, her softness, blurs of motion and blackness and a scent of flowers that smelled as warm and comforting as the sea.

Day Three Hundred Seventy-Five

The Beauty of the Blue

Reed moved in with Marisol, and together they rebuilt the Welcome Wanderer, brick by brick by brick, Samantha at their side. Thanks to the volunteer work he'd done with Lance and Clione, he knew exactly what one does to make a wall. They found as many of the hostel's books as they could and dried them in the sun, page by page. It was Marisol who found the Murakami book, wet again but Luz María's expert repair had held up even in the second deluge. Marisol wrapped the volume carefully in brown paper and left it for Reed to find atop the refrigerator, with the one word "Yours" written in pencil on the top.

A fisherman found Lance's body six days after they'd visited the bridge, and after a futile attempt to contact his family, they buried him in the same makeshift cemetery that so many of the villagers had made their final resting place. Marisol and Reed had dressed it as best as they could. Marisol had combed her dead lover's hair and kissed his lips, and the village priest babbled his mumbo jumbo and they made the sign of the cross and placed Lance Canyon to rest.

When Reed asked Marisol why she wasn't weeping, she answered, "Because that is not Lance, it is only a container, something useless to me. The man I love fled this world long ago. Why should I be so sad now?"

But Reed felt as if a part of himself were being buried as four villagers took their shovels and covered the once-powerful body with earth. They had come from Punta Allen; almost everyone in attendance was connected to someone whom Lance or Clione had saved. They all wore black, and they brought bright flowers and crosses and plastic saints to place on the earth, when the hole had been filled in. It seemed ironic to Reed that Lance, who had scoffed at religion, who bragged about being a sinner headed for the fires of Hell, would become a saint in death, loved and respected by so many. Stories of Lance's strength and his heroic actions spread throughout the tiny town, getting larger and larger, stronger and stronger, with Lance more superhuman as each person told the tale, until in a few months he was thought to have had Samson's strength, a man who was in the process of lifting the entire van to safety, passengers and all, when he had been overcome by an enormous wave of biblical size and carried off to sea.

Curiously, no stories were told of the girl, the writer, save the one that the brother of the chicken seller had told about how she saved his son, and it was quickly forgotten by the town. In a few months, most people thought there had only been one savior in the beat-up Jeep that had arrived just after the van had plunged.

Marisol cooked meals for Reed and helped him to eat them. She combed his hair and took out clothes in the morning for him to put on. He held the hoe and mixed cement, his muscles straining, as Marisol poured water into the concrete dust and turned the powder into the gray mud that would hold their walls together. Together, they rebuilt the walls, doubly thick, filling the hollows between the cinder blocks with empty plastic bottles, which added strength and helped insulate against the searing heat of the sun. They pounded nails, sawed wood, carried paint cans from the hardware store, and little by little, the Welcome Wanderer came alive again. The 1940s-era refrigerator had survived unscathed. When power finally returned they plugged it in and were rewarded by the hum of cooling Freon.

As soon as the walls were up, Reed began working on the bookshelves. He took long planks and varnished them layer on top of layer until they seemed to contain the sun itself, then nailed them with brackets into the cement so that they would not come loose again. The hostel looked like the cabin of a yacht when they were finished, there was so much varnished wood. They filled the bookshelves with paperbacks in English and Spanish that they collected from hotels in Cancún and Playa. They put books outside and let people take them or borrow them or add to the pile as they chose. Reed felt good as the sweat turned his T-shirt clammy, and he liked the feel of a hammer or sledge in his hands. Marisol would look up at him from time to time, their eyes would meet, and they would smile.

In the evenings, they made slow, sensual love and listened to a battery-powered radio instead of watching television. They fell asleep in their hammock, in plain sight, with only the mosquito gauze pulled over them for privacy. They woke up to the sun's rays pushing through the new palm leaves, each morning so much like the rest that it became a blur. Long after it had expired he found his immigration card tucked into his passport, and he left it there, not bothering to renew it. Reed forgot how many days or weeks or months he'd been there. He forgot about Laurel. At times it was even difficult to remember what his address in Boston had been. Sometimes he remembered the heavyset girl, Cindy, and Sharon, who had almost ruined things for him and Clione. Where was she now? What country? Probably in some other youth hostel, offering her smile and her body to whomever would prolong her travel a few weeks more. He could barely remember what she looked like.

But Clione remained, helping and haunting him. She appeared sometimes when he and Marisol were making love, a warm breeze and the scent of guava. He could hear her voice in the wind. His orgasms became longer and more intense when he let himself slip into those memories of her, pretending he was inside Clione instead of Marisol. He could almost see her beneath him, a shadowy silhouette, and when he finally told Marisol about these feelings, instead of being upset, she nodded.

"I see Lance too," Marisol whispered, then pressed her lips to his. "She'll always be with you. I know that. It's a good thing." She drew a spiral on his chest and kissed his nipple and whispered, "*En nuestros corazones*. Lance and Clione, they live within us now."

They went together to the riverbank where the van had plunged in and made two small shrines above the waterline, simple white crosses of painted pine. Marisol suggested plastic flowers, but Reed insisted that they be real.

"Better no flowers than plastic ones," he said, and Marisol eventually acquiesced. At first he went every week, taking the Punta Allen collectivo van, two bouquets cradled on his lap as if they were children. He would get off at the bridge, pluck up the old, desiccated flowers and let them float away in the river, then arrange the new ones in their place. Then he'd sit for a few hours at the edge of the river, looking out at the sea. He brought Clione's journal with him, reading the pages over and over, cover to cover as if it were a bible.

When the van came by on its return trip he would flag it down, arriving back at the Welcome Wanderer before sundown. Eventually, as things picked up at the hostel, the visits fell off. First once every two weeks, then every month. Part of him said that Clione would have wanted it that way, and another part was just accepting the comfortless finality that the dead do not return.

Once he arrived to find two men standing there. Only after they'd told him their names did Reed remember them as Lance's friends, the ones they'd met volunteering to build the houses at the village. They had brought plastic flowers, thin spindly bouquets, but Reed left them there. The three men hardly spoke and shortly after Reed arrived, the other two men nodded, said goodbye, and returned along the pitted road toward Tulum. After they had left Reed noticed that they had placed on Lance's cross two fresh cans of beer.

Reed created a fund at the local bank so that the young boy Clione had saved could attend school full time in Tulum rather than split his time between fishing and home-schooling in his village. The boy's name was Memo and he had an aptitude for drawing portraits, which Reed hoped might turn into a directed profession someday. Perhaps the boy might study art in Europe or America; at least he would have options open to him that no one else in the village had.

Immigration officials eventually came knocking at the Welcome Wanderer; no coincidence that it was just days after he'd refused to give a police officer a bribe and instead requested — and promptly paid — a ticket for having a license plate that was not properly attached. He and Marisol were married with no ceremony, no reception, no gifts, just a piece of paper that meant the difference between staying together and being apart.

"That's the only *good* reason to get married," Marisol had said, laughing, the night that it was finalized. "To circumvent the law."

They put candles on the hostel's picnic tables and told the night's guests it was the anniversary of the reopening of the hostel, and someone started a round of "Happy Birthday, Welcome Wanderer" that left everyone laughing. That night they took a taxi out to the beach and swam together in the warm, dark waters, a ritual purification.

As if Clione had willed him her love of the water once she no longer needed it, Reed discovered that he had lost all fear of the sea.

* * *

It was in late October when Reed returned to the riverside to visit the two crosses and reread the only book he had ever loved. He had gotten a ride with an uncle of Memo's, who said he was just doing an errand and could bring him back in a few hours. The two men were silent most of the way, with Reed looking out the window on the passenger's side, studying the mangrove swamp and the shimmer of the sunlight onto the waxy green leaves.

When the beat-up pickup truck dropped him off he stood at the dusty edge of the road for a long time. The van was still submerged in the shallow water, rust spreading out over the paint in ever-widening circles like hives. Sand had built up around it, making a white bar around the scene of the accident as if someone had poured milk into a puddle of greeny-blue sea. A few fish, no bigger than fingers, shimmered as they swam through the shallows.

When the blowing dust from the wheels of the pickup had disappeared completely, Reed walked to the two graves. He knelt and touched them each, running his fingers over the weathered crosses. The whitewash had been stripped off by the winter's salt spray and the baking sun. Already the grain had begun to rise up out of the sanded wood, the ridges easily discernible beneath his touch.

"I'm back," he whispered.

He brushed away the detritus that had collected and then placed the bouquet of daisies and marigolds at the one for Clione. He pulled a can of Sol from his jacket pocket and popped open the fliptop.

"Something for both of you," he mumbled, bothered by the awkward one-sidedness of gravesite visits. He came to fulfill an obligation to the living, not the dead. He did not believe in something beyond. Nor did Clione nor Lance, and yet he felt obligated to continue the Mexican ritual. Marisol believed, as did the villagers. It was not as if the crosses had any genuine connection to the lives they signified. Clione was not here any more than she was anywhere else — at the Welcome Wanderer, or out there somewhere in the ocean. Reed came so that other people passing by that spot would notice the crosses, so that they would remember that two people gave their lives so that a boy and some other passengers could live.

After a while, he walked down to the edge of the ocean, Clione's journal in hand. Initially, he had spent most of his visits sitting next to the graves and marveling at the pelicans that could soar mere inches above the glassy surface. He watched how they dove, plunging in and reversing direction as they hit the water like corkscrews. Frigates with their V tails flew high above in the cerulean blue. Plovers and sandpipers trotted along in the foam at the shore. He read a page or two of the journal as a meditation. Sometimes he brought the Murakami book with him and reread the sections that he and Clione had read in the hammock together months before.

Yet each trip brought him closer to the sea. He would walk with Samantha near the shoreline, laughing as the dog — now healthy — pounced on unsuspecting crustaceans and crunched them up in her teeth. Then he was wading, then taking off his shirt and shoes, and finally swimming. The weight of the water helped him to hold himself upward, and with a full breath of air he would rise up like a balloon instead of sinking down. When a guest left a beat-up mask and snorkel at the hostel, Reed started bringing them along with him and found he could float for hours on the surface looking down into the depths at all the fascinating creatures there. Samantha hated seeing him drift out of reach. She was terrified of the water and would wait anxiously on the shore and then jump into his arms as soon as he was back on land.

As the months passed, swimming became so rhythmic and natural that at times he felt as if he were making love, as if the water were caressing him in soft thrusts and yielding pressures. He learned how to pull himself crossways through rip currents, felt the exquisite tautness of his muscles after a long swim. He tasted the salt in his mouth, the fishiness, the seaweed. When he came out of the water it was as if he'd been hollowed out, devoured: All he wanted to do was gorge himself with food and pull Marisol to the floor, bury himself inside her. Sometimes he wondered how he ever could have felt afraid of something as natural, as perfect and primal, as the sea. Only Samantha's frantic yelps as he walked in made him remember that he too used to fear this vast, enormous force in front of him.

Old and semi-rigid, the mask was not particularly comfortable, but it fit snugly on his face and kept the water out. Reed stripped off his T-shirt and tucked it under a saucer-size piece of bleached coral, then sat and let the sun soak into his skin. He ran his fingers along the coral chunk, felt the glassy edges prick his skin. He pulled his hand away sharply and sucked at the blood until it slowed. It always amazed him how something as sharp as coral could become the velvety soft beach sand. Pure alchemy.

He entered the water, ignoring Samantha's panicked whining as he got further away. He let the waves splash around his ankles, then his knees, then his thighs. The sensation of water between his toes felt relaxing now. Adjusting the strap of the mask, he made sure that it fit snugly around his face and then took it off and spat in it, rubbing the saliva around with a finger to prevent fog. He rinsed it, then put the mask on, bit down on the snorkel, and gently dove in.

Already the fish were collecting around his hands, swarms of them, tickling at his skin. With slow strokes he moved outward, following a puffer as it hovered over the bluish landscape below. The bottom here had more sand than other parts of the coastline, in part because of the river nearby, and partly because the area was shielded by a slightly higher coral reef. The whitecaps would smash against that barrier first, then slowly roll in toward shore.

He followed the jagged path of a crevasse where a plate of thin rock had broken in two; beneath it the water was deep blue. Reed's heartbeat quickened when he saw a green moray, as thick as his thigh, gracefully cross from one side to the other. Tucked up underneath a bright pink patch of coral was a spiny lobster, its shell tiger-striped, its antennae curled back over its body as if it did not want to be seen. He felt as if these creatures held messages for him, told in a language he could not yet quite understand.

He let the current carry him, drifting, watching the bottom, the sun warming his back. Occasionally, he lifted his head and checked the shore for the telltale pickup truck, but it didn't arrive. The water deepened, the colors shifting from the bright neons to muted yellows and blues.

Something different near the bottom caught his eye. Reed pushed against the current to get a better look at what he first thought was a dead diver, but when he got closer he realized that it was a tank and buoyancy vest. He looked at it for several minutes before understanding that it was the same tank he and Clione had lost a year ago: Lance's diving gear. They'd been diving farther north, but the currents had carried it here.

Or no, Reed thought, *maybe it's me that's wrong. Maybe this is where we were?*

He couldn't remember. But the oddity of it, of finding *this* spot, finding that very tank, made his skin prickle for several minutes as he tread water above the site. He remembered the manatee, the shark, the sense of utter panic as it had approached, how worried Clione had been when he'd first awakened. How she'd told him about being "late" on the ride home.

He remembered the sense of loss he'd had as they continued silently back toward Tulum. A flood of memories. His fear of the water, that awful sense of dread that he'd had when he looked out into that midnight void or felt the clamminess grab hold of his toes. There below him was the very same tank they'd used. He'd forgotten all about it until now.

Now he knew he would appreciate watching a shark slice through the depths like a living torpedo, graceful and sleek like an underwater jaguar. He understood how they rarely attack, how magically they trace the scent of blood. How could Clione ever have been attracted to him when he had been so terrified of everything she loved so much? Only now could he see what she saw when she put her head below the surface and began to swim.

Taking a deep breath, he dove down toward the seafloor. Almost immediately, he realized that the bottom was much, much deeper than he'd thought. His ears popped once, then twice, then pain tore at his head as if it were going to explode. He stopped fighting, let the air in his lungs pull him back up toward the surface. He broke through the whiteness and inhaled, felt the air and the wind, and his ears were normal again.

He looked back at the shore, expecting the pickup to be waiting, but the only motion was Samantha anxiously trotting back and forth, desperate to join him but too afraid of the water to even let her paws get wet. A white egret swooped out of the sky and landed, coiled its neck like a spring, and began stalking fish. He remembered that Clione had told him that diving is in the legs, that you need to lift them up into the air to get the downward thrust, let gravity do the work. Treading water for a few minutes, Reed inhaled and exhaled, saturating his blood with additional oxygen. It made him feel slightly lightheaded. When he was ready, he took a last look at Samantha and then turned and pushed his legs upward, toes pointing at the sky. He plunged downward, but the strong current already had pulled him off the target and he aborted the dive. The attempt gave him hope: If he could line himself up right over the tank, and if he made a straight shot down, he might get close enough to grab hold and pull it up to the surface.

He located the tank again and treaded water while looking down at it through the mask. Then he hyperventilated through the snorkel until he felt dizzy, and quickly snapped his legs upward. The result was a smooth glide down, deep and straight, much faster than he ever expected. The water temperature changed twice as he descended, significantly colder down deep than at the surface. He kept one hand on his nose to equalize the pressure, blowing continually to keep his eardrums from imploding. His ears made a funny squeaking sound inside his head, as if air were coming out of a balloon. The dive tank seemed to be rising up to meet him.

As he neared it, he could see that a branch of antler coral had snagged around the tubing connecting the regulator to the mouthpiece and had become an anchor. The buoyancy vest still had air or it wouldn't be floating, but the coral was strong, and without a jolt or intense wave action, it couldn't lift up enough to float free. Downy green seaweed coated the tank like fine pubic hair. Barnacles and limpets dotted the once-shiny steel. A few brightly colored fish circled in and out of the vest cavity as if claiming the equipment as their own.

When the momentum of his dive petered out, Reed was only a few yards above the tank. Clawing at the water with his hands and kicking his feet, he forced himself downward until he could grab hold of the slippery nylon. His hands couldn't find purchase on the algae, but as the current pulled him past he reached out and grabbed onto the hose of the octopus, holding it as a drowning sailor reaches for a buoy. Using the weight of the water to spin himself around, he oriented himself feet downward, head up, as if he were walking underwater. Planting his feet on each side of the twisted coral trunk, he grabbed the vinyl jacket of the vest and thrust upward.

There was a sharp pop, audible even underwater, and the antler coral branch toppled slowly to the sandy seafloor. Reed fell backward, the weight of the tank unexpectedly shifting over his center of gravity, and only slightly buoyant. He felt a sting in his left leg and saw a curl of purple blood rising up from the heel. He had transgressed: The reef, a sentient organism, was defending itself.

Reed tried to swim upward, his lungs starting to spasm, the involuntary reaction pushing him to breathe even when there was no air, but the tank made ascent impossibly slow. He would never make it up without dropping the vest. Just as he decided to let go, his fingers hit the second stage of the regulator and there was an explosion of white bubbles.

The tank still had air!

Reacting as Lance had taught him in that frigid pool, Reed shoved the mouthpiece between his lips and inhaled. The air tasted metallic and stale, but it was air.

He was breathing!

Reed started laughing underwater. He was fine!

Breathe! He'd been so focused on returning to the surface that he never considered checking to see if the tank still functioned. *Breathe!* He let a long stream of bubbles escape and watched as they climbed upward, expanding as they went from golf balls to silver plate-size saucers until they disappeared.

Breathe!

Everything around him seemed intensely beautiful: He felt ashamed to have torn that piece of coral from its base. The tank belonged down here now. *Breathe!* Fish had made it their home. The larger shelf of coral was so vivid, its layers of color and texture like an oriental rug that the reef and the sea had woven over the centuries. How could he have violated it? The odd swirls of yellow-green brain coral mixing with the fluttery blossoms of flesh-pink anemones, the jagged ridges of box coral overlapping with the delicate fringe of feather worms. *Breathe!* Reed saw things more intensely, as if he were not merely an observer, but as if the reef, all its myriad of life, were a part of him, and he a part of it. He let go of the tank and watched it slowly spin, like a person on a space walk, as he let himself drift with the current. He looked down and surprised a cluster of yellow-and-black angelfish and a school of pink squirrelfish that were hugging the base of the coral shelf. He kicked, fighting his way back to the tank, and inhaled again.

Breathe!

In the distance he spotted tuna, their silver bodies speeding through the blue.

How amazing that he could see this, that he could have been this lucky in his life. How easy it would be for him to still be sitting at the edge of a pool, each day just like the next, each sunset slipping by him unseen. He realized that it was all because of a girl, all of it just a random collision of events that might never have led to anything if he hadn't also been willing to see what lay out there. The smile of the old woman, the taste of the orange, the softness of Clione's lips and the scent of her hair as it fell around him, all these things came back to him in a flood, all kinds of memories. He felt Marisol's caresses on his neck and shoulders, saw the love in her eyes. He'd been so lucky, so incredibly lucky. To have had the chance to share his life with such special people, to be able to enter their lives.

What he'd written to Laurel was all wrong, he thought. Love isn't whatever works. It was a living thing, a reaction of two elements mixing and becoming one.

He'd been so blind.

Love is letting someone change you forever. Change the course of your life. Mark you indelibly. It was like the egg on its epic fallopian journey that allows just one selected sperm inside its membrane, just one, and then the membrane locks and everyone else is on the outside. Inside, a whole new process begins. Life. That's what love is. When someone slips inside you and you're never again the same.

A sense of supreme calm suffused him. He felt rapture.

This is how it happens.

This life, this reef and the colors and the people and fish. Water surrounded him, whispered to him, tickled him like a lover. He let himself go, kept drifting farther and farther from the corroding tank of oxygen until he realized that he no longer needed it.

It was so obvious, like something he'd known all along. There was nothing to fear. There never had been anything to fear. Nothing would hurt him. He realized in a flash of eureka the trick the abalone uses to shellac its shell with the sea.

Gratitude welled up inside his chest until he thought he would explode. He watched intently the patchwork symphony of color and shimmering light that was the coral reef unfolding below him, then turned his gaze forward and into the face of the deep beautiful blue.

The Tulum Sunset

3 oz tequila
1 oz triple sec
½ oz Damiana liqueur
juice of ½ lime
fresh guava puree
fresh pineapple juice
1 splash grenadine

A lovely Tiki-style drink. Shake tequila, triple sec, Damiana, guava puree, and lime juice until deeply chilled. Pour into Collins glass filled with ice. Top with pineapple juice, and the splash of Grenadine. Garnish with cherry and/or pineapple slice arranged so that it looks like the sun setting in a pink and yellow sky.

reprinted by
permission of the
Grand Medallion Cancún

The End

Thanks to the Reader

If you're reading this page, chances are you've finished the book and the very first person I want to thank is *you*. It's a commitment to involve yourself in a novel's world for days or weeks, and I am humbled and honored that you chose to take the time. If you liked the book, *please* take a moment to recommend it to your friends on social media and sign up at my author Facebook page.

www.facebook.com/RayBartlettAuthor

Also *www.Kaisora.com, @kaisoradotcom,* and on other social media.

Though I can't promise to reply to each and every email or post, I'd love to hear from you! I'd also love to come speak at your school, graduation, book club, or nearest bookstore. Invite me!

If you are reading this book for free, please consider making a donation to support great work at *www.RaymondBartlett.com/donate,* via credit card or PayPal. Every donation makes a huge difference in the life of this author. The hard copies still make great gift ideas, and if you purchase through me I can even sign them! It's an extra special way to give that extra special someone a unique gift they'll have the rest of their lives.

Lastly, thank you for being part of a community that values fiction in a world that frequently doesn't. Too often authors fail to acknowledge that it's because of *you* that all the years spent writing a book become rewarding. Thank you so much for being part of what makes writing so special for me.

Acknowledgments

I would like to first thank my family for their help, understanding, encouragement and support in all ways and at all hours. Al Waitt, editor, publisher, and friend, huge thanks for your keen eye and patient suggestions on the long road to print. Sena Desai Gopal, your enthusiasm, energy, belief and insights couldn't have come at a better time. Zora O'Neill, your knowledge of Yucatán was invaluable. Jessica Ryan, thank you for catching so many Spanish errors that might have otherwise slipped through. Giles Carwyn, your plot sorcery and eye for drama helped enormously in making this novel have current and flow rather than eddies. Todd Fahnestock, your industry knowledge and willingness to help was fantastic. Marina Katayeva, your naming suggestions, artistry, and inspirations made all the difference, always at just the right time. Jim Nidositko, thank you for instantly "getting" this book and being so excited to spread the word. And a dear thank you to Missy Brownson and the sweet gals of the Frankfort book club for such a fantastic show of Southern hospitality. Meg Tyler, your word artistry is unparalleled. Eva Schegulla, thank you for such a kind and helpful edit and great suggestions. My parents, who proofread it carefully and found a number of things I might have missed.

So many helpful readers: Daphne, Tracy, Tascha, Shanna, Gemma, Amy, Christine, Tristan, Loren, Brett, Melissa...to list only a few by name. There are other people not listed who have read the book and helped by providing feedback, suggestions, or muse whispers: you know exactly who you are. *Thank you.*

Lastly, thanks too to the amazing people and wonderful places in Tulum, Yucatán, and Mexico. I am honored to have spent so many days, weeks, and months crisscrossing your highways and staying in your beautiful, sleepy little towns and cities, making such amazing friends.

For Book Clubs and Discussion Groups

As *Sunsets of Tulum* was heading to the publisher I shared a few copies with friends and family and asked them to get the word out. Little did I know that mere weeks after that, a group of total strangers would have been so enthusiastic that they crowdfunded a plane ticket to get me out to their Frankfort, Kentucky book club. Despite a few travel disasters (delayed plane, lost luggage) the literary evening went off without a hitch and we had a fantastic time: I made pitcher after pitcher of Tulum Sunsets, we laughed and discussed the book, we talked about writing in general, and I even gave the club an Argentine tango lesson (one of my other passions besides writing). More than one person in the group told me it was "the best book club ever." I have to agree. It rocked.

For me it was more than just a book club. That Thursday confirmed what I've always thought about the process of reading: that it is like taking a walk in the woods, different for each person. A birder looks up through binoculars. An entomologist looks down with a magnifying glass. Someone elderly might walk slowly, see the rocks and roots as hurdles, whereas a young girl might dash down the path not worrying at all about tripping, overwhelmed by the greenness and the mystery of what lies around the next corner. A walk is different with the seasons. So too is reading a great novel.

So if you are part of a book club, please know that I would love to join you for an evening as well. I'm even running a promotion: June 30, 2016, I'll do a drawing among all the entries for people who signed up for my e-news at www.SunsetsofTulum.com – just fill in your info and be sure to choose the "Book Club contest" option from the "Select Interest" pull down. The lucky winner will get me for 1 hour at their book club via Skype (or in person if it's within Massachusetts), plus a signed copy of the novel.

Thank you for your commitment to the community of books and to each other. Fiction matters. As do you.